HOUSE OF FEAR

EDITED BY
JONATHAN
OLIVER

HOUSE OF FEAR

EDITED BY
JONATHAN OLIVER

NINETEEN NEW STORIES OF HAUNTED HOUSES
AND SPECTRAL ENCOUNTERS BY:

Lisa Tuttle
Stephen Volk
Terry Lamsley
Adam L. G. Nevill
Weston Ochse
Rebecca Levene
Garry Kilworth
Chaz Brenchley
Robert Shearman
Nina Allan
Christopher Fowler
Sarah Pinborough
Paul Meloy
Christopher Priest
Jonathan Green
Nicholas Royle
Eric Brown
Tim Lebbon
Joe R. Lansdale

SOLARIS

First published 2011 by Solaris
an imprint of Rebellion Publishing Ltd,
Riverside House, Osney Mead,
Oxford, OX2 0ES, UK

www.solarisbooks.com

ISBN 978-1-907992-07-0

Cover by Luke Preece

10 9 8 7 6 5 4 3 2 1

A CIP catalogue record for this book is available from the
British Library.

Designed & typeset by Rebellion Publishing

Printed in the US

CONTENTS

INTRODUCTION

I'VE NEVER SEEN a ghost, I've never stayed in a haunted house, and I don't believe in revenants seeking revenge from beyond the grave, yet the supernatural in fiction continues to fascinate me. There's nothing better than the fright you get from a really good ghost story; certain scenes in Stephen King's novel *The Shining* took my breath away and the last line of Ramsey Campbell's classic ghost story, 'The Trick,' froze me with fear. However, while the ghost story has the fear of 'the other' at its heart, it is also fundamentally concerned with ourselves, for what are ghosts but the memories of lives lived and losses suffered? Grief and coping with loss are at the heart of several stories here: Chaz Brenchley explores the tragic death of a friend in 'Hortus Conclusus'; in 'An Injustice' by Christopher Fowler, a haunting provides more than an intrepid group of ghost-hunters could have hoped for, while in 'The Room Upstairs' Sarah Pinborough explores a locked-room mystery through the sorrow of a grieving widow, and Eric Brown shows us that there is indeed a life after death in 'The House.'

Revenge is often a theme that crops up in ghost stories and in this collection we have some unusual takes on this trope. 'The Windmill' by Rebecca Levene is a genuine howl of anger that speaks eloquently about crime and punishment; 'Moretta' by Garry Kilworth reveals an interesting twist that I certainly didn't see coming the first time I read the tale, and while 'Pied-à-terre' by Stephen Volk isn't necessarily a story of supernatural revenge, its warning from beyond certainly speaks of a desire for justice.

Ghosts as symbols of our own mortality also speak to us of ageing and the failure of the mortal flesh. This theme is chillingly and powerfully explored by two stories in this collection: 'Florrie' by Adam Nevill, in which the past tenant of a house draws the new owner into its influence, and 'Trick of the Light' by Tim Lebbon where the sight of a face at a window prompts a journey into darkness.

With two of our American contributors we have something a little more outré, an encounter with entities that may not be entirely human. The influence of Ray Bradbury is evident in a story that is really about a yearning for the hereafter and the fantastical, 'Driving the Milky Way' by Weston Ochse, while Joe R. Lansdale channels the spirit of Arthur Machen into a story that nevertheless has its roots in Texas. The figure of the unknowable other is also present in the Aickmanesque 'The Muse of Copenhagen' by the brilliant Nina Allan.

Let us not forget in our discussion of the supernatural, however, that the location of the haunting is often as important as the haunting itself. Lisa Tuttle's unsettling 'Objects in Dreams may be Closer than they Appear' features a house that may or may not exist, but which still draws on the desires of the characters in the tale; 'Villanova' by Paul Meloy takes us on holiday to a static home in France, there to reveal a terrible family secret; 'In The Absence of Murdock' by Terry Lamsley features a very strange house and a haunting that verges on the comic and surreal; Jonathan Green takes us into the territory of gruesome horror with a visit to 'The Doll's House,' while Robert Shearman's 'The Dark Space in the House in the House in the Garden at the Centre of the World' sees our protagonists learning what it is to be human through their encounters with the supernatural.

Questions of what constitutes a haunting, and even what constitutes a house, are explored in the compelling and complex stories by Christopher Priest, 'Widow's Weeds' in which a stage magician finds himself possessed by a most unusual haunting, and 'Inside/Out' by Nicholas Royle, where that which the protagonist perceives and the spaces he finds within and outside of himself comes together in a truly unsettling tale.

So now that you know what awaits you within, dear reader, it only remains for you to step up the front door, knock and await for that which lives here to answer your call.

OBJECTS IN DREAMS MAY BE CLOSER THAN THEY APPEAR

LISA TUTTLE

Lisa Tuttle understands that, for a ghost story to work, it has to be as much about the human protagonists as any supernatural entities that arise. It's all very well going for the scare or the sudden chill, but at the end of the day a house is a place where people live, whether it's haunted or not. In the disturbing story that follows, Lisa writes about two people falling out of love and how the strange house they find affects them in a way they couldn't even begin to imagine

SINCE WE DIVORCED twenty years ago, my ex-husband Michael and I have rarely met, but we'd always kept in touch. I wish now that we hadn't. This whole terrible thing began with a link he sent me by e-mail with the comment, "Can you believe how much the old homestead has changed?"

Clicking on the link took me to a view of the cottage we had owned, long ago, for about three years – most of our brief marriage.

Although I recognized it, there were many changes.

No longer a semi-detached, it had been merged with the house next-door, and also extended. It was, I thought, what we might have done ourselves given the money, time, planning permission and, most vitally, next-door neighbours willing to sell us their home. Instead, we had fallen out with them (they took our offer to buy as a personal affront) and poured too much money into so-called improvements, the work expensively and badly done by local builders who all seemed to be related by marriage if not blood to the people next-door.

Just looking at the front of the house on the computer screen gave me a tight, anxious feeling in my chest. What had possessed Michael to send it to me? And why had he even looked for it? Surely he wasn't nostalgic for what I recalled as one of the unhappiest periods of my life?

At that point, I should have clicked away from the picture, put it out of my mind and settled down to work, but, I don't know why, instead of closing the tab, I moved on down the road and began to discover what else in our old neighbourhood was different.

I'd heard about Google Earth's 'Street View' function, but I'd never used it before, so it took me a little while to figure out how to use it. At first all the zooming in and out, stopping and starting and twirling around made me queasy, but once I got to grips with it, I found this form of virtual tourism quite addictive.

But I was startled by how different the present reality appeared from my memory of it. I did not recognize our old village at all, could find nothing I remembered except the war memorial – and that seemed to be in the wrong place. Where was the shop, the primary school, the pub? Had they all been altered beyond recognition, all turned into houses? There were certainly many more of those than there had been in the 1980s. It was while I was searching in vain for the unmistakable landmark that had always alerted us that the next turning would be our road, a commercial property that I could not imagine anyone converting into a desirable residence – the Little Chef – that it dawned on me what had happened.

Of course. The Okehampton bypass had been built, and altered the route of the A30. Our little village was one of several no longer bisected by the main road into Cornwall, and without hordes of holiday-makers forced to crawl past, the fast food outlet and petrol station no longer made economic sense.

Once I understood how the axis of the village had changed, I found the new primary school near an estate of new homes. There were also a couple of new (to me) shops: an Indian restaurant, wine bar, an oriental rug gallery, and a riding school. The increased population had pushed our sleepy old village slightly up-market. I should not have been surprised, but I suppose I was an urban snob, imagining that anyone living so deep in the country must be several decades behind the times. But I could see that even the smallest of houses boasted a satellite dish, and they probably all had broadband internet connections, too. Even as I was laughing at the garden gnomes on display in front of a neat yellow bungalow, someone behind those net curtains might be looking at my own terraced house in Bristol, horrified by what the unrestrained growth of ivy was doing to the brickwork.

Curious to know how my home appeared to others, I typed in my own address, and enjoyed a stroll around the neighbourhood without leaving my desk. I checked out a few less-familiar addresses, including Michael's current abode, which I had never seen. So *that* was Goring-by-Sea!

At last I dragged myself away and wrote catalogue copy, had a long talk with one of our suppliers, and dealt with various other bits and pieces before knocking off for the day. Neither of us fancied going out, and we'd been consuming too many pizzas lately, so David whipped up an old favourite from the minimal supplies in the kitchen cupboard: spaghetti with marmite, tasty enough when accompanied by a few glasses of Merlot.

My husband David and I marketed children's apparel and accessories under the name 'Cheeky Chappies.' It was exactly the sort of business I had imagined setting up in my rural idyll, surrounded by the patter of little feet, filling orders between changing nappies and making delicious, sustaining soups from the organic vegetables Michael planned to grow.

None of that came to pass, not even the vegetables. Michael did what he could, but we needed his income as a sales rep to survive, so he was nearly always on the road, which left me to take charge of everything at home, supervising the building work in between applying for jobs and grants, drawing up unsatisfactory business plans, and utterly failing in my mission to become pregnant.

Hard times can bring a couple together, but that is not how it worked for us. I grew more and more miserable, convinced I was a failure both as a woman and as a potential CEO. It did not help that Michael was away so much, and although it was not his fault and we needed the money, I grew resentful at having to spend so much time and energy servicing a house I'd never really wanted.

He'd drawn me into *his* dream of an old-fashioned life in the country, and then slipped out of sharing the major part of it with me. At the weekend, with him there, it was different, but most of the time I felt lonely and bored, lumbered with too many chores and not enough company, far from friends and family, cut off from the entertainments and excitement of urban existence.

Part of the problem was the house – not at all what we'd dreamed of, but cheap enough, and with potential to be transformed into something better. We'd been jumped into buying it by circumstances. Once Michael had accepted a very good offer on his flat (*our* flat, he called it, but it was entirely his investment) a new urgency entered into our formerly relaxed house-hunting expeditions. I had loved those weekends away from the city, staying in B&Bs and rooms over village pubs, every moment rich with possibility and new discoveries. I would have been happy to go on for months, driving down to the West Country, looking at properties and imagining what our life might be like in this house or that, but suddenly there was a time limit, and this was the most serious decision of our lives, and not just a bit of fun.

The happiest part of my first marriage now seems to have been compressed into half a dozen weekends, maybe a few more, as we travelled around, the inside of the car like an enchanted bubble filled with love and laughter, jokes and personal revelations and music. I loved everything we saw. Even the most impossible, ugly houses were fascinating, providing material for discussing the strangeness of other people's lives. Yet although I was interested in them all, nothing we viewed actually tempted me. Somehow, I couldn't imagine I would ever really live in the country – certainly not the practicalities of it. I expected our life to continue like this, work in the city punctuated by these mini-holidays, until we found the perfect house, at which point I'd stop working and start producing babies and concentrate on buying their clothes and toys and attractive soft furnishings and decorations for the house as if money was not and could never be a problem.

And then one day, travelling from the viewing of one imperfect property to look at another, which would doubtless be equally unsatisfactory in its own unique way, Blondie in the cassette player singing about hanging on the telephone, we came to an abrupt halt. Michael stopped the car at the top of a hill, on one of those narrow, hedge-lined lanes that aren't even wide enough for two normal sized cars to pass each other without the sort of jockeying and breath-holding maneuvers that in my view are acceptable only when parallel parking. I thought he must have seen another car approaching, and taken evasive action, although the road ahead looked clear.

"What's wrong?"

"Wrong? Nothing. It's perfect. Don't you think it's perfect?"

I saw what he was looking at through a gap in the hedge: a distant view of an old-fashioned, white-washed, thatch-roofed cottage nestled in one of those deep, green valleys that in Devonshire are called coombs. It was a pretty sight, like a Victorian painting you might get on a box of old-fashioned chocolates, or a card for Mother's Day. For some reason, it made my throat tighten and I had to blink back sentimental tears, feeling a strong yearning, not so much for that specific house as for what it seemed to promise: safety, stability, family. I could see myself there, decades in the future, surrounded by children and grandchildren, dressed in clothes from Laura Ashley.

"It's very sweet," I said, embarrassed by how emotional I felt.

"It's exactly what we've been looking for," he said.

"It's probably not for sale."

"All it takes is the right offer." That was his theory: not so much that everything had its price, as that he could achieve whatever goal he set himself. It was more about attitude than money.

"But what if they feel the same way about it as we do?"

"Who are 'they'?"

"The people that live there."

"But you feel it? What I feel? That it's where we want to live?"

I thought about the children – grandchildren, even! – in their quaint floral smocks, and nodded.

He kissed me. "All right!" he cried, joyously, releasing the hand-brake. "Let's go!"

"Do you even know how to get there?"

"You've got the map. Direct me."

My heart sank. Although I had the road atlas open in my lap, I never expected to have to use it. Michael did not understand that not everyone was like him, able to look at lines and coloured patches on a page and relate them to the real world. His sense of direction seemed magical to me. Even when the sun was out, I had no idea which way was north. On a map, it was at the top. In the world, I had to guess at right or left or straight ahead.

"I don't know where we are *now*," I objected. "We need to stop and figure it out."

Fortunately, we were approaching a village, and it offered parking space in front of the church, so that was easily done. Michael had no problem identifying which of the wriggly white lines was the road we'd been on, and where we'd stopped and seen the house, and with that and the location of the village we were in, he was able to perform some sort of mental triangulation that enabled him to stab a forefinger down on a blank place within the loops of spaghetti representing the nameless country roads. "There," he said with certainty. "It's got to be there. An OS map would show us exactly, but anyway, it shouldn't be hard to find. We'll just drive around until we spot it."

We drove around for the next two or three hours. Round and round and round. The same route, again and again, up and down the narrow roads, some of them like tunnels, they were so deep beneath the high-banked hedges, until I was dizzy, like a leaf swept away in a stream. Deep within those dark green lanes there was nothing to see except the road ahead, the deep, loamy earth with roots bursting through on either side, and the branches of trees overhead, through which I caught pale, gleaming shards of sky. The house remained hidden from view except when Michael drove up to higher ground, and found one of the few places where it was possible to see through, or over, the thick, ancient hedgerows that shielded nearly every piece of land from the road.

There it was, so close it must be just beyond the next curve of the road, yet forever out of our reach. The faint curl of smoke from the chimney inspired another yearning tug as I imagined sitting cosy and warm with my dear husband beside a crackling fire. I could almost smell the wood-smoke, and hot chocolate steaming in a mug.

I was hungry, thirsty and tired of stomping my foot down on an imaginary brake every time we met another car. There was a chill in the air as afternoon began to fade towards evening, and I wondered if we'd be able to get lunch anywhere, and made the point aloud.

He was impatient with my weakness. "We'll get something afterwards. Surely they'll invite us in for a cup of tea when we get there. They can't have many visitors!"

"If we could find that house by driving around, we would have found it already. You've already taken every turning, and we've seen every farm-yard and tumbledown shed and occupied house in the whole valley."

"Obviously we've missed one."

"Please, darling. It'll be dark soon. Look, we need to try something else. Why not go to Okehampton and ask an estate agent?"

"So now you're assuming the house is for sale."

"No. I assume it was for sale some time in the past and will be again in the future, and it is their business to know the local market. It's a beautiful place. We can't be the first people to have asked about it."

"No, but we will be the ones who get it!"

No one knew the house in the offices of the first two estate agents, and the man in the third one also stated there was no such cottage in the valley where we claimed to have seen it – that area was all woods and fields, he said – but there was something in his manner as he tried to fob us off with pictures and details of ever more expensive houses located twenty miles away that made me think he was hiding something, so we persisted, until, finally, he suggested we go see Mr. Yeo.

Mr. Yeo was a semi-retired property surveyor who had been in the business since before the War, and knew everything worth knowing about every house in this part of Devon. He lived still in the village where he had been born – Marystow – a name we both recognized, as it was one of the places we'd passed through a dozen times on our futile quest. So off we went to find him.

He was an elderly man who seemed friendly, happy to welcome us in to his home, until Michael revealed what we had come about, and then, abruptly, the atmosphere changed, and he began to usher us out again. The house was not for sale, we would not be able to visit it, there was no point in further discussion.

"But surely you can give us the name of the owners? An address to write to?"

"There b'ain't owners. He's not there."

I thought at first 'he' referred to the owner, unused to the way that older inhabitants of rural Devon spoke of inanimate objects as 'he' rather than 'it.' But Mr. Yeo made his meaning clear before sending us on our way: the perfectly desirable house we'd seen, nestled in a deep green coomb, did not exist. It was an illusion. We were not the first to have seen it; there were old folk and travellers' tales about such a house, glimpsed from a hilltop, nestled in the next valley; most often glimpsed late in the day, seemingly near enough that the viewer thought he could reach it before sunset, and rest the night there.

But no matter how long they walked, or what direction they tried, they could never reach it.

"Have you ever seen it?"

Mr Yeo scowled, and would not say. "'Tis bad luck to see 'im," he informed us. "Worse, much worse, to try to find 'im. You'm better go 'ome and forget about him. 'Tis not a good place for you'm."

Michael thanked the old man politely, but as we left, I could feel something simmering away in him. But it was not anger, only laughter, which exploded once we were back in our car. He thought Mr. Yeo was a ridiculous old man, and didn't buy his story for an instant. Maybe there was some optical illusion involved – that might explain why we hadn't been able to find the house where he'd expected it to be – but that was a real house that we'd seen, and someday we would find it.

Yet we never did. Not even when Michael bought the largest scale Ordnance Survey map of the area, the one for walkers that included every foot-path, building and ruin, could we find evidence that it had ever existed. Unless he'd been wrong about the location, and it was really in a more distant coomb, made to look closer by some trick of air and light...

Even after we moved to Devon – buying the wrong house – we came no closer to solving the mystery. I think Michael might have caught the occasional glimpse of it in the distance, but I never saw it again.

I SHOULDN'T PRETEND I didn't know what made Michael's thoughts return to our old home in Devon, because I had been dreaming about it myself, for the same reason: the Wheaton-Bakers Ruby Anniversary Celebration. We'd both been invited – with our respective new spouses, of course – to attend it at their house in Tavistock in four weeks' time. I didn't know about Michael, but I had not been back to Devon in over twenty years; not since we'd sold the house. The Wheaton-Bakers were the only friends from that period of my life with whom I'd kept in touch, although we saw each other no more often than Michael and I did.

I'd been pleased by the invitation. The party was in early October. David and I had booked a room in an inn on Dartmoor, and looked forward to a relaxing weekend away, with a couple of leg-stretching, mind-clearing rambles on Dartmoor book-ending the Saturday night festivities. And yet, although I looked forward to it, there was also a faint uneasiness in my mind attached to the idea of seeing Michael again, back in our old haunts; an uneasiness I did not so much as hint at to David because I could not explain it. It was irrational and unfair, I thought. My first marriage had not worked out, but both of us, or neither, were responsible for that, and that failure had been come to terms with and was long in the past. There was no unfinished business between us.

When the weekend of the party arrived, David was ill. It was probably only a twenty-four-hour bug (it was going around, according to our next-door neighbour, a teacher) but it meant he couldn't consider going anywhere farther than the bathroom.

I should have stayed home and tended to him, like a good wife – that is what I wish I had done. But he insisted I go. The Wheaton-Bakers were my friends. They would be sorry not to see me. We wouldn't get our money back for the hotel room – that had been an internet bargain. And he didn't need to be tended. He intended to sleep as much as possible, just lie in bed and sweat it out.

So I went. And I did enjoy myself. It was a lovely party; the Wheaton-Bakers were just as nice as I remembered, and they introduced me to other friendly, interesting people, so I never felt lonely or out of place for a moment. Michael was there, but he'd been seated at a different table, and struck up conversations with a different set of people, so although we'd exchanged greetings, we'd hardly done more than that. It was only as I was preparing to leave that he cornered me.

"Hey, you're not leaving!"

"'fraid so."

"But we've hardly spoken! You're driving back to Bristol tonight?"

"No, of course not." I told him where I was staying.

"Mm, very posh! I'm just up the road, nylon sheets and a plastic shower stall. Want to meet and have lunch somewhere tomorrow?"

I was happy to agree. We exchanged phone numbers, and he offered to pick me up at my hotel at ten. "If that's not too early? It'll give us time to drive around a bit, see how much the scenery has changed, before deciding what we want to do."

There was a familiar glint in his eye, and I was suddenly certain he meant to take me back to look at our old house, and maybe one or two other significant sites from our marriage. I didn't know why he felt the need to revisit the past like that – the past was over and done with, as far as I was concerned – but I didn't say anything. If he needed to go back and see with his own eyes how much time had passed, to understand that we were no longer the people who had fallen in love with each other, then perhaps I owed him my supportive, uncomplaining companionship.

Anyway, I thought it would be more fun than going for a walk by myself or driving straight back home.

The next morning, I checked out, and left my car in the car park. There was no question that we'd go in his: I remembered too well that he'd always disliked being a passenger. His car was better, anyway: a silver Audi with that new-car smell inside, soft leather seats and an impressive satnav system. Something by Mozart issued softly from hidden speakers as we he headed down the A386 before leaving the moor for the sunken lanes I remembered, winding deep into a leaf-shadowed coomb.

"Remember this?" he asked, as the car raced silently along. It was a smoother ride than in the old days.

"I'm glad they haven't dug up all the hedgerows," I said. "I was afraid Devon might have changed a lot more."

He frowned, dissatisfied with my answer. "Didn't you click on that link I sent you?"

"Yes, I did. I saw our old house – didn't I send a reply?"

He shrugged that off. "I thought you might have explored a bit more widely. Not just the village, not just the street view, but moving up and out, looking at the satellite pictures."

"It's a busy time of the year for us, with Christmas coming. I don't have much time to play around on the internet. Although I'm sure it's very interesting."

"It's more than just 'interesting.' You can see things that aren't on other maps. The aerial shots – do you remember how we had to go up to the top of the hill to see it?"

I understood. "You're not talking about our house."

"You know what I'm talking about." He touched the screen of his navigation system and a calm, clear female voice said, "You are approaching a cross-roads. Prepare to turn right."

"You found it?" I asked him, amazed. "How?"

"Turn right. Follow the road."

"Satellite view on Google. I zoomed in as much as I could – it wasn't easy to get a fix on it. Street View's no good – it's not on a road. But it's there, all right; maybe not in exactly the place we kept looking for it. Anyway, I have the co-ordinates now, and I've put them into my system here, and... it will take us there." He grinned like a proud, clever child.

"How, if it's not on a road?"

"Prepare to turn left. Turn left."

"It will take us as close as it can. After that we'll walk. Those are good, sturdy boots you have on."

"Take the first turning to the right."

"Well done, Sherlock," I said. "Just fancy if we'd had GPS back in those days – we'd have found it, and... do you think they'd have accepted our offer?"

"Bear left. At the next crossroads, turn right."

Despite the smoothness of the ride, as we turned and turned again – sometimes forced to stop and back up in a *pas-de-deux* with another Sunday driver – I began to feel queasy, like in the old days, and then another sort of unease crept in.

"Haven't we been along here already? We must be going in circles," I said.

"And when did you develop a sense of direction?"

"Prepare to turn right. Turn right."

The last turn was the sharpest, and took us off the road entirely, through an opening in a hedge so narrow that I flinched at the unpleasant noise of cut branches scraping the car, and then we were in a field.

There was no road or path ahead of us, not even a track, just the faint indication of old ruts where at some point a tractor might have gone, and even they soon ended.

"Make a U-turn when possible. Return to a marked road."

Michael stopped the car. "So that's as far as she'll take us. We'll have to rely on my own internal GPS the rest of the way."

We got out. He changed his brown loafers for a pair of brilliant white sports shoes that looked as if they'd never been worn, took an OS map out of the glovebox, and showed me the red X he had marked on an otherwise blank spot. "And this is where we are now."

"Why isn't it on the map?

He shrugged.

I persisted. "You must have thought about it."

He shrugged again and sighed. "Well, you know, there are places considered too sensitive, of military importance, something to do with national security, that you're not allowed to take pictures or even write about. There's an airfield in Norfolk, and a whole village on Salisbury Plain –"

"They're not on maps?"

"Not on any maps. And those are just the two examples I happen to know. There must be more. Maybe this house, or the entire coomb, was used for covert ops in the war, or is owned by MI5, used as a safe house or something."

My skin prickled with unease. "Maybe we shouldn't go there."

"Are you kidding? You're not going to wimp out on me now!"

"If it's so secret that it's against the law –"

"Do you see any 'No Trespassing' signs?" He waved his arms at the empty field around us. "It's a free country; we can walk where we like."

I took a deep breath, and thought about that airfield in Norfolk. I was pretty sure I knew the place he meant; it was surrounded by barbed wire fences, decorated with signs prohibiting parking and picture-taking on the grounds of national security. It was about as secret as the Post Office Tower. I nodded my agreement.

It was a good day for walking; dry, with a fresh, invigorating breeze countering the warmth of the sun. For about fifteen minutes we just walked, not speaking, and I was feeling very relaxed when I heard him say, "There it is."

Just ahead of us, the land dropped away unexpectedly steeply, and we stopped and stood gazing down into a deep, narrow, wooded valley. Amid the turning leaves the golden brown of the thatched roof blended in, and shadows dappled the whitewashed walls below with natural camouflage. If we hadn't been looking for it, we might not have seen it, but now, as I stared, it seemed to gain in clarity, as if someone had turned up the resolution on a screen. I saw a wisp of smoke rise from the chimney, and caught the faint, sweet fragrance of burning wood.

Michael was moving about in an agitated way, and it took me a few moments to realize he was searching for the best route down. "This way," he called. "Give me your hand; it's a bit tricky at first, but I then I think it should be easier."

I was suddenly nervous. "I don't think we should. There's someone there."

"So? They'll invite us in. We'll ask how long they've had the place and if they'd consider selling."

I saw that the notion of an MI5 safe house was far from his mind, if he had ever believed it. He wasn't even slightly afraid, and struggled to comprehend my reason for wanting to turn back.

"Look, if you want to wait for me here..."

I couldn't let him go by himself. I checked that my phone was on, and safely zipped into my pocket, and then I let him help me down to the first ledge, and the one after that. Then it got easier, although there was never anything as clear as a path, and on my own I'm certain I would have been lost, since my instinct, every time, was to go in a direction different from his. He really could hold a map in his head. At last we emerged from a surprisingly dense wood into a clearing from which we could see a windowless side wall.

I fell back and followed him around towards the front. Pebbles rolled and crunched gently underfoot on the path to the front door. I wondered if he had a plan, and what he would say to whoever answered the door: was he really going to pretend we were interested in buying?

Then I looked up and as I took in the full frontal view, I knew I had been here before. It was the strongest wave of *déjà vu* I'd ever felt, a sickening collision between two types of knowledge: I knew it was impossible, yet I remembered this visit.

The memory was unclear, but frightening. Somehow, I had come here before. When my knock at the door had gone unanswered, I'd peeked through that window on the right, and saw something that made me run away in terror.

I could not remember anything of what I had seen; only the fear it had inspired was still powerful.

Michael knocked on the door, then glanced over his shoulder, impatient with me for hanging back.

I wanted to warn him, but of what? What could I say? I was in the grip of a fear I knew to be irrational. I managed to move a little closer to Michael and the door, telling myself that nothing could compel me to look through that window.

We waited a little while, but even after Michael knocked again, more loudly, almost pounding, there was no reply. I relaxed a little, thinking we were going to get away with it, but when I spoke of leaving, he insisted, "Not until I find out who lives here, what it's all about. There is someone here – I can see a light – look, through that window –"

I moved back; I wouldn't look.

"I think I can smell cooking. They're probably in the kitchen. Maybe a bit deaf. I'm going to try the back door. You coming? Suit yourself."

I didn't want to stay, but wanted even less to follow him around the back, so I waited, wrapping my arms around myself, feeling a chill. The sun didn't strike so warmly in this leafy hollow. I checked my phone for the time and was startled to see how much of the afternoon was gone. I wondered if I should call David to warn him I'd be late, but decided to wait for Michael.

I didn't like to keep checking the time because it made me more nervous, but at least five minutes had passed when I felt I had no choice but to walk around to the back of the house to look for him.

I had no sense of *déjà vu* there; I was certain I'd never seen the peeling black paint that covered the solidly shut back door, or the small windows screened by yellowish, faded curtains that made it impossible to see inside.

"Michael?" I didn't like the weak, wavering sound of my voice, and made myself call out more loudly, firmly, but there was no reply. Nothing happened. I knocked as hard as I could on the back door, dislodging a few flakes of old paint, and as I waited I listened to the sound of leaves rustling in the wind; every once in a while one would fall. I felt like screaming, but that would have been bloody stupid. Either he had heard me or he hadn't. Either he was capable of reply – could he be hiding, just to tease me? – or he wasn't. And what was I going to do about it?

As I walked back around to the front of the house I was assailed by the memory of what I had seen when I looked through the window the last time I was here – if that had ever happened. I'd seen a man's foot and leg – I'd seen that there was someone inside the house, just sitting, not answering my knock, and the sight of some stranger's foot had frightened me so badly that I'd run away, and then repressed the memory of the entire incident.

Now I realized it must have been a dream that I recalled. It had that pointless, sinister atmosphere of a bad dream. Unfortunately, it now seemed like a precognitive dream.

Nothing had changed in front of the house. I got out my phone and entered the number Michael had given me. As I heard it ringing in my ear, I heard the familiar notes from 'The William Tell Overture' sounding from inside the house. I clenched my teeth and waited. When the call went to his voice-mail, I ended it and hit re-dial. Muffled by distance, the same tinny, pounding ringtone played inside the house, small but growing in volume until, once again, it was cut off by the voice mail programme.

I knew what I would see if I looked through the window, so I didn't look. I wanted to run away, but I didn't know where to go. It would be dark soon. I had to do something.

The front door opened easily. Tense, I darted my gaze about, fearful of ambush, although the place felt empty. To my right, I could see into a small, dark sitting room where an old man sat, or slumped, in an armchair.

He was a very, very old man, almost hairless, his skin like yellowed parchment, and appeared to have been dead for some time. It would have been his foot I would have seen if I'd looked through the window: his feet in brand new, brilliantly white sports shoes. But even as I recognized the rest of the clothes – polo shirt, jeans, soft grey hooded jacket, even the phone and car-keys in his pockets – I clung to the notion of a vicious trick, that someone had stolen Michael's clothes to dress an old man's corpse. How could the vigorous fifty-eight-year-old that I'd seen a few minutes ago have aged and died so rapidly?

I know now that it is what's left of Michael, and that there is no one else here.

I am not able to leave. I can open the door, but as soon as I step through, I find myself entering again. I don't know how many times I did that, before giving up. I don't know how long I have been here; it seems like a few days, at most, but when I look in the mirror I can tell by my hair that it must be two months or more.

There's plenty of food in the kitchen, no problems with plumbing or electricity, and for entertainment, besides all the books, there's an old video-player, and stacks of videos, as well as an old phonograph and a good collection of music. I say 'good collection' because it might have been planned to please Michael and me, at least as we were in the '80s.

Having found a ream of paper in the bottom drawer of the desk in the other parlour (the room where Michael *isn't*) I decided to write down what has happened, just in case someone comes here someday, and finds my body as I found his. It gives me something to do, even though I fear it is a pointless exercise.

While exploring the house earlier – yesterday, or the day before – I found evidence of mice – fortunately, only in one place, in the other sitting room. There were droppings there, and a nest made of nibbled paper, as if the mouse had devoted all its energy to the destruction of a single stack of paper. One piece was left just large enough for me to read a few words in faded ink, and recognize Michael's handwriting, but there was not enough for me to make sense of whatever he was trying to say.

PIED-À-TERRE

STEPHEN VOLK

Stephen Volk does ghosts like nobody's business. He is, after all, the writer behind the legendary TV 'hoax' Ghostwatch, *the drama series* Afterlife *and the forthcoming film* The Awakening. *Here Stephen presents us with a story that is a cry for justice, a common theme in tales of revenants, but 'Pied-à-terre' isn't so much a call for vengeance from beyond the grave, as a deeply affecting story whose ghost continues to call to us long after the tale is done.*

SHE PUT HER sunglasses on and raised them onto her head as she consulted the Google Maps print-out diligently folded and tucked between pages ninety-eight and ninety-nine of her A-Z. Leaving the Underground, she turned right into Fulham Road and followed the blue arrows, the print-out clutched in her hand. She hurried past Pizza Express, Nando's and the Nat West, mentally ticking off the landmarks, then took a right into North End Road before crossing to the other side of the street. On the Tube map it hadn't looked far from Hammersmith where she'd parked the car in a multi-storey just outside the congestion zone – *clever girl!* –

but she hadn't made allowance for the delay at Earl's Court, and now she was concerned about being late for her appointment.

Typical, she could hear Rollo saying when she told him. *Not typical, actually,* Miriam thought, as if answering him back, which she never did. *I'm never typically late, Rollo. You know that. I'm always really punctual, you know that.* She felt a little rash heating her neck as she even thought it, and felt foolish and annoyed at herself for feeling foolish and annoyed.

She knew why she was feeling like this – on edge, twitchy. It was because, just before driving to London, she and Rollo had had a row. Not a major one. Not a really major one, but a row nevertheless. It had always been the plan they'd do this together. But when it came to it, Rollo was on his laptop. *You go and look, I'm busy,* he'd said, not taking his eyes from the illuminated screen. *I'll see it later. I don't care. You make the decision. You can make a decision, can't you?*

Yes. But that wasn't the point. She'd *wanted* to do it together. They were husband and wife. That's what husbands and wives *did*. Look at houses together. Make the decision – *together*.

But now she started to think she was being unfair. Why was she always so unfair? He was probably back there, still on his computer, still working. And she'd done the two-hour drive to London – of course, why *not* her? She had nothing else to do. And he probably wanted to get it done today so that they could spend a nice Sunday together relaxing in the garden with a jug of Pimm's and the Sunday papers littered around them on the grass. That's probably what he was thinking. He was probably thinking of her.

The sun blinked behind red brick chimney stacks and black slate roofs, back-lighting television aerials and satellite dishes.

The street, as she walked along it, gave her a faint pang of nostalgia, unremarkable and unspectacular though it was. Certainly not salubrious. Just the kind of street of Victorian (or was it Edwardian?) houses you found all over London, with bay windows on the ground and second floors, and a plain, square, attic window above that. She could already picture the attic room; she had been brought up in a house not dissimilar in Tottenham, near Black Boy Lane, equidistant between Spurs and the MFI her parents used to frequent every weekend in their devotion to DIY. She recognised the type of apologetic yard they had in front of them cordoned by squat brick walls, barely big enough to house your wheelie bin – presumably now their sole purpose other than collecting weeds and straggly, dying plants. As if dying plants were some sort of design feature and envious neighbours peeked between net curtains deciding they had to have them to keep up with the Joneses.

37 Shorrold's Road, SW6...

Miriam read the address on the information from the estate agent.

37...

She raised her sunglasses again and squinted at the numbers on the doors or in cheap plastic decals on the gates. But there was no reason to, now she could see ahead of her a 'FOR SALE' sign, and since it was the only one in the street, made a bee-line for it.

For a moment she felt slightly woozy and lowered her shades back onto the bridge of her nose. Perhaps she'd inadvertently stared right into the sun or something –

that was it, probably – because she was suddenly aware of a pain just above her right eye, a tooth-achy pain that she got sometimes when her sinuses were blocked, or, perhaps now, when there was a lot of pollen in the air. Was there a lot of pollen in the air?

She wanted to get inside. Indoors. Rest her eyes. Dry eyes. Itchy eyes, now. Get rid of this damned headache. Where had it come from all of a sudden?

She saw no doorbell, so she rapped the knocker. To her surprise, the door opened an inch under the ever-so-slight force. It had been left on the snib, as her mum used to say. *On the snib?* Did anyone even use that expression any more? *On the snib.*

"Hello?"

She prodded it ajar and stepped gingerly into the narrow hallway, feeling a refreshing coolness spreading over her back where the sun used to be.

"Hi."

A cheery face popped out from the doorway of what was obviously the sitting room. Nice face. Nice smile, Miriam thought instantly.

"I'm Suzy, from the estate agent's." A hand extended to shake hers. Young hand. Perfect fingernails. Soft.

"Hi. I'm Miriam Lehr. Did we speak on the phone?"

"Did we...?"

"I don't know. I don't think so."

"Oh..."

"I think it was a man."

"Oh, then you're right. It wasn't me!" Suzy from the estate agent's chuckled. Miriam did the same, as best she could.

She liked the sound of the girl's laughter, though. It said, I'm a bit flaky but I'm all right, you can trust me.

She didn't think it was a ploy. It was just the way the girl was. There was no 'side' to her – another of her mum's expressions that Miriam wasn't entirely sure wasn't past its sell-by date.

"You don't mind, do you?"

"No," Miriam said. "No. Why should I mind?"

"Good." Suzy from the estate agent's had the ring of her car keys round one finger, jangling like jewellery when she moved, hugging the house specifications to her chest. Miriam fleetingly saw something else clutched there – a greeting card still in its cellophane wrapper. She could make out the words 'Mum' and '50' on it above the estate agent's cuff. "Right, then. Do you have any questions up front, or do you want to look around in your own time?"

"I'd like to look around in my own time, if that's all right."

"Be my guest. And anything you want to know, please fire away. That's what I'm here for." Suzy smiled and the smile was as nice to see as her laughter was to listen to.

"It's warm, isn't it?" Miriam fanned herself with the A-Z.

"Yes. I love it."

"It's a bit too much for me, actually."

"Is it? I love it. I'm a bit of a sun bod, I'm afraid." Suzy made a face, like it was a character fault of hers. A nice air of self-deprecating charm, there, under the confidence – both things Miriam envied. Deeply.

"I can tell." Miriam had noticed the other woman's tan as soon as she'd seen her. "Have you been abroad?"

"No. I had a great day this weekend windsurfing. Got myself a new sail!"

Miriam would have liked to hate her for saying that, and for slightly miming the action, but it was said in a completely un-showy manner, with almost childish glee. A guilty secret she wanted to share. And who could be mean-spirited enough to begrudge her that? In all honesty, with her perfect teeth and lipstick, Miriam thought, the young woman beside her had everything going for her. She was trim. Fit. Beautiful. Possibly still full of memories of the beach – the sport, the swim suits, yellow sand on wet skin, the sound of crashing waves, the boyfriend – wine (sparkling wine?), kisses... Obviously something blissfully romantic...

She pretended to be taking in the room but she was really taking in Suzy out of the corner of her eye, in her smart dry-cleaned business suit and shirt, top button undone, healthy tan and glowing good looks, her sun-loving glow, lush nut-brown hair swept from that side parting, draped over one eyebrow. It made her think how sickeningly pale she herself was, with her too-long body and too-short legs stuck in ugly running shoes instead of the polished high heels Suzy wore, showing off her shapely calves.

"How long has this house been on the market?"

"A week."

"Has there been any interest?"

"A bit." Suzy grinned cheekily. The grin said: I'm bound to say that, aren't I? I'm not going to tell you nobody else is interested, am I? I'm doing my job. You know the game.

Miriam had started to give her surroundings the once over and wasn't impressed. Everything was dark. Dark wood, dark carpets. Never the taste of anybody born since 1970, she thought. Perhaps it was an old person's house. An Asian family. She didn't know why she thought that, but there was the smell of cooking in the air, curry perhaps, from next door even, or was it the long ingrained smell of dog? *Wet* dog?

A nail stuck out of the wall where a painting once hung. What kind of painting? And where was it now? Sold? Sold so that someone could eat? So that a mother could feed her children? She wondered what else had been removed. Where were the owners anyway? Where were the signs of them? There should be children playing, toys, something. Even the absence was an absence...

Miriam rubbed her arms, eager to move on. "Right."

"Right, Mrs Lehr... Upstairs? It is Mrs Lehr?"

"Yes, it is."

Hadn't she noticed her wedding ring? Women usually did. It was the first thing they noticed. But then, that's no guarantee you want to be called *Mrs*, is it? There were plenty of married women who wanted to be called *Ms*. There were plenty who retained their maiden name, too. Probably thinking they were hanging on to their beloved 'independence,' but to Miriam it sounded non-committal, like clinging onto their old name was an escape plan, a glider in the attic.

She climbed the stairs behind the estate agent, noticing her calves again. Perfect. Muscular. Not rugger-player's legs like hers, as her husband called them. Miriam was mesmerised for a few minutes by the way her ankles rose out of the high heels, leaving a little gap as she went from step to step, and by the way her slim hips jutted gently from side to side.

"This is the master bedroom. Nice size, again," Suzy said. "How long have you been married, if you don't mind my asking?"

"Not long. Only six months." Miriam followed her into a room with heavy net curtains over two large windows. The filtered sunlight fell on a large double bed with cheap, ungenerous pillows and a hideously drab duvet which Miriam tried to blank out of her consciousness. She wondered how long ago the bed had been made. That morning? Had the man lain sweating against the pillow? Had they made love? Perhaps – ghastly thought – the stains were still under there, drying...

"Oh. That's nice. So you're still quite newly-fangled?"

"I beg your pardon?"

"Newly-fangled. With each other?"

"Oh, no. Not really. We've known each other for a while. About four years, in fact. We know each other well. He used to live in a flat with some other blokes and I used to live with my mum and dad."

"So this is your first home together? Lovely."

"No, I won't be staying here. Not a lot. Maybe occasionally, if we come up for the theatre and we can't get a late train back, sort of thing. But mainly it's for my husband, you see..."

"Lovely."

Miriam looked at the flowers on the bedside table and felt sure they were the work of the estate agent in a vain attempt to brighten up the place. It didn't quite work, but it was a gesture. Suzy was good at her job, and she cared, that was obvious. Miriam wondered if she did those little touches in her own home. Wondered if she had a husband or boyfriend – *windsurfer* – tanned, successful, waiting for her when she got home from work and kicked off those high heels and rested those perfect calves.

"We have a cottage in the country," Miriam said.

"Near a place called Marshfield, just off the M4. That's our main home."

"Sounds gorgeous," Suzy cooed, interlocking her fingers and raising her shoulders to her ears. "Does it have a thatched roof and stuff and roses round the door, and a pond with ducks in?"

"Not quite." Miriam laughed. "But there are ducks within walking distance."

"Waddling distance."

"Feeding distance. Just a stream. It's a nice little routine we've got into, throwing breadcrumbs to them on the way to getting our paper in the morning."

"Now I'm envious," Suzy said.

"Well, Rollo got to the stage in his career he wanted to move out of London. We both did. For our sanity, he said. But he still needs somewhere to lay his head during the week. Just a *pied-à-terre*. You can't commute a two-hour trip each way, every day, can you? That's asking for trouble."

"Absolutely." Suzy smiled a big smile like she'd forgotten about doing so and suddenly realised the fact. "Bathroom?"

Miriam followed.

"You'll miss him during the week, though."

"I will. Of course I will, but this is more about creating quality time together, as a couple. That's our priority. That's what we've talked about. That's our plan."

"Lovely."

Suzy opened the door to the bathroom and Miriam stepped inside a box-like room with brown cork-tile walls and an avocado bath and sink.

The colour combination she found massively claustrophobic, and the window, daubed opaque with gloss paint – (so badly done, look, God, not even *neatly* done) – conspired to make her feel vaguely, definitely trapped. What's more, the boiler in the airing cupboard, she was sure, was physically pulsating, the heat a Mecca for bedbugs. The combination of which meant the nausea she'd experienced earlier welled up again, the unwelcome pulsing in her forehead back with a vengeance. Searing, this time. Unrelenting. Her skin tightened across the front of her head...

KA-CHUNK!

What was that? What was it?

Then, hush... a kind of hushing, pitter-patter...

Her head twisted round, almost cricking her neck.

She stared wide-eyed at the sink. At the taps.

"What's that noise?" Miriam said.

"What noise? I didn't hear anything."

"You did. You must have. It was really loud. Like something turning on somewhere. A clunk."

Suzy slowly shook her head, mouth downturned at the edges.

"Like a tap running. It's stopped now," Miriam said.

"I didn't hear anything."

"Are you sure?"

"I didn't hear a thing. Honestly."

Miriam stepped closer to the sink and vigorously turned both taps on full.

Stupid. What are you like, eh? Stupid!

She took a deep breath and fluttered her fingers quickly under the water and wiped her cheeks. Reaching out, she covered her face with a towel that was old and hard and cheap and past its best, then quickly put it back on its rail. The ghost of a towel. A shroud.

She turned the taps off again. CLUNK.

"I'm sorry. I..."

"Don't worry."

"I don't know what I..."

"Don't worry," Suzy said, smiling. "Onward and upward?"

Miriam nodded. "Please."

Following, she pressed the index finger of her right hand against the place that was now agony on her forehead, holding it there and massaging it the way Astrid, her friend the aromatherapist, did.

"Just the central heating, I expect," Suzy said. "I put it on boost to take the chill off. It's probably just the pipes expanding, that's all."

"Rollo says I'm too jittery. Too jumpy by half. He tells me to calm down. But I can't help it."

"Of course you can't."

Miriam listened to the silence of the house, and she wasn't sure whether that pleased her or made her more nervous. She wasn't entirely sure anything would put her at ease now, because as she followed the estate agent up the stairs to the top floor, the air seemed to become thinner and hotter, all the fresh air and life sucked out. *Shroud*, she thought again. *Ghost*, she thought again – and tried to rid herself of those words, and those thoughts, but they wouldn't go away.

And anyway, why did Suzy have to boost the heating? Did the family no longer live here? Had they absconded? Fled? What makes a person flee? A family, *flee*?

"This could make a nice office. For Rollo," Suzy said, walking towards the grimy Roman blinds covering the attic window. "Desk here, overlooking the street. His space. His den."

Miriam tried to see the glass-topped trestle table, right

there. Tried to see Rollo's laptop, open, on top of it.

"How did you meet?"

"Whuh?"

"You and your husband."

"Oh. In work. We worked together. Venom Records. I was in the accounts department. Boring. He was on the management side. Much more impressive." Miriam's mobile phone emitted a bleep and she delved into her handbag to fish it out.

"I thought that was him now, but it isn't." Her eyes narrowed as she thumbed the tiny keys. "I don't recognise the number. Probably someone trying to sell me something..." She switched it off and put it back in the dark where it belonged.

"So you don't need to be in London, too?"

"No, I was made redundant. No, I was happy about it. I'll get a job locally," Miriam said. "In a shop or a garden centre or the pub... I'm not bothered..."

Then, again, just as she'd begun to forget it, tooth-achy pain spread up her brow and across her scalp like running water seeping along fissures... along unsheathed nerves... she felt as though her skull was open to the elements, to the dark.

TSCH-TSCH-TSCH-TSCH...

"Are those footsteps?"

Suzy turned to look at her with a frown deeply etched on her face.

"I'm sure they are. Listen. Footsteps. Downstairs!"

Suzy kept staring at her. The frown didn't go away.

Don't be stupid. You're imagining things. You imagine things.

Miriam flinched. Shut her eyes. Tried to stiffen, straighten her back.

"Mrs Lehr? Miriam?"

She couldn't look at Suzy any more. She couldn't stay in the room any more. It was crushing in on her, like a great cement block pressing down on her head. Some rollercoaster was doing a figure of eight inside her. Some wave was coming up through her chest and she had the terrible feeling that when it hit she was going to collapse, and she feared that, feared it desperately and ran from it – ran from the room.

Gulping air, she hung onto the chest of drawers on the landing as if it were a piece of driftwood.

"Are you all right, Mrs Lehr?"

"Yes, I'm all right." Miriam closed her eyes again, tighter this time. "I'm being silly. I'm always being silly..."

"Why do you say that? What's wrong?"

"Nothing's wrong. Look, I don't like the feel of this house."

"Don't you?"

"No, I don't. I really don't. I don't like it. There's something about it. I can't explain. I don't have to explain! I don't think it's what we're looking for. At all, actually! I'm sorry..."

"Well, maybe a studio flat might be more suitable? More in your price range?" She wished Suzy would leave it, *just leave it, just shut up*. "We've certainly got some of those on our books. Perhaps if you came in with your husband..."

"No. No! – you don't understand..."

"Well, this is a big decision for you to make all on your own..."

"I know! I *know*, all on my own. But I have to!" She could tell how pathetic that sounded. Knew how pathetic it was. *She* was. "You can't possibly..."

She looked into Suzy's eyes and Suzy waited for her to speak. Why did she wait like that? Why was she even interested, this beautiful girl – interested in *her*?

"You see, the thing is, the thing is I've got to get this right. It has to be the right decision, for us as a couple. It *has* to be. I don't want to get it wrong because... because I *always* get things wrong." Miriam felt her lower lip quivering. "I know it probably sounds pathetic to you, but you're not me and it's different for you and I want to please him, for once. I want him to be pleased with me. I want him to say, 'Good girl, brilliant.' I want him to go, 'My god, if I was there that's exactly what I would've done.' Not..." *Why the hell did you do that? You idiot! Can't I trust you, ever? Can't you do anything?*

Miriam caught her own breath in a gasp.

Not wanting to let it out. The words. The thought, even.

She felt Suzy's hand on her shoulder, on the muscle just beside her neck, pressing where it hurt. Where everything hurt. And felt the heat lifting, the soreness cooling. But still she couldn't open her eyes. Maybe it was the only way to say things, when she couldn't see the world, any of it. Just...

"He's not always like that, but sometimes..." Miriam said, wiping her eyes with the heel of one hand. "And I'm not always a moron, but I am sometimes... I know I am, and I don't blame him for getting irate. And when he's irate he loses it and words come out and I know he doesn't mean them. Not really." She gulped on her inhale and shuddered. "Why am I saying this? God..."

Suzy's fingers squeezed, but she said nothing.

"Most of the times it's okay because I know he loves me. Most of the time..."

Bang!

Suddenly Miriam's head exploded, hit by a fist. Her eyes sprang open, glazed, pupils contracting with terror into pin-pricks. Her breath, caught between an exhale and an inhale, knotted in her throat. A metal rod shafted through her spinal cord, lifting her to her feet.

The door had slammed.

The door *downstairs*. The front door.

"What was that?"

"Mrs Lehr?"

She swung round to look at Suzy, but Suzy just stared at her. Of course she did. What did she hear? Nothing.

"Miriam?"

The naked light bulb hanging over the stairwell went off.

Ghost!

She held her breath. She felt her bladder loosen. A squirt like acid inside. In some organ inside her. Some substance. Some poison wanting to get out. *Please.*

Just as suddenly the light bulb came on again.

Then off. Then on again.

Please!

She bleated. Pulse pounding.

"Miriam, what is it? You're frightening me. Say something."

But she didn't. Couldn't.

Instead she toppled, caught herself, stumbling, ran downstairs – almost leaping the entire first flight of steps and risking breaking her ankle in the process. But she wasn't even thinking about that. She was thinking about the dog-smell that was back, and the nail in the wall, and the absent picture, and the absent *family*, and careering down the next flight –

Clinging to the banister rail because her feet were hardly touching the floor now –

Swinging round the newel post, not even letting the half open door to the master bedroom (smelly duvet, net curtains, bed bugs) catch her eye. Didn't want anything catching her eye, ears, nose, throat, senses, brain, especially brain –

Desperate to get to the front door, desperate to find the front door and open it and be free –

She was there.

She could see it.

The front door, closed – as she knew it would be, *must* be – with day, sunlight, life beyond.

She ran towards it – *please!* – hands stretched out with fingers splayed in front of her until they found the wood, spidering to the Chubb, the lock, the *snib* – all that now stood between her and –

KA-CHUNK!

Again!

She froze. Turned. Back to the door, the Chubb, the snib. Eyes pulled open. Eyes unable to close.

Staring down the tunnel of malignant wallpaper – turning the narrow passage at the kink at the electricity meter, down one step – back into the kitchen (where she hadn't set foot!), lit from the yard (what yard?) where she could see her...

Nail... Family... Shroud...

Ghost!

Oh, Jesus Christ!

A man bent over the sink – twenties, overweight, puppy-fat, paunch – head arched in profile, eyes unblinking, staring down at the running tap. Holding up a spoon and looking at it. Polishing it on his sleeve and looking at it again – and looking through it, *past* it – at *her*.

Oh, Christ!

The ghost lowered the spoon.

She felt pee ooze into her knickers. And she thought, *don't let me be afraid. I don't mind dying, God. Dying is fine: just don't let me be afraid...*

"Mrs Lehr?"

The young man placed the spoon on the stainless steel draining board and wiped his hands on his jacket. He walked towards her in a shuffling motion. A little gawky, she thought. A gawky ghost. His long-toed winkle-pickers – all the rage recently – clicking on the tiled floor.

Tsch-tsch-tsch-tsch...

He took her hand and shook it.

"I heard a voice upstairs. I was starting to get a bit spooked, to be honest. I thought the house was empty. What time do you make it?" He looked at his watch. "Only, when you weren't here on time I phoned the office. Couldn't get a signal indoors, so I went up the street. Is something wrong?"

Miriam walked past him to the staircase and stood with her back to him. Suzy hadn't followed her down.

"In the time I was out, you came in. Obviously," the young man said. "I wondered why the lights were on. They tried to phone you, by the way, the office, did they?" Miriam didn't answer and hadn't moved. "My name's Olly, by the way."

"Suzy?" Miriam called up the stairs.

"Excuse me, Mrs Lehr..."

"I was with your colleague... She's –"

"Colleague?"

"She took me upstairs."

"No. I don't think so."

"Yes. She showed me round the place. Room by room. She's up there. I was with her."

"No, Mrs Lehr. That's not possible. It's just me."

"Don't be ridiculous."

She turned to look at him and he was pale. His eyes flickered, avoiding hers, the way people did at funerals. The way people looked when they had bad news.

"Do you want a cup of tea or coffee? The owners made me one before they took themselves off to the London Eye. I was just cleaning up. They said to offer you one. Nice people." He edged past her, holding his tie flat to his stomach. "Sit down and let me explain. Not that I can. Not really."

He switched on the kettle to bring it back to the boil. Miriam came into the kitchen, but remained at the door.

"Have you heard of Suzy Lamplugh?" the young man said. "She was an estate agent. She went missing on the last Monday of July 1986. Nobody ever found out what happened to her. It's a mystery. Wasn't until 1994 she was officially declared dead, presumed murdered."

Miriam decided she would sit down after all, and felt her way to the nearest chair like a blind person.

"She went out to show someone a property. The last entry in her diary said, '12.45 – Mr Kipper – 37 Shorrold's Road O/S.' 'O/S' meaning she was going to meet him outside."

"Suzy Lamplugh," Miriam said as the kettle rose to a shriek. "It was in the news for ages. Years... Suzy Lamplugh..."

"Her white Ford Fiesta was found about a mile from the office outside another property in Stevenage Road. No sign of a struggle. No trace of her. Nothing. To this day."

Miriam thought of the face she first saw, so tanned, so healthy. So – her throat tightened at the idea – alive.

"To be honest I don't know much about it. Just what they say in the office. Apparently Suzy's parents set up a charitable trust in her name. I think her mum got an OBE for it."

"It was her mum's birthday," Miriam said.

"Was it? You know more than me."

Miriam held the image of the greeting card still wrapped in cellophane in her head. Didn't want to explain. Explain? She couldn't *explain* anything.

"She's been seen before," Olly said. "In this house, I mean. Other people in the business. I always thought it was bollocks. Sorry."

"Don't be," Miriam said. "She was a very happy girl. She had a wonderful smile. She wouldn't want anybody to be sad. I think she was probably an amazing person."

Neither of them noticed that the kettle had boiled.

Even now, so soon, Miriam felt all her impressions of Suzy starting to fade. The words, the voice, the images. Was it real, what had happened? Or passing, like the heat of the day? A memory, like a yesterday, a yesterday that visited today. A feather she tried to grasp even now, but the very act of grasping sent it floating away, again, and again...

"1986," Olly said. "I wasn't even born."

"I was three."

"Nobody who knew her works at the office any more. But we keep a small picture of her by the copier machine. To remind us."

"To remind you of what?"

"I'm not sure. Just her, I suppose," he said.

Miriam stood up and walked back into the hall. She didn't know why she touched the banister rail, resting her hand there, but she did.

"Do you think she even knows she's dead?"

Hunched over in his chair in the kitchen, Olly shrugged.

"I mean, what do ghosts want?" Miriam thought aloud.

"Perhaps they don't want anything. Perhaps they're just drawn to places they've been, they're familiar with, and do what they did in life, over and over... like a kind of loop tape. Like a scratch in a record you can't get out of... Ever..."

"She was happy. She'd been windsurfing." Miriam sensed her eyes prickling again as the word hung in the air like a heartbreak, and knew this time it wasn't the pollen. She turned slowly to look at the sunlight-bleached world beyond the front door and squinted slightly in preparation to entering it, hearing waves unbidden, imagining the fondest of kisses, imagining sand on skin all over again. "I need to go now."

"Cool. No problem." Olly stood up, both hands thrust in jacket pockets, then one checking his mobile phone for messages. "Can I drive you anywhere?"

"No. Thank you."

"Are you sure?" He pushed the chair under the kitchen table. "Well. I'm sorry we couldn't come up with the goods, Mrs Lehr. Not on this occasion." He shot his cuffs, ran his finger round the inside of his collar. "Do you want us to keep your details on record? Er... I take it you're not interested in the property?"

He saw himself reflected in the dark lenses of her sunglasses as she held out her hand.

"I'll take that as a 'no,' then," he said.

* * *

BY THE TIME she reached the multi-storey in Hammersmith she'd already decided she wasn't going to tell Rollo. He'd call her gullible, silly, neurotic, certifiable. Foolish. Worse. It was pointless. He wouldn't feel anything for Suzy. A career girl with everything ahead of her? Why would he care about *her*? He'd just grunt like he grunted and shook his head when she got weepy over an old black-and-white movie. Yet he'd shed tears happily over a goal at the cup final and not think anything abnormal about that.

She would simply tell him the house in Shorrold's Road wasn't suitable. End of story. That was all he needed to know. And she wouldn't phone him before the return journey. She didn't want to talk to him right now. Or was she being – (that word)...

You're not being weak, Miriam. He's a bully, he always has been, you know that, and you have to be strong.

Miriam nodded. Gripped the wheel. Adjusted the rear view mirror.

He gets a kick out of belittling you. Don't let him. This isn't the only life you can have, it's just the one you've chosen right now and you can un-choose it.

She felt Suzy's hand resting on hers on the steering wheel. So much smoother and softer than her own.

Miriam. You're a strong, beautiful lady. You can do this. You can change your life. You can turn this corner. I know you can.

She drove down the ramp of the multi-storey and let the barrier take her ticket, not relishing the drive ahead, heading into the rush hour.

Then, as she joined the traffic, she decided not to take the M4 at all, and headed somewhere else, with a clarity of mind that startled her.

HABITUALLY, OLLY LUMB rearranged the fridge magnets when he arrived home and he wasn't about to change the habit of a lifetime. He found an 'S' and a 'U', then an 'R' and an 'F' to go with it. Then he found a large red 'M' to spell 'SMURF' but had to move a magnetic fried egg to keep the photograph of The Boy after his first haircut in position. He loved that picture. Tintin, he called it. Cartoon boy. It made him smile.

His wife was cooking and she got a kiss on the back of the neck, just above the chain of the necklace he'd bought her for their last anniversary.

Didn't want to share the day with her, though. Didn't know why.

There was nothing illicit or untoward in his contact with Miriam, nothing romantic. He wasn't even attracted to her – God, no. It just seemed a private thing. What happened today, to the two of them. He wanted to process it, let it sink in, get it settled and ordered in his brain because it didn't feel ordered now, not even after he'd popped the cap of that ice-chilled Belgian beer they'd brought back through the Tunnel.

Then he would tell her. Maybe. If it felt right. But only if it felt right. Maybe it was something he'd keep to himself. Not like an affair or a secret, more like walking through a graveyard and not wanting to step on a grave. You knew the person underground wouldn't care, but somehow, weirdly, that didn't matter. It was just something you didn't want to do. And this felt the same.

"What's wrong?"

He looked up from his bottle of Ename.

"You're quiet."

"Am I? Don't mean to be."

When he'd first made love to his wife she'd said, "If I were a cat, I'd purr!" and he loved that, that memory. He basked in it. From the very beginning he wanted to love Fran and protect her, save her. Make her feel safe, that was it. That was it exactly. Though she'd no doubt laugh uproariously if he said it that way. He went over and kissed her again, this time on the lips.

"You know what? I love you," he said.

"That's better."

"That *is* better."

"Now go and switch off *Octonauts* and tell The Boy his tea's ready. Hector!"

As he did as he was bidden, Olly was wondering several things. Most of all wondering why the ghost appeared to her, Mrs Lehr, and not him. He'd been to the property several times in the last few years and seen nothing. He'd stood in that empty house and that's all it was – an empty house. Nobody spoke. Nobody appeared. So it troubled him. Why do they appear to some people and not others?

Then he remembered the moment he shook Miriam's hand to say goodbye, and how he'd seen the little flinch of pain in her cheek. And how he'd looked down for a fraction of a second and had seen the bruising on her wrist and forearm. Pink, dark blue and purple. The result of a fall or some accident, he'd thought, or perhaps not an accident at all.

* * *

MIRIAM TURNED OFF Black Boy Lane into the street she knew of old. It was notoriously bad for parking, but she found a place instantly.

She rang the doorbell, thinking how to say she wanted to stay a while, she wasn't sure how long, before going back to the West Country. But the truth was, she was now certain, she never wanted to go back to the West Country, or see Rollo, her husband, ever again. Yesterday had visited today, and now she wanted today to visit tomorrow, if that made sense. And if it didn't, tough luck.

A woman opened the door and embraced her. For a fleeting moment she smelled of Suzy, of Suzy's embrace, of Suzy's hair, and Miriam felt for the first time in a long time she wasn't scared any more.

"Hello, Mum."

For further information about the work of The Suzy Lamplugh Trust, and to donate, please go to:

http://www.suzylamplugh.org/

IN THE ABSENCE OF MURDOCK

TERRY LAMSLEY

Terry Lamsley is an extraordinary practitioner of the supernatural. His roots are in M.R. James, Robert Aickman, Ramsey Campbell and the tradition of the English ghost story, yet there is a surreal and almost comic thread to Lamsley's fiction that reminds me of the films of David Lynch and Mike Leigh. 'In The Absence of Murdock' is a very strange story indeed, at once urbane (urban even), but at the same time the fiction's reality threatens to dissolve into a terrifying world that none of us would ever understand.

"OH, IT'S YOU, Franz, come on in."

"I've come to see Jerry. Is he at home?"

"Of course he is. Where else would he be? He's always at home nowadays, remember. He's upstairs, waiting for you, I expect."

Franz gave his sister a curious look. "How do you know that?"

"I suggested that he call you or another of his old friends."

"Is something wrong?"

"Possibly. Probably," Barbara said, pulling the front door shut behind him.

Franz said, "I can hear it in your voice. And Jerry sounded very strange when he phoned."

"Yes, I expect he did."

"Are you going to tell me what it is?"

"The problem? Well, I'm not sure about that. I'd better let Jerry explain. It would sound better coming from him."

"Really? Why's that?"

Barbara gave Franz a wild, slightly irritated look. "Please," she said, "go on up. He'll be pleased to see you."

"You seem almost embarrassed about something, Barbara."

"Not really, no – it's not that, exactly – but we've both been under a bit of a strain recently, for the past few days, in fact."

"It shows."

"Well, you're here now. Perhaps you can sort things out."

Franz started to climb the stairs. "I'll try, at least," he said.

Barbara waited until he was passing the chair lift waiting at the top of the stairs before she called out, "Thanks for coming, Franz. Jerry will be so pleased to see you."

Franz said, "So you said, just now."

He walked along the landing, stopped outside his brother-in-law's room, and waited a few moments before lifting his fist and rapping rather loudly on the door.

"Is that you, Franz? Come on in."

Franz walked in to the room Jerry called his office. It resembled an office in as much as it contained a large desk covered with a certain amount of paper and a typewriter. Jerry called himself an 'old fashioned' writer. He claimed to despise computers and people who used them and was proud of his antiquated method of producing his and Murdock's scripts. As far as Franz could remember, Murdock transferred the finished script to respectable Word form, but Jerry was not supposed to be aware of that. Murdock was not present, but Franz thought he could detect the faint smell of the man's horrible cigars hanging in the air.

Jerry was sitting in a wheelchair near the window. The heavy curtains were drawn and the only light in the room came from a big lamp hanging over the desk.

Franz said, "What have you been up to, Jerry?"

"Not a lot. We've just about put the new series to bed, I'm pleased to say."

"You didn't invite – summon – me here to tell me that."

"True enough. I'd forgotten what an extremely no-nonsense sort of person you were, Franz. Forgive my attempted polite small talk."

"Barbara thinks you've got a problem."

"Hum. Well, it's not exactly a problem. One that you might be able to solve, that is."

"What is it, then?"

"Something inexplicable, Franz."

"Go on then, astonish me."

"Okay. Murdock has gone missing."

"He's walked out on you? Doesn't surprise me at all, you can be a pain in the neck at times, as I'm sure you're aware. I'm surprised that the working relationship has lasted so long. He's probably had enough – or too much – of you. Needs a break. I expect he'll turn up in his own good time."

"I fear not."

"Why?"

"The circumstances of his disappearance were... peculiar."

For some reason Franz found this funny. He laughed and said, "Just what exactly is on your mind, Jerry? Do you want me to go and look for him?"

"No, that may not be necessary, but I'd like your opinion. Just let me explain."

"Do, by all means."

Jerry put his hands together in a prayerful attitude, tapped his fingers together one by one, then hauled his wheelchair around so it was exactly facing Franz. Franz supposed he was attempting to appear relaxed, but he had the same mildly embarrassed expression on his face that Franz had seen on his sister's face a few minutes earlier.

He said, "I assume you know how we work together, Murdock and I?"

Franz had watched an episode of the comedy Murdock and Jerry were responsible for, *Dead Funny Ted*, set in a funeral parlor run by a doddering old fool called Edward, in a picturesque seaside town populated almost entirely by elderly people. He had found it gormless and not the least bit funny, but he didn't think it necessary to tell Jerry that. Besides, the public were supposed to love it. Instead, he said, "I read something somewhere, in one of the TV Sunday supplements I guess, how you work as a team. About how you read the papers together in the morning in search of ideas and then get down to work in the afternoon."

Jerry nodded, "Murdock enjoys what he calls 'our daily disaster sessions.' Always seems to be something terrible happening somewhere. You have to laugh."

"I believe it mentioned something about that, too."

Jerry permitted himself an uneasy smile of satisfaction on hearing this. "That's right. That gets us going. Anyway, we both have our different roles. I provide the plots and situations and Murdock handles the characterization and dialogue. Believe it or not, he's good at jokes. Or, rather, a humorous turn of phrase. Myself, I'm less so."

Jerry paused as though he expected Franz to make some comment. Franz didn't, so Jerry continued, "It always worked well enough for both of us. We were just about finishing up on our fifth series, you know."

"I didn't."

"Yes, it's been what you might call a runaway success."

"That's very good."

"We were working on putting the finishing touches to the last episode a few days ago. Murdock was going through his paces, speaking every character's part aloud, as he has always insisted on doing, searching about for the humor in the situation we've reached in the script. I had turned my chair away from him and wheeled it up to the window for some fresh air. My lungs and heart, as you know, are not good, especially in the presence of Murdock's cigar smoke."

"I don't know how or why you stand it."

"As I said, we have to work as a team, all for one and one for all. Murdock says he can't think without a smoke and we each need the support of the other. It's the way we get things done."

"Humm. It once occurred to me that he might use those particularly pungent cigars to hide another more personal smell."

"Barbara told me she sometimes has the same suspicions. She keeps her distance."

Franz, resisting the temptation to yawn, said, "Anyway, carry on."

"It's going to be a bit tricky explaining the next bit. Barbara, usually so sympathetic, can't follow me at all after this point. Anyway, see what you think."

"You had your back to Murdock and you were looking out of the window."

"I was doing a bit of free thinking, I call it, searching for inspiration, letting my mind wander, and was not really aware of my surroundings. While I was daydreaming I realised that Murdock's voice had stopped and the room had fallen silent. Even when he's not mumbling away to himself, Murdock fidgets about and makes noises. He giggles to himself and coughs and sighs a lot. I couldn't hear a thing from him, so I looked round to see if he was alright."

"And he wasn't."

"No, he really wasn't. He wasn't there at all."

"He'd left the room."

"He certainly wasn't in it. It took me just a few seconds to establish that fact. Then I smelt burning and that worried me, as you can imagine. I thought the house might be on fire. But then I saw smoke rising from over there" – he pointed – "just where Murdock had been sitting, and I found a cigar end smoldering on the carpet."

Franz leaned forward and rested his hand on his forehead in hope of concealing the smile that he couldn't avoid. Jerry said, "What's the matter?"

"Nothing, please continue."

"Yes, well, I had to call Barbara then, because if I reached down for it I risked falling out of my wheelchair.

I mean, I could have killed myself, it was that risky. My condition is very delicate. Luckily she heard me and ran up at once." He pulled a peculiar face, like a cautious rat sniffing the air, then said, "There's what's left of the cigar. I thought I'd better keep it." He stretched out and slid a large glass ashtray towards Franz.

After giving the tray and its content a brief inspection Franz said, "Why?"

"Why did I keep it? I suppose as some sort of evidence."

"Evidence of what? Surely, at that time it didn't occur to you that something had gone wrong."

"Oh, yes it did. No doubt about it. There was a *feeling* in this room. Barbara noticed it, I think, but she didn't say anything, so as not to upset me even more, bless her."

"She could see that you were upset, then?"

"I couldn't hide it. And she was furious about the burnt carpet. I tried to explain but she didn't, couldn't, understand what had happened and I was too confused to make much sense. I mean, I wasn't sure myself. She got the message that Murdock had gone after dropping his cigar but she wasn't much surprised because she's said many a time that the man was a clumsy lout."

"Well, let's face it, she's not far wrong."

Jerry looked mildly disapproving of that. "Murdock has his faults, no doubt about it, but together we bring in the money. I may not be around much longer, and there's seven years left before the mortgage on this house is paid. I frequently have to remind Barbara of that when she criticizes Murdock."

"Anyway, you say he's gone missing for the moment," Franz said.

"I said he's vanished."

"And you saw and heard nothing when he went?"

"Umm, well, there was a slight sound, just before I looked round and found he had gone. At least, I think so."

Franz was tired. It had been a long, hard day in the library where he had been doing some research since it had opened at nine in the morning. He took a discreet look at his watch and found it was now almost eleven in the evening. He got out of his chair and yawned. Jerry got the message and said, "You are leaving. I'm sorry to have kept you. It was good of you to come."

"What was it, though, this sound you heard?"

Jerry sought the precise expression to describe the noise he thought he had perceived, then said, "It was like a sharp inhalation and exhalation of air."

"Of breath?"

"Almost certainly."

"Like a sigh, then. Perhaps Murdock's last sigh? Or gasp?"

"It's no joke. I'm deadly serious about this."

"I'll go away and think about what you've told me, but perhaps, if Murdock really has disappeared or had some sort of accident, wouldn't it be better to call the police?"

"No, no way am I having anything to do with them. They'll question me and I will have to tell the truth and they'll think I'm mad. Do you think I've gone insane?"

"It crossed my mind," Franz confessed, "but I think it more likely you just got it all wrong. Maybe you fell asleep for a short while that day and Murdock left without waking you."

"He couldn't do that. He makes too much noise, I told you. He bellows about and blunders into everything. Knocks things over."

"He's a big man. Anyway, I'm off now. I'll have a fish about and I'll be in touch."

"What do you mean 'fish about'?"

"I'm not sure. I'll see if I can dig into things a bit, if you know what I mean?"

"I don't. But that's fine. Thank you, Franz. I'm sorry to have off-loaded all this on you. But I felt I had to tell someone who was not too... judgmental."

Franz slipped out of the room and almost ran downstairs. At the bottom he found his sister waiting for him.

"What do you think?" she said. "Has he told you the whole story?"

"He told me too much. More than I can believe."

"When he called me up on Wednesday, to extinguish a cigar Murdock had dropped, I had no idea that he was up there alone. Usually I hear Murdock leaving the house. He can only manage three stairs then he has to have a rest. Like a bloody elephant coming down. And he usually calls out goodbye to me before he leaves. I didn't hear a thing that day."

"Perhaps he was in a hurry for some reason. Late for an appointment. Wanted to get away without causing a fuss."

"I expect you're right, but people do disappear under odd circumstances. Strange things do happen, Franz."

"Not to me, they don't. I've lived for almost fifty years and nothing remotely strange has ever happened to me."

"That's why I suggested Jerry get in touch with you to hear his story. You're so down to earth. Jerry believes what he says, though. I can't get him away from that."

"He's delusional, in my opinion. Not that I know anything about unusual psychological states. But you said yourself you've both been under a lot of strain recently. Perhaps he's been working too hard."

"We were doing okay before Murdock went missing, Franz."

NEXT MORNING, SUNDAY, Franz lay in bed until just before noon, thinking about the work he was planning to do on his new project and trying not to think about Jerry or Murdock. It was a perfect day for working indoors, with a constant drizzle falling outside. But, after he had dressed and eaten a late breakfast, he phoned Barbara and asked for Murdock's address. As it happened, it turned out to be quite near where he lived. After establishing that Murdock was not answering his phone, he told Barbara that he was going to call round to see what, if anything, was going on.

"Murdock probably isn't aware that he's caused this upset, Barbara," he told her. "I'll see if I can get him to explain himself."

"That's really good of you, Franz, but be careful."

"*What?*"

"You heard what I said."

"Are you suggesting Murdock might pose some sort of threat?"

"Not really, no. But we don't know what might happen next, do we? I mean, the man's disappeared, hasn't he?"

Franz put the phone down, grimaced at his reflection in a mirror, and went out to his car.

FRANZ RECOGNISED THE spot as soon as he saw it. He'd passed it many times going in and out of town. A thirty yard square of grass, still covered by an inch of grimy snow from weeks before. It was surrounded by a mixture of bungalows and cheaply built houses of various vintages, with little or no individual parking space, so their occupants had to squat their vehicles in front or on a makeshift, crumbling area of cement set in among the unkempt grass. The higher walls of a larger and grander estate recently built behind loomed above them, giving the impression that the older group of houses had clung on where they were not wanted.

After finding space for his car on the cracked cement, Franz looked about for number 15, which proved to be the largest of the bungalows. Obviously the scriptwriting didn't bring in as much money as he had supposed or, for some reason, Murdock chose to live in one of the less salubrious parts of town.

Franz walked in the continuously drizzling rain through a creaky gate and up to Murdock's front door. As soon as he rapped his knuckles on the glass, something, probably a small animal, went berserk in the hall beyond. He could hear it leaping and scratching frantically. He tried to get sight of it through the letter box, but the view was blocked by a flap of canvas hung behind the door. He whispered what he hoped were words of comfort to the creature, whatever it was, which only made it wilder in its desperation. Franz withdrew and took stock of the rest of the building, which was much bigger than he had supposed, by circumnavigating it. When he got around to the front door again, he was pretty sure that Murdock was not at home. He tried peering into the gloom beyond the front windows when a voice said, "Would you be looking for Mr. McFee, by any chance?"

It took Franz a few seconds to recognise Murdock's surname, it was so long since he'd used it.

He turned and saw a bald man in a boiler suit carrying aloft an open umbrella. He said, "Yes, have you any idea where he is?"

"No," the man said. He seemed to be measuring Franz up carefully.

Franz said, "There is some kind of animal in there that obviously wants to be let out."

"That will be Mr. McFee's dog, Rasputin."

"Is it hungry?"

"If Mr. McFee is not at home and it's not been fed, then it will be, yes."

"Is he in the habit of going away and leaving it?"

"No. He gives my lad charge of it."

"Your lad?"

"I'll fetch him. He's got a key." The man went swiftly off towards the house next door and returned at once with a boy of about fourteen huddled up next to him under the umbrella. "This is the feller, Clive," he said. "Says he's a friend of Mr. McFee."

Franz saw at once that Clive, unfortunately, was not all there. His father's words seemed to mean nothing to him and he stared steadily at the ground in front of him.

"Clive is a bit slow, but he loves that dog. Mr. McFee isn't here to let him in, but if you say so he'll open the door and let it out."

"Well, certainly, yes, let's do that."

The man said, "Go on, Clive," and the boy sauntered away holding the key out in front of him. A moment later, the dog burst out of the open door like a flood of bathwater, and squirmed round and round Clive's legs. The boy knelt down and Rasputin licked his face voluptuously.

"It doesn't bark," Franz observed. "Why's that?"

"Mr. McFee had it operated on, I believe."

That seemed an odd remark to Franz. "I'd better take a look round in the house, to make sure nothing unfortunate has happened," he said and, when the man made no objection, he made his way into the bungalow.

The stale smell of Murdock's cigars hung about the place, particularly the kitchen, which was obviously the room most used. A few small piles of dog shit were scattered about on the floor, which Franz grubbed up with some paper towels. Not as many turds as might be expected, but then the dog hadn't eaten for possibly three or four days. Franz opened the fridge. Not much there either – some wilting salad, a pint of milk beginning to turn blue and a few cheese rinds. Relics of meals. Obviously, Murdock was not a fancy eater. On a shelf next to the refrigerator he spotted some tins of dog food. He eased the lid off one and turned its contents out into a saucer and set it down on the linoleum.

The large table obviously served Murdock for many purposes, as its entire surface was covered with books, magazines, DVDs, some dirty mugs and dishes, a computer and various other, to Franz, unrecognisable electrical gadgets. Two large scrapbooks of newspaper cuttings contained reviews of *Dead Funny Ted*, some of them surprisingly ancient, and reports of various disasters, both at home and in distant parts of the world.

Having seen enough of the kitchen, Franz set about inspecting the rest of the house for signs of a possibly sick or even dead Murdock, perhaps in the bedroom.

The bungalow was surprisingly spacious, and contained more rooms than Franz had expected. Some of them were completely empty. Murdock hadn't even bothered to put bulbs in the light sockets, others contained oddments of furniture stacked without thought any which way. Murdock lived a far more desolate life than Franz had imagined. And this from a man who laughed a lot. But not, Franz reminded himself, at particular jokes and incidents. He seemed to find amusement in life itself.

At the rear of the bungalow Franz became confused; someone, Murdock presumably, though he didn't seem a likely candidate to be a master of DIY, had fitted neat partitions into two rooms to divide them up into a number of smaller spaces. Finding his way round them in the semi-darkness kept Franz fully occupied for some time and he was relieved when he came upon a wooden door which he took to be at the back of the house. He tried the handle, found it wasn't locked, and hurried through it, only to find himself in a large, windowless room lit only by some slight luminescence originating in what at first he took to be some indoor plants. He stopped to get a better look at them and saw that in fact they were what appeared to be the upper – in fact the topmost – branches of a large tree and, looking down, he realised that they continued down into a space below the bungalow.

Bemused, he ventured forward a couple of steps and peered into what he thought might be a cellar and saw that the space below was too wide and deep to be anything of the kind. He could see a very long way down – so much so that he felt himself reeling. His fear of heights made him almost topple forward and it was with some effort that he managed to scramble back towards the door. He held his right hand up to his brow as his head had, for some reason, begun to ache and glared again at the branches that protruded through the floor.

He noticed that some of them were beginning to move and sway a little where they were closest together, at the back, and thought he could see a clump of something in amongst them, like a platform, or maybe it was – could it be – a nest? It appeared to be a good four feet across and three or more feet deep.

Yes, he knew then that that was what it had to be, some kind of nest made of branches and the tattered remains of what appeared to be curtains, bed sheets and various scraps of clothing. And the reason that the branches were swaying and bending was because something, some creature, had been aroused by his presence, and was coming out of its nest to investigate the cause of its disturbance.

After a couple of quite violent shudders the nest tipped forwards at the side nearest Franz, far enough for him to get a glimpse of what could have been the top of a large hairless head and perhaps the tips of the fingers of a chubby, grasping hand.

Franz must have fled then, though he had no memory later of going through the wooden door and closing it behind him. He found himself in the partitioned rooms trying frantically to find his way out.

He fumbled and tumbled about in the near darkness for some time then, before he managed to relocate Murdock's kitchen, where he stopped for a moment to listen for any sounds of anything following him. There were no indications of that at all. All around him was perfect silence.

He sat at Murdock's table just long enough to recover his breath and steady his head, then left the bungalow, slamming the door behind him.

He found the father of the boy who had gone off with

Murdock's dog waiting for him near the front step. The man, still holding his umbrella, looked at him and said, "You've cut your hand. It's bleeding all down your jacket."

Franz couldn't think of anything to say to this but he realised it was true. He held the key out to the man who took it and said, "I'll give it to the boy."

Franz nodded.

"He's not in there dead or anything, then, Mr. McFee?"

Franz shook his head this time.

"Don't worry about the dog. My boy will look after him in the meantime."

This time Franz forced himself to speak.

"Does he go into the house to collect it?"

"My boy? No, *never*. Mr. McFee wouldn't want him to."

"Hum. Does he often go away, Murdock? I mean Mr. McFee."

"Oh, from time to time, yes. That's when he tells my boy to look after the dog. Usually he gives him something to buy food for it. We don't have much money."

Franz reached into his pocket for his wallet. He had no intention of going back into the kitchen where the tins of dog food were stashed. He held out a note and said, "Is that enough?"

"I should think it will be, yes. Have you no idea when your friend is coming back, then?"

Franz shook his head again and went off to his car.

HE DROVE HOME slowly, cautiously, not really concentrating on what he was doing. His mind was on other things. At one point he drove off the main road, down a side street and stopped while he sorted through his thoughts. What had he seen back in the bungalow? A hallucination, or some kind of tableau devised by Murdock to scare away burglars? It would certainly have that effect but surely it would be better placed in the front of the building instead of hiding away behind a maze of wooden partitions where he, Franz, had only come across it as an afterthought, after searching the whole bungalow.

It then seemed to him that perhaps it had been that his brain had simply misinterpreted the information it was receiving and things were not as they seemed. He had never experienced any kind of hallucination before but that seemed a more reasonable solution to what he now began to think of as his 'vision.' He thought that might be the explanation for all such visions, religious and otherwise. If he, a determinedly unbelieving person, could think he saw such sights, then surely it could happen to anyone?

He drew comfort from that thought. He even began to wish he had stayed a little longer in Murdock's back room and even considered returning to take another look, but decided not to.

And he wouldn't mention anything about his visit to Barbara, apart from telling her that he had not been able to contact Murdock at all. No point in upsetting her even more.

He went back to the main road and drove home.

THE PHONE RANG twice that evening, but Franz did not answer it. He felt guilty and slightly irritated about not doing so but his mind was not sufficiently calm to deal with his sister and her worries. He was certain it was her who was calling, as hardly anyone else ever did.

Next day, Monday, he worked on his computer at home, and in the afternoon returned to the library to continue his research on his project. When the library closed, he went to a supermarket to buy supplies. He was loaded down with bags of food as he approached his front door, behind which he could clearly hear his phone ringing. Flustered by the urgent sound, he tried his best to get to it in time, but fumbled with his key and almost dropped some of his bags. Meanwhile, the phone stopped ringing.

He knew he ought to call his sister but was still unready to do so. No doubt she would call back.

She did, almost an hour later. This time he picked up the receiver.

"Hello, you're there at last then," Barbara said, then seemed to whisper something that he didn't catch.

"Sorry, could you repeat that?"

"No, Franz, it doesn't matter."

"I went round to Murdock's place yesterday. He wasn't there. No sign of him. Did you know he has a dog, though? That was a surprise. He's never seemed to me to be a pet-loving sort of person."

"No, he's never mentioned a dog to me. What kind of dog?"

Franz realised he had no idea. The boy had run away with the creature so quickly he'd not been able to get a look at it. He explained as much to his sister, who did not sound particularly interested.

"Anyway," she said, "I'll be able to ask him about it. He's back now."

"What!"

"Yes, it was all a misunderstanding. He's been ill and he didn't want to tell us for some reason, so he slipped away."

"Slipped away?"

"And he's done it again now. He's coming to see you. He should be there in ten minutes."

"Ten minutes."

"That's correct. Stop repeating what I say, please."

"But why would he want to come here? Did you give him my address? He's never been here before."

"No, I didn't need to. He must know it. Anyway, he's heading in your direction now. He left as soon as you answered the phone and I told him you were in."

"But Barbara, you shouldn't have done that."

"Why on earth not?"

"I don't want to see him. I *particularly* don't. The bastard. What does he want with me?"

"Franz, it's not like you to talk of anybody like that. He said he just wants to thank you."

"For what?"

"Oh, I don't know. For caring enough to take the trouble to call on him?"

"Did you tell him I'd done that?"

"Not that I can remember, no. I didn't know you had."

"He was supposed to be ill, wasn't he?"

"Perhaps he was too ill to answer the door."

"No, he bloody wasn't."

"Franz, what's got into you? You're not normally like this."

Realising he had to end the conversation to prepare for Murdock's visit, Franz gruffly apologised, said he'd probably call her back later, and put down the phone.

He went round his house, checking all the doors and windows were shut and pulled all the curtains on the ground floor. Then he went up to his bedroom to watch and wait.

HE WAITED IN the darkest part of his bedroom and kept watch on the street in front of his house. After about ten minutes, a small unmarked white van drew up against the opposite pavement. The driver turned off the engine but didn't get out immediately, confirming, somehow, Franz's guess that Murdock was the occupant of the vehicle. This proved correct when the door suddenly swung open some time later and Murdock's huge bulk clambered into view. He was dressed in some kind of duffle coat with a hood concealing his face, but Franz recognized the shuffling glide of his feet as he went round to the back of the van and opened the rear door. The dog ran out.

It doesn't look too happy, Franz thought. It had its tail between its legs and slunk along with its belly almost touching the ground. Murdock closed the back of the van and crossed the street towards Franz's house with the dog following close behind.

Franz moved backward a couple of steps, fearing he might be visible from the street. Murdock moved up to his front door and Franz expected him to knock or ring the bell, but it didn't happen.

Guessing that Murdock was reconnoitering his house, Franz waited to see what move his visitor would make next. After a long silence, he heard his letter box squeak. Then Murdock appeared in his little front garden again, pursued by the dog. As he got to the point where the garden ended and the street began, he stopped, turned, looked up to where Franz had concealed himself, and raised an arm in some sort of salute. At the same time the hood fell back and Franz saw that he was smiling broadly, almost laughing. He turned, crossed the street, let the dog in the back of the van, got in himself and drove away.

After waiting a few minutes in the dark, Franz ventured out of his bedroom and went downstairs without turning on any lights. He saw that a folded piece of paper had been posted through his letterbox. There was enough light from the street lamp outside his house for him to see, when he unfolded the paper, that there was nothing written on it at all. But he got the message.

He spent the next half hour going round his house with a little torch and filling his rucksack with essentials for travel. He made sure he had his passport, credit cards in his wallet, and some folding money.

Then, after checking to make sure there was no sign of the white van anywhere nearby, he ran out to his car and drove swiftly away. After parking in the airport lot, he checked the departures board, then walked up to the Scandinavian Airlines stand and bought a one-way ticket. He wasn't sure how long he was going to be away, but it was definitely time he took a break He'd decided he had a lot to get away from.

NEXT MORNING, AT about eleven o'clock as usual, Murdock lumbered into Jerry's room without knocking, with a selection of daily newspapers under his arm. He lit a cigar, sat down close to Jerry's wheelchair, and spread the papers on the table in front of him.

"Anything especially grim today?" Jerry asked, genuinely expectant of some entertaining bad news.

Murdock made a play of searching through the sheets of paper as he said, "Well, not much actually, it's been a good day for the world, all thing considered, but I did spot one small item of interest. Now let me see... ah, here we have it." He held up a page of newspaper and said, "It seems a 747 came off the runway in Oslo last night and hit a luggage vehicle."

"Much harm done?"

"A few people hurt in the ensuing fire but only one fatality."

"Oh. Hardly worth mentioning, then."

"It says here that the dead man was believed to be carrying an English passport but the body was too badly burned to be identified. Next of kin have yet to be informed."

"They'll soon sort that out," Jerry said, without much interest.

Murdock, who seemed to be very pleased about something, perhaps just himself, said, "I expect they already have done."

Downstairs, sounding faintly mournful and further away than it actually was, a phone began to ring.

FLORRIE

ADAM L. G. NEVILL

If anybody has proved the persistent popularity of supernatural fiction, then it is Adam Nevill. His three novels, Banquet for The Damned, Apartment 16 *and* The Ritual, *have all received critical and commercial success. Adam's love for the genre comes through in every one of his tales and the story that follows proves his mastery of the form. The place where Florrie lives is, at first glance, not all that remarkable, but once her story is told, you'll never forget her.*

FRANK REMEMBERED HIS mother once saying, "houses give off a feeling," and that she could 'sense things' inside them. At the time, he was a boy and his family had been drifting around prospective family homes. He only remembered the occasion because his mother was distressed by a house they had just viewed; if not hurried away from, to get back to the car. But all he could recall of the property now was a print of a blue-faced Christ within a gilt frame; the only thing on any of the walls. And the beds were unmade, which also shocked his mother. His father never contradicted his mother on these occasional matters of a psychic nature, though his father never encouraged her to hold forth on them either. "Something terrible happened there," was his mother's final remark once the car doors were shut, and it was never mentioned again. But Frank had been perplexed by the incongruity of a house belonging to Christians issuing an unpleasant 'feeling.' Surely the opposite should have been true.

Frank amused himself trying to second guess her intuition about the first home he'd ever owned. He knew what his Dad would say about the 120% mortgage he'd arranged for it. But once it was fixed up, he'd have them down. To *his place*. His own place, after ten years of shared accommodation.

The narrow frontage of grubby bricks faced a drab street, cramped with identical terraced houses leaning over a road so narrow that two cars from opposite ends struggled to pass each other. But a final jiggle of the Yale key moved him out of the weak rainy light to enter the unlit hallway, its air thick with trapped warmth. A cloud of stale upholstery, thoroughly boiled cauliflower, and a trace of floral perfume descended about him.

He assured himself the house would soon exude the scents of his world: the single professional who could cook a bit of Thai, liked entertaining and used Hugo Boss toiletries. Once he'd ripped out the old carpets, stripped the walls, and generally 'torn the shit out of it,' as his best friend, Marcus, had remarked with a decisive relish, the house would quickly lose the malodour of the wrong decade, age group and gender.

Enshrouded by weak light about windows begrimed with silt and a thicket of silvery nets, before he managed to place a foot inside the front room, he realised the place had not been cleared of the former owner's furniture. There had been a mistake. It was like he had mixed up the dates and stepped into what was still someone else's home; as if *she* still lived there. "Pure 'seventies Nan," Marcus had commented with a grin on his face, the evening he'd visited to assist Frank's purchasing decision between this two-up, two-down terrace, and an ex-council property in Weoley Castle that needed an airstrike more than a first time buyer.

Poking from a Bakelite fitting, he found the chunky light switch, which was the same colour as the skirting boards, kitchen cupboards and the fittings: vanilla ice cream left too long in a freezer drawer, or the plastic of artificial limbs used until the 1970s. The ceiling fixture emitted a smoky glow from inside a plastic shade, patterned with all the colours inside a tin of fruit cocktail.

As he stared at the cluttered room, his distaste and irritation swiftly fashioned fantasies of destruction towards everything inside: the rosewood sideboard; the gas fire grill that resembled the front of an old car, with plastic coals that would glow in the hearth; the ancient television in a wooden cabinet, the small screen concave like a poorly ground lens in a pair of NHS spectacles; the tufted sofa, exhausted and faded from a thing plush and dark four decades prior, but now sagging into the suggestion of a shabby velour glove, dropped from a giant's hand. It all seemed offensive. An affront to taste. An issued intention to drag him backwards in time, choking him with disenchantment and despair as he went, kicking.

Beneath his feet the dark red carpet swirled with green fronds that reminded him of chameleon tongues. He looked down at it, into it. The carpet absorbed most of the dim electric light. And it also seemed to suck the emotion out of Frank. In the dusty gloom, he felt chastened. Embarrassed and feckless, as if he had made an inappropriate remark in polite company. He steadied himself against a wall, the paper old and fuzzy against his fingers; the vine pattern no longer lilac on cream but sepia on parchment. About him the warmth and powerful fragrance of the room intensified, as did his curious guilt. Momentarily, he was overwhelmed with remorse too, as if made to observe the additional distress his destructive thoughts had inflicted upon someone already frightened and long persecuted. He wanted to apologise to the room, out loud.

Only the sound of a delivery truck, reversing and beeping outside, stirred him out of his inexplicable shame. The unpleasant feelings passed and he surveyed the room again. *Where to start?*

Before he could pull up a single carpet tack, the furniture would have to be removed. All of it. He reached for his phone. This also meant the terrible Formica dining table with extendable flaps would be in the second downstairs room, along with the hideous quilted chairs. He checked: it was. "Fuck's sake," he whispered, then wondered why he'd kept his voice down, as if told to by an adult.

He jogged up the narrow stairwell to expel the onset of fatigue, presumably caused by the stifling air. Or because his limbs demanded reparation for the accumulation of stress he'd endured for months preceding the exchange of keys.

The master bedroom remained choked by the immense walnut-veneered wardrobe he'd seen on repeat viewings. Beside the towering wardrobe stood the teak dresser in defiance. A bed that had survived the Luftwaffe's bombing of munitions factories on the nearby Grand Union Canal appeared implacable and vast enough to fill most of the floor space.

One quick look around the door of the second bedroom confirmed a total repudiation of the estate agent's promise that the house "would be emptied by the time of your possession," because the room was still being used in absentia by the previous owner as a depository for cardboard suitcases, Christmas decorations from the 1970s, candlewick bedspreads, candy-striped linen, and knitting paraphernalia.

On the tiny landing under the white hardboard loft hatch, he went cold and wondered if the old woman had moved out, or maybe even come back. "Went to a retirement home, I think," the wanker that was the estate agent, Justin, of Watkins Perch and Manly, had said when Frank had asked about the former occupant. So why hadn't her relatives collected her things?

Because she had no one at the end.

An unwelcome notion of age, its indignities, and its steady erasure of who you had been, and the recycling of the tiny position that had been your own in the world, overwhelmed him. The same tragic end game might befall him. One day. *Right here.* A sudden acute empathy with a loneliness that was absolute disoriented Frank. And it took a conscious effort to suppress the awful feeling. He went downstairs, quickly, wiping at his eyes.

To listen to an answer machine at the estate agents. He left a curt message. Then turned about in the living room and forced a change of tack in his thoughts, by visualising the renovation he and Marcus intended: wooden floors, white walls, wooden blinds, minimalist light fittings, dimmers, wall mounted TV, black and white movie stills in steel frames on the walls, leather furniture, a stainless steel kitchen, a paved yard for outside dining, a spare room for his gadgets, guests and neat closet space, and nothing in the master bedroom but a bed and a standing lamp. Danish stylings throughout. Clean lines, simple colours. Space, light, peace, modernity, protection.

He had his work cut out.

ON THE FRIDAY of his first week in the house, the former resident's furniture was still in place, as it had been for long enough to leave the carpet dark beneath the sofa and solitary armchair in the living room. He hadn't been able to begin stripping the walls of the living room or bedrooms. Until the furniture was hauled away, the kitchen was the only part of the house he could dismantle. Though he had become fond of using the kitchen to make egg and chips, which he'd not eaten since he was at school, and he also liked to listen to the radio in there. So he'd staved off pulling down any of the old wooden cabinets with their frosted glass doors. There was something cosy and confirming about the cupboards and the little white stove. And anyway, Marcus would arrive the next morning, Saturday, with his tools, so Frank had decided to postpone the destruction until then.

He needed groceries too, for the weekend. Hadn't organised himself enough to conduct a proper shop at a supermarket, so he'd been dipping in and out of the local shop, called Happy Shop, at the end of the road to feed himself. This would be his fourth trip up there in a week. *Or was it more than that? Didn't matter.* And he was due a treat. Which might just be the Arctic Roll he'd been eyeing up in Happy Shop the day before, or was it on Wednesday? He couldn't be certain; nothing really defined any one day during his first week in the house. They'd all been slow and reassuringly pleasant.

And he found himself looking forward to his excursion to the strip-lit cave that was Happy Shop, run by a smiling Hindu man, that hoarded forgotten treasures from any seventies childhood. Going round the local shops was the furthest he'd ventured all week, too, because the house was immensely warm and safe and he'd come to consider the world outside the front door as not being either.

After six months without annual leave, he'd quickly slumped into a routine of slouching on the sofa each morning to watch the greenish TV screen, too. It was his first opportunity to relax in months, which must have accounted for his torpor. The house untied his knots wonderfully; he slept like he was in a coma for an hour after lunch, until his shows came on. Not that he'd ever seen any of them before, due to work, but he'd quickly discovered preferences on the five terrestrial channels available.

In the cupboard under the stairs he'd found, and laughed at, a tartan shopping trolley on wheels, beside a carpet sweeper he was sure he could flog on eBay to a retro nut. But having to fetch and carry so many tins all week from Happy Shop made the idea of using the trolley incrementally less amusing. Before he left the house on Friday, he even paused outside the cupboard and wondered whether anyone would see him with it rattling along the pavement behind him.

Inside Happy Shop, his usual tastes deserted him. The idea of sushi, or stir fries, or anything with rice and coconut milk, or anything that had been messed about with, like the curries and chillies he was always eating, all running with sauce... turned his stomach. Revolted him. Instead, he'd spent his first week eating tinned pink salmon and a brand of white bread he remembered as a kid, and had believed wasn't even sold anymore. There had been tinned rice pudding, a Victoria sponge, ice cream packaged in cardboard, and Mr Kipling French Fancys for pudding during the week too. A taste for condensed milk and individual frozen chicken pies had been rediscovered. And he'd bought, for the first time in his life, a round English lettuce.

Birdseye fish fingers and a tiny bag of minted peas landed in his basket; they had four baskets at the front of the shop that smelled of newspaper and tobacco. A tin of mandarin segments, strawberry Angel Delight – *they still sold it in sachets!* – a box of PG Tips, and a jar of Mellow Birds coffee went in next. He avoided anything with onions in it as he'd recently gone right off them.

To his growing haul he added some Pledge furniture polish that he remembered under a sink in his family home, and realised he missed its smell; the veneered walnut finish on the wardrobe would come up a treat, as would the rosewood sideboard and teak dresser once he got busy with a duster.

He'd become fond of using the cupboard above the cooker as a space for treats too; he could dip into it while he watched telly in the afternoon. Inexplicably, the true purpose of the cupboard seemed to have suggested itself to him. In Happy Shop, he bought a bag of Murray mints and a Fry's Turkish Delight especially for it.

Almost done. What else did he need? Washing up liquid. He seized one of the green and white plastic bottles of Fairy Liquid. He hadn't seen that packaging in years, and when he smelled the red nozzle the fragrance of childhood summers made him instantly giddy as overexposed images flowed from his memory: running in swimming trunks, grass blades floating in a paddling pool, the plastic bottom blue, the water warm, suffocating with laughter as he was chased by his brother who squirted him with water from a Fairy Liquid bottle, trying to swim in the paddling pool – though the water was never deep enough and his knees bumped the bottom – then lying face-down for five seconds before springing up to see if his mum was worried he'd drowned. He saw deck chairs in his mind, with his mom and nan in them, watching, smiling. He was rewound to such an extent, he even thought he could smell the creosote on the garden fence, that tang of burnt oil and timber.

And then he walked home, dreamy, taking short steps with his head down, as if wary of hazards underfoot, until he snapped out of it and walked normally.

WHEN MARCUS KNOCKED at ten, Frank jumped up from the kitchen stool, but couldn't account for why he was so nervous. Was being silly, but it was as if opening the front door was suddenly a cause of great anxiety. He hovered for ages, scarcely breathing, in the hall beside the thermostat that looked like something from an instrument panel at the dawn of space travel. When Marcus peered through the letter flap, Frank was forced to open up.

"Fuck's going on?" Marcus said, when he saw the kitchen. "I bought the tiles and units with me. This shit should be long gone by now. Your stuff can't stay in my garage forever, mate."

Frank had convinced himself he could somehow delay, or persuade Marcus not to engage in the splintering of wood and crowbarring of those kitchen cabinets that must have been up there for decades. They were in good nick. Nothing wrong with them, so it seemed such a waste. And he wanted them left alone for another reason that had been nagging at him as Saturday approached: gutting the kitchen just felt *wrong*. Bad. Like violence. Like bullying. But he still helped Marcus break them away from the walls, because he was too embarrassed by his own sentimentality to defend them, but felt like crying as they did their worst.

When they found the handwriting behind the first cabinet – *Len and Florrie, 1964* – he went into the bathroom with moist eyes and smothered his face inside one of the big lemon yellow towels he'd found in the airing cupboard.

Looking at the three wall cabinets and row of cupboards, piled like earthquake wreckage in the yard (particularly the sight of the pale unpainted wood that had been facing the kitchen wall since 1964), hit him as hard as the sight of a dead pet once had, rigid with the terrible permanence and unfairness of its final sleep, when it was still *loved*.

Indifferent to the inscriptions left by Len and Florrie – they had found four – Marcus cracked open the tins of white emulsion and began painting. As Marcus worked, Frank realised he despised his best friend.

They never had time to vandalise another room that weekend, and it was just as well, because his relationship with the house changed the night following their desecration of the little kitchen.

* * *

THE FOLLOWING MORNING, while he sat, doleful, over some toast and a mug of tea in the newly painted starkness of the kitchen, his stainless steel units piled in the middle of the room, he mused it was as if he'd just dreamt someone else's dreams.

Throughout the entire night he'd passed through a dark muddle of images mostly lost to him in the morning, but he did partially recall scenarios filled with the smoke of Silk Cut cigarettes, the clack of Scrabble tiles, and the same Matt Monro song playing on a continuous loop from a black tape recorder with spatters of white paint upon it. *Born Free.* He'd been a guest on *The Price is Right* too; was somehow inside the show, but also watching himself from the sofa. It had been his goal to win a small caravan. Then he was stood upon the yellow lino of the kitchen floor, counting pages of Green Shield stamps before he'd woken. Or thought he'd woken. Because there had been someone in the bedroom with him. Talking to him between sharp intakes of breath. A small indistinct figure stood at the foot of the bed when he jerked awake from the first dream to enter another he was sure was real at the time, with him fully awake within it.

In the second more vivid dream, the figure left the room quickly. So quickly, with its hands clutched over its face, he never saw its progress. It seemed to just reappear in the doorway as a hunched silhouette, lit by ambient light rising up the stairwell. And when the figure turned to him the face remained dark, but the crouching outline was visible. It was a woman, for whom he felt a rush of tenderness and affection and remorse, despite the shock she had given him by appearing at the foot of his bed like that. He was stricken with the same feeling of abandonment he remembered on his first day at school.

The dream continued until he stood behind the small figure in the spare room, in which she had bent over to mooch through plastic bags. "You need to get ready. And I can't go without it," she'd said, but never turned around.

He woke up at seven and realised he'd not seen the figure's face once, but discovered his own to be briny with dried tears. He'd gone downstairs to the smell of fried sausages that competed with the stink of new paint, though he hadn't cooked a single sausage in the house. Must have been the neighbours.

THE DREAMS TURNED nasty on Sunday and Monday night, brought by the kitchen cupboards being left outside in the rain. Like his mother's vibes about other people's houses, he just instinctively knew that was the cause of his troubled sleep.

On Sunday night, the figure came back into his room. But her agitation and grief had intensified within the room. He'd woken to find her leaning over his face with her hands clasped across her mouth, behind which she issued grunts. He suspected a glimmer of an eye had been visible, but he saw no other features.

And he'd sat up, his heart hammering, convinced it was an actual intruder, only to see the figure fade into the dark centre of the wardrobe.

All the lights had come on upstairs and he'd conducted a search of the entire house, but there was no one in the building with him.

On Monday night what might have been the figure of the elderly woman was inside his room again, but on its hands and knees this time. Or he may have dreamed about a wounded animal, because he awoke to hear something mewl and fumble about under the curtains, though he could not see it and just lay stiff with fright in bed as round and round it went on all fours, bumping the wall in its distress.

The figure eventually went out of the bedroom very quickly and scurried across the landing; he saw the last of it and was sure it had been a dog. Nothing else could run that fast. He had been terrified, but compelled to follow, and had looked inside the spare bedroom from the doorway and seen the figure of the old woman again, but on all fours with her back to him. She searched for something amongst boxes of vinyl photograph albums he had never seen before. She was covered in a grubby housecoat and eventually held an object in front of her lowered face like she was trying to see a tiny item in front of her eyes in the darkness. Either that or she was putting something into her mouth. He couldn't tell which, but she was breathing hard between the grunts.

When he spoke, the figure turned quickly and showed him milky eyes like those in the head of a dead sheep, and she bared teeth that didn't belong in a human mouth.

He came awake underneath the eiderdown in the master bedroom with his fingers stuffed inside his own throat.

ON TUESDAY MORNING he carried the broken kitchen furniture back inside the house and dried the wreckage with a tea towel. It was felt as necessary as rescuing a drowning cat from a canal.

Mail from the Macmillan Nurses and from a council mobility service arrived on Wednesday morning addressed to Mrs Florrie White. He put the letters on the kitchen counter, in a neat stack beside the small toaster; he'd repaired the unit as much as possible and leaned it against the wall. It was at a tilt and didn't help the house much, but he couldn't bear another night of it being outside in the cold. The new steel kitchen units went outside and into the yard. Of course it could not be a permanent arrangement, but he couldn't settle until the swap had been made.

He spent Tuesday to Thursday on the sofa, listless and melancholy, drifting through afternoon television shows for the modicum of comfort they provided, before he took long sleeps with the gas fire on; its glow and little clicking sound reassured him more than anything he could remember. The naps he would often awake from, because the figure in his dreams would mutter to itself at the top of the stairs. Though he could never remember what it said when he awoke and there was no one up there when he looked.

Frank also spent a lot of his time staring at the pattern on the kitchen table and thinking of rooms he'd occupied as a student; the cohabits through his twenties with two girlfriends long gone; the house-shares with strangers with whom he had no contact now. In the increasingly indistinct crowds in his memories there had been an alcoholic who only consumed extra strong cider and Cup-a-Soup, and a fat girl who ate like a child at a tenth birthday party and spent hours locked in the bathroom. He could no longer remember their names. Or the faces of the girlfriends. He tried for a while until he moved to the living room and fell asleep in front of *Countdown*.

On Thursday evening, he refused to take a call from Marcus. There had been another four since the previous weekend. All unanswered. For some reason Marcus and his calls were irritating him to such a degree, he put his iPhone in the cupboard under the stairs, inside a box of wooden clothes pegs. He hadn't had enough time to think things through about the house and could not abide being rushed.

His sleep went undisturbed until the weekend and he found himself watching ITV from seven to nine, before going up to bed. Happy Shop kept him fed with its inexhaustible variety of memory and flavour. And when Marcus arrived on Saturday morning, Frank never answered the door, lying on the floor of the living room with the curtains shut. At the end of his second week off work, he called the office from the public phone outside Happy Shop, to say he wasn't coming back.

ON THE MONDAY of his fourth week in the house, he finally went out for tools. Not to renovate the property, but to try and repair the kitchen. It could not be put off any longer. But the act of leaving the house was excruciating.

Twice the previous week, when he'd been cooking in the wrecked kitchen, he'd looked up, convinced he was being watched from the doorway, as if caught doing something wrong, or eating something he had been told not to. The imagined presence had been seething with a surly disappointment and was dark with hostility. That room had become the focus of an intensification of the restlessness growing since the Saturday he had assaulted the cabinets. The kitchen was the heart of the house and he had broken it.

There was no one physically inside the house with him. Could not possibly have been, but the repeated sounds of small feet padding about the lino while he'd napped in the lounge during the afternoons, suggested to a region of his imagination he little used, that a bereft presence was repeatedly examining the kitchen. He actually worried the first time he'd heard the shuffle of feet that the former owner had escaped the retirement community, or worse, and let herself back into what she believed was still her own home.

Frank recovered quickly from the sudden frights, and within the confines of the comfortable womb of the terraced house eventually found this supervising presence acceptable. Deserved. Nor could he think of a single reason to doubt his instincts that amends had to be made. Within the house, such things were possible.

But functioning and navigating his way around the world outside of the house, of what no longer felt so familiar, defeated him. When he went out for tools, his actual attempts to move on the Pershore Road wasted him before he reached the bus stop in front of the bowling alley.

Unpredictable tides of energy and the staring eyes of pedestrians and motorists, all filled with smouldering threats, seemed to pull his thoughts apart and compress him to a muttering standstill. He was thinking of too many things at the same time, but then forgetting one train of thought at the same time another began.

The pressure the city exerted was tangible. Uncomfortable, like a head-slappy wind on a hilltop or a coat pocket caught on a door handle. Unless he was inside the house or Happy Shop, he didn't fit in anywhere and was in everyone's way. His recent life had been reduced to quick forays outside the house for very good reasons, because he was unable to cope with anything else and he wasn't wanted anywhere else. Never had been. The house had opened his eyes. And there was now something wrong with one of his legs; a pain that started inside a hip. So he should keep off it.

The further he ventured from the house to buy the tools, the greater his physical discomfort and confusion. Frank lit endless cigarettes. Silk Cut. He'd started smoking again at the weekend, after being driven by an unstoppable urge to light up during the National Lottery. At the bus stop, fat pigeons scurried around his feet and watched him with amber eyes.

After boarding a bus, he made his way upstairs and with his bad hip it was like trying to stand upright in a rowing boat. Sitting by the window, as the bus trundled toward Selly Oak, where he knew there was a DIY store, he looked down to the streets for women wearing tight skirts and leather boots; the sight usually made him dizzy with longing. Now the women and their clothes just appeared to him as ordinary, and he felt dead to the previously strong images. It led to an incredulity that such a part of himself had ever existed.

From a seat in front of him, a mobile phone began to ring in a girl's handbag. It distracted Frank from what seemed like important, meaningful thoughts he could barely remember a few moments later. He groaned. The girl began talking in a loud voice. "Oh, Jesus," he said. Frank wanted to take the phone from her hand and drop it out of the window, to hear it smash on the asphalt below.

Muttering under his breath to prevent himself from swearing aloud, he was forced to listen. The girl's voice was controlled and sounded too much like a prepared speech to be part of a natural discourse. There were no pauses, or repetitions, or silences; just her going *blah, blah, blah,* and addressing everyone on the bus. It was not a phone she was holding, but a microphone. It was the most disappointing thing about getting older; to still be confronted by these childish things. These increments of self-importance and vanity he saw all about him whenever he left home.

By the time he reached the Bristol Road, he felt sick from an aversion to everything around him. A hot loathing. But a fascination too, and a pitiful desperation to be included. In one mercifully brief moment, he wished to be burnt to ash and to have his name erased from every record in existence. He was rubbish. No one wanted him around. He dabbed the corner of one eye with a tissue and wanted to go home. Back to the house.

As the bus brushed the edge of Selly Oak he fell asleep. And woke to find the vehicle had trundled and wheezed into streets he didn't recognise. He'd slept through his stop and found himself in a bleak part of Birmingham he had never seen before. Somewhere behind Longbridge maybe? In a panic, he fled down the stairs, alighted, and then stood beside a closed factory and a wholesaler of Saris.

Everything here was inhospitable. Anger choked him. *Can I not leave the house without a map?* He'd lived in the city for ten years, but he recognised none of this. It was as if the streets and buildings had actually moved while he slept on the bus to disorient him.

He followed a main road in the opposite direction the bus had taken, but grew tired and turned his face to a wooden fence surrounding a building site and suffered a paroxysm of such powerful contained rage it left him with a broken tooth and cuts on the palms of his hands.

Clenching his jaws together and grinding his teeth, he'd felt the enamel snap at the side of his mouth. His cheeks filled with grit. But when the tooth snapped, the tension passed from his body, leaving him confused and expecting shock-waves of agony. But there was no pain and he decided against going to a dentist. He didn't know where the dentists were in the city. He then noticed the little half-moons of blood on the inside of his palms, made by his own nails. It had been so long since he'd bitten them. They were like unpleasantly feminine claws. How could they have grown so much and he not noticed?

Trying to retrace the bus route and find a familiar landmark, he became hopelessly disorientated. He went into a tacky women's hairdressers, the only place he could find that offered him any sense of reassurance, to ask for directions. The girls in heavy make-up exchanged glances when he was unable to speak. He just stood there and trembled before them. After throwing his arms into the air in silent exasperation, he left the shop, crimson with shame. Speech only returned to him at the curb, where he stood muttering. Some people stared. A taxi took him home.

These things never used to happen to him, but he had a notion that the potential for such a slide had always been in place. In the back of the taxi he hid his face inside the lapel of his overcoat and bit his bottom lip until his eyes brimmed with water.

TWO DAYS LATER, though it might have been three or even four days, someone knocked on the front door for a long time. So he hid on the floor of the spare room. Then he could hear three voices talking in the neighbour's garden and knew they were trying to look through the back windows of the house.

For the rest of that afternoon he chain-smoked Silk Cut, didn't relax until it was dark outside and Coronation Street's theme tune boomed through the living room. The thought of going further than the end of the road made him nauseous, so he stopped tormenting himself with the idea.

He tried again to put the cabinets back up on the walls, but made his fingers bleed. He went upstairs to wash them, but couldn't remember why he was upstairs when he arrived on the landing. He went and lay down on the bed instead. And around him the smell of perfume, of old furniture, stale carpets, and chip fat clouded. The radiators came on upstairs with a gurgle. He felt safe and he closed his eyes.

Sometime that night, Florrie came into the room on all fours and climbed onto the bed. She sat on his chest and pushed a thin cold hand inside his mouth.

DRIVING THE MILKY WAY

WESTON OCHSE

Weston Ochse's roots are firmly anchored in the great American weird tale. If you've never read Weston's stories before, you're in for a real treat, for while his fiction seems effortless and simply told, there's a real depth and complexity to his work that calls to mind the stories of such greats as Ray Bradbury and Theodore Sturgeon. 'Driving the Milky Way' features an unusual take on the haunted house and brings us a moving tale about friendship and loss.

IT STARTED WITH a sneeze.

Chicken George, whose real name was Henry, Flipper Gordon, named as such because of his webbed toes, Frank Just Frank and Bach, whose real name was Sebastian but demanded they never call him that on fear of death, all heard it at the same time. Out in the wide open desert scrub of Arizona, there was no mistaking a sneeze for any other sort of naturally occurring sound.

They'd been playing Cowboys and Indians, with Flipper and Bach channeling the spirits of Cochise, Geronimo and a thousand other bad-ass Apaches. Both the boys wore leather belts around their heads and had used some spit and dirt to work the red sandy soil into the skin of their faces. They carried hollow yucca shoots with the seedpods rattling on the ends, which they waved around in a mad melding of a Mexican maraca and a Don Quixote lance.

Chicken George and Frank Just Frank were the cowboys. They didn't have proper hats, but made up for it by channeling John Wayne – hooking their thumbs through their belt loops and walking stiff-legged, dead-eye stares promising violence from their almost real weapons. Chicken George carried a molded plastic machine gun circa 1920s, the kind that had made the Valentine's Day Massacre famous. And Frank Just Frank wore a gun belt with two glistening silver toy cap guns.

The side of the hill was covered in clumps of buffalo grass and the occasional yucca plant with leaves like razor-sharp tongues. Chicken George and Frank Just Frank hid behind them when they were ready to shoot. Flipper and Bach hid behind them when they were preparing to spear their enemy, which they did at the end of each battle. Even if they were shot a hundred times with the machine gun, they'd somehow manage to thrust the rattling ends of the lances into the cowboys' chests.

But when the sneeze came, it was no longer Cowboys against Apaches. It was now everyone against the sneeze.

When it came again, they rushed the top of the hill, transformed from the mythology of Americana to a screaming host of berserker Vikings. They figured they'd come upon another kid hiding out, spying on them. They never guessed that they'd encounter the front end of what they'd learn later to be a 1961 Dodge

Travco Recreational Vehicle. The radiator was long gone, leaving the fan blades sticking forward without a protective shield. They'd rusted to a stop in the position of a cross, and like any group of eleven-year-old boys, they'd yet to reach the point where the cross didn't really matter, so the sight of it drew them up short. There was no rubber on the wheels. Nor was there any windshield. In fact, the RV was so rusted it had begun to turn green, with deep reds and ambers interspersed like it was a calico iron cat.

"Get out of the way. Can't you see I'm driving here?" came a girl's voice.

The boys glanced at each other and grinned.

"You got to pay a toll first," Flipper growled. He was the tallest and tried to peer into the cab of the RV, but the angle was all wrong.

"I ain't paying nothing. My daddy owns this property and he says I can go wherever I want."

Bach shared a conniving look with the others, then crouched low in the grass and began to circle the RV.

Frank Just Frank trained both pistols on the vehicle.

George couldn't help but say, "Whatcha going to do, Frank, kill the RV? I think it's already dead."

"My RV ain't dead," the girl piped back. "It's just old, is all."

"Piece of shit is about to fall apart," Frank Just Frank said.

A fierce Indian cry went up. George and the others grinned madly. But their grins turned to dismay as the cry was cut short, followed by the sound of flesh meeting flesh, and then howling. Bach appeared from around the side of the RV with his hands on his face, blood gushing from his nose.

A girl not even two-thirds the size of Frank Just Frank, who was the smallest of them, stepped out the side door and put her hands on her hips. Red pigtails sprung from the side of her head like devil horns. Her skin was tanned the color of cow hide. Freckles danced across her cheeks.

"Which one of you is gonna be next?"

HER NAME WAS Emory Lowenstein, but boys and their love of nicknames eventually turned Emory into Auntie Em. It was midsummer when they all met. The homes in their part of Cochise County resided on ten acre plots along dirt roads between the towns of Sierra Vista and Bisbee on the American side of the border and Naco on the Mexican side. Auntie Em had just moved to the area, but none of the boys lived there. They'd come to spend the summer with their grandparents. For Chicken George and Bach this was their first summer. Bach was from San Diego and Chicken George was from Tucson. Frank Just Frank and Flipper Gordon lived in Phoenix. Sometime around the end of May through the beginning of August the boys' parents would send them all down to spend a carefree summer under the desert sky. More than a simple vacation, the parents enjoyed the grandparents' ability to provide free babysitting. It was 1977, inflation was at eleven per cent, the cost of a gallon of gas was up ten cents in the last three years, and Jimmy Carter was the president. The parents had to work.

On Friday of the week they met Auntie Em, all the boys were invited over to her house to eat barbeque chicken and to tell ghost stories. They were asked about their nicknames. Bach and Flipper Gordon's were the asiest to clarify. Flipper even removed his shoes and howed everyone his webbed toes. Next came Frank, who was from a family of Franks, with Frank Seniors and Frank Juniors and a Frankie and a Franklin. Frank didn't like all the additional qualifications to his name and had decided that he would just go by Frank, so he became Frank Just Frank, regardless of his desire to be merely Frank. Chicken George's name was derived from the miniseries Roots, which everyone had watched the previous January. His real name was Henry Scoggins, but when there was a fight, he could be found dancing around the edges, egging the combatants on just like Chicken George had done in the series. Later that night, with the Milky Way spread above them and marshmallows roasting on the ends of mesquite branches, they sat around a fire pit on patio chairs while Em's father, who was a professor at Cochise Community College, explained what the Apaches believed when they'd looked at the same wide sky.

"The Apaches believe the Milky Way is a trail made of departing spirits who are on their way to the afterlife. *Yolkai Nalin* is the Apache goddess of death and what comes after; she controls the Milky Way and chooses those who are allowed to journey there."

Although he went on to explain the history of the Apache, the kids didn't pay too much attention after that. Their minds were awhirl with all the new possibilities the Milky Way presented. No longer was it just a band of stars too difficult to conceptualize. It had become supernatural. It had become something they could relate to. The words *goddess of death*, *departing spirits*, and *afterlife* succeeded in inspiring ideas that would set them on a course rest of the summer.

The RV became their world. For as rusted and dilapidated as it was, sitting in the middle of a high plain of desert scrub, it was all theirs. No one wanted it. Auntie Em's father had left it where he'd found it when he'd bought the property and had no plans to have it removed. The desert and its crawlies greeted them in all directions. The RV made them feel safe. And unlike when they were at home, they could be themselves. Because although they knew that they weren't really grown up, without their parents and grandparents around to constantly remind them of that fact, they felt a little less like children.

The metal skin of the RV had been stripped in places, leaving a hard metal skeleton. The roof was long gone, except for a cross-strut attached to the frame. The interior had been gutted and little remained of the original luxury. A metal bench along one side of the middle and a larger one across the back were all that was left of the couch and the bed that had once made this a travelling home. The place where the bathroom had been was nothing more than a hole. This, they stayed away from; although any evidence of its previous use was long since gone, the very idea of it was gross.

When they weren't playing around the RV, they were digging. Frank Just Frank and Bach brought shovels. Using the RV as the center, the five of them would march into the desert in straight lines, looking for ancient Indian burial sites. Whenever they spotted something like a mound of dirt or a scrap of cloth sticking from the ground, they'd dig. But try as they might, they never found any bones, much less ancient artefacts.

Finally, when the month of July was about to melt into August and there was just two weeks left of summer before school started, they gathered around the RV.

Auntie Em sat behind the wheel. The others lounged around inside, protected from the sun by a tarp they'd tied across the roof.

Bach, who was as undeterred as a terrier after the rumor of a rat, arrived last. "What's everyone doing? We have a two-mile hike ahead of us."

"And tomorrow another two-mile hike," Chicken George said. He sat on the floor, his legs pulled up, his chin resting on his knees.

"And then another the day after." Frank Just Frank shook his head. He took a sip of water from an old Army canteen, then handed it across the seat to Em. "This is getting old. If you'd have told me that I'd spend my summer digging holes in the desert, I would have called you a liar."

"Now look who the liar is," Em said, handing back the canteen.

Frank Just Frank grinned. "No kidding."

Bach let his shovel fall to the dirt and climbed aboard. "Fine, then. What do you want to do instead?"

Ever since that night in June when Em's father had planted the seed in their minds, they'd done little besides look for Indian bones. Their repertoire of fun things to do had evaporated and no one had any better ideas.

Except Flipper Gordon.

"Boob sweat," he said.

"Excuse me?" Em asked.

"I think we heard him," Chicken George said laughing.

It was no secret that Flipper Gordon's sixteen year old cousin, Miranda, was staying at his grandparents' house. She'd come two weeks ago and Flipper Gordon found it difficult to think of little else. At least once each day since she'd arrived, he'd waxed sophomorically about how much she'd filled out. That she was related meant little to his thirteen-year-old libido.

"You talking about your cousin again?" Frank Just Frank asked.

"Maybe."

"Maybe, hell. You know that it's illegal to think what you're thinking," Em said.

"Is not. This is America and I can think whatever I want."

"I doubt that the founding fathers ever considered boob sweat when they drafted the Bill of Rights," Em countered.

Chicken George, who'd been lying on his back in the bed of the RV, rolled over, propped himself on one elbow, and grinned. "What about Adrian Barbeau's boob sweat?"

Everyone was silent for awhile, Even Em. After the appropriate amount of reverence for the weekly appearance of Adrian Barbeau's boobies on the television show *Maude*, it was Frank Just Frank who broke the silence.

"So what about the boob sweat?" he asked, his voice almost a whisper.

"I wonder if it's different than other sweat," Flipper Gordon finally said. After receiving looks from the other four, he added, "Think about it. It has to be. The sweat under your arm stinks, but the sweat in other places doesn't."

"Your butt sweat stinks," Chicken George said, garnering laughter from the rest of the crew.

Bach giggled.

"Can't you be serious for one moment?" Flipper Gordon shook his head in disgust.

"And you're being serious with boob sweat?" Em rolled her eyes.

"Absolutely."

"Boob sweat is no different than any other sweat. I can tell you that," she said.

All four boys turned towards her. They looked her in the eyes for a long moment, then as if it were rehearsed, their gazes dropped a foot until they were fixated on her budding chest. They stared as if they'd just now noticed that they'd been there.

"Hey!" Em brought both hands up to cover her chest. Everyone except Flipper Gordon averted their eyes and laughed self-consciously.

"Flipper!"

He started like he'd been jolted with electricity. He looked at her sheepishly. "Sorry."

Em rolled her eyes. "Jesus Christ on a Big Wheel. How would you like it if I stared at your penis?"

They sat in the RV the rest of the day, joking and telling stories about when they were younger. Most of the stories they'd already heard before. But the heat made everyone laconic and they didn't really care what was being said. They just liked the companionship.

The next morning, Auntie Em was an hour late getting to the RV, but when she came, she was running, her face flush with excitement.

"We have bones," she said, breathlessly.

When asked to explain, she went on to tell them about how her father had told her, the night before, that several students had found some bones while they were hiking near the border. The college was going to send a team to investigate, but they couldn't break away from classes until tomorrow.

"Which gives us today to find them," Frank Just Frank said.

The only problem was that the directions weren't exact. After several calculations and referencing the survey map they'd been using to record their dig sites, they determined that the spot was ten miles away. Sitting in the shade of the RV was hot enough. Each of their excursions to dig a hole had been death-defying experiences and the farthest they'd ever travelled was two miles. Crossing ten miles of desert in the middle of the day might as well have been crossing the face of the sun. All the boys' faces fell as they realized that they'd never be able to do it.

"Then we do it at night," Em said.

They all looked at her. Flipper Gordon shook his head. "My grandma would kill me if she found out."

"Then don't let her find out," Frank Just Frank said, climbing on the bandwagon. "If we leave at midnight, that will give us six hours to get there, dig up the bones, and bring them back. Walking ten miles will take us about two hours. Counting two hours to get back, that leaves us two hours to dig up the bones. We can totally do this."

Everyone accepted his logic and began to make plans for the trip. Flipper Gordon, however, said that there was no way he could make it. Ever since his cousin had come to stay, his grandmother had been keeping a sharp eye out for boys and possible midnight trysts, and he'd never be able to leave undetected. It was decided that he'd arrange to have a sleepover with Chicken George, whose grandparents liked to drink beer and slept so deeply they couldn't hear their own dog barking outside their window all night.

They congregated around the RV at ten minutes after midnight. Frank Just Frank and Em had flashlights. Flipper Gordon and Chicken George carried shovels. Bach carried arguably the most important items: the map and the empty rucksack from his grandfather's Korean War stash, which they'd use to retrieve the bones.

"Don't we need a compass?" Chicken George asked.

"We don't need one." Frank Just Frank shone the light on the map and traced several roads. "All we have to do is walk straight across the desert and bisect these three roads here. When we see a windmill, which isn't on the map but should be here," he said, placing his finger in a spot seemingly in the middle of nowhere, "we'll be almost there."

"How do you know so much?" Em asked.

"Boy Scouts. I used to love maps until I quit."

"What made you quit?" Bach asked.

Frank Just Frank was silent for a while, but finally answered. "I couldn't make those fake Indian belts."

"Yeah, and the scout leader liked to give out special merit badges," Flipper Gordon snickered, but no one joined him.

Auntie Em and Bach exchanged a look, but said nothing.

They headed out. Auntie Em and Frank Just Frank took the front, with the rest falling in line behind them. Thus began a stumbling, tripping affair through the desert. They soon discovered that although the ground might look flat, it rolled across hidden slopes and holes just large enough to capture and twist a foot. By the time they took their first rest at the first road, Chicken George was limping from a lightly sprained ankle and Bach was limping from being stuck in the leg by a yucca plant. Flipper Gordon had let his imagination run raw and was seeing giant tarantulas hiding in every dark shadow. It became apparent that their earlier estimation of the time it would take to get there had been highly optimistic. Still, no one wanted to quit yet.

After a ten minute break for water, they took off again.

By the time they reached the third road, Frank Just Frank snapped off the light and held up a hand for them to stop. The dirt road was higher than the surrounding desert.

"Get down," he said, flattening his face against the dirt slope.

Then the night got brighter as headlights fired down the road. Soon they could hear the low rumble of an engine as a vehicle began to creep towards them. The suspension squeaked roughly as the tires crunched across the gravel.

When it had been out of sight and earshot for roughly ten minutes, Frank Just Frank lifted his head. The quarter moon caught his grin. "That was a close one."

"Who was it? Are they after the bones too?" Flipper Gordon asked.

"Probably drug dealers. My grandpa says they're thick as cockroaches on the border." Chicken George stood and stared worriedly at the road.

Frank Just Frank shook his head. "I don't know who they are, but it can't be good for us, whoever they are. Let's just stay away from them." He got up on one knee and checked both directions. "Come on." He took off across the road.

Soon the others joined him on the far side, where they sat panting more from fear than exertion. They'd never been out alone at this time of night. More importantly, they'd never been this close to the border at night. Each of their families had warned them that they could get stolen by Mexicans if they strayed too close, so the border, although an invisible line in the sand, took on a ponderous psychological weight.

Above them the Milky Way spread out in a spiral of hot white lights. Away from the city and in the middle of the night it was breathtaking. Here, as they lay on their backs on the way to offer salvation to a pile of old bones, the idea that the Milky Way was a pathway to the afterlife didn't seem so fabulous. Away from the conveniences of culture and the technology of society, it seemed like it might be real.

Each of the kids secretly hoped it was so.

Each of the kids also secretly hoped their plan wouldn't work.

"MR. GORDON," THE judge began. "Your wife claims that reconciliation attempts have been fruitless. She asserts that you've done nothing that the court has asked of you, nor have you sought counseling on your own. Is this true?"

Sam Gordon nodded.

His lawyer added, "If it pleases the court, please record that my client nodded in the affirmative."

"Not so easy," the Judge said. He leaned onto his bench. "Mr. Gordon, your wife claims that you haven't been home for any extended period of time in the last three years. She says you've been spending all your time, especially time you should have been working, in a desert down in Cochise County. Tell me, sir, just for my edification, what is it down there that makes you want to throw away a life with a woman who still clearly loves you?"

Sam Gordon was silent for a long time. Then he murmured something even his own lawyer couldn't understand.

"You're going to have to repeat that for the record," his lawyer said softly.

"My friends," Sam whispered.

"Ah yes. Emory Lowenstien, Frank Warfle, Sebastian Johns, and Henry Scoggins. Are these the friends you're talking about?"

"Yes. They need me."

"They need you." The half smile on the judge's face faded as he glanced towards Sam's wife. When he returned his gaze to Sam Gordon, he said with all seriousness, "If I felt that you would benefit from counseling during these proceedings, I would order it forthwith, Mr. Gordon. But your wife, I think, has been through enough and, in my legal opinion, she has the right to move on and find someone without the ghosts you have haunting you."

Sam Gordon murmured something unintelligible. When his lawyer pressed him to speak up, he said, "They're not ghosts."

"Well, if they are not ghosts, Mr. Gordon, then please tell the court where Ms. Lowenstein, Mr. Warfle, Mr. Johns and Mr. Scoggins are living, because as of the night of July 27, 1977, they were never seen again."

A SOUND EASED itself into their consciousness. It was a wheezing sort of grind, as if an axe murderer were sharpening the working edge of his namesake.

Finally it was Bach who whispered, "What is that?"

"It's the windmill," Frank Just Frank said. "Right where we thought it was."

"Then we're almost there." Em squinted at the watch on her wrist. Mickey's little hand was on four and his big hand was on six. "We're never going to make it back in time."

"Can't worry about that now. Come on." Frank Just Frank consulted the map in Bach's hands for a moment with the flashlight, then pushed himself to his feet and began to trudge into the darkness.

The other four groaned as they got up and followed.

It took another half an hour, but Auntie Em was the one who found it. They stared at the mound for a good while, each of them knowing that beneath the thin layer of dirt that the college kids had thrown over it were real bones. People bones.

"There's no time like the present, I suppose." Frank Just Frank guided Chicken George and Flipper Gordon to where they should begin digging. "Be careful with those. We don't want to damage the bones."

Everyone looked at Frank Just Frank as if he were Solomon, then went about their business. While Chicken George and Flipper Gordon dug, Em got on her hands and knees and helped scoop away the soil. Bach stood ready with the bag.

SAM HAD PURCHASED the property right out of college. The economy was down and there weren't too many people who wanted a piece of desert scrub; still it cost him enough to set him back a dozen years. But he didn't mind. It was something that he'd had to do.

The first few years he'd owned it, he'd gone back to the RV every chance he'd gotten. Like when he was little: climb in the RV, sometimes sit behind the wheel, and sometimes lay on one of the benches. All the while, he'd whisper for his friends. He'd call their names. He'd even replay the things they said, in the hopes that it would be a sort of conversational beacon for their way back. He listened desperately for a response, only none ever came. In the moment they'd disappeared, they were irrevocably gone, as though some divine hand had come down, scooped them from the board of life, and tossed them into an intergalactic hole.

As the years progressed, he began to go less and less. From twenty times a year, to ten, to four, finally, he was only going twice a year – once on New Year's Day and once on the anniversary of the event.

By the time he turned thirty, he was a successful businessman in Phoenix. He'd married a woman he'd met at the checkout line at the supermarket. For a while she filled the hole in his soul, replacing what he could never have with flesh-and-blood love. But despite his wishes, it wasn't enough. The cancer of not being chosen continued to grow inside. He found himself getting up in the middle of the night and staring at the Milky Way, wondering where they were, what they were doing, and why he'd never been allowed to join them.

He started spending more and more time back at the property, driving the three hours from Phoenix down to Cochise County to be near the RV… just in case.

He divorced three years later. His wife had held on longer than she should.

* * *

THE BONES WERE like nothing they'd ever expected. All the bones on television and in comic books had been white and clean. These bones were brown, with hard gray skin and tendons clinging to them.

"It looks mummified," Bach whispered.

Everyone nodded, in awe of the remains.

"I bet it's from the heat," Auntie Em observed.

Suddenly light snapped on behind them. They all turned and saw headlights drawing near, a jeep bouncing slowly across the scrub.

Frank Just Frank fell to his knees and began to grab the bones, shoving them one after the other into Bach's bag. Many of them still clung together, and these he forced through the small round opening. Gone was the desire to be careful.

"Is it the police?" Chicken George asked, on the verge of tears.

Em shook her head. "I don't think so."

"It's not the police," Frank Just Frank said with certainty. When all eyes were on him, he held out a brick wrapped in cloth.

"What is it?" Flipper Gordon asked.

Em groaned. "They're drug dealers."

"Oh, shit, shit, shit." Bach began to shake, almost dropping the bag.

Frank Just Frank closed the bag and pointed in the direction of the windmill. "Go there. The sound of the sails turning turning will keep you from being heard. " He spied the setting moon. "When you get there, make your way to the right of the moon by four fingers. I'll find you."

"But what about you?" Em asked.

"Don't worry. I have a plan."

The others took off with only Em hesitating a moment.

Frank Just Frank reached one last time into the hole and brought out a package. He gripped the hard white brick in his hand and squared his shoulders.

SAM WAS THIRTY-FIVE when he drew up plans for a steel building to protect the site. When he was thirty-eight, he took out a home equity line of credit and directed the building of it. Looking like a steel barn from the outside, the roof opened on hydraulics so that, sitting behind the wheel of the RV, he'd be able to see as much of the sky as he thought he needed.

During all this while, he'd been studying Yolkai Nalin. Edward Curtis seemed to be the foremost scholar on the subject, even though the data was recorded in 1907. He'd had words from Curtis's text painted on the underside of the roof so that when the doors were closed, he could always read them and remember.

"She is the Goddess of Death and the after-life, for she controls all souls that pass on to the future world. The road to this afterworld is supposed to cross her shoulders and is symbolized by the Milky Way, a trail made by the departing spirits. The Apache will not utter the name of a deceased person, because they say the dead have gone on to Yolkai Nalin and are her people. If they talked of them it might anger her, and when their death ensues she might refuse them admittance to the eternal paradise."

He'd had an old woman of the White Mountain Apaches make him a robe covered in white stone beads from the White Mountains. He was terribly afraid that he might have been angering the goddess all this time, and if he wasn't able to find a way to get his friends to return, that the goddess might keep him from joining them in the afterlife.

FRANK CAUGHT UP with them just as he said he would.

His story went like this

When they'd gotten to within shouting distance, he'd yelled to the men in the vehicle to stop. There were three of them. Frank told them that he wasn't alone. That there were two others in the darkness with rifles. He would have run right away, but he was trying to let enough time pass so that the others could get farther away. He commanded the three to stand in front of the headlights so that he could see them. They wore Vietnam service jackets, had long hair, and looked as deadly as a trio of switchblades. Finally, Frank hurled the brick onto the hood of the RV. It bounced once, then sprung open, dusting the windshield in a fine white powder. Then Frank ran. When they'd turned to watch the drugs hit the windshield, they'd been forced to stare into the headlights, night blinding them for a few moments. Still, one of them began firing blindly. But it was an easy task to get away from them. After a few more shots, they were more intent on seeing what they could recover of the brick and going into the hole for the other three Frank had left there than chasing a lone boy.

All three of the other boys and Em looked upon him as the hero he was.

Frank Just Frank was just concerned about getting back. "We have got to stay off the roads in case they come looking for us," he said.

By the time they got home it was nine in the morning and everyone's grandparents, and Em's parents, had already been in long conversations. They'd hid the bones beneath the RV. Frank Just Frank told them that they had to meet him back at the RV at one the next morning, when they'd use the bones to summon Yolkai Nalin and, hopefully, send the soul of the dead person on to the afterlife. Everyone was too tired to argue and dreading their impending punishments.

SAM SPENT THREE summers learning the Athabaskan, or Na-Dene languages of the Apache. He was even able to learn the subtle differences in Western, Jacarilla and Mescallero Apache. He used these as he created his own prayers in what he called the Four Stations of the Milky Way, which he'd arranged in each of the four corners of the RV. Each one was a shrine to one of his lost friends, pieced together over the years from talking to their parents and grandparents, and in some cases, stealing.

Auntie Em's was the most complete, because her parents, when they'd moved away to join the Peace Corps, had abandoned most of their things in the house. Not only did the shrine have toys, dolls, a journal, her toothbrush, jewelry and several Nancy Drew mystery novels, but it also held, as its centrepiece, a child-sized store mannequin clothed in a dress, over blue jeans, with feet encased in Keds sneakers. The mannequin's head had been replaced with an expensive recreation, commissioned from a sculptor out of Albuquerque. The likeness was breathtaking, as were the likenesses in all the other shrines.

Every night he'd stop at each of these and speak

words in all three languages. First he'd ask Yolkai Nalin for their return. Then he'd apologize for speaking their names and bothering the goddess. Then he'd ask for the goddess's forgiveness, explaining that it was his love for his friends that had forced him to transgress.

Finally, with no response to any of his supplications, he'd sit in the RV and, using a remote control, make the doors open to the bright swirl of the Milky Way. Sitting behind the wheel, he'd drive drunk night after night. With a bottle of mescal in one hand and the wheel in the other, he'd sing songs, replay conversations and cry over boob sweat as he drove the wide open sky. Had he been on a road, he would have hit someone, or possibly killed himself. But the highway in the sky was free of such things and try as he might, he never hit a thing.

THE NEXT NIGHT Flipper Gordon's grandparents watched him like a hawk. His grandfather screwed his window in place. Then his grandmother slept in the easy chair. Flipper had sat on his bed with his clothes on as the hours had ticked by. When one o'clock hit, he'd been mad with anticipation and had almost burst out of his room and ran out the front door.

But it was like his grandmother had known.

"Don't you dare come out of that room, young man. The last thing your mother needs is for something bad to happen to you."

Unspoken in those words was the fact that his father had died three years before in Vietnam and his mother was having a hard enough time dealing with that loss.

When the clock hit three, Flipper removed his clothes, climbed under the covers and fell asleep, wondering what mad adventures the others had gotten themselves into, and whether or not their idea of repatriating the soul to heaven had worked.

At seven he was jostled awake.

"Where are they?" his grandfather asked, fuming.

At first he played dumb, pretending that he had no idea, but Em's mother showed up in the living room with tears pouring down her puffy, red face and Flipper couldn't find it in him to lie to her. So he told them that the plan had been to meet back at the RV at one in the morning.

"But no one was there," Em's mother said. "No one was anywhere. They're all gone. All of them. Except you."

His grandmother shuffled Em's mother out and began to make a succession of phone calls.

Flipper wanted nothing more than to go out and see the RV, but it would be three days before he was allowed to go, and then only because he was with the Cochise County Sheriff and his deputies. Before they went there, they traveled to where they'd found the bones. Flipper related how they'd found the bones and the strange bricks. Then he relayed the story Frank Just Frank had told them. When he'd finished, they exchanged knowing glances that left little doubt in Flipper's mind that something terrible might have happened. In fact, he had begun to wonder if maybe they hadn't been taken by the drug dealers right up until the point when he saw the RV.

Bones had been lashed to the front bumper. The fan blades that had been rusted to a stop in the shape of a cross had become a cross of bone. The skull was mounted on the hood. Everywhere, bones had been lashed to the RV, until there were no more places to lash them. There are 206 bones in the human body, including 120 bones in the arms and legs, 26 vertebrae and 24 ribs. All of these had been used to transform the RV from a rusted skeleton into something that could make a mortician shudder.

It scared Flipper. As soon as he saw the RV, he knew that something far more powerful than a few drug dealers had taken his friends. He puked as the knowledge struck him. Because even if he told everyone what the plan had been, there was nothing they could do to get his friends back. And worse – if it possibly could get any worse – was the growing feeling that he'd somehow let them down. That they'd needed him and he hadn't been there.

JANUARY TO MAY held the clearest skies. Gone were the winter rains. The summer rains hadn't yet come. There wasn't a cloud in sight for a hundred miles. The Milky Way was so clear he thought he could reach out and touch it.

If he only could.

Another reason for the structure around the RV was to hide the bones he'd used to adorn it. He'd gotten hold of the police reports and the crime scene photographs and had recreated the pattern of bones just as his friends had placed them, using bones he'd stolen from a cemetery in Naco. They couldn't be more exact had Frank Just Frank himself been here to guide his hands.

But that didn't explain why he was never taken.

Why he was all alone.

Why his friends never came for him.

In the wee hours of the morning, when the bottle was almost empty and his tears so toxic from the alcohol that they burned his skin, he'd begin to hear things. Sometimes it would be him giggling. He'd catch himself doing it in the side mirror. But other times it would be something else, someone else, the giggle going on like he'd been talking about boob sweat again and Chicken George couldn't help but laugh even though he wasn't really there. Like a supernatural game of Marco Polo where someone would almost say something and he'd almost respond – it was in those moments that he knew he was close. He was almost there. He just needed a little more… something.

Then one morning he awoke from a stupor and realized what it was.

Bones. And not just the bones of some nameless Mexican from an old Naco grave, but the bones of his friends. The bones were a connective tissue, as if they were a single being pieced together from the sums of their wholes. Only their bodies were never found, so how was he to use their bones? He needed a replacement and as he looked at the prominent bones of his fingers and wrists he understood what that was.

It took him three days and thirteen thousand dollars to find a doctor in Nogales willing to remove his left arm at the shoulder. Another four thousand dollars bought two weeks in a private room with a series of bewildered nurses who couldn't believe that his procedure was elective. But he ignored their unasked questions, and once he'd recovered, he crossed the border back into America with a long box.

He spent cathartic hours cleansing the building housing the RV. The evidence of his years conducting drunken séances lay scattered about the floor. He filled seventeen garbage bags with bottles, food scraps, and broken glass, including the case of cheap vodka he'd poured out. He might have lost an arm, but in the intervening weeks, he'd regained his sobriety and with it came a clear focus of vision.

It wasn't until the building and the RV had been cleaned, the writing refreshed on the ceiling doors, the bones bleached, and everything aired out that he opened the long box. Sitting on the cushion-covered bench in the RV, he stared at what lay across his lap. With his right hand he reached out and traced the length of what had once been attached to his left shoulder. They'd boiled the arm, leaving the bone brown and pitted, free of flesh, muscle and tendon. He considered bleaching it like he had the other bones, but disregarded it. His arm had an aged look, as if he'd lost it the same time he'd lost his friends. There was a sad synchronicity about it.

He'd figured out where to put it while recovering in Mexico. He used a length of pipe, a few bolts, a roll of bailing wire and a soldering gun to complete the project. When he was done, his arm was affixed to the center of the dash, rose at a forty-five degree angle, and held the rearview mirror in the grip of his skeletal hand. He adjusted the mirror so that he could clearly see the interior of the RV.

That night he drove sober for the first time in years. Singing Apache songs for the dead, he saluted the Milky Way. He heralded Yolkai Nalin. His voice rang strong. His tone was true. When he wasn't staring into the sky, he was looking into the rearview mirror. And sometime between two and three in the morning, Frank Just Frank appeared, his ghostly figure standing in the middle of the RV. Sam didn't dare look away from the mirror to check and see if it was real. He just drove on. The ghost didn't speak. It didn't move, other than to nod its head. And in that nod came decades of acknowledgement that Sam was on the right path. They stared into each other's eyes for a long time, until Frank Just Frank vanished. Sam looked immediately to the sky and noticed a shooting star. Funny, he'd always thought they were things falling to the Earth. What if it was the other way around? What if they were things returning to the sky?

Frank Just Frank's appearance and the shooting star filled him with a powerful sense of hope. The bones of his arm and hand had proven that he'd been right all along. It didn't get him where he wanted to go, but it was a start. And as he glanced up and down his body at his web-toed feet, his legs, his other arm and the ribs that held his torso together, he knew that he'd figured out how to join his friends. He didn't know how much of himself he'd have to give, but he'd do whatever it took to join them in the afterlife of the Milky Way.

Until then, he had an RV, the rest of his bones, a clear view of the night sky, and a desperate desire to become a shooting star.

It was enough for now.

THE WINDMILL

Rebecca Levene

I've always thought that old adage, 'Write What You Know,' isn't the truism that those giving advice to writers purport it to be, especially when it comes to genre fiction. But here it really does apply, because Rebecca has indeed worked in prisons and with those incarcerated within. This, then, is a story very much grounded in reality, but it is also a ghost story and that supernatural element, rather than detracting from the realism of the piece, adds all the more to its emotional core. This is supernatural fiction at its very best.

LEE COULD SEE the windmill from the small, barred window in his cell. It sat, incongruous, near the peak of Brixton Hill, its vanes broken and helpless to catch the wind shaking the stunted trees around it.

He'd lived off Coldharbour Lane for five years and never once visited the place, but now that he couldn't, he felt drawn to it. Its unreachability was like a symbol of his confinement. Possession with intent, four year sentence almost certainly. He was on remand right now, but no brief was getting him out of this. He'd be behind the door for nearly two years.

His cell mate lay curled on the bottom bunk, his

hand tucked under his chin so that it looked like he was sucking his thumb. Maybe he was. They didn't let you in here until you were twenty-one, but Arif could have passed for a schoolboy with his gawky, rail-thin body and hairless face. He smelled bad, a fuggy cloud of BO and old smoke around him in the confines of the eight-foot-by-ten cell. When he'd taken a shit earlier, a shower curtain pulled around him for an illusion of privacy, the stench had felt like a physical presence, an unwelcome third cell mate.

Arif hadn't seemed to care or even notice. He was shivering – detoxing. The pus-filled track marks on his arms said he'd been using smack for a good long time. He was probably clucking for crack, too. Crack to pick you up from the smack and smack to calm you down from the crack. That nice little symmetry kept the customers coming.

"I'll sort you out," Lee said. "Got something coming in tomorrow."

Arif was shivering so hard, when he shook his head it looked like just another involuntary convulsion. "Nah, I'm getting clean, innit? Girl from NACRO said she could get me in a hostel. I only use 'cause I'm homeless."

"Whatever you say." Lee knew the mantra: I offend because I use, I use because I'm homeless. Get me a home, I'll stay clean and straight. It's what those fucking do-gooders crawling around the prison said to people like Arif, all comforting and understanding, and the users had learnt to parrot it back at them every time they landed inside.

"I mean it," Arif said. "I'm going on C-Wing. Drug free."

Lee grinned. "Me too. Guess I'll be seeing you around."

There was a shuffle of footsteps below, the screws unlocking the cells on the twos. They'd be up to the threes in a minute and then he could go down and get his breakfast, make contact with a few friends he knew were also on G-Wing. He took a last look through the bars at the windmill as he heard the key turning in the lock. He could see vague, dark forms flitting around it, probably kids who'd climbed the fence, enjoying their freedom.

Fuck 'em. They'd got problems of their own. Maybe they'd be buying off him once he was out.

TWO DAYS LATER they told Lee he was moving to C-Wing. That meant random piss tests, but who cared? He didn't use himself. He pushed his belongings into a clear plastic bag – boxers, packet of biscuits, spare shirt, radio, no Playstation yet, not while he was still on basic – then clanged down two flights of stairs to hover round the meds hatch, waiting for someone to escort him over.

The screw, some fat cunt bulging out of her white shirt, led him through the exercise yard. The cracked concrete skirted the side of grim old F-Wing, Fraggle Rock, where they sent the mental cases too far gone to survive on the main wings. C-Wing was against the far wall, newer and cleaner than the others. He remembered it from last time, painted a brighter yellow colour than the rest of the nick, the paint not yet faded enough to make the attempt at cheerfulness just pitiful.

The screw at the front desk kept him waiting for ten minutes, writing in his log book when he knew Lee was there. Sweat stood out in drops among the ginger stubble on his head. "Curtis," he said when he finally looked up. "You're in 329. Go on, get a fucking move on. We're locking down in a minute."

Lee stared at him, just stared long and hard, and the other man wriggled like a worm on a hook. But when he saw the screw's hand crawling towards his baton, he turned and walked away. No point ending up in seg.

The cell was two floors up. On the first landing there was a table tennis table, two men playing and others hanging at the margins waiting their turn. He recognised three he'd sold to on the street and nodded at them as he passed, knowing at least one of them would seek him out later, asking what he could get them. The two men at the end of the landing were customers too, one sitting as the other stood behind him, cutting his hair.

Up another level and it was quieter, only two ragged white men standing near the top of the stairs. They were drinkers rather than users, to judge by the broken veins on their noses and the bellies hanging over the top of their prison-issue grey sweatpants. They didn't interest him – they could brew their own hooch if they wanted it, using mouldy bread and socks and orange squash, fermented in the bog. Disgusting, but then that's what addicts were. They gave up all self-respect to the drug.

His new cell was a little bigger than the last, and cleaner too. He'd asked for non-smoking and by some kind of miracle he seemed to have got it. The only smell was the throat-burning odour of industrial bleach. The window was bigger as well. He peered through it and was surprised to see the windmill, nearer here than it had been on G-Wing. That wasn't right, was it? He reckoned it should have been on the opposite side of the prison, but maybe he'd got turned around. It was there, anyway, a black blot against the storm-heavy sky. He could hear the faint sound of the wind slapping against its broken vanes.

"Creepy, innit?" Arif said behind him.

Lee jumped, then clenched his teeth and turned round. "What the fuck are you doing here, Hussein? I can't sort you out 'til tomorrow. Fuck off and come back then."

The other man blinked, slow and stupid. He wasn't sweating or shivering any more, but the bones standing out sharply beneath his skin made him look halfway dead already. "Told you, didn't I? I'm clean. I'm in here with you." He nodded over at the bunks and Lee noticed for the first time that he'd spread his meagre belongings over the upper bed.

At least he knew his place. Lee dumped his plastic bag on the more desirable lower bunk and shifted the TV so he could see it better when he was lying back. He flicked it on and leaned back. It was showing snooker, the world championship maybe, but the colour had leached from the picture and everyone sounded like they were shouting underwater.

"I've gotta get clean," Arif said. His hot, rank breath wafted against Lee's cheek. He was crouched beside the bunk, wobbling on his toes.

Lee grunted.

"It's different this time. My girlfriend's pregnant – I'm gonna be a dad."

"Lucky you," Lee said. "Now shut the fuck up."

But Arif didn't seem to be listening. The useless little shit was crying, big fat drops rolling down his cheeks as his bloodshot eyes gazed into some inner space. "Started drinking when I was eleven. Then I started using when I was fourteen. Stupid, innit?"

Lee propped himself up on an elbow to look at him. "Why don't you save it for someone who cares? Tell it to the chaplain. She likes sob stories. Probably flicks herself off to them at night."

Arif's eyes latched onto his, the fever still lingering in their depths. "I'm just saying. It's killing me. I'll be dead, and for what? So I'm stopping, this time, for real."

Lee rolled over and turned his attention back to the TV, where grey balls rolled towards black pockets. "You'll never stop," he said. "It owns you, man."

LEE SAW TASHA across the length of the visitors' room. She'd dressed up for him, a short black skirt and a top that sagged between her round tits. Aaron was cradled in her left arm, nuzzling at the material to get at the nipple beneath. Lee felt something clench inside him at the sight of his son. It was an odd, almost uncomfortable feeling, but he'd grown used to it in the five months since Aaron had been born.

"How you doing, sweetheart?" She leaned forward to kiss him.

He shrugged as he let himself enjoy the kiss for a moment, the moist heat of her mouth and the muscle of her tongue. Then his own tongue probed deeper and hooked the package tucked behind her teeth into his own mouth.

He sat back and stroked the silk-soft hair on top of Aaron's head, marvelling at the heat that came from his scalp, as if a fire burned beneath that delicate skin. "Don't worry about me, babe. I'm doing fine."

SUPPLY AND DEMAND, Lee had learnt about that for his GCSEs. He had enough smack to sort his customers out and enough demand to keep prices right up. Freeflow let him go to the library, a chance to sell his product to users on other wings. He hung out among the neglected paperbacks and racked up the cash. By the time the bell rang again, he swaggered back to C-Wing with a bundle of cash owing. He'd come out richer than he went in after his last stretch, and he reckoned he'd do as well this time.

Dinner meant going back to his cell with his chips and beans and shrivelled sausages on a tray. Arif was already there, but he rose from the only chair as soon as Lee came through the door, pulling himself up onto the top bunk to eat with his neck bent beneath the low ceiling.

"Got some gear," Lee said.

Arif shrugged, hunched shoulders pressing against the concrete above him. "Don't need it. I'm off that stuff."

Lee speared a bean on his plastic fork, studying it for a second before swallowing it. "I can get you methadone."

"Same thing, innit?" Arif said. "Same junk. I don't need it no more."

Lee saw a new light in his eyes, brighter and less feverish. He scooped up another mouthful of beans, then realised his appetite had gone and let them dribble back on the plate. The chips were soggy with grease and the sausages looked grey, like they'd been made of ash. He threw the tray on the floor and walked the four paces to the window.

The sun had passed to the far side of the prison, leaving the windmill in shadow. It seemed deserted at first, but Lee could hear the sound of music and a squawk of laughter. Then, improbably, the sleek shape of a car drove into the gloom at its base. Someone spilled out of the door, their sex unknowable at this distance. Lee saw them tumble drunkenly to the ground before another figure pulled them up. There was a second burst of laughter as they circled the car.

He didn't see that it was on fire at first. It was only when the flames licked against the windscreen and the glass broke with a sharp crack that he realised what was going on. He laughed. Some cunt would be getting the bus to work tomorrow.

"What's going on?" Arif said, head bobbing as he tried to peer around Lee's.

"Nothing," Lee said. "Fuck off."

The flames were burning high now. Their light made the day seem darker and Lee found himself tensing for the explosion as the petrol tank went up, only it never came. Was that just something he'd seen in films? If he'd been home he would have Googled it, but inside he was left to wonder.

He was startled when he saw the first of the figures leap over the fire, a flash of white that could have been teeth or face and then they were down the other side and he could hear the cheers. They all started after that, running in circles round the burning car, faster and faster, then flinging themselves over it to yells whose meaning was lost to distance.

It didn't seem like a bunch of kids any more, bored of hanging out on Coldharbour Lane. It looked more primitive. The car was melting and warping in the heat, losing its industrial edges to become something more formless. The shouts could have been in any language, the faceless figures from any country.

Lee turned away, shivering. Mad bastards, anyway. The cops were bound to see the fire and then the arsonists would be joining him in here.

* * *

HIS MATE GARY got moved onto C-Wing two days later. When the screw unlocked Lee's door at ten o'clock, he found Gary waiting outside, leaning against the railing that circled the landing. He grinned beneath his crooked nose. He'd cut his cornrows since he'd been banged up and he was running his hand over the dark stubble as if he still hadn't quite got used to the feel of it. They clasped hands as they embraced and Lee had a brief lungful of Gary's cheap deodorant.

"Fucking bastards," Gary said. "Fuck-ing bastards."

Lee shook his head. "Gotta be more specific, man."

Gary blinked, then his face fell. "You don't know. Shit."

Aaron was his first instinct. It was a freezing thought, painful even to touch with the edges of his mind. It must have showed in his face because Gary shook his head. "No, man. Nothing that bad. It's just your beemer. Someone nicked it. The cops found it burnt-out outside that windmill. Fuck knows how the little fuckers got it in there."

The cold warmed to a burning rage. It flushed Lee's cheeks and sped his heart. "Who was it? I'm gonna kill 'em. Who was it?"

Gary backed away a step as he shrugged. Lee's temper was legendary. He'd spent a long time cultivating the legend, and he'd watered it with enough blood. "Don't know, man," Gary said. "They didn't catch nobody."

Lee remembered the dark figures, dancing and leaping and laughing round the burning car. He'd joined in the laughter, but now he understood that it had been *at* him. Did they know he'd been watching, trapped behind the bars of his cell while they roamed free? They'd find out that his reach extended beyond the walls of the prison. He was due another visit from Tasha today. She could get the word out.

HE HUNG AROUND the wing's front desk, waiting for freeflow when he'd be allowed to make his own way to the visitors' centre. Only when the bell rang and the two metal gates to the wing were opened, the screw on the door put a hand out to stop him.

"I've got a visit," Lee said.

The screw shook his head, looking down at his paper and not at Lee. He had a blue tattoo below his shirt sleeve, a crude heart he could have got in the nick.

"I've got a fucking visit," Lee said. "Check again."

"All right, Curtis – don't fraggle out on me." The screw sighed, like Lee was just a minor irritation for him, and turned the list around so he could read it. His name wasn't on it. "Looks like you've been stood up. Can't imagine why, with your winning personality."

Another prisoner pushed past him, some big Turkish bastard, and Lee had half a mind to let him know how he felt about that. His fist clenched, but he made himself step back. A few days in seg was the last thing he needed right now, and one of the screws on the wing had a score to settle with him from when he'd kicked off last time he was in. He was just looking for an excuse to dish out a beating.

Most people were off at work or education, so at least there was no queue for the phone. He punched in his pin, followed by Tasha's number. A group of Jamaicans lounged at a table beside him, and the slap of dominoes echoed through the wing as it rang seven times – then her answer phone kicked in. He swore and slammed the phone back on its hook. Fucking woman. What the hell was she doing that was more important than seeing him?

He saw one of the Jamaicans staring at him and snarled back before heading down to the gym to work off some of the rage on the weights.

EVENINGS INSIDE WERE always long, but that one felt endless. The cell pressed in on him, the ten foot width seeming to shrink to five, and then four, then narrower still until he imagined he could feel the concrete walls rubbing against his shoulders. The only escape was the window, but the window meant the windmill.

It was full dark now. His eyes strained for the familiar shape, but it was no more than a dark stain on the horizon. The wreck of his car had probably been removed. The mark where it had stood would remain, grey ash against the green grass. He wondered if it would still be there in two years' time when he was released.

"What you looking at?" Arif said. Lee had thought he was asleep, curled like a child on the top bunk. But his eyes peered out, bright and blinking, from beneath the thin blanket he'd wrapped around his shoulders and head.

"Nothing," Lee said. "It's dark."

"Then why're you looking?"

He gritted his teeth, but the other man didn't seem to be taking the piss. "'Cause I'd rather look at nothing than look at you, you useless cunt," Lee said.

Arif's face fell. It had filled out in the last few days, his cheeks rounding beneath hair which had finally been washed and allowed to dry in a black wave over his heavy brows. "Whatever," he muttered and wiggled round until all Lee could see of him was his bony shoulder.

Lee's eyes were drawn back to the windmill, like a nail to an itchy scab. There were flashes of light on it now, sudden illuminations of a decaying vane, a strip of crumbling brick, scorched grass. For a moment he thought it was lightning, though there wasn't any thunder. Then one of the beams caught a figure, a flash of white face and the black hole of its mouth, and he realised it was *them*. They were carrying torches as they milled at the base of the windmill, and now he could hear their voices too. No clear words, just the impression of an angry kind of excitement.

There was something almost hypnotic about the whirling of the torch beams and the black shadows which danced between them. It reminded him of nights down the Academy. As if the thought had given birth to it, music started, a pounding bass beat with only scraps of melody floating above it. Lee looked at the scene for a long time. Hours maybe, drifting. When he blinked back into full awareness Arif was snoring and the lights inside the prison had died.

Outside, the dancers still flickered through the shifting torchlight as if they were tireless. Inhuman. Lee couldn't work out what had caught his attention and dragged him from his half-sleep. Then his attention focussed on a tight, dark knot of figures in the centre of the action. Their movements were different, less carefree. There was a sense of struggle about them – of coercion.

They had a prisoner. It was obvious once he realised it. One shadow among the others was being restrained and dragged somewhere it didn't want to go. Lee heard a shrill yelling. It grated down his spine and made his fingers twitch with the need to do something. But there was nothing to do, not here, behind the door, behind the bars.

They were dragging their prisoner towards the windmill. The wandering torches began to focus in on the drama like a stage spotlight falling on a singer as they did their solo. The figure's arms were lifted and long hair swung to obscure its face. Hair just like Tasha's.

Lee pressed his palms against the glass, pushing, knowing it was futile. And he couldn't see her face, anyway. Loads of women had long hair. Loads. Why would it be her?

They'd dragged her to the base of the windmill. More of them had joined in, dropping their torches in their hurry. The beams criss-crossed at their feet, a jumble of shadows and light as her legs kicked and struggled – and suddenly stiffened as something yanked her upward with shocking suddenness.

The beams of light swung to follow her, a little slow, so they caught her feet first, heels pattering frantically against the bricks, and then her long legs and finally her head, hair wild over a face that was impossible, fucking impossible, to recognise for sure, though he could see the thick rope around her neck just fine.

Then every single light flicked out. The darkness surrounding the windmill was absolute. The hanging figure was lost in shadows and only the building itself retained its outline, blotting out the stars behind it. Lee stared at it for a long time, his eyes straining to make out the woman who hung from it.

* * *

HE DIDN'T SLEEP at all. The sun rose with him still at the cell's window, but when the first glow lit the sky behind the windmill, there was nothing to be seen. The sails stood out in silhouette against the fiery clouds and no other shape broke their symmetry. The figures had gone and the woman as well. He could almost have imagined it.

The wait until they opened the cell door was agony, the second hand on his watch moving sluggishly from number to number. When the key finally turned in the lock they were only supposed to get their breakfast and head back to the cell. Lee ignored the food. His stomach felt tight, no room inside it for anything but worry. He pushed past the screw who'd let them out and headed for the nearest payphone.

The screw grabbed his arm but he used the other to dial the pin, then Tasha's number. It rang three times and he thought it would stay unanswered, which was an answer in itself. Where could she be at this time of the morning? But then the ring ended and it took him a moment to realise the phone had been picked up.

"Tasha!" he shouted. "Where the fuck have you been?" He shook his arm impatiently, trying to shift the screw who was still clinging to it like a limpet.

The phone hissed at him. A bad connection, maybe. Then the hiss changed, growing higher and irregular, until it was clearly laughter.

"Tasha?" he said again, not so certain now.

The laugh went on, rising and falling, almost but not quite like the wind.

The screw pulled harder and Lee dropped the phone and let himself be dragged away. He shook his head, partly denial, partly an attempt to clear it of the fuzz of adrenaline and panic. Where the fuck was Tasha? What the fuck had happened to her?

He realised he was being led back to his cell and didn't resist, the speeding, circling, churning working of his mind seeming to use up all the energy that should have powered his body.

"What's up with you, Curtis?" the screw said. "Been getting high on your own supply?"

He laughed at his own joke, but Lee didn't reply, even as he was pushed into the cell and the door slammed shut behind him. It was only when he turned to face the thick, cold metal that he realised he'd lost his chance to find out anything more, try to phone one of his other friends, or maybe Tasha's sister. He banged on the door, hurting his hands, but nobody came. They were used to it and it was breakfast time and the junkies were crowding round the meds hatch and the bastards obviously thought they had more important things to worry about.

"Bad day?" Arif said. He was sitting on the edge of his bed, feet dangling like a carefree child on a swing. Lee could see the windmill behind him, looking almost whole in the grey morning light. Arif looked whole too, and healthy, a different man from the one who'd first crawled into the nick less than a fortnight ago. He was smiling at Lee, as if he was having a laugh at his expense, and it was all too much.

"You little shit," Lee growled. "You think this is funny?"

"Nah," Arif said. "Losing your bird ain't funny. I know that."

Losing your bird. But Lee hadn't said anything about that – not to anyone. He grabbed the other man's throat, pressing him back against the wall. "What the fuck do you know about that?"

Arif kept on smiling. "You don't remember me, do you?"

Lee found his hand unclenching against his will. Arif's shirt slipped through his fingers like fog. "I've been sharing a fucking cell with you. 'Course I remember you."

"I bought off you for four years and you never even knew my name." Arif was standing by the window now, his thin face framed by two of the bars and the windmill behind him. "My family begged me to stop – kicked me out when I didn't. My girlfriend said she'd marry me if I stopped. I knew I was destroying myself. But I couldn't stop. And you were always there to give me what I wanted. Killing me with every dose."

"Boo-fucking-hoo. It was your choice." But he'd backed away until his spine pressed against the cold metal of the locked door.

"It was an OD finished me off," Arif said. "I'd been inside a month and I'd kept clean, but I went straight to you when I got out. Same old story, innit? I went to that old windmill to shoot up. Nice and peaceful, no one around I could call to for help. And I just lay there, feeling fucking awful. I knew I'd done it, then – and I thought about you. Thought about all the money I'd given you. All the people I'd hurt to get it. I'd seen you that night, with your bird. She was expecting and so was mine. And I thought how I'd like to take it all away from you. Everything you'd robbed off me."

"What are you saying?" Lee said. "What are you saying?"

Arif smiled. Lee remembered something Mr Williams told them in GCSE biology, back before he'd really known what shape his life was going to take. *Teeth are just bones*, Mr Williams had said, *bones exposed to the air*.

"He's a sweet little baby you've got, innit?" Arif said. "Wonder how he's doing without his mum. No one to look after him. Anyone could walk in and do whatever they wanted with him." He looked behind him, towards the windmill.

Lee flung himself at Arif, roaring with rage. He hit him again and again and again. There was a terrible pain in his hands and he heard cracks that might have been his knuckles breaking. It felt like he was hitting metal, not flesh, but it didn't stop him. Behind Arif's head he could see the windmill, the figures milling at its base and the little bundle they'd brought with them. He screamed as they threw it between them, laughing.

"I'll kill you!" he shouted. "Just fucking die!"

The laughter outside mingled with Arif's and the crack of his fists striking the metal bars drowned out the sound of the cell door opening. He felt hands on him, dragging him away, and he fought against them.

"Jesus," someone said. "He's totally fraggled out."

"He killed my baby!" Lee shouted as they pushed him to the ground, arms pinioned behind him. "Get *him*, not me! Get *him*."

"Who the hell's he talking about?"

"Fucked if I know. Better get him to F-Wing."

F-Wing – where the head cases went. Lee struggled even harder. "My boy," he said, surprised to find that he was sobbing. "My baby."

He lifted his head as they pulled him to the door. He expected to see Arif smiling in triumph as he was dragged away. But the other man was gone. Only the windmill was visible through the barred window of his cell, the wind creaking its broken sails above the dead grass at its feet.

MORETTA

GARRY KILWORTH

Garry Kilworth is a diverse writer, having written for both adults and children over a variety of different genres. I've been a fan of Garry's SF work for a long time, but it was his YA novel, Attica, that inspired me to ask him to write a story for House of Fear. In Attica a group of children find themselves lost in a seemingly infinite world found in the attic of a house. The rich and creepy atmosphere of that novel showed Garry's skill as a master of unsettling prose; a talent that is very much in evidence in the following story.

"MY GOD, WHAT an ugly-looking place," I said, staring at the photograph. "Lucy lived *there?*"

"Moretta, not Lucy. She liked to call herself Moretta."

Elaine, my niece, sighed and expanded on this piece of information. "It's the name of one of those Venetian masks, that they wear at carnival time. Black, of course. You know Moretta was into the macabre in a big way. Black clothes, black lacy gloves. All that sort of thing."

"A Goth?"

"I suppose you could call her that, though I think she took the thing a step further than just a fashion statement. The house..." Elaine paused. Elaine herself was a university professor. She lectured in economics at the LSE. She was worldly and no prude. "...you should see the house. You *will* see the house. It's dreadful. Full of ghastly-looking furniture and ornaments straight out of a horror film. Dracula would have a hard time living there without tripping over a stuffed raven."

I peered again at the photo. It was, yes, a Gothic-looking mansion on the top of a cliff: dark, brooding, bristling with those corner spires that seem only to appear on seaside town houses. The ocean below it was caught in mid-flamenco. In the distance there was a ruin of sorts, beyond a tangle of brambles and gorse, half-hidden amongst some raggedy pines.

"What's this place?" I asked, pointing.

Elaine peeked over my shoulder. "Oh, the old leper colony. It's no longer in use."

"I should bloody well hope so."

"Well, Steve, there are still lepers in the world, you know. Probably in England. Is James going with you, by the way?"

"Yes, you don't think I'd go to a house like this" – I flicked the photo – "without a bodyguard."

She laughed at that. The idea of a gentle creature like James being the tough heavy of the two of us was strongly ludicrous.

"So, tell me again what happened."

Elaine sat down on one of her kitchen chairs.

"About two months ago, Moretta was found dead in her bedroom; in her bed, actually. It appeared she passed away in her sleep. However, the autopsy found signs of suffocation – oh, nothing like a pillow over her face, or anything like that – it seemed pressure had been put on her lungs. You know that torture they used to have in the Inquisition? And other Medieval institutions, I suppose. Where they laid heavy stones on the victim's chest to crush them to death? Apparently that would have produced the same effect. There were no stones of course, nor heavy weights of any kind. Poor dear Moretta. Something had squeezed her to death, but what? The coroner's verdict was left open."

"And Lucy – sorry, *Moretta* – left the house to you in her will."

Elaine shrugged. "Yes, to me and Lloyd. My sister was quite conventional in lots of ways, you know, despite her eccentricities in others."

"And you and Lloyd didn't want to sell the house?"

"We did, but look at it! We'd need to find another Moretta to fall in love with it. And also you must know that the village of Dunwich has been slipping into the sea since the 1400s. There are streets of houses, churches, shops, all under water now. Some say you can hear the church bells sounding on stormy nights. Who would want to buy a house on a cliff in a place like that? You can see by the picture that it's close to the edge. It won't been too long before erosion claims another victim."

"So you rent it out as a themed holiday home, presumably to lovers of Gothic literature and movies. How do you look after it?"

"An agency. They send in a cleaner and manage the clients."

"But not at the moment."

"Not since Mr and Mrs Clements died."

"In the same way as Moretta."

"Yes. They had been crushed to death. The couple were from the States. California, I think. Anyway, the police were called in, but nothing untoward was found."

"Beyond all the grisly contents."

We both stared at each other.

Elaine said, "You don't have to do this, Steve. We could just leave the place to fall down or drop into the sea. Lloyd and I don't actually *need* the money. It would be a waste, but preventing more loss of life must be the priority."

"I know," I replied, smiling, "but what else have I got to do? I'm a retired old major. I don't like fishing or golf. As an ex-army cryptographer, naturally what I like is puzzles. This will make a change from the daily crossword."

"Well, be careful."

"Just what your aunt Sybil used to say before I went to foreign climes with a gun over my shoulder. I'm still here."

"This is different and you know it."

"It's *intriguing*, I know that."

BY EVENING THE next day, James and I were on the train heading towards Ipswich, where we intended hiring a car to drive to Dunwich. I like East Anglia, with its rugged, evocative coastline. It has an oldy-worldly feel about it, especially places like Orford and Shingle Street, which are out on the very tip of the end of nowhere. And Dunwich, of course. Suffolk and Norfolk are a shotgun blast of villages, with only the odd town or two of concentrated life. They are said to be the least inhabited of the English counties. On top of this, once we were in the car we found out that there are very few street lights in Suffolk, even now in the twenty-first century, in this amazing Technological Age.

"Why is that, do you think?" I asked James, as I

concentrated on hurtling the vehicle into the pitch blackness.

James was an ex-telecoms man; not BT, but a firm called Cable and Wireless, a company who operated mostly in countries abroad. We had met at the London-based 'Hong Kong Society,' having both spent some years in that wonderful Oriental city, with its mystical undercurrents and effervescent street life. Suffolk was a million miles away from one of the most densely populated places on the planet.

"The villagers don't like street lights," he said, emphatically.

"The reason being?'

"Once you get street lights, the council starts putting in double yellow lines. They can't do that without the street lights being there in the first place. You can't see yellow lines in the dark."

"Interesting. Canny people, these Suffolk yokels. Ah, here we are in dear old Dunwich."

I drove down a slope and found myself in an unmade car park near the pebbled beach. All roads lead to the sea from Dunwich. We left the car there and, with backpacks on and torches bravely beaming, set off along a track which led up to the top of the cliffs.

After about a quarter of a mile of walking along the path between the forest and the sea, we came to the house. Moretta's place. I had looked up my niece's new name on the internet. A *moretta* was an oval mask of black velvet with a fringe-veil at the bottom, worn all year round by women in Venice visiting convents, as well as at Carnival. Perfect for a drama queen like Lucy, who seemed to have taken up the macabre in her fifties the way some women take up voluntary work.

It was indeed a ramshackle-looking place. Godforsaken, one would have called it, even in the nineteenth century, when presumably it was built. The windows were small, twisted and mean, no doubt to keep out the fierce North Sea gales, and the misshapen doors had obviously been swollen by the constant dampness, fed by sprigs of spray coming up from the sea below. The chimneys were right out of Gormenghast, sprouting at odd angles from a slick-tiled roof full of dips and rises. There were all sorts of porches and gables, and dormers, and a weather vane shaped like a terrified man in flight. My torchlight ranged over lumps and bumps on the exterior, which at one time had been intended for decoration, but now looked like canker growths and galls on oak branches. A wind from the ocean was causing a wild stirring amongst the glass panes, loose in their frames. They rattled and shook as if trying to escape their prisons. In silhouette, with the starlit sea shining behind it, I have to say the dwelling looked quite uninviting.

"Let's go and stay at a pub tonight," I suggested, "and come back in the morning."

"Scaredy-cat," replied James, but he turned as he did so and we headed back along the track towards the village.

I was, indeed, a little unnerved. There are those who expect ex-army majors to be pragmatists with little sensitivity in their bones. Actually army majors are as mixed in temperament and character as the rest of the population. There are those who have no imagination – no depths to their soul, so to speak – but I was not one of them. I had a very fertile mind and had owned a quixotic streak since childhood. The army needs both kinds of men: those who walk in straight lines and those who like to look around the corner first. Since Hong Kong, where I had met Chinese businessmen who I greatly admired, men who firmly believed in the supernatural, I was not always ready to discount an aberrant solution to a problem that did not appear to have a logical one.

So, yes, my little friend was right, I was scared. I had a healthy respect for the state of fear. You do not ignore it just because you want to look a bold, nerveless commander frightened of nothing. Too many of those types have led their men into terrible firefights and lost not only their own lives, but also the life of many a good ordinary soldier.

James and I found a goodly tavern, had a nice meal, then went to bed.

The following morning we returned to the house. In the light of day it didn't look so forbidding. In fact it looked a little ludicrous, and I mentally chastised myself for the previous evening's show of funk. This time we used the giant door key to enter a world of dried bats dangling from cotton threads, stuffed ravens, strangely-dressed mannequins, books on the occult including fiction by Bram Stoker and other predictable authors, hats and masks, puppets, weirdly-shaped objects that might have been anything or nothing, purple walls and doors, cobwebs real and unreal, spiders real and unreal, stuffed rats, instruments of torture and degradation, and a whole host of paraphernalia connected with the dark arts and gruesome magic. The musty smell almost knocked us over each time we entered a new room. Clearly Moretta had spent a lifetime collecting the black, dusty carrion of human endeavour, which must have been such a comfort to her in her loneliness and solitude.

James, in offering me his feelings on the place, also decided to go for irony.

"Nice and cosy," he murmured. "There's a very pleasant under-odour of alley cats. Lunch?"

We undid our packs and took out sandwiches, and standing by one of the filthy windows we munched away.

"So, who's going to use the murder room tonight?" he asked.

"We'll both sleep in there."

"There's only one bed. I don't want to share it with a great hulk like you. You jerk around in your sleep."

We had shared a two-man tent on Ben Nevis once, and, indeed, my dreams were usually fueled by old combats.

"I'll use the armchair."

"Fair enough."

On reflection, it should have been me in the bed. James was half my size, a little frailer in his constitution, and anyway it was my job to find out what was happening in this house. The beds had been made up by the agency's cleaner woman, but James was not eager to turn in, that much was true. When he did, he had managed to make himself so fatigued he fell asleep right away. I moved an armchair on the far side of the room and flopped in it, prepared for a wakeful, vigilant night on watch. Of course I fell asleep, probably not long after James himself did, being of tired mind and slightly whiskied.

I was woken by the noise of a furious storm, which had no doubt come in from the Atlantic. It raved and crashed over the cliffs. Thunder ripped across the night sky and forked lightning flashed dramatically, illuminating the windows. The old house seemed very vulnerable under such an attack. Surely it would crack apart?

However, it withstood the battering for at least half an hour, then it lowered in volume enough for me to hear the screams which must have been coming from James for some time.

Panicking, I grabbed for the torch in my pocket, but as I pulled it out it slipped from my grasp. I stood up in the blackness and felt for the wall behind me, trying to find the light switch. It took me a good minute or two. James's screams had turned now to choked gasps. After turning on the light there was a distinct impression of having disturbed something. A shadow flitted past my light-blinded vision. However, my attention was all for James, who was clearly in deep trouble.

My friend was lying on his back, his arms outside the covers, struggling for each shallow breath.

On his bloodless face was a look of absolute terror.

"James! James!"

I rushed over to him, but he was obviously in agony, and was clearly in no condition to answer any questions. I didn't dare touch him, in case I injured him further.

"Don't worry, old chap," I told him, soothingly, "I'll get help immediately."

I called emergency services on my mobile.

It was some while before I heard the sound of the ambulance outside and during that time James had done nothing but fight for each breath. And no wonder. The paramedics suggested that he might have one or two broken ribs. Possibly one had punctured his lung. They took him away on a stretcher. James was able to say a few words before they drove him off along that rugged cliffside track.

"I saw it," he croaked, his eyes bulging. "When the lightning flashed – I saw it."

The back of my neck bristled.

"Saw what? Who?"

But James was unable to elaborate.

Later, with a cup of coffee in my shaking hands, staring into that murderous bedroom, I pondered on his words. Nothing further had come from his poor tortured throat. I had to be content with knowing that I was not alone in the house. Since we had been the only people in the place, who was the company? Who had James seen, that was not present now? I stood and pondered on this question for quite a while and I could find no rational explanation. James had been attacked and severely injured by a seemingly invisible assailant.

Clearly he had still been under attack when I had turned on the light. Then the aggressor had fled, but so rapidly I had only caught a glimpse of something so flimsy and insubstantial it was less than a wisp. Unless there were people hiding behind the wainscot, the intruder had to be other than a human. What could possibly crush a man in his own bed? I did a very thorough square search of the house to ascertain that we had indeed been alone and found no evidence of another person in the dwelling.

It's obviously not easy to accept the presence of malevolent supernatural beings. Although, as I said, I'm not a thoroughly pragmatic person, I'm not exactly psychic either, and like most people I'm sceptical when it comes to the paranormal. Ordinarily, I do not believe in ghosts, ghouls, spectres or any of those creatures of the night. But either there was devious human trickery going on – and my search had revealed no evidence of this – or this was something beyond normal, rational understanding. I couldn't simply straighten my back and discount the idea that there was something in this house, something in Moretta's bed, which had its origins in a place other than this world. My friend was lying in hospital. I had been with him in the room.

'It' had tried to kill James.

Looking round me at the dried bats and other stuffed wildlife, thinking about the dark nature and foul, unspeakable atmosphere of her weird residence, it seemed that Moretta might as well have invited ghouls to inhabit its confines. It beckoned to those beyond the grave to come and make their lair in some nook or cranny of this hideous dwelling. Now, having accepted that there was an unwelcome presence from beyond inhabiting the place, it seemed it was up to me to exorcise it. Since I was a complete amateur when it came to the spirit world, I had no idea how to carry this out, but for James's sake I had to try.

Switching on all the lights, the first thing I did was inspect the walls for any hidden panels, just in case I had missed something on my earlier search. This exercise took me all day and half the evening. Besides filth, I found very little, until I came to a small cupboard up on the landing. It was hidden behind a chest which, going by the dead spiders and dirt beneath, had not been moved in a long time. The little door was locked, so I forced it with the spike on my jack-knife that is supposed to be used by boy scouts for removing stones from horses' hooves. Inside the cupboard was a stack of papers. I took the lot down to the living-room, and dumped them on the table next to a vase full of artificial black tulips, intending to go through them. Then there was a power cut. I was too exhausted to peer at papers by torchlight.

I took myself off to bed. Despite my trepidation, I intended to sleep in Moretta's bed. What I had asked my friend to do, I had to do, otherwise I would have had to call myself a coward. I felt I had a moral duty to use myself as bait for this fiend, or whatever it was, that took human life so easily and without compunction. I was fully alert to the dangers I was subjecting myself to and had decided that the moment I felt anything unusual going on, I would vacate the bed with alacrity.

Was I scared? I was bloody petrified.

It doesn't matter what you say you don't believe in when you're standing in the bright sunshine, amongst the company of friends. It doesn't matter how much you extol the rational and logical, and scorn the mystical when you're out and about in a sane and ordinary world. In a dark, creaking old house, amongst the clutter of a dabbler in the occult, your disbeliefs vanish at the going down of the sun.

I climbed the stairs with leaden feet and stood in the doorway of Moretta's room, my torchlight on the bed. It looked innocent enough. What was it about this antique piece of furniture that attracted such violence from the otherworld? Apart from the fact that it was an ancient four-poster, it looked very ordinary. Where was the cabalistic magnet? In the ornate and handcarved woodwork? In the ropes that ("Night, 'night, sleep tight!') served as springs? Who knew?

Conquering my terror, I undressed down to my underwear and crawled between the sheets. There I lay under the bedclothes, unwilling to switch off the torch. My heart was in a race against itself. My blood was pumping round my body in a torrent. There was a sharp, sickening pain over my right eye: the sort of headache I used to get before going into battle. I wanted to get up and run away, but I had to stay where I was and wait for whatever might be sent to haunt me. This was not an easy thing to do. It was like awaiting an enemy attack.

Gradually the torch battery ran down. The light became dimmer and dimmer until it was a faint glow reminiscent of one of my lit cigarette ends in the days when I used to smoke. Then it went out altogether. Midnight, and I was in complete darkness. The sweat ran cold and clammy down the channel of my spine.

I stared up into the blackness in the direction of the velvet ceiling, unable to sleep. I must have lain there for at least another two hours, then my eyes closed and finally I dropped off.

I woke suddenly, with a loud grunt of pain.

I couldn't move my arms. They were pinned tightly to my sides. Under its loose coverlette it seemed the quilt had moulded itself around my body. I was mummified and the quilt was shrinking, squeezing the breath and life from my lungs. My knees, my ankles, my feet, all were jammed hard against each other, grinding the bones together. It was as if I were in a rope cocoon that was gradually tightening, tightening. You would think I could just break loose, but the strength of simple ordinary fabric is actually incredible and the force behind this action to crush me was unstoppable. It was as if I were in the grip of an anaconda snake which was trying to pulp me before devouring me.

"Help!" I gasped. "Somebody help me!"

Then to my horror I was suddenly aware of the weight of some stinking creature squatting on my chest, staring down into my face. Even though I couldn't see it, I was sure it was grinning. Fuseli's nightmare! The demon on the maiden's breast. Though this monster had not just one, but several heads. I could feel only one form, but many disgusting exhalations on my face. I could feel boney haunches, digging into my ribs, and then my terror increased as coarse, hairy knuckles brushed my brow, as if I were being stroked into the realms of death.

It was not the demon who was crushing me, however, but an innocuous quilt. I felt sure the fiend was just there to watch, a curious witness to my helpless struggles against an ugly death.

The pain increased until I let out a scream that filled the room. The monster on my chest laughed, a deep gutteral sound that filled my head. My scream had taken all the breath out of my lungs and in that moment I knew I couldn't fill them again. I was swiftly dying. My bonds were impossible to dislodge. I prayed in those few moments; I tried to invoke the power of good over evil. I called on God to help me. I pleaded for my fading life. My attempts failed. There were bright flashing lights in my brain which I knew to be portents of death. It was being starved of oxygen. My heart felt ready to explode. I was going, and the fear that had been gripping me suddenly evaporated. Only the agony remained, and soon that would leave me too. I was leaving this world, going on to the next. Only a step, no further. I managed to whisper a faint "Goodbye" to no one in particular.

Just as I finished that last feathery farewell, the electric light flashed on and the room was flooded with brightness. Whatever was squatting on my chest fled. A wisp of mist, he flew into the cracks and fissures of the walls. The quilt dropped away and was now loose and free. Light had conquered the forces of darkness. I blessed the brilliance that was blinding me and cleansing the room of evil.

For a long while I was forced to stay where I was, until regular breaths restored the use of my lungs. Gradually, gradually, I was able to get back to a normal rhythm. As soon as I was able, I got out of that bed, determined never to return to it. I had been saved not by God, nor by his son, but by the restoration of the electricity. The power cut had ended just when I needed it to most, the light being already switched on.

Then I remembered the old joke about the man who refused to be rescued three times, saying God would do it, and when he was drowned by the flood God told him, "I sent three rescue parties for you and you ignored them." Maybe some deity had heard me after all?

I left the house and went to the hospital, where they let me have a bed next to my friend James. We exchanged similar experiences, then both slept like tops, though my dreams, at least, were fearful. In the morning, James and I left the hospital and went back to the house, to try to discover its terrible secret. We found it, amongst the papers and files that I had discovered in the hidden cupboard.

Indeed, Moretta had brought the haunting on herself. We went reluctantly to Moretta's bedroom and under a thin top coverlet we uncovered the blood quilt. There were brown marks still visible on some of its patches. They looked like maps of unknown regions. Not every patch had an old blood stain though, for there were those malefactors who had been hung, and not shot, and others who had suffered strangulation by the garrotte. Still, a good many bore the evidence of their former owners' executions. Several still had their bullet holes, even now unstitched. Just one patch, from some country which had yet to reach a humane way of executing its murderers, had the jagged rent of a sharp instrument just below the position of the heart.

In her untiring search for ever more experiences of the macabre, Moretta had made a patchwork quilt. A friend of hers had written to her and told her that she was making a bedspread out of T-shirts purchased in cities around the world.

I LOVE NEW YORK.

I LOVE LONDON.

I LOVE ISTANBUL.

Moretta went one better. She made a quilt, not of love, but of hate. Moretta had researched and located the shirts and vests of executed murderers. She had then purchased these items from those who had removed them from the corpses, hoping to turn a profit. There are always people in this world who know the symbolic value of evil, to worshippers of religions like voodoo and other cults that follow Satan's teachings.

Moretta's blood quilt became more than a symbol.

She had fashioned an instrument of execution for the pernicious dead who wanted revenge on the living.

ELAINE HAD THE quilt burned on a bonfire. Then the house was boarded up and never again rented out to anyone. She called me two years later and told me that the sea had at last claimed yet another victim. A storm had eaten away a chunk of the cliff and Moretta's house had joined the parts of the town that had fallen under the waves. James and I drove down to look at the spot, but there was nothing to see.

HORTUS CONCLUSUS

Chaz Brenchley

There's a beautiful line in Chaz Brenchley's story that really gets to the heart of the piece: "The dead don't go away." And that's the thing about ghosts, because what they really are is the persistence of memory. In this tale of loss and grief, Brenchley explores how the dead continue to affect us, often hanging on long after we thought we had said goodbye for the last time.

SOMETIMES AN IDEA is just bad from the beginning, a road that only goes one way.

Sometimes, a friend phones up with an invitation you really can't refuse.

"Johnny. What are you doing, August?"

"August?" This was April. "I don't know," I said, "I haven't –"

"Good," she said. "You have now. Houseparty."

"What? Where?"

"The Rectory, of course. Where do you think? There is only ever one house, and only ever one houseparty, and we are it."

"Mel, we can't just keep on..."

"Of course we can. We have to. This time it's the garden, okay? I've already said, we're all going."

THAT? WOULD BE Mel, oh yes. Signing people up, making promises on our behalf, committing us all.

And this would be us, oh yes, falling into line because she didn't allow the option and neither did the situation. Mel and Rob, Mark and Catriona and Harriet and me: Charlie's Angels, people used to call us. And now Charlie was dead and it was his mum who needed angels, and – well. Here we were, come August, all in a minivan together. One party, indivisible.

The last time we'd done this we called it a painting-party, but we did a lot more than decorate. The Rectory was a classic Victorian pile; it had been Charlie's home all his life and his parents' for a decade before that, and I'm not sure any of them had ever thrown anything away. When we first visited, the house seemed comfortably, interestingly full; now, to an elderly widow with burdensome memories, it had become just another burden. Painting was our excuse; we were cheerfully ruthless, clearing rooms and filling skips, and if we all knew we were getting the house ready for the market, at least none of us actually had to say so.

She would sell, she would move – but not yet, not this year. Which meant that we had time for this too, for a garden party.

Charlie's big old teddy bear was ours to keep, to share, to pass around. Today he hugged the gear lever, getting in the driver's way and in everybody's eyeline. Charlie's absence was so explicit, so defined, it was almost a presence in itself. Of course he was the ghost in the machine: benevolent and grateful, or I thought so. Pleased to see his friends looking after his mum. How else should he feel?

IT WAS MID-afternoon when we pulled in to the Rectory driveway. There might no longer be a rector here, but the house still dwelt in the shadow of the church. Parishioners' bones had made the bed beneath the gravel drive, where this stretch of land was salvaged from the mediaeval churchyard; the house declared its ecclesiastical interest from the frowning displeasure of its roofline to the iron-studded door and the stone steps that rose up to find it, both liberated from an earlier incarnation of St Jude's itself.

The woman waiting to greet us on the top step, she too might have stood for that same broken linkage, something taken away. Age had closed its fist on her since Charlie's death; she was turning in on herself, harbouring her sorrows. Perhaps a move, a new home, would revive her – but in private, I thought she would dwindle even faster. Loss was something to lean on: what would she do without her morning visit to Charlie and her long-late husband, where they lay side by side just beyond the wall there, under the east window of the apse?

Still. For now she was bird-bright, sharply pleased to see us: "Mel, dear, peacock *blue*? For your *hair*? I don't know, I give up, I really do... Well, never mind. Give me a kiss and if you've had any more tattoos don't show them to me, nasty disfiguring things... Catriona, put those bags down and leave them for the boys – yes, I know Mark's just a long streak of water, but at least he has *leverage*, do you see?... I've put you all in the same rooms, of course. No, Rob, I didn't make the beds, but you'll find fresh linen waiting. I – oh."

Her abrupt silence came on sight of Charlie's teddy. She held out her arms wordlessly; I handed him across and slipped by her into the cool height of the entrance-hall, my arms full of rucksack and my head full of memories.

Sometimes I thought we shouldn't keep coming back; sometimes I couldn't imagine keeping away.

CHARLIE HAD NABBED the attics long ago, for himself and his friends. Servants' quarters and lumber rooms: as a kid he'd run riot up there. As a teenager – well. For his mother's sake, discretion ruled.

In his adulthood, we were the friends he brought. We'd seen him here often and often, drunk or stoned or on a caffeine high, drowsy or electric or giggling with lust. Sex always made Charlie laugh, it was part of that charm he worked, to draw us close and keep us. In his last days we'd moved him to a ground-floor room to save his mother trailing up and down stairs all day, but if his spirit lived on anywhere in this house, it was up here that we'd find it.

Bare narrow steps, mean chilly rooms: it was odd how welcome we'd always felt here. There were more comfortable guest rooms below, but these were ours. Sloping ceilings and faded wallpaper closed around us like enveloping arms, familiar and homely. Voices echoed down the corridor: the loan of a charging cable, a demand for the bathroom, an offer of jelly babies and a shot of vodka...

Voices echoed in my head, too, more intimately; shadows flickered in the corners of my eyes. My room had been Charlie's room, still was.

By the time we trooped downstairs, we were settled enough already to sweep up our hostess and usher her outside, despite all her efforts to distract us with tea and scones, homemade jam and cream and conversation.

"It's the garden we came for, Mrs P. We've only got a couple of weeks, and it's a lot of work. We'd best take a look at it, at least..."

The front of the house was no concern of ours: trees and shrubs and grass that a neighbour kept trim on her behalf. At the back, though, was a great walled kitchen-garden that must once have fed the Rectory, and half the parish besides. Now it was rank and derelict. She struggled just to turn the key in the lock of the gate: "We always meant to tackle this, but my husband died, the silly man, and Lord knows I'm no gardener. Charlie promised to take it on, but you know what he was like, always another grand plan that never came to anything. And then he got sick himself" – *and died himself*, though she couldn't quite bring herself to say that – "so..."

So we had to lend a shoulder, to drive the gate open against the rust of hinges and the drifts of time: and beyond was a jungle contained, a wilderness in a bottle, nature rampant within boundaries.

A greenhouse ran all the length of the south-facing wall, not quite an orangerie but the next best thing, steam pipes for winter warmth and the skeletons of fruit trees espaliered against the brickwork. Time or wind or some more deliberate hand had shattered half the glass: no matter. There were six of us, and we'd all fixed broken windows in the past. We could fix this.

Beyond the greenhouse, it was only growth. Growth could be uprooted, earth turned over.

"The sleep of reason breeds triffids," Rob said, surveying six-foot stems that seemed to be surveying him back. Unflatteringly.

"But with his nails he'll dig them up again. When he wakes." That was Mel, the smallest of us and the most confident. "Don't worry, pet. I'll wake you. Tomorrow. We'll get a start tomorrow. Not right now. Right now is back to the house for scones and cream, right, Mrs P...?"

LATER WE DRIFTED out again, cool glasses in our hands and the low evening light to draw us, Mrs P chasing us out of the kitchen, Harriet wanting a smoke and all of us wanting something we couldn't find in the house, something more.

"I really can't see Charlie in a garden." That was Harry, blowing smoke-rings into the breeze. "Well, doing this, of course: getting high on gin and dope and company. But not, you know, not *gardening*."

"No, of course not," Cat said. "Even his mum knows he never would have done it. He wouldn't have wanted to. It was his secret garden when he was a kid; you remember he showed us where he used to get over the wall?"

Showed us and led us, or some of us, one of us, me. I didn't say so. It had been our own private place, his and mine, when we wanted to escape the party, but the others didn't need to know that now.

"He would've kept it that way," Cat went on, "for himself, for his own pleasure, something guarded in his heart; Charlie always wanted things he didn't have to share..."

Her voice faltered then, and she glanced at me. I just smiled back at her, all grown up, invulnerable.

Undergrowth and overgrowth tangled around our legs like something conscious and deliberate, wanting to keep us out or maybe just wanting to keep us.

Rob said, "What we need, we need men with scythes."

Mel snorted under his arm. "Give you men scythes, soon enough we'd have men without feet."

"We could get in a rotovator, then?"

"No, we can't. We don't want to bequeath Mrs P nothing more than a ploughed field. There must still be paths and beds under all this, that we can restore. Proper Victorian kitchen garden, I want to leave behind us when we're done."

"In two weeks? Mel, you're dreaming..."

Even so, we went from the garden to the garden shed, to see what survived in the shape of tools and equipment. I was last out through the gate, leaving it open behind me, deliberately standing wide.

It slammed shut at my back, almost before I was safely through.

Everyone turned to stare; I just shrugged. Maybe I'd tugged it loose after all and a gust of wind had caught it, or its own momentum carried it on. Maybe it just liked to be closed at night.

Maybe I hadn't really felt any sense of animus behind me, and it was just imagination feeding on twilight and absence at the end of a strange day.

NEXT MORNING WE were up astonishingly early, fed and coffee'd and outside before the sun had risen above the high garden wall. Armed with spades and shears and a single instruction from Mel: "Hack and slay. No quarter."

All day we did that. We started out cheerful, pleased with ourselves, amused by our own industry; banter died slowly in the sunlight, and by day's end we were a grim crew at a laborious task.

Mrs P came out with a tray in the last of the light. "Enough now, you've done enough for one day. I can't believe the difference already. Girls, you can use my bathroom to clean up, leave the other for the boys; but I thought you'd be glad of a glass of – oh, dear Lord," she broke off, looking at me. "What in the world have you been doing to yourself?"

"Your garden hates me," I said, shrugging. "Don't worry, it's only scratches. Thorns, mostly." I was wearing my scars with pride, stripped to the waist and now suddenly wishing that I wasn't. She'd seen me in less, but not streaked with blood.

"This wasn't a thorn," she said, taking my hand irresistibly, frowning at where the ball of the thumb was torn open.

"No, that was a nail on an old rotting bit of wood buried in the leaf-litter."

"A *nail?* You should see someone about that. I'll call Dr Farjeon..."

"No need," I said. "He gave us all tetanus boosters when we were nursing Charlie." She knew that; we'd made her have one too.

"Well, mind you wash it out properly, and disinfect it too. Have Rob dress it for you, you'll only make a mess if you try to do it yourself."

"Yes, ma'am..."

*   *   *

AFTER DINNER, CAT sprawled on the sofa with her feet in Mark's lap. Mel said, "I'll play martyr tonight, if someone else does it tomorrow. One of us has to keep Mrs P company, and those two will be asleep in ten minutes, you know they will."

I did know it. And I knew her too, how tired she was, how determined not to admit it. I was weary and sore myself, but even so I headed off with Rob and Harriet because somebody had to, this was what we did. What Charlie had taught us, the pattern he'd set. However we spent the days here, evenings we wound up down at the Blue Boar. Even when he was sick and we were nursing, there was a pub shift. That mattered to him, and so we did it; and now? Well, now it mattered to us, apparently, because it had mattered to him. Or else for some deeper reason, pattern recognition, something.

We sat in the old settle below the window, and I drank Guinness because I'd given blood that day; and the others teased me about being clumsy or unlucky or just a lousy gardener; and we did our duty by Charlie until the landlord grew bored with us, threw us out, closed up at our backs.

We rambled back along the lane, three abreast and daring the world to send traffic at us, defying it, staring it down. And came crunching up the Rectory drive at last, unaccountably safe, feeling wonderfully protected; and Harry said, "Anyone up for a joint in the garden before bed?"

"Not me," Rob said quickly. "Mel needs rescue."

I was fairly sure that he'd find Mel fast asleep; I was fairly sure, too, that he just wanted to join her. Emulate her. I could have done the same myself, but Harry needed to smoke, the dope was her excuse for the tobacco, and leaving her alone would only rub her face in it.

So I heaved the garden gate open and the two of us
went through, to squat on an upturned wheelbarrow
and survey our handiwork by moonlight.

"I hope Charlie doesn't mind," she said slowly.

"Mind what, that we're helping his mum?"

"That we're helping her leave, maybe – but I was
thinking about this." A waft of a glowing red end
to indicate the ruin that we'd wreaked. "This was his
playground, and he always kept it private. We went
everywhere together, but he never brought us in here."

He brought me. I didn't say so, of course; only, "
don't think he'd mind. I really – ow!"

"Oh, God, sorry, was that me?"

She shifted the joint conspicuously to her other hand
but I shook my head. "Not a spark. Something, though
A mosquito, maybe."

"In *Surrey*...?"

I shrugged, and peeled my hand carefully away from
my neck, where I'd slapped at the sting of it. There
was something on my fingers, sure, and my skin was
burning. I didn't really think it was a mosquito.
thought maybe a plant had spat venom at me, like a
cobra. I didn't think they had venom-spitting plants in
Surrey, any more than I thought they had mosquitoes
but still: that was how it seemed, a packet of poison
hurled at me from the dark.

DAYS PASSED, AND it wasn't just me. People cut themselves
on rusty tools, dropped bricks on sandalled feet, had to
be untangled from rampant briars. At first we mocked
our own clumsiness; then we joked about the garden

poltergeist; then we stopped joking.

Actually, we pretty much stopped talking about it at all. Silence indicates denial, rejection, no consent at all. We turned away from what was unbearable and sought refuge in refusal. If we didn't admit it, of course it wasn't happening.

If it wasn't happening, then of course it couldn't be happening worst to me. I might limp on both feet simultaneously, I might carry blood into the shower and bruises out at the end of every day, but still: no acknowledgement meant no surrender.

And still the work got done. Relentlessly, grimly, enduringly. We stripped the jungle back to stubble, found old brick ways and borders laid between. Dug and turned the earth, washed down the brick, brought order rising out of chaos.

And still...

"You put that down," said Mel, gently and firmly taking a spade away from me. "You'll only lose a toe, you know you will, and I like you whole. Besides, I've got another job for you."

So I spent the morning measuring panes of glass in the greenhouse and counting how many were broken, counting back to be sure; and then driving to town and finding a glazier and waiting while he cut what we needed.

Back at the Rectory, I set to work picking out the clinging shards and scraping down old putty. Mel saw me at it and came over frowning, but I forestalled her. "Look," I said, "teeny-tiny panes, they're barely larger than my hand. What harm can I do myself with these?"

It was meant to be rhetorical, but for a moment I thought she'd tell me anyway. In the end she just said, "Wear gloves," and stomped away.

* * *

That became my job, then, restoring the greenhouse. I scraped and sanded and painted woodwork, I swept and scrubbed and whitewashed the interior, but mostly I reglazed the frame. Little by little, pane by pane: painstaking work, it suited my mood and my skills together.

I did wear gloves, despite the heat. Stripped down else to shorts and Factor 50, the only other protection I clung to was my shades. With the sun behind me I worked in my own shadow, but I'd have been blinded none the less by the fierce light jagging off a thousand panes of glass all around me.

My back to the sun, to the garden, to my friends. I could hear them, of course, call and response, and the soft murmurs of private conversation. I could turn and join in, take a break any time...

I could do, but mostly I didn't. I worked in a kind of deliberate isolation, an exaggeration of the determined mood that had settled on us all. They didn't talk much; I barely said a word from dawn until dusk. They worked harder than they'd planned to, paused less often, found less fun than they had hoped for; I was reluctant to stop at all. Even at dinner or in the pub, it felt as though I faced a different direction.

At night, my room – well, it had been Charlie's. It still was Charlie's, though we had taken everything we could away from it. Mrs P had offered me another when he was sick, and again after he died; but this was the room I'd always slept in, with him or without him. It would be worse than refusal, it would be betrayal to leave him now.

So I spent my nights in his absence, and my days in the ruin of his playground, scouring that as we had scoured this. Painting him over, washing him away. It would have been a wonder if I hadn't seen him, at least in my mind's eye.

In fact I saw him reflected: little shimmers of movement, moments of stillness, in all those many panes of glass. I might have mistaken his figure for anyone's, for Rob or Mark or Cat as they worked in the garden behind me – but that would have been deliberate, a denial too far. Pattern recognition: we can't turn our backs on that. Besides, sometimes he was just too small, smaller than Mel, even: a child still, a child in his garden.

Besides, I'd seen him before. At night, in the dark of the windows of his room, a reflection poised behind me; or in the bathroom, a blur in the steamed-up mirror when I showered, gone when I wiped the glass.

The dead don't go away. I knew that, I didn't need to see it, to see it and see it, to wear it written on my body. And yet, and yet. I still didn't get it: not until I carefully fitted the last little pane of glass into its frame like the last piece of a jigsaw, the final fragment of mosaic. And stepped back to see the picture complete, the greenhouse entire at last – and saw his reflection one more time, saw him eye to eye in front of me, complete and entire and just that little moment before the glass blew out in the shape of his silhouette, as though all his body had punched clean through the frame.

If I hadn't been wearing the sunglasses, I'd have been blinded for real. As it was, I was pierced and pierced, a thousand splinters all up and down my body.

There was a lot more blood, then, and pain not quite like anything. There were screams, and a dreadful urgency all around me. There was a frantic drive, blood on the seat and foolish apology; a hospital, Casualty, nurses with tweezers and one more jab, a needle that lent me a little welcome distance.

Then there was time, weaving in and out of bed, not my bed, not Charlie's; and then another drive and we were all back at the Rectory. I was lying on the long sofa on my own, everyone keeping a little too much distance, and an inquest of sorts going on all around me, interrogation under oath.

Mrs P said, "You all claimed that he fell in through the glass, but that's not what happened, is it? Johnny was outside, yes, but that whole frame was broken from the inside out."

Into the silence, one voice dropping one word, like a pebble to break a sheet of glass: "Yes."

That was Mark, the quietest of us, the one who wouldn't lie to her. She knew.

It was Mel who picked the story up. Taking responsibility. She said, "We didn't want to tell you, but there's been... something, a spirit, a presence, out there all through. Not a friendly presence. We've all felt him – *it*, I mean, it – and we've all got scars to show for it. This was just... worse, an escalation, something we can't shrug off. And it's always been hardest on Johnny, and –"

"No," Mrs P said. "Wait. You mean, you think it's *Charlie?*" And then, against our silence, "Yes, you do. But no. You're wrong. Of course you're wrong. How could you even think that? Charlie loved you all, he loved *you,*" and she said that directly at me, like a weapon, like a javelin. I had no defence. "He wouldn't do this. Even if..."

* * *

THERE WAS NOWHERE to go from there. Not for her, not for us. I wasn't moving anyway: just lying still was drearily, dreadfully uncomfortable. No way I was going up to bed tonight, to any bed, let alone Charlie's. This sofa was long enough, broad enough for me.

I was deeply, intimately glad when at last they all peeled away and left me. They didn't want to, they knew they left that silence hanging, that accusation unresolved; but things close down, time slips away, leaves you with nothing to hold on to. Mrs P went to bed, and one by one the others followed.

Me, I lay awake a long time, listening to the soft murmur of the radio and staring at soft, unreflective velvet curtains, glad beyond measure not to have windows or mirrors to be looking at.

I didn't move much the next day, either: just out into the sunshine, to sit on the front lawn beneath the lilac and let heat soak into my bones, drugs into my tissues.

That night, we went to Mrs P as a delegation, apologetic, armed with a cardboard box.

"You were right," Mel said. "Of course it wasn't Charlie. We were digging, and we found these," a set of bones: not a full skeleton, but enough to say that this was a human once. A long time ago. "I don't suppose we'll ever know what happened," she said, "but there must have been some reason why he was buried beyond the churchyard, not in consecrated ground. He might have been a suicide, perhaps, or an executed murderer. Or a victim. Maybe he was killed and buried secretly in the garden there, and that's why he haunts the place. Maybe that's why the garden's been abandoned all this time, I think it must be..."

It was clever, the way she handled it. No answers, only a series of proffered questions and the bones themselves, dark and mute, exposed and unrevealing. Enough to settle Mrs P's distress. She'd take the bones to the rector, no doubt, and have them securely reburied under a burden of prayer. She might do some fitful research into the history of the house, maybe construct her own story from a missing stableboy and a brutal incumbent. There was sure to be something she could work with.

And meanwhile she would leave that difficult gate locked, and hasten her own intent to leave. A ghost in the garden, some other family's lost sorrow would be the last spur that she needed, to set her own sorrows at her back and move away.

WE'D COME DOWN when the time came, to help her pack up the house and go.

At least, most of us would. Not me.

GOING HOME, I sat up front all the way, riding shotgun, privileged by pain. In the back, under all our bags, was one more box that we didn't dare leave behind in case she found it at last, what was left of Charlie's secret collection. All through his teenage years he'd picked up bones as they surfaced in the garden; I was fairly sure he'd deliberately dug for them along the wall that divided Rectory from churchyard, where the harvest would be richest. How else would he ever have found skulls? What we'd sorted out to give his mum had been the pick of his collection, enough to look convincing as a body.

We couldn't have left her with the truth – which was why I couldn't go back, for fear of what I might be taking with me, undeniable this time.

Like the story we'd given his mother, the truth was all questions. Maybe Charlie really didn't like what we'd done to his secret garden; maybe he was upset that his mother meant to move. But I thought it was more personal, a tempest aimed at me. Envy, resentment maybe because he got sick and I didn't, I had the life that he'd lost. And had come back robust and happy in the company of friends, to his own home yet, to rub it in.

He wasn't letting me leave so lightly, not leave him behind again.

We drove away north, and I sat in the front and never looked behind me. Never needed to.

Every time I glanced in the side-mirror of that van, I saw Charlie's eyes stare back at me.

THE DARK SPACE IN THE HOUSE IN THE HOUSE IN THE GARDEN AT THE CENTRE OF THE WORLD

ROBERT SHEARMAN

You may know Robert Shearman from his work on the BBC's flagship show Doctor Who, *and his episode 'Dalek.' But what really excites me about Shearman is that he is, hands-down, one of the best short story writers working in and out of the genre. His debut collection,* Love Songs for the Shy and Cynical, *blew me away, reminding me of the best of Walter M. Miller Jr, Jonathan Carroll and Fritz Leiber, while each story was uniquely... well, Rob. What follows is an unusual story of a house in a garden and how the people within that house find out what it is to be human.*

i

LET'S GET SOMETHING straight, right from the outset, okay? I'm not angry with you. Mistakes were made on both sides. Mistakes, ha, arguably, I made just as many mistakes as you. Well, not quite as many, ha, but I accept I'm at least partly to blame. Okay? No, really, okay? Come on, take those looks off your faces. I'm *never* going to be angry with you. I promise. I have wasted so much of my life on anger. There are entire aeons full of it, I'm not even kidding. And it does nothing. It achieves nothing. Anger, it's a crock of shit.

Isn't it a beautiful day? One of my best. The sun's warm, but not too warm, you can feel it stroking at your skin, it's all over your bare bodies and *so* comforting, but without it causing any of that irritating sweaty stuff under the armpits. Though I do maintain that sweat's a useful thing. Look at the garden. Breathe it in. Tell me, be honest, how do you think it's coming on? See what I've done, I've been pruning the roses, training the clematis, I've been cutting back the privet hedges. Not bad. And just you wait until spring, the daffodils will be out by then, lovely.

No. Seriously. Relax. Relax, right now! I'm serious.

The apples were a mistake. Your mistake, my mistake, who's counting? My mistake was to set you a law without explaining why the law was being enforced, that's not a sound basis for any legal system. Of course you're going to rebel, right. And *your* mistake, that was eating a fruit in which I had chosen to house cancer. Well, I had to put it somewhere. You may have wondered about all those skin sores and why you've been coughing up blood and phlegm. Now you know. But don't worry, I'll fix it, see, you're cured. Poppa looks after you. As for the apples, good source of vitamin A, low in calories, you just wait til you puree them up and top them with sugar, oh *God*, do I love a good apple crumble. I'm not even kidding!

Keep the apple with my blessing. As for the cancers, well, I'll just stick them in something else, don't worry, you'll never find them.

Give me a smile. We're all friends. Smile for me. Wider than that.

And so, are we good? Cindy, and what is it, Steve? I think we're good. The fruit is all yours to eat. The air is all yours to breathe, the flowers are all yours to smell. The beasts of the world, yours to name and pet and hunt and skin and fuck. We're good, but there is one last thing. Not a law, ha ha, I wouldn't call it a *law*, ha ha, no, okay, no, it's a law. Don't go into the forest. The forest that's at the heart of the garden, the garden at the centre of the world. The forest where the trees are so tall that they scratch the heavens, so dense that they drown out the light, where even the birds that settle on the branches come out stained with black. What? Why? Because I said so. What? Oh. Yes, fair point. Because at the centre of the forest there stands a house, and the house is old, and the house is haunted.

Okay.

Okay. I'll be off then. Night, night, sleep tight. Don't let the bedbugs bite.

SO THEY WENT into the forest the very next morning, man and wife, hand in hand, and they dropped apple cores along the way so they could find a path back again. "Like Hansel and Gretel!" said Cindy, because God had told them all his favourite fairy tales when they'd just been children, he'd tucked them up tight in beds of leaves and moss with stories of enchanted castles and giant killers and heroes no bigger than your thumb; "you can be Gretel," agreed Steve, "and I'll be Hansel!" And the trees were so tall and so dense and so black, and they were glad they were doing the hand holding thing together, it made them both feel warm and loved. And they didn't know for how long they walked, it may have been days, and they worried they might soon run out of apple cores, but presently they came across the house, right there at the forest's heart. And it was a magical house, a structure of red brick and thin chimneys and big bay windows and vinyl sided guttering. It didn't look very haunted; "it's probably quite nice inside," said Cindy, and Steve agreed, but he held on to her hand tightly, and both hands began to sweat. They went up to the front door, and peered their way through the panel of frosted glass, but they couldn't see anyone, nothing inside was moving. Steve rang the doorbell, and Cindy called "Hello!" through the letterbox, but there was no answer, and they were both about to give up, turn about, pick up their apple cores and go home, when the door swung open anyway at their touch. It didn't creak, the hinges were too good on that door.

Cindy and Steve wondered if they could squeeze themselves into something as small as that house, they'd been so used to the sheer size of the garden that was their world. And they exchanged glances. And they shrugged. And they went in.

In the kitchen there were two places set for dinner, and at each place there was a bowl of porridge. "Like Goldilocks!" said Cindy, because God really hadn't stinted himself in his fairy-tale-telling; "you can be Goldilocks," said Steve, "I'll be the bear!" They ate the porridge. They both privately wondered who

the porridge belonged to. They both wondered if the
porridge belonged to the ghosts. They thought they
should go home, but it had started to rain. So they
decided there was no harm in staying a little longer; they
inspected the sitting room, the bathroom, a nice space
under the stairs that could be used for storage; "Hello,"
Cindy called out, "we're your new neighbours!" And
they looked for the ghosts, but saw neither hide nor hair
of a single one. The rain was coming down hard now, it
was a wall of wet, and it hit the ground fierce like arrows
and it was so dark outside you couldn't see where the
rain might have fallen from, how it could have found
its way through so dense a crush of treetops. And the
apple cores were gone, maybe they hadn't been dropped
clearly enough, maybe the birds had eaten them, maybe
they had long ago just rotted and turned to mush. So
they had no choice, they had to stay the night together
in a haunted house, maybe they could find their way
back to their own garden in the morning, maybe.

The bedroom was big. There were two large
wardrobes, and there was a dressing table with a nice
mirror to sit in front of and do make-up, and there was
a huge bed laden high with blankets and pillows. Cindy
and Steve got under the covers.

They both listened out for the ghosts in the dark.

"I'm frightened," said Cindy, and reached out for
Steve's hand. And Steve didn't say he was frightened
too, that his stomach felt strange, stuffed as it was with
porridge, that his skin felt strange, too: tingly and so
very sensitive with a mattress underneath it and sheets
on top of it and this smooth naked body lying next
to it, brushing against it, tickling its hairs, yes oh yes.
"Don't be frightened," said Steve, "I'll protect you,

my Snow White, my Rapunzel, my unnamed princess from Princess-and-the-Frog," and he kissed her, and they had never kissed before, and they explored each other's mouths much as they had explored the house, with false bravado, and growing confidence, and some unspoken sense of dread. They pushed their tongues deep into each other's dark spaces. And slept at last. And dreamed of ghosts. And of what ghosts could even possibly be.

ii

SO THIS IS where you are! I couldn't find you! I didn't know where you could be, I thought maybe you were in the maze. You know, that maze I made for you, with all those tall hedges, cylindrical archways, and any number of delightful red herrings. The maze, yeah? I thought, they're playing in the maze, it's easy to get lost in the maze, what a hoot! So I waited for you at the exit, I thought you'd come out eventually, I'd surprise you by saying boo! And I waited quite a long time, and one day I thought to myself, you know what, I don't think they're in this maze at all. The maze I made for them. So where could they be?

I felt a bit of a prawn, I must say, waiting outside a maze for six months all primed to say boo. Getting the exact facial expression right. I got a bit bored. I made a lot more cancers and viruses to keep my mind occupied. Oh, and I made the antelope extinct. Hope it wasn't a favourite.

But, no, you've found the house! And good for you. Oh, did I say that you shouldn't come to the house? Did

I? Doesn't sound like me, hang on, trying to think, no.
No, I can't imagine why I would have said that. You
want a house, with what, rooms and floorboards and
curtains and shit, then you go for it. Much better than
a maze. Really, *fuck* the maze. I want to hear you say it.
Say it with me. Fuck the maze. *Fuck* the maze. That's it,
so you can see, I've no problem with the maze at all. I'm
not even kidding! You have whatever you like, I never
want to hold you guys back, I love you, I'm crazy about
you. You have your house, a house with a roof to keep
the rain off.

(In fact, sorry about the rain. Not quite sure what that's
about. Very frustrating, must be leaking somewhere up
there, the sky's cracked, got to be. And yeah, I can hold
the rain back, but the thought of that crack, at that
poor cowboy workmanship, it makes me a bit cross,
quite *angry*, and when I get angry, it seems to rain all
the more, and you know what? It's a vicious circle.)

And you've found the wardrobes! Picking through the
cupboards as if they're yours, and they *are* yours, of
course they are. Look at you, Cindy, no, I mean, *look*
at *you*. All those dresses, all those shoes. That skirt,
ha, that doesn't leave a lot to the imagination, ha, that
really emphasises your, um, ha, hips, ha ha! And make-
up, too. Though? If I can? Make a suggestion? The
lipstick. Goes on the lips. Hence the name, yeah... And
you, erm, Steve, you look nice, too.

No, not *all* the house is haunted. Did I give you?
That impression? No, the kitchen's fine. The bedroom's
fine. The sitting room, fine. Bathroom, ha, there are no
bogeymen lurking behind the toilet cistern. No, it's the
attic. It's the attic that has all the ghosts in. You haven't
found the attic yet? You didn't know there even *was*

an attic? Well, there is. I wouldn't go looking for it, though. No good will come of it. Sometimes you stand underneath that attic, at the right spot, you can feel the temperature drop, there'll be a cold chill pricking over your skin. There'll be a sickness in your throat, your heart will start to beat uncomfortably fast. Listen hard enough, press your ears up to the ceiling, you can hear *whispers*. The whispers of the dead. No, I wouldn't bother, you just stick with your mercifully spook-free lavatory, you'll be fine.

Is that the time? I should go. It's a long way back to the garden, and it's getting late. No, how kind, shouldn't stay for dinner, maybe next time. But how kind. What a kind thought. How lovely. I'll get back to my maze, my silly little maze, that'd be best. Better hurry, it's pissing down out there.

'Night, 'night, then. You be happy. Be happy, and stay happy. You both mean the world to me. 'Night, 'night, sleep tight. Don't let the bedbugs bite.

IT TOOK THEM four days to find the attic. It was difficult. No matter whereabouts they stood they felt no chill or nausea, and their heartbeats remained frustratingly constant. Eventually it took Cindy balanced upon Steve's finer shoulders, reaching up and prodding at the ceiling – a painstaking operation, and one that took a lot of straining and swaying – before Cindy said that beneath the wallpaper she felt something give. They cut away the wallpaper with a kitchen knife. They exposed a hatchway – small, neat, perfectly unassuming.

It hadn't been opened in a long time. No matter how much Cindy pushed at it it just wouldn't move; Steve at last had to help, crouching down with Cindy on his shoulders and then springing up tall, sending his wife fast up in the air and using her as a battering ram.

The rather dazed Cindy poked her head through, and Steve called up, "Can you see anything? Can you hear anything?" Cindy remembered the fairy tales she'd been told, Jack climbing his way up a beanstalk to dangers unknown, Aladdin lowered into the darkness whilst his uncle stayed safe up top. "No, nothing," she said. Steve got up on to a table and climbed through the hatchway after her. There were a few nondescript boxes piled up, mostly cardboard; they contained years-old fashion magazines, clothes, toys, a stamp collection, stuff. If there was a chill, it was only because they were away from the central heating. If there was a whispering, it was just the lapping from inside the water tank, or the sound of wind playing against the roof.

And if they were disappointed, neither Cindy nor Steve said they were. They went back to their ordinary lives. Cindy learned how to use the kitchen, she'd make them both dinner from tins she found in the cupboard. Steve found a DIY kit, and would enjoy banging nails into things pointlessly with his hammer.

And in bed they continued to explore each other's bodies. Steve discovered that Cindy enjoyed it when he nibbled on her breasts, but that he should stop well short of making the blood thing leak out; for her part, Cindy quickly learned that sucking at appendages rather than biting down hard and chewing was always a more popular option. They examined and prodded at each and every one of their orifices, and into them would experiment inserting opposing body parts; they found out that no matter what they tried to stick up there, be it tongue, finger or penis, the nostrils weren't worth the effort. And soon, too, they realised that it was better to do all of these things in the dark, where the ridiculous contortions of facial expressions on their spouse's face wouldn't put them off.

They listened out for the ghosts. They never heard them.

One night Steve woke from his sleep to find Cindy wasn't there. He put on his favourite silk dressing gown from the wardrobe, went to look for her. At last he found her in the attic, sitting on the floor, rocking back and forth as she cried so hard. At his approach she started, turned about, looked at him with startled teary eyes. "Where are our ghosts?" she begged to know. "Where's the chill, the sickness in my stomach? I can't feel anything. Why can't I feel anything at all?"

iii

YOU WERE THINKING of a nursery, right? The attic for a nursery, that was the plan?

Oh, sorry, didn't mean to make you jump! Coming round unannounced, very rude, but I tried the doorbell, and there was no answer, and I thought, shall I just pop in anyway, why not, good friends like us don't need to stand on ceremony. I can see why you didn't hear me. You're pretty busy. Pretty... entwined, there.

Don't stop on my account. I can wait. You finish off, I don't mind, I'll watch. Oh. Oh. Suit yourselves.

Speaking of which! I can see that you've discovered the joys of sex. Which is nice. I'm a little surprised, ha, by your choice of *partners*, I mean, doesn't it strike you as a bit incestuous? You crazy kids, what will you get up to next! I don't mind. I don't mind at all. I mean, it makes me wonder why I invented the zebu in the first place, you don't fancy the zebu, all those dewlaps? It could have been a baby zebu that's growing inside your stomach this very moment, imagine what *that* would have looked like!

Oh, you didn't realise? Yeah, you're pregnant. Congratulations! Some men don't like women when they're pregnant, but Cindy, I must say, you look *great*, all shiny and hormonal like that, all your body parts swelling every which way. And yeah, well done too, Steve, yeah. And you're going to need a nursery. Which is why, I'm sure, you had only the best intentions when you ignored my *advice* and went up into the attic. And why not, good choice. Babies are great, but take it from me, they're annoying, they cry a lot, there's a lot of noise and sick, keeping the baby up in the attic out of earshot is a good plan. Clear away the boxes, there'll be room up there for all those baby things babies seem to like. It's all just junk, there's nothing in there to worry about.

Except, of course, for that *one* box. The one with the padlock on. Now, you two and I have had a bit of a laugh, haven't we? It's all been fun. But this time I'm really telling you. It's a padlock. That's a big fucking hint. You are not to open the box. You are not to open the box. I forbid it. I absolutely forbid it, and yes it's a law, it's an order, it's a commandment from up high. Leave the box alone. No matter what you hear inside. No matter what the ghosts inside the box say to you.

Lightening the mood! – any ideas for a name for the baby yet? No? Well, I'm just saying. You want to name it after me, you can. Call it God, or Lord, or Jehovah, or some such, and I'd be honoured.

The daffodils are out. They look beautiful.

Well, I can see you have things to do. Some of which will no doubt make you drowsy, you'll be wanting to sleep soon. So, you know. 'Night, 'night. Sleep tight. Don't let the bedbugs bite. No, I really mean it, I'm not sure, but I think I put cancer in a few of them, the bedbugs are riddled with cancer. You see a bedbug, you *run*.

SO THEY SMASHED the padlock, and straightaway they heard them, the whispers inside – and there were so many, there was so much chatter, the conversations were all overlapping so they couldn't make out what was being said! "Open the box!" said Cindy, too eagerly, and "I'm trying!" Steve snapped back, and it seemed such a fragile little box, but now the lid was heavy, they pulled together and the lid raised an inch, and husband and wife had to prise their fingers painfully into the little gap to stop it from shutting again. And the whispers seemed so loud now, how could they not have heard the ghosts before? And they both felt a bit ashamed of that. Ashamed that they'd been carrying on with their lives quite pleasantly, cooking and hammering and shagging away, and had never paid the ghosts any attention. Cindy looked at Steve, and smiled at him, and thought, *I wonder if I'll find someone new to talk to.* And Steve looked at Cindy, smiled back, thought, *I wonder if their orifices will be prettier.* Because they both loved each other, they knew they did; but how can you tell what that love is worth if you've nothing to compare it to?

They took strength from each other's smiles; they heaved again; the box opened.

The whispering stopped, startled.

Inside there was a house. Not a proper house, of course, but a doll's house. And it wasn't *quite* like their house; it, too, had red bricks, and thin chimneys, it had windows and guttering, but they could see that the sitting room was smaller, there was less wardrobe space in the bedroom, the toilet had a broken flush.

There was no one to be seen.

"Talk to us!" said Cindy. "Come back!" said Steve.

They wondered if they could squeeze themselves into something as small as that house. And they exchanged glances. And they shrugged. And they went in.

iv

God didn't talk to them for a long while after that.

There was lots of fun to be had in the haunted doll's house.

Their new neighbours were very kind. Their names were Bruce and Kate. Bruce and Kate knocked on the door one day, said they'd heard people had moved in next door, wanted to welcome them, hoped they'd be very happy. They invited them round to dinner. Cindy and Steve didn't know what to bring, but they found a bottle of old red wine in the back of one of the kitchen cupboards, and Bruce and Kate smiled nicely at it and said it was one of their favourite tipples. Kate made a really lovely casserole, "nothing fancy, just thrown it together," and Bruce laughed and said Kate's casserole was a secret recipe, and it was certainly better than anything Cindy could have come up with. Bruce was in charge of dessert. Bruce and Kate showed Cindy and Steve around their modest house, and it wasn't much different to Cindy and Steve's, only in the bathroom their flush *did* work, Cindy and Steve felt a little bit jealous. And Bruce and Kate had a seven year old daughter called Adriana who was quite pretty and very polite and did ballet and whose drawings from school were hung on display for all to see with fridge magnets. "Can see you're expecting!" said Kate to Cindy, and Cindy agreed she was; Kate said it'd be nice for Adriana to have a new friend to play with, maybe. Bruce and Kate were dead. They were dead, but they didn't seem to know they were dead. Cindy and Steve could see right inside them and there was nothing but ash in there and their souls were spent. They smelled of death, their eyes rolled dead in their heads, they waddled awkwardly as they walked. Adriana was dead, and when at Kate's indulgent prompting she agreed to show the new neighbours a few choice ballet steps it was like watching a broken puppet splaying cack-legged across the floor. "Well done!" said Kate, and clapped her dead hands, and Bruce laughed the most cheery of death rattles, and Cindy and Steve were good guests and clapped and laughed too.

Bruce asked Steve what he did for a living, and Steve said that he was between jobs. And Bruce was very kind, he got Steve an interview at the bank where he worked. And Steve spent the day sorting money and counting money and giving money to people through a little glass grille. He'd never seen money before, but he liked the feel of it, and in return for his hard work he was given money of his very own. Steve determined he would try

hard to collect an awful lot of it. And the bank manager
was very nice, and congratulated Steve on his efforts,
and gave him a promotion, which basically meant that
Steve gave more money to different people through a
slightly bigger glass grille. And the bank manager was
dead, and the customers were dead, and Bruce was
still dead, of course, Bruce being dead wasn't going to
change in a hurry. And Steve would sometimes after
work go out with Bruce to a pub and get pissed.

And Cindy wanted to work at the bank too, but Kate
told her she'd really be better off staying at home and
looking after her baby. And Cindy could feel it kicking
inside, and decided it was high time she let the baby out,
she couldn't be sure but she thought it had been kicking
inside there now for *years*. She went to the hospital and
the doctors were dead and the nurses were dead and all
the patients were dead, and some of the dead patients
were so ill that during their stay at the hospital they died
again and somehow got even *deader*, that was so weird.
And a particularly dead nurse told Cindy she had to push
the baby out, and that she was being very brave, and that
they were having this baby together, and *push*. And out
came the baby, and the baby was crying, and still kicking
away, and the nurse cooed and said it was a beautiful
little girl, and Cindy felt a sudden strange rush of love for
her child, a stronger love than she'd ever known before,
stronger than anything she'd felt for Steve or, even, God;
but the baby was dead, it was dead, Cindy was given
it to hold and it rolled its dead eyes at her and burbled
and sneezed and Cindy could see there was no soul to it,
just ash. "I don't want it," she said to the dead nurse, "I
don't want this dead baby," and she thought of how this
ashen soulless corpse monster had been feeding inside

her stomach and she felt sick. The dead nurse told her again the girl was beautiful, she was such a *beautiful girl*; "You keep it then," said Cindy. But apparently that just wasn't an option, and Cindy had to take the stillborn little parasite home and feed it and pet it and read it fairy tales and give some sort of shit when it screamed.

And Steve didn't like their new baby daughter either – he *said* he did, and he played with it, and sat it on his knee, and asked after it when he came back home pissed from the pub – he didn't say *anything* against the baby at all, come to think of it; but Cindy knew he must hate it, because she hated it, and they were one flesh, weren't they, they were soulmates, they were *one*. And they still had sex, it was a little more routine than before, even a bit desultory – but Cindy didn't mind, she wasn't quite sure what part of the sex process had resulted in this baby growing inside her in the first place; she thought that if they did the sex thing very quietly, almost without passion, almost as if they weren't really there at all, then they wouldn't draw attention to themselves. Then no future daughter would see.

Cindy stayed at home. Cindy felt trapped. Cindy remembered the fairy tales she'd been fed when she was a child. Damsels with long hair locked away in high towers, princesses forced down to sleep on peas. Mothers pressed into bargains with grumpy evil dwarves who wanted to steal their first-born. Cindy didn't meet many dwarves, no matter how hard she looked – not at the supermarket, not at the kindergarten, not at the young mothers' yoga group that the erstwhile Kate had persuaded her to join. Cindy knew that the dwarves wouldn't have been much use anyway, the dwarves, too, would have been dead.

"I love you," Steve would say to Cindy, each night as they got into bed, and he meant it.

"I love you," Cindy would say back, and she meant it too.

Steve had met someone at work, a little cashier assistant less than half his age. He didn't expect her to like his whitening beard and his receding hairline and his now protruding gut. She fucked him at the office Christmas party, and he told her it had to be a one-off, but she fucked him three more times in January, and an astonishing fifteen times in February, she was really picking up speed. "Tell me you love me," she'd say afterwards as she smoked a fag, ash in her ash, and he'd say he did, and he thought that maybe that was even true, just a little bit; she'd wrap her corpse legs around him and her dead matted bush would tickle the bulge of his stomach, and then he was inside her, he was inside something that felt warm and smooth but he knew was really so, so cold and was rotting away into clumps of meat. He thought her death would infect him, he hoped it would. He wished he had the sort of relationship with Cindy where he could talk about his new girlfriend, who bit by bit was becoming the very centre of his world, the little chink of garden at the heart of his day. But Cindy had never been one to share things with, nothing of any importance. And some nights he'd cry.

Once in a while they'd try to escape the doll's house. But they couldn't find the exit. They took their dead daughter on a holiday to Tenerife, but there was no exit there, not even as far away as Tenerife. When their dead daughter was older, and wanted holidays of her own, with disreputable-looking dead boys who had strange piercings and smelled of drugs, Cindy and Steve took their very first holiday alone. They went to Venice. They drank wine underneath the Rialto. They were serenaded on a gondola. They made love in their budget hotel, and it felt like love, too. It felt like something they could hold on to. And sometimes, back at home, when Steve cried at night, or during the day when Cindy stared silently at the wall, they might think of Venice, and the memory made them happy.

This account focuses too much upon the negatives, maybe. They had a good time in the haunted doll's house, and the ghosts were very chatty, and some of them were kind.

v

"HELLO, HELLO!" BEAMING smiles all round. "Well, here we are! Here we all are again!" A clap on the host's back, hearty and masculine, a kiss on the hostess' cheek just a little too close to the mouth. "So good to see you both, I'm not even kidding! I brought some wine, where would you like it?"

They showed him the house. He made appreciative noises at the sitting room, the kitchen, the bedroom. He admired the toilet, Steve pointed out to him the flush, and how he'd fixed it with all the DIY he'd learned. They settled down at the kitchen table and ate Cindy's casserole, and they all agreed it was really good.

"Well. Well! Here we all are again."

God was wearing a sports jacket that was meant to look jaunty, but it was two sizes too big for him; God looked old and too thin; the jacket was depressing, it made him look diminished somehow. The wine he'd brought was cheap but potent. The conversation was awkward at first, a series of polite remarks, desperate pauses, too-big smiles and eyes looking downward. The wine helped. They began to relax.

Cindy asked if they could return to the garden.

"Go backwards?" said God. "I don't know if you can go *backwards*. You crazy kids, what will you think of next!"

They laughed, and shared anecdotes of mazes and apples, of fairy tales told long ago.

God mused. "I think the idea is. If I think about it? I think, the older you get, and the more experienced you get. And the more you realise how big the world is, and how many opportunities are in front of you. Then the smaller the world becomes. It gets smaller and smaller, narrowing in on you, until all that's left is the confines of a wooden box." He coughed. "You could say that it's a consequence of maturity, of finding your place in the world and accepting it, of discovering humility and in that humility discovering yourself. Or, maybe. Ha. It's just a fucking bad design flaw. Ha! Sorry."

He drank more wine, he farted, they all laughed, oh, the simple comedy of it all.

"But," God said, "this world isn't all there is. It can't be. There must be a way out. At the very centre of the world, there's a dark space. Don't go to it. Don't go. It isn't a law. I'm not, ha, forbidding you. But I think," God said, and his voice dropped to a whisper, and he looked so scared, "I think there are ghosts there. I think the dark space is haunted."

"Well," said Steve, eventually. "It's getting late."

"It *is* getting late," said Cindy.

"No doubt you'll be wanting to get back home," said Steve. "Back to your garden and whatnot."

"Back," said Cindy, "to your maze." She took away God's wine glass, put it into the sink with a clatter.

God looked sad.

"I'm dying," he said.

"Oh, dear," said Steve.

"That's a shame," said Cindy.

"I've been mucking about with too many cancers. I've got nobbled by the ebola virus, I've come down with a spot of mad cow disease. It's all the same to me. I've been careless. Too careless, and about things that were too important." He coughed again, gently wiped at his mouth with a handkerchief, looked at the contents of the handkerchief with frank curiosity. He blinked.

"Shame," said Cindy again.

"And I wanted to see you. I wanted to be with you, because we're family, aren't we, you were always my favourites, weren't you, you're my favourites, did you know that? I'm crazy about you crazy kids. I miss you. I miss you like crazy. We never had a cross word. Others before you, others after, well. I admit, I got angry, plagues, locusts, fat greasy scorchmarks burned into the lawns of the Garden of Eden. But I love you guys. I love you, Cindy, with your big smile and your deep eyes and your fine hair and your huge norks and your sweet, sweet-smelling clit. And you, what was it, Steve, with your, um. Winning personality. If I have to die, I want to die with you."

His eyes were wet, and they couldn't tell if he were crying or rheumy.

"This world can't be all there is," he breathed. "It can't be. I have faith. There *must* be a way out." He opened his spindly arms wide. "Give me a hug."

So they did.

"Because," said God. "You loved me once. You loved me once, didn't you? You loved me once. You loved me. Tell me you loved me. Tell me you loved me once. You loved me. You loved me. You loved me."

THEY BURIED THEIR father in the back garden that night. It wasn't a grand garden, but it was loved, and Cindy and Steve had planted flowers there, and it was good enough.

Then they went indoors, and they began looking for the dark space at the centre of the world. They'd been to Tenerife and to Venice, they'd seen no dark spaces there. So they looked in the kitchen, they cleared out the pots and the pans from the cupboard. They looked in the bathroom behind the cistern. They looked in the attic.

They decided to go to bed. It had been a long day. And Steve offered Cindy his hand, and she took it, a little surprised; he hadn't offered her a hand in years. They both liked the feel of that hand holding thing, it made them seem warm and loved. They climbed the stairs together.

They looked for the dark space in the bedroom too, but it was nowhere to be found.

They got undressed. They kicked off their clothes, left them where they fell upon the floor, stood amidst them. They came together, naked as the day they were born. They explored each other's bodies, and it was like the first time, now there were no expectations, nothing defensive, nothing to prove. He licked at her body, she nuzzled into his. Like the first time, in innocence.

She found his dark space first. It was like a mole, it

was on his thigh. He found her dark space in the shadow of her overhanging left breast.

She put her ear to his thigh. Then he pressed his ear against her tit. Yes, there were such whispers to be heard! And they marvelled that they'd never heard them before.

She slid her fingertips into his dark space, and they numbed not unpleasantly. He kissed at hers, and he felt his tongue thicken, his tongue grew, all his mouth was a tongue. They both poked a bit further inside.

They wondered if they could squeeze themselves into something that was so small. They looked at each other for encouragement, but their faces were too hard to read. They wondered if they could dare. And then she smiled, and at that *he* smiled. And they knew they could be brave again, just one last time. They pushed onwards and inwards. And they went to someplace new.

THE MUSE OF COPENHAGEN

Nina Allan

It's wonderful to discover a new writer who understands the traditions of supernatural fiction, while bringing something new to the field. There is something Aickman-esque about Nina's story, but while you can feel the presence of that master of the genre there is also a bold and original voice here. 'The Muse of Copenhagen' proves that Nina Allan is an exciting new writer in the genre of the weird.

I DUMPED MY holdall on the back seat of the taxi and got in beside the driver. When I told him where I wanted to go, he seemed surprised.

"Southshore?" he said. "I thought Mr Gouss was away?"

"My uncle's dead," I said. "He died at the weekend. I'm here to take care of the house."

I thought it best to get the facts out into the open. People in small communities are invariably curious about each other and if I tried to keep my business a secret it would only make them gossip all the more.

Everyone in St Lawrence knew my Uncle Denny. Whether they would remember me, I was less sure. Southshore had been my home throughout my boyhood, but I hadn't been back to the house for a decade, not since Anka's funeral. Uncle Denny packed up and left soon afterwards, dividing his time between his houses in Athens and Marseille. I never questioned him about his voluntary exile. Once I was past my teens, we didn't tend to discuss our personal lives all that much. What we talked about mostly was stamps.

After Anka's death, we didn't see each other so often either, but we kept in touch fairly regularly by letter and then later by email. He usually phoned at Christmas and on my birthday, but his last call came out of the blue. It was a bad line. I couldn't make out who it was at first. I put that down to the lousy connection, but as the conversation continued I realised it was more than that. Uncle Denny sounded weird. Furtive somehow, as if he was afraid someone might be listening in on what we were saying. He also seemed older. My uncle was getting on a bit, that was true, but he had always been fit and healthy, and the last time I saw him, in a restaurant in Geneva, he could have passed for sixty or even younger. Now suddenly he sounded ninety, and on his last legs.

"I've called to tell you you'll get everything," he said. "I've made sure you'll inherit the lot. But I want you to clear the house, Johnny. I want you to promise. And you mustn't touch anything yourself. Get a firm in. Don't worry about the money, that's all been arranged."

"Steady on a moment, will you? I haven't got a clue what you're talking about."

"I'm talking about when I'm dead, of course. Get rid

of it all. If I had my way, I'd burn the house down, but it's too late for that."

"This is crazy, Uncle Denny. Are you trying to tell me you're ill?"

"Not so far as I know. I just wanted to get things settled, that's all. You never know what's round the corner, do you? Especially at my age."

"You'll live to be a hundred."

"God forbid." He laughed then, and immediately he sounded more like himself. "How are you, Johnny?"

I said I was fine, which I mostly was. I'd been working my way around to breaking the news of my divorce, but I didn't want to do it over the phone and now didn't seem like the right time in any case. Uncle Denny had been fond of Ginny, and when I received the news of his death a week later my first thought was one of relief, that at least now I wouldn't have to tell him my marriage was over.

My second thought was that my uncle had predicted his own death. The thought made me go cold all over.

SOUTHSHORE WAS NEVER a grand house, but it had a sizeable chunk of land attached to it, and its westerly aspect meant that its narrow, high-ceilinged rooms were always full of the pearlescent, rain-coloured light particular to the estuary, even in summer. During the war, the house was requisitioned as a convalescent home for wounded soldiers; afterwards it was turned into a hotel. The business was successful for a while, but it began losing money in the mid-seventies, and by the time my uncle bought the place it had become run down almost to the point of dereliction.

I knew that Uncle Denny had been married before, very briefly, to a woman named Lily Betts, but I was scarcely more than a toddler at the time and I had no memory of her. It was Anka, of course, that I remembered. Anka was Danish, and some twenty years younger than my uncle. I don't know if Uncle Denny left Lily Betts to be with Anka, or whether his first marriage was over anyway. It was something that was never talked about. But my uncle often repeated the story of how Anka fell in love with Southshore at first sight. They were driving back to London after a day in the country and Anka saw the house out of the window. She made my uncle stop the car, telling him this was the house she wanted to live in and that they had to buy it. Less than two hours later Uncle Denny was putting his signature on a draft contract in an estate agent's office in Maldon.

I think Anka loved eastern Essex because its level greenness and eroded coastline reminded her of Denmark. You say Essex and people think immediately of Ilford and Romford, the commercial wastelands of the London commuter belt. But the country around the Blackwater estuary is a flat, watery spread of narrow inlets and offshore islets, salt marshes and open grassland. Because of the constant steady ingress of tidal erosion, there is no coast road, and three of the four railway branch lines from Maldon were closed down during the Beeching reforms. The place bears a mantle of secrecy. Anka used to refer to it as her haven.

I never questioned what drew her to my uncle. Linden Gouss was a handsome man, generous and sharp-witted. He was also a highly successful businessman. It was only after Anka died that I wondered why they'd never had children of their own. I supposed there must have been some physical obstacle, some gynaecological complication. The idea of asking my uncle for details made me wince with embarrassment.

I PULLED MY suitcase out of the car and on to the gravel. A playful breeze was tripping in off the mudflats, bringing with it the familiar dense reek of bladder wrack. The sky was wide, clouded with bands of cirrus, opalescent as a late Turner. The house reared up before me like a mirage, like a faded Polaroid, and suddenly I felt emotions rising in me, a wave of feeling that could have been to do with my uncle's death or with Ginny leaving, but that seemed to be connected with neither, that seemed to come from much further back, from that sun-drenched afternoon in late August when I was summoned to the headmaster's office and told that both my parents had been drowned in the Victoria ferry disaster.

I paid off the cabby and stood with my back turned as he drove away, not wanting him to see how shaken I was.

Only when the taxi had passed completely out of earshot did I continue on up the drive and into the house.

What with the place having been unoccupied for so long I suppose I'd been prepared to find it in a bit of a state, but it was quite the opposite. The parquet looked recently polished, the air was filled with the scents of furniture wax and fresh chrysanthemums. There was a small stack of post on the hall table, all of it addressed to me, the various bills and legal permissions sent on to the house as promised by my uncle's solicitor in

Maldon. Everything looked cared for, pristine, and I remembered that as well as the annual heating and plumbing inspections Uncle Denny had employed a cleaner, some local woman from the village, to come in once a week to run a vacuum cleaner and a duster around and generally keep an eye on the place.

It must have cost him a small fortune over the years. It would have been cheaper to keep a *pied-à-terre* in London, not to say a great deal more convenient. I found myself wondering for the hundredth time why my uncle hadn't just sold the place and been done with it.

I placed my luggage at the foot of the stairs and went through to the back. I felt on edge rather, starting at the slightest sound, although what I was expecting to encounter I had no idea. My uncle's body had been cremated in Marseille, under the strict instructions that there should be no funeral service. He left a letter for me, apologising for his strange request but pleading for my understanding.

'*I can't stand the thought of it,*' he wrote. '*All those vultures standing around saying things they don't mean and polishing off the last of my Sauternes. I don't want it, Johnny. And you and I know that the important things have already been said.*'

I guessed that when he spoke of the important things he was referring to our final telephone conversation. Once more I felt that odd frisson of disquiet, that after calling me he had sat down and written that letter, knowing in some mysterious manner that we had talked together for the last time.

I supposed the mystery was all in my head. There was nothing that unusual about an old man coming increasingly to realise that time was running out on him. If so-called psychic premonitions were what you were after, you only had to turn on the television or open a newspaper. What was harder for me to admit was how pleased I had been, not to have to drag myself all the way down to the south of France, to make stilted small talk with a bunch of strangers, to do all of it alone, without Ginny.

It wouldn't have surprised me to discover my uncle had somehow known about that too, after all, and that his most likely reason for not wanting a funeral had been to spare me the trouble of attending it.

The back rooms were as clean as the hall. In the kitchen, the pedal bin under the sink was fitted with a fresh liner, and the fridge and one of the overhead cupboards had been stocked with a small store of basic provisions. Had my uncle informed the cleaning woman that I would be coming? I put on the radio, tuning it to a jazz station I liked, then filled the kettle and spooned sugar and instant coffee into a mug. The mug was one of Anka's, the Royal Copenhagen beakers she always used for hot drinks at bedtime, or for Bovril when I was ill. The mugs were simple in form – straight white porcelain cylinders with a narrow gold band at the rim – but they were functional and elegant and I had always loved them. The very act of handling one of them gave me a sense of coming home, though I had forgotten all about them until now. I waited for the kettle to boil, thinking how these few small acts of ownership – playing some music, making coffee – had already altered the atmosphere of the place, shifting it from the past into the present.

I reminded myself that Southshore was mine now, not just the house but everything in it. It was only then that

I started to wonder about my uncle's odd instructions, the way he had insisted I dispose of everything. I had not dwelt on his words at the time, mainly because I had other things on my mind but also as I had not the slightest expectation of his dying. Now I was forced to ask myself what he had meant by it all. Surely he had not intended me to literally get rid of every last object in the house; the porcelain mugs, for instance? As I thought about this I realised something I had not realised even five minutes before: that *I did not want to get rid of the mugs*, that they were important to me because of the memories they held, and selling them would be a betrayal. It would be like selling off a part of my past.

Southshore would be full of such things: objects that contained within them the essence of my whole childhood and of such deep personal significance that the idea of parting with them was unthinkable.

I could not believe that this was what my uncle would have wanted. When my parents died, Uncle Denny did everything in his power to make a new and secure home for me at Southshore. I could not imagine him wilfully forcing me to give up any part of it.

I came to the conclusion that there was only one explanation for my uncle's request: there was something in the house that he hadn't wanted me to know about. He hadn't had time to remove it himself, and in his weakened condition telling me to dispose of everything must have seemed a viable solution.

I considered the obvious things – evidence of marital infidelity perhaps, or criminal activity – but found neither of them particularly convincing. It wasn't that I didn't think Uncle Denny capable of such misdemeanours

– I tend towards the belief that anyone is capable of anything, given the right circumstances or incentive – it was just that they seemed insufficient grounds for such drastic action. Anka was dead. It could hardly matter now if I happened to discover that half a lifetime ago my uncle had been unfaithful to her. The same logic would apply if he had once embezzled funds or even killed a man: he could hardly be made to answer for it now.

I think it was then I decided I was not going to abide by my uncle's wishes. There was nothing about them in his will, after all. Surely it was up to me now, to decide how I wanted to dispose of my own property and to do so in my own good time?

Beneath the avuncular exterior, Denny Gouss had been a powerful and determined individual, the kind of man who had grown used to getting his own way. I rationalized his last words to me as a failure of nerve, the fear of dying, which is after all the ultimate loss of control.

I CHECKED THAT the TV was working, made an omelette for supper, and as evening began to fall I poured myself a glass of Frascati from the bottle I had found in the fridge and went out into the garden. The wide lawns to the front of the house were kept regularly mown and trimmed, but Anka had always insisted that the acreage at the back be left free to go wild. It was a large stretch of land, running all the way down to the sluggish, briny waters of the estuary, a riot of yarrow and thistle and stringy red campion. As a boy I had found it enchanting.

I turned to look back at the house, and was surprised to see a light burning in one of the upper windows. I had been upstairs, just briefly, to deposit my holdall in the room I still could not help thinking of as my bedroom, but I didn't remember switching on any lights. I went slowly inside, placing my empty wine glass on the draining board and passing through to the hall. At the foot of the stairs, I hesitated. One of the house's anomalies and something my uncle had never got round to fixing was that you couldn't turn on the upstairs hall light from downstairs. As a child I had always dreaded that blind rush up the darkened staircase to get to the light switch, a failure of nerve of my own that Anka had occasionally liked to tease me about. Now, to my own wry amusement, I found that the fear had returned. There was a cupboard up there on the half landing, an odd little store room that during the day I had often used as a hideout but that at night, for some reason, became terrifying in my imagination. As I crept past it now, on my way to the shadowed recesses of the upper floor, the door to that cupboard seemed carved from pure blackness, the velvet rectangular entrance to an endless void.

I reached the top of the stairs. As I fumbled for the light switch, I thought I caught a glimpse of a figure darting away from me along the landing. I drew in my breath, feeling not so much the threat of being attacked as the terror of being silently observed, in a lonely place, by someone I had not known was there.

I was somehow convinced the figure had been a woman.

Finally, I managed to get the lights on.

"Hello," I said, though my voice came out as a choked whisper. The landing was empty. The door to my room was standing slightly ajar.

I crossed the landing and peered inside. The bedroom seemed as empty as the hallway. A vaporous, tungsten light hung in the room's angles and corners like shreds of spider silk, and through the top right hand pane of the window I could see the flat white plate of the moon rising above the estuary.

I told myself that this was the explanation, that the light I had seen from the garden was simply the moon's reflection in the window glass. I flicked the light switch by the door, banishing the moon to outer darkness, then closed the curtains and sat down on the bed.

The room was the same but different. The bed and the wardrobe occupied the same positions they had always done, but the glass-fronted bookcase had been moved to the opposite wall, and at some point during the years of my absence someone had taken down the small framed aquatint of a steam train crossing a viaduct that had been in the room ever since I had been brought there on the evening following my parents' funeral. Years later I discovered that the print was an original Ravilious. The knowledge that my uncle had placed this valuable object in my room, just because he thought I might like it, that its colours and subject matter might be reassuring to me, and regardless of its monetary value, made me respect and love him all the more.

The disappearance of the picture made me sad. I looked once more around the room, wondering what else might be missing. I leaned forward, running my hand over the polished walnut surface of the bedside cabinet, sliding out the little drawer, remembering how easily it flowed upon its runners at the start of every summer, how by September it would scarcely open, crammed solid as it was with the usual vacation detritus: paperback horror novels, half-filled exercise books, innumerable cellophane envelopes of foreign commemoratives.

The drawer opened easily now. It seemed, at first, that there was nothing inside it at all, then I noticed a single sheet of ruled notepaper, yellow with age and with a single line of writing across the top.

My dearest Johnny, it read. *Today when I went to the village –*

It was Anka's writing. I knew it at once, from the hundreds of notes and amusing postcards she had sent me when I was at school. There was no date, nothing to tell me exactly when it had been written, although I supposed it must have been shortly before she died or I would have been bound to have come across it on a previous visit.

I wondered what had made her stop writing the letter, what had happened to her in the village. She was still a young woman when she died, not yet fifty, and as I stopped being a child and passed into puberty it was Anka who formed the basis of my first tentative and guilty sexual fantasies. It was not just that she was beautiful, with the pale skin and very fair hair typically associated with Scandinavians. She was also fun to be with, had a ribald sense of humour and enjoyed playing practical jokes. Those girls of my own age that I encountered – the sisters of friends or day pupils at the school I attended – seemed with their chapped lips and adolescent inarticulacy to be ignorant and coarse by comparison, and in any case I had no idea how I might go about approaching one of them. Anka I could talk to and touch, because talking and touching had always been a part of our relationship. I had even seen Anka naked once, when I barged into the bathroom just as she was stepping out of the shower. I was fourteen at the time and had never seen a naked woman outside of the fleeting glimpses offered to me by the airbrushed photographs in the ladmags that some of the senior boys kept stashed in their lockers. My cheeks flared up like a forest fire but Anka just laughed, and coiled herself sedately in a pale blue towel.

There was also a second incident, soon after my sixteenth birthday. I was in bed with a summer cold and feeling rather sorry for myself. Uncle Denny, as so often, was away on business, but Anka kept me well entertained, and I found I was glad we had the house to ourselves. I sensed a new dimension in our togetherness, something that had not been there before, something exciting and vaguely dangerous. One afternoon – we had been eating our lunch off trays and listening to the radio – Anka slipped off her sandals and climbed up on the bed with me. She leaned back against the headboard, her eyes closed, her shoulder pressing lightly against mine as she began telling me about the people she had known, the life she led in Denmark before she met my Uncle Denny and came to England.

"I was an artist, a sculptor," she said. "I bet you didn't know that, did you? My bronze of 'The Young Lucifer' won first prize at my graduation show. Shall I open the window wider? You're feeling a little feverish."

She rested her hand against my forehead as if to check my temperature then moved it slowly across my face, stroking my lips and eyelids with the tips of her fingers. "You know it's strange, but you remind me a little of my Lucifer. It's something about your mouth, I think. You have a beautiful mouth, Johnny, did you know that?

Your lips are fuller than the lips of most men. They are like rose petals."

She pressed her palm against my mouth, then slid her hand sideways so that her little finger rested in the crack between my lips. Her other hand, whether by accident or on purpose I did not know, was pressing down on the duvet close by my groin. Sweat burst out on my forehead and under my arms and my penis began to get hard. I lay there, motionless apart from my swelling member, frantically insisting to myself that whatever happened next would be all right, because Anka was not really my aunt, she was just my uncle's wife, and my uncle's second wife at that.

Then suddenly the pressure on the bedclothes vanished and she was gone. I heard her running lightly downstairs, and then seconds later the sound of car wheels crunching on gravel. I remembered then that Uncle Denny was due back from Amsterdam that evening; apparently he had caught an earlier flight.

Everything seemed normal at dinner. Uncle Denny was in a talkative, jokey mood as he often was after a trip, and Anka played along just like always. But at some point during the night I was woken by the sound of them arguing.

"You're not to touch the boy," said Uncle Denny. He sounded cold, angry, utterly unlike himself.

"Your precious brother's precious son," Anka said. She made a strange noise, something between a cry and a laugh, and then fell silent. I think my uncle might even have struck her. It was the only time I ever heard them fighting, and for some reason it terrified me. I screwed my eyes shut and pulled up the covers, trying to block out not just the sounds but the sense of what was happening. A short time after that I went back to sleep.

My uncle left on business again three days later. I both hoped and feared that Anka would use this opportunity to pick up where she had left off, but she acted as if the whole strange episode had never happened.

I WATCHED *NEWSNIGHT* and then went to bed. I thought of phoning Ginny to let her know where I was, should she need to contact me, but in the end I decided against it. I knew I was just looking for excuses to call her. If Ginny needed me for any reason she would ring my mobile. I thought I would have trouble sleeping, but the worry proved groundless. I woke just after eight, feeling rested and curiously optimistic about things, filled with a sense of wellbeing I hadn't experienced in months, and certainly not since Ginny moved out. I supposed the change of scene was doing me good.

I ate breakfast in the kitchen and afterwards began my inspection of the house. I had planned to make a detailed inventory, but I quickly realised that such a task would take me weeks and possibly months to complete. It wasn't just the number of things, it was the difficulty of categorizing them. Some, like the Mackintosh chair in my uncle's office and Anka's pretty little Sheraton writing desk, were valuable antiques that I knew should be put into secure storage until I decided what I wanted to do with them. Others – my uncle's books, the photographs of him and my father as students at Oxford – were less of a worry in financial terms, but no less vital in the matter of what they meant to me personally.

The problem was it was all of a piece. It was not the

individual objects that carried significance, so much as Southshore as a whole, as an entity. I wandered through the rooms, picking things up and putting them down again, and the longer I went on the less I felt able to make a firm decision about anything.

I began to develop a theory that there was no secret hidden in the house, just this poignant physical detritus of time's passing. I could keep everything, or keep nothing, it would make no difference. The time had come to let it go, to turn it over to the auctioneers.

My uncle's odd request was really quite simple: he had wanted me to let the house die with him.

This idea was so liberating it was like a weight being lifted from me. If I had been the kind of person that believes in ghosts, I might almost have concluded that Uncle Denny was somewhere close by and approving my decision, but in reality I supposed it was simply the relief that comes with any resolution of a difficult problem: I had decided in effect to give up on it, and I was glad.

I heated some soup for lunch and reviewed my plans. I had reckoned on being at Southshore for some weeks. There were a couple of sales I would need to attend later in the month, but other than that, my business did not necessitate me being in London. Indeed, I had welcomed the time away as an opportunity to take stock, to recuperate at least in part from the aftermath of my breakup with Ginny. In the light of recent events, however, there seemed little point in staying on. A day or two should now be sufficient, just long enough for me to organize the removal and storage of the more valuable pictures and furniture. I also wanted, if I could, to contact the cleaning woman my uncle had hired and arrange for her to continue her weekly visits. The rest could stay as it was until the house was sold. There were a few things, some small keepsakes, that I wanted to take back to London with me, but these were barely enough to fill a cardboard box and I thought I would probably find one of those in the store cupboard on the landing. I went to look, but discovered the door to the cupboard was locked. I could not remember it ever being locked in the past, but dismissed this as a minor annoyance. The key would be here in the house somewhere, it was bound to be. I could hunt for it later.

I washed up the dishes and tidied the kitchen then decided I would take a walk into the village. St Lawrence didn't offer much in the way of shopping facilities, but there was a post office and general store which sold most of the basics, enough to tide me over until I left. I also felt the need for some fresh air. I had been stuck inside all morning, and it wasn't until I opened the front door that I realised how bright and warm the day was. I took the short cut into the village, a narrow footpath skirting fields and then cutting down through the new estate into what passed for the High Street.

Like my bedroom at Southshore, the village was the same and yet different. The pub had been completely refurbished, the telephone box by the garage had disappeared. The post office store, though, was still there and still doing business.

"Did you find everything you needed?" said the woman behind the counter. "We were ever so sorry to hear about your uncle."

"Yes, thank you. At least he had a good long innings." I smiled, doing my best to seem friendly, but not wanting to get drawn into conversation. Although I knew it was inevitable, I still found I couldn't get used to the idea of people talking about me behind my back. I was glad I had already made the decision to go back to London.

"We were all quite shocked, actually," the woman persisted. "Especially as Annie said she saw him the other week."

I stared at her, not comprehending. "What on earth do you mean?"

The woman shrugged, looking uncomfortable. "Anne Mellors, the lady who does the cleaning. She saw lights on up at the house. She thought your uncle was back for good."

"I'd like to have a word with Mrs Mellors, actually. I'd be grateful if you'd ask her to call."

I gathered up my purchases and left, not waiting for the woman to reply. I knew my behaviour would seem rude to her, but I felt unable and unwilling to excuse myself. Not only were the locals talking about me, they were trying to make fun of me, too. Perhaps it was something they did to all Londoners. I wouldn't have minded that so much – I was leaving anyway. What enraged me about their little haunted house joke was that it had been made at my uncle's expense. I even found myself wondering if it had been this Mrs Mellors who had somehow switched on the upstairs light the evening of my arrival, but of course that was stupid. In any case, if they were trying to scare me they would have to do better than that.

I stormed back across the fields feeling furious, and wondering how I could get my own back, but by the time I reached the house my anger had cooled. In a year the house would be sold, and none of this would matter anyway. I resolved to forget all about it.

I booted up the computer in my uncle's office so I could check my emails and deal with some of the more urgent correspondence, then spent the rest of the evening watching television. I went to bed at around one o'clock, so tired that I fell asleep with the light on. Half an hour later I woke with a start, unsure for a moment of where I was, and then uncomfortably aware of the lamp shining full on my face. I leaned over to switch it off, and in the fleeting afterglow I caught a glimpse of a woman, standing beside the bed. I snapped the light back on immediately but there was no one there.

I fell asleep again and dreamed of Ginny, a row that ended in sex, a petulant, angry coupling that felt like a continuation of our fight. As I struggled in her arms I became aware that strands of her hair had become caught on my shirt buttons, that I was tied to her and could not get loose. The hair, though, was not short and dark like Ginny's own, but long and light, glass-coloured, and as I looked down at her, spread on the bed, I saw the woman I was with was not Ginny after all, but Anka.

I tried to roll away but there was no room to move.

"It's okay," Anka said. She reached up and touched the side of my face. "It's okay, Johnny."

I could hear her voice, so clearly it was as if she was actually there in the room with me, and I could smell her breath, the woody, aniseed scent of a particular garden herb she liked to nibble. Her hands gripped my buttocks, pulling me astride her. I bent to kiss her, grinding my mouth down on hers and closing my eyes. I came almost at once. Ginny and I hadn't made love in almost three months and my orgasm hit me so hard it was like hoof beats against my skull. I tried to wake up, then realised I was already awake. The inside of my thigh was sticky with semen.

I WAITED FOR it to get properly light and then I called Ginny.

"Don't laugh at me, Gin," I said. "But I think the place is haunted."

She sighed. "What are you calling for, Johnny? I thought we'd agreed."

It was strange, but the sound of her voice, so familiar, so familiarly irritated, was enough to bring me back to reality. It was also enough to remind me that the Ginny I still missed was not the Ginny that now actually existed, no matter how much I tried to fool myself. The connection between us was broken. It had been stupid to call.

"I'm sorry," I said. "It's just a bit weird, I suppose, being back here after all this time."

"And I'm sorry about your uncle. He was a nice man. Go back to London, Johnny. You can leave all this stuff to the lawyers, make them earn their fee for a change."

"That's what he said, too. Uncle Denny, I mean."

"Well, there you are, then."

There seemed nothing more to be said. I said goodbye and ended the call. I felt both wretched and foolish, wretched for having to be reminded yet again that it was over between us, foolish because if I had wanted to look an idiot, calling my ex-wife at the crack of dawn and raving about ghosts seemed the perfect way of going about it.

I got myself up and dressed, then called the solicitor in Maldon and told him it was my intention to sell the house as soon as it had passed through probate. When he asked if I intended to live there or rent it out in the meantime, I said no. I added that I was concerned about my uncle's pictures, and asked if he could recommend anyone to store them for me.

"I'm glad you brought that up," he said. "The current period of insurance has almost expired, and the policy your uncle put in place is very expensive. It would make a lot more sense to put the paintings and antiques under separate cover." He said he would email me some details later that morning.

When I had finished dealing with the solicitor, I began gathering together those few of my uncle's possessions that I intended to take back with me to London. There weren't many. The two days I had spent rifling through drawers and cupboards and picking over the remnants of the past had given me a distaste for the whole business and I was tempted to leave as I had come, empty handed. In the end though I knew there were some things I would regret forever if I didn't save them, and it was these things – the university photographs, and pictures of my parents on their wedding day, an early pastel by Ivon Hitchens, the six Royal Copenhagen mugs – that I put together on the kitchen table ready to pack. This brought me once again to the problem of what to pack them in. There were some bin liners under the sink and in the understairs cupboard I found the old nylon carry bag Anka had always used for her vegetable shopping, but neither of these were really suitable and I resigned myself to hunting down the key to the locked store cupboard.

I began at the top of the house, with the ebony bureau in Anka's old dressing room, and worked my way down from there. It was not a pleasant task. Most of the things in Anka's room had clearly not been touched since her death, and my fumbling among her underwear and jewellery had a feel of grave robbery about it. In any case, the key was not there. Neither was it in my uncle's games table, nor in the fifty-drawer apothecary's chest at the end of the hall, nor was it in the bathroom medicine cabinet, nor in any of the dozen or so cupboards or chests or chiffoniers in the three main guest bedrooms.

I nearly gave up at that point, and had it not been for my dislike of being beaten I almost certainly would have done. In any case, I decided I had been coming at the problem from the wrong angle, concentrating on the *where* instead of the *who*. Given that Anka had died before him, the person most likely to have locked the cupboard was my Uncle Denny. It seemed odd and not a little ironic that the one room I hadn't looked in so far was my uncle's office.

I made a cursory search of the bookshelves and the large wooden filing cabinet, and then began to go through his desk. There wasn't much there, of course. All his legal papers and anything concerning his business activities had been packed up and removed to the Marseilles house a decade before. But if anything that made the things that were left behind seem all the more poignant. There was a stack of my old school reports, a postcard I'd sent to him and Anka during a class trip to the Norfolk Broads, my uncle's onyx inkwell, the letter opener in the shape of a crocodile that I once coveted so much I stole it, only to smuggle it back into his desk during the black-coated small hours of the following morning.

And there, in the secret drawer that had stopped being a secret when Anka showed me how to open it by pressing and then sliding a certain piece of the lustrous maple marquetry, were my uncle's stamps.

UNCLE DENNY ALWAYS used to joke that he gave up serious collecting on the day I first outbid him at an auction.

"This is where I throw in the towel," he said. "Time to leave it to the professionals."

We were drinking champagne at the bar of some hotel in Knightsbridge, celebrating my Trinidad Red. Uncle Denny was still based mostly in London then, still living at Southshore. Anka was still alive. I laughed, and protested he had taught me everything I knew, that the game would be no fun without him.

"But it's not a game for you though, is it, Johnny? That's where you and I differ, and that's why I'm getting out now."

He was right, in a way, I suppose. Philately had always been my uncle's hobby, a break from the jet-powered world of international investments, a place where he could occasionally be foolish and let down his guard. Whereas I had chosen to pour my own modest accretion of what Anka called the Gouss instinct for moral suicide into the peculiar business of buying and selling stamps. It was true that Uncle Denny had taught me a lot. But at some point it was inevitable that I would overtake him.

I felt sad when I found the album, but at the same time it made me smile. I always liked to think that Uncle Denny had not given up the game entirely, that he still made the occasional purchase on the sly. Now it appeared that my suspicions had been correct.

It was just a slim album, and the most of what it contained was if not second rate then unexceptional, issues my uncle had kept, I suspected, more for sentimental reasons than out of any hope that their value would increase.

There were a couple of nice things, though: a Gagarin first day cover displaying the famous 'yellow Vostok' error, a Hitler skull stamp that I thought was almost certainly genuine, a strip of three fifty-cent McKillips, an artist's commemorative that showed the complete New York skyline including the twin towers, issued at the end of August 2001 then hurriedly recalled on September 12th.

It was an odd little collection, with something of the macabre about it. I turned the page, curious about what else might have taken his fancy. There was a yellow Romanian beetle stamp with three torn perforations, an unfranked Limoges Bleu, and a stamp with Anka's face on it.

I did not recognise her at first. What caught my attention was the sight of a stamp I had never seen before. I leaned forward to get a closer look, then examined it through the magnifying loupe I always carry in my right breast pocket.

The stamp was Danish, and of a relatively scarce denomination. Its design featured the face of a woman, a detail from an oil painting. The woman looked familiar, and because I was seeing her out of context I wondered at first if it was some opera singer or minor film star that I was looking at. Then suddenly I realised it was Anka, her exact likeness.

The artist's name, Mikkelsen, was printed in silver along the stamp's left hand margin. I had never heard of him, but that did not surprise me; it was my uncle that knew about art.

I fetched my uncle's Gibbons, still in its old place on the top of the filing cabinet, and began leafing through. It was an old edition, fifteen years out of date at least, but the stamp was not a new issue, and it didn't take me long to find the listing. The stamp was one of a set of five, issued in nineteen-sixty-six to commemorate the art of Arne Mikkelsen. The other stamps in the set featured a white castle, a raven with a rose in its beak, a flying horse, and a wizened witch with agate-green eyes. The stamps were listed as common. In view of that it seemed odd that they were unknown to me.

Gibbons had nothing to say about Mikkelsen, of course, but a brief search online told me that he had been an artist and book illustrator, made popular throughout Scandinavia for his representations of subjects from Norse mythology. He died in nineteen-fifty. The centenary of his birth in nineteen-sixty-six was marked by the issue of the five commemorative stamps, together with a lavishly illustrated catalogue of his work, entitled *Fantasme*.

It took me a little more time to unearth the original paintings, but in the end I found what I was looking for on a website published by a Danish museum. The woman depicted on what I was coming to think of as Anka's stamp was Maryane, a beautiful succubus who, according to legend, had enticed and then enslaved a number of powerful merchants and princes in Copenhagen, wearing them away to madness and then to dust.

The painting was called 'The Muse of Copenhagen.' My first assumption was that Anka had been

Mikkelsen's model, but I now knew that this was impossible: Mikkelsen had died before Anka was born.

Her mother then, or grandmother? I realised I knew nothing at all about Anka's background. What puzzled me most was why Uncle Denny had never told me about the stamp, had never shown it to me. It crossed my mind that it was this, after all, that my uncle had been wanting to hide from me, that the stamp was the secret. I reached for the idea, but it eluded me. None of it made any sense.

Suddenly I felt very tired. I switched off the computer and closed my eyes. My head drooped forward on my chest as I listened to the quiet sounds the house made when it was resting: the sighing of the floorboards, the rattle of steam in the hot water pipes, the sly whisper from the open chimney. When I first came to Southshore as a child I was disappointed not to hear the sound of the sea, but Anka told me it was because of the marshes.

"The water is heavy with sand," she said. "The sand steals its voice."

Her words haunted me for a long time. I found I was unable to rid myself of the image of old father Neptune, his beard clogged with mud, his throat choked with the dark, glistening quicksand of the Blackwater estuary. I dozed where I sat, not quite conscious, the pale fingers of the dying autumn brushing my face. I told myself I mustn't drop off, there were still things I needed to do before I left.

A hand was gripping my shoulder. I jerked awake.

"Johnny," she said. "You look just like a naughty schoolboy, falling asleep in your seat at the back of the class."

She sank to her knees at my feet. Slowly I reached

out for her, burying my hands to the wrists in her glass-coloured hair.

TIME PASSED THEN, but I don't know how much. Hours or days, possibly weeks. I know that, on the morning after Anka first came to me, a woman arrived at the house, and that following a moment's panicked confusion I realised it must be the Mrs Mellors my uncle had employed to do the cleaning. I remembered I had asked to see her but couldn't recall exactly when that had been. She asked if I would be wanting to keep her on and I said yes. I also asked her if she could get in some shopping. When she asked what I would like her to buy, my mind went completely blank. I knew I probably needed food, but I didn't feel hungry.

"Just get what you got before," I said. "It doesn't matter. Anything you like."

She looked at me strangely but she took the money I offered and returned an hour or so later with three bags of groceries. I don't remember seeing her again.

During the days, I sorted through my uncle's possessions, arranging his letters in date order, cataloguing his pictures. These tasks absorbed me while I was engaged in them, but afterwards I often had the sense of working in circles, repeating a thing incessantly with no hope of ever bringing it to completion. Anka was both there and not there. Sometimes she was physically present, at other times I was aware of her only as a kind of itching in the back of my mind, the sense that she was close by but could not be seen. Sometimes she brought me tea in the porcelain mugs, and when I mentioned that it tasted odd she said it was fennel tea, made from the herb in the garden that she liked to chew.

"It's good for you," she said. "It will clear up those scabs on your arms."

I told her there were no scabs on my arms, but when I took off my shirt that night I saw she was right, that the skin of my forearms had become dry and abraded, its surface busy with small red lesions.

"It's the damp climate," Anka said. "It's nothing to worry about."

As the days grew shorter I felt listless and sad, but in bed with her I never seemed to tire.

In the afternoons I dozed on the book room sofa. One afternoon towards the end of November I awoke out of troubled dreams to the knowledge that I was in the house alone. I opened the kitchen door and looked out, certain that I would see Anka down by the water as I often did, foraging for herbs or simply standing with folded arms, gazing out over the estuary.

I asked her once if she was looking towards Denmark, but she just laughed and said she had been in England so long she had more or less forgotten what Denmark was like.

On that day, though, there was no sign of her, there was just the grey water – the grey water and the grey sky, folded together like one grey blanket on top of another.

I should go, I thought, but the idea refused to take hold. I closed the door and came back inside. There on the table in front of me was the missing Ravilious, the little steam train crossing its viaduct in the winter twilight. I picked it up, mystified as to how it had got there, then turned it over to look at the back. The picture itself appeared undamaged, but someone had scrawled some words on the hardboard backing. The felt tipped marker that had been used to write them was lying uncapped on the floor under the table.

'*Johnny*,' I read. '*The key.*'

The key to what? I thought. *Key to the problem? Key to the road map? Key to the door?*

It was my uncle's writing, I knew that. But Uncle Denny was dead. He had been dead for weeks now, for months. Possibly years.

Like a mud dredger churning the sands of the estuary I scoured my mind for a memory, the memory of my search for the key to the locked store cupboard. The cupboard had not been locked before, but now it was. I never did find the key. I had stopped looking when I found Anka's stamp.

I went groggily up the stairs to the half landing, convinced that when I reached the little store room I would find it open. It wasn't, though; it was locked, just as before. I took hold of the handle and shook it, rattling the door in its frame. The lock held firm. I stood back from the door, aiming a hefty kick at its lower panel. Pain coursed up through my leg, curling itself in a ball when it reached my knee. I felt weak from fatigue, as if I had just climbed a mountain. Aside from my ferocious couplings with Anka it had been a long time since I attempted anything more strenuous than changing my location from one silent room to another.

I retraced my steps to the kitchen. In the cupboard under the sink there was a rubber plunger and a small assortment of household tools: a pair of pliers, a steel claw hammer, two screwdrivers. I took the hammer and the heavier of the screwdrivers and went back up the stairs. Somehow I managed to jam the flattened tip of the screwdriver into the narrow space between the door and its frame. I worked it into the crack until it held firm, then struck out with the hammer as hard as I could. It missed the screwdriver by a couple of inches, bludgeoning the doorframe with a resounding crack. A long pale splinter of wood dropped to the floor. I froze, terrified that Anka would sense what I was doing and appear at my side. When nothing happened, I tried again, this time bringing the hammer down squarely on the handle of the screwdriver. There was a tense, splintering sound, and after a couple more blows the lock gave way.

I was drenched in sweat, my shirt clinging to my back in damp patches. I remembered stories that had thrilled me as a boy, adventure yarns by Rice Burroughs and Rider Haggard in which men left for dead and half blinded by madness stumble on an oasis in the desert, outrunning the demons of sunlight and thirst by a hair's-breadth miracle.

But this was no oasis, this was a cupboard, and the inside of the cupboard was as I remembered. There was one small window, high in the exterior wall. Watery light ran through it, revealing to me a stack of mildewed suitcases, the cardboard packing cartons I had been so keen to get my hands on, and the large blanket chest that had always been used for storing spare bedlinen. The blanket chest was made from antique pine. Anka had brought it with her from Copenhagen.

I lifted the lid. The body of the chest was filled with dried fennel stalks, a deep layer of them. An odour rose up, the pungent, aniseed scent of the tea Anka made, but intensified to the point of foulness. Nestled side-by-side in the straw were two humped, pale objects, each about the size of a melon. I picked up the one nearest to me. It was dry to the touch, and light as balsa. As I lifted it closer, the rank smell of the fennel intensified.

It was an animal of some sort, or at least it had been. What remained was a desiccated husk, the shrivelled limbs drawn up, bunched together like the limbs of a foetus. The skin crackled where I touched it, like cellophane, a mass of parched wrinkles.

I turned it over. The thing's mouth was partly open, revealing a horde of pointed yellow teeth. They seemed too many, those teeth, and needle-fine, crammed inside the mouth like splinters, the teeth of some small but particularly unpleasant carnivore. The thing's face was shrunken as a raisin and mottled with liver spots, but still I found no trouble in recognising the face of my Uncle Denny.

As I stood there gazing down at him, one tiny foot kicked out feebly, blood-warm against the hollow of my palm.

I sprang back, horrified, hurling the thing to the ground. It rolled rapidly away from me, disappearing beneath the mound of suitcases. A moment later I heard it scrabbling frantically for purchase as it tried to right itself. I shoved the chest backwards against the wall, trapping the loathsome creature in the space behind.

I began shifting the cardboard boxes, using them to form a barricade around the blanket chest. Then I went downstairs to fetch some kindling. There had been a stack of newspapers in the kitchen but they seemed to have disappeared and I supposed Mrs Mellors had taken them for recycling. In the end I used what remained of my uncle's papers, tearing them into strips and stuffing them into the spaces between the cartons. I worked as quickly as I could. I knew I didn't have much time.

*   *   *

I LEFT THE house by the back door, cutting down through the garden and striking out across the water meadows. I struggled over the unkempt ground for a mile or so then rejoined the road. My shoes were sodden through, the lower portion of my trousers streaked with mud. The sun was going down, by then, a glaucous orange, glistening on the still water of the estuary like spilled syrup. The light of the rising fire was small by comparison, although I had no doubt that as the darkness deepened its power would grow.

I managed to hitch a lift as far as Maldon, where I spent the night in a bed and breakfast before travelling back to London the following day. Late in the afternoon I received a phone call from my uncle's solicitor, informing me that Southshore had burned to the ground.

"I'm afraid it looks like arson," he said. "Local youths, probably. I know this must be very upsetting, but I'm happy to tell you at least you're still fully insured."

I wanted to ask if anything had escaped the conflagration but I did not quite dare. I hoped the silence from my end of the line would be taken for shock.

A week before Christmas I attended a stamp fair in Basel, where I was able to acquire a complete set of the Mikkelsen commemoratives. The dealer was Danish. We discovered we had acquaintances in common – the stamp world is a small and sometimes uncomfortably intimate one – and quickly found plenty to talk about. He seemed fascinated by my interest in the Mikkelsen painting, and invited me out to stay with him and his family in Copenhagen the following summer, so that he could take me to the National Gallery and show me the original.

"The Muse is really very powerful," he said to me. "She has this energy about her, you know, an internal fire. I visit her quite often, actually. Sometimes I think she's going to step right out of the painting."

He laughed, and I laughed too. I thanked him for his invitation, and told him I would be delighted to accept.

AN INJUSTICE

CHRISTOPHER FOWLER

There are forgotten parts of London, and it is in these places that the most extraordinary stories are often found. In the remarkable and powerful tale that follows, Christopher shows us what happens when an urban legend – a story of spirits and the power of the supernatural – evolves into something far more sinister and much more dangerous.

WE ALWAYS USED to meet in The Intrepid Fox, even when we'd been ghost-hunting all night. Me, Shape and Ali would bed down for a long session with bottles of cider, and argue about London's pagan history, but as we got progressively more drunk the discussions about Wiccan mythology and Aleister Crowley and spirit dowsing would get blurred together with complaints about slashed student funding, climate change and the Labour party's lost ideologies. By the end of our evening nothing made sense any more, and we would totter back to our respective flats.

Shape was always finding a new crusade to fight, and this month was no different. He'd heard that Ali and I sometimes went ghost hunting and announced that he wanted to join us. Having Shape on your side isn't always a good thing. He gets excited for a while, but his enthusiasm ebbs just as fast and you get left with the wreckage he's created. As soon as he heard about our trips out to country houses, he wanted to find a revenant in a London house.

"Why is it that only abbeys and castles get visited by ghost hunters?" he asked. "Forget the rich, we need to liberate the spirits of the poor and do some good in the world." And for once he had an idea about how to find such a place. He had decided that spirits were probably most drawn to properties built on ley lines, those tracks of spiritual energy that supposedly attract strange occurrences, and as there was a massive crossover point behind Euston Station which made the ground there more susceptible, that was the place to start looking.

So on Friday night, somewhat against my own will, the three of us met up and headed to Euston station.

Shape was striding ahead in his strappy Camden boots and long black leather coat, and Ali and I had to almost run to keep up with him. Now that he had joined us, he automatically assumed leadership.

"See, the area has always been really poor because the government needs to contain the working classes and deliberately trapped them here by forcing rents up in the surrounding areas so they couldn't move," he reckoned, zooming along the centre of the pavement. "And the poor are more prone to visitations by past spirits."

"I don't understand," said Ali, "why would they be more likely to see ghosts? I thought ghosts appeared because of an injustice."

"No, it's because the working classes are traditionally more superstitious," Shape explained, as if talking to a child. "The streets of ancient London followed the leylines, and they were traced over by hedgerows and canals. The low marshlands were poor areas largely because they flooded regularly. Water and fog brought illness, deaths created superstitions; that's why ghost stories were more associated with say, the poor East End and the areas around railway termini rather than the city's prosperous North."

"Wow, I never thought of it like that," said Ali. But she was always the first to admit she wasn't much of a thinker.

"I have some questions," I said, because I knew how Shape got if you let him have his way. He needed to be challenged, otherwise he would just walk over us. He was like that all through school, and he was like it once we were together on the same course at St Martin's. He's probably even worse now that he's in banking. We don't speak any more.

Shape sighed in annoyance. "You always do have questions, Max."

"First, how are we going to find a house with a revenant, and second, how do we gather the physical evidence we need?"

"Look, are you on board with this project or not? You could get amazing material for your degree show."

"Yeah, I'm on board. But I just don't see how we're going to pull it off from a practical point of view."

"Don't worry, we'll have plenty of time to work out the physical side of things later. First we need to find the right house."

I liked Shape then because I thought he cared about the world. He helped set up an innovative fund for earthquake victims at St Martin's and started a huge viral campaign to save the sacred white rhino – okay, so neither of those projects actually worked out, but the ideas were there. He always said he wanted to do some good in the world, like Bob Geldof and Bono. Shape's parents were uber-rich, but he said he never took a penny off them because they voted Conservative. They wanted him to go into banking right from the start but he defied them by taking up textile design, and now they were really angry with him, which made him really happy.

We were walking down Coburg Street, going towards Starcross Street. There were Indian restaurants and corner pubs, and rows of low two-floor Victorian houses with their ground floors converted into shops. I looked at the upstairs windows and saw dirty net curtains, rain-stains, ragged lines of washing on blue and red nylon lines, bicycles on balconies. Quite a lot of Indian kids. There was a big council estate just behind them, ugly modern utility buildings sticking above the slate roofline of the terrace.

"According to the book, this is the spot where seven separate ley lines cross," said Shape. "We should start here. Ali, go up and ask those kids if they know of any strange occurrences happening in the houses around here." He pointed to a hoodie gang in shiny blue track suits loitering outside a halal butchers.

I watched Ali hesitate. She didn't want to look like a wimp in front of Shape, because she was kind of in love with him even though he barely noticed her, so she went over to talk to the kids. We watched her talking to them for a minute or so. She came back.

"I couldn't understand a word they said," she admitted. "They have this funny accent." Ali was quite posh and hadn't spent much time in London before she got accepted at St Martin's. She probably never had much of a chance to talk to Asian people in Norfolk, where her folks lived, not unless they were her mum's cleaners or something.

"That'll be the working class slang they use. You fail, Ali. Three fails and you're off the team, okay?" She looked shamefaced at Shape, and mumbled an apology. "Okay, I can see I'll have to sort this out. What we'll do is look for the houses that sit exactly on the confluence of ley lines. That's where the presence of revenants is strongest."

It was grey and brown and drab around here, and just starting to rain, but I was intrigued about what we might find, and anyway we had nothing better to do today. We reached another row of houses (they all look the same), clean and still and quiet, but these ones had black iron railings and brown brick basements you could see down into. The corner sign said Phoenix Street. Shape raised his eyes at me when he saw that. There was a shop at one end selling weird fruit and fat knobbly vegetables, most of which I wasn't familiar with.

"Go in there and ask the guy if they've had any spectral activity in this zone," said Shape.

Spectral activity? I thought. *Suddenly he's the expert on ghost-hunting, and designating tasks out to his employees? Where was he when Ali and I spent a freezing night in Lesnes Abbey waiting for the ghost of a monk to appear?* This is how it always was with Shape. The night in the Abbey hadn't gone well. I thought the cold air might drive Ali into my arms for warmth at least, but all she talked about was him.

Shape peered through the window at the shopkeeper. "He looks Indian, which means he'll be more spiritually in touch with such things," he told us. "There's no

point in asking white people, they no longer have access
to their souls."

So I went into the Am-La Grocery Store. It was the
most cluttered, overstocked store I'd ever been in. The
bored boy behind the counter was barely-visible under
red and silver lottery tickets and chocolate bars. He
was watching a blurry bootleg Bollywood film on the
tiny monitor above his head. I bought a packet of mints
because I felt a bit embarrassed, and asked him. "Excuse
me? We're doing some research for a student project?
And we were wondering if you ever heard about there
being any ghosts around here?"

He turned to me with sleepy eyes and realized he'd
been asked something unusual. "Ghosts?" he repeated,
like he was trying out the word.

"Yeah, we heard there's a ghost in one of the houses."

I had trouble understanding what he was saying
because he had a strong accent and spoke so fast, but
part of it was (I thought): "The house down the street,
man, the empty one. There's some old lady who haunts
the place." And he pointed back along the street. "She's
down there," he said, emphasizing with a jab of the
finger. "We see her at the window sometimes. In the
basement. Real scary."

I was pathetically excited; I'd found our first lead.
Why did I put so much store by winning Shape's
approval? I went back out, where Shape and Ali were
sheltering from the rain. "He says there's the ghost of
an old lady that appears just down here, they see her
sometimes and she's really scary."

"Well, of course I knew we'd find her," Shape said
casually. "Doesn't he know which house?"

I didn't want to go back in the shop and ask him

again, so I said "Let's just take a look. Where are the ley lines the strongest?"

Shape took out his book and followed the scribbly map he'd made. "Two houses from the end," he said with absolute certainty, so that's where we went. We peered down into the basement but the room was dark behind the curtainless window and we couldn't see in.

"It doesn't look like anyone's living there," said Ali.

"Maybe the living residents couldn't handle it," Shape replied, opening the gate and going down. "The manifestation probably drove them out. They didn't tell anyone because they were scared of looking crazy. That's what usually happens in these cases, you know."

Shape always acted like he was the only living authority on these things, even though he was new to ghost-hunting. Ali and I had been doing it for ages, while Shape was off getting involved in lots of other stuff, student activism that mostly involved wildly unmanageable plans and half-hearted complaints rather than anything that instigated positive action. "I must challenge the lies and expose the truth because I'm the only one who cares." That was his mantra, but he never seemed to expose anything except his own inability to finish what he started. Basically he would try anything if he thought it would annoy his parents.

"What if it's got a burglar alarm?" I asked, worried.

"Max, these are working class people who haven't anything worth stealing, why would they have an alarm? All they have left is their dignity." He reached the bottom and peered in through the dirty glass. He checked his book again. "Yeah, this is definitely the right house." He wiped the window with the end of his scarf. "The rooms are empty, probably between tenants."

We ventured down the stairs behind him and looked in. I could see a room lined in brown wallpaper and dirty wall-to-wall reddish carpet. A fireplace. Some cardboard boxes and dirty rags on the floor. A ratty-looking sofa. An open doorway led into something darker, a hallway I guessed.

Shape was trying the front door, but of course it was locked. He shone his key-ring torch through the gaps. "It's bolted. We'd have to go in through the window. That's just got an old-fashioned catch."

"That's breaking and entering," said Ali, concerned.

"No, not if it's empty, it's squatting and that's completely legal," Shape told her. "Besides, if there's a problem with the police I'll just tell them who my father is. We'll need some tools. We can come back another time for that."

"We need to hold a proper watch first," said Ali. "We don't bring equipment for that because we need to verify the site. In other words, we have to see or hear something that will convince us the place has a spirit connection, otherwise we could waste weeks just hanging around at a dead venue."

"Okay, we do that, then if there's any evidence of spirit manifestation, we come back and break in, yes?"

And suddenly we had a plan. We returned the same night at nine, went for a few beers in the corner pub and then headed back down to the house in Phoenix Street. A couple of Indian teens were hanging on the opposite pavement as usual, looking like they were waiting to pull drug runs. Shape opened the gate and we went down to the basement. We had these green nylon tripod stools that looked like small umbrellas but folded out, making it easier to sit for ages; the main part of ghost hunting is sitting around.

We were in the greatcoats we took to Glasto last year, so we'd be warm and dry if the rain started up again. We set a small pocket torch beside the window and angled it so that the beam was shining into the room. Then we settled down to wait. It smelled of rotting vegetables down in the well of the basement, and I could hear rats snuffling about somewhere.

Nothing happened for the first half-hour. Then Ali said she saw something. "Where?" asked Shape.

"Just in the corner, like a change of the shadow or something." She tilted the torch and tried to see, but whatever there was, it wasn't there now. "See, it was lighter by that wall and it went dark for a moment. Really, I saw a change," she told him, anxious to be believed.

The thing about ghost-hunting is, just as you're about to give up for the night you always think you're about to see something, and you end up staying one more minute. You become convinced that if you pack up to go, you'll miss the moment. And that's what nearly happened here. Shape was bored, I could feel it, the rain had started up again and the last Tube was going soon. Ali kept moving the torch around, and Shape kept telling her to leave it alone, and something caught Shape's eye. "Turn off the torch," he hissed at Ali, and leaned into the window, searching the room. And we unconsciously mimicked him, one on either side.

And then, suddenly and shockingly, we saw it. A woman's ghostly face, impossibly drawn, blank and paper-white, right in front of us, just an inch the other side of the glass, its mouth a dark 'O,' hair wild, mad eyes wide – a textbook ghost. And something more – a sense of ancient tragedy, there for a second only and then gone, vanishing into nothing.

"Whoa!" We fell back off our stools, then packed up and shot up the stairs so fast that we embarrassed ourselves. We were shaken, but after a minute Shape was jazzed and wanted to go back down. "We all saw it, didn't we? The manifestation? We should go and take another look."

"No," I said, "we have to get the equipment. We can come back tomorrow night."

"But what if she doesn't reappear?" Ali twisted her rainbow-coloured braids anxiously.

"They're drawn to the life-force of the living," said Shape, suddenly the expert again. "Max is right, we'll come back tomorrow."

We returned home and over the next day we collected what we needed. Infra-red equipment, night-vision digital recorder, barometer, EMF detector, hydrometer, spirit wind chime, motion detector, talcum powder, a decent clock. We'd have liked a thermal imaging scope to find cold spots, but they were too expensive. Shape was impressed.

We arranged to meet at 11:00pm outside Euston station. Ali and I got to carry all the equipment. The rain had died down to a thin, greasy drizzle that made the sodium-yellow pavements slippery. We headed over to the house, and noted that neither of the houses on either side had their lights on, which was a good thing if we were about to take up house-breaking. Luckily, the bad weather had forced the hoodies off the streets.

Shape had brought a crowbar with him, and led the way down into the basement. He pushed one end under the rotting wood of the window sill and the catch popped, that easy, although we knew it would be harder to shut again. He had trouble opening the window, though, because the wood was damp and swollen, but eventually the three of us managed to work it up a little so that we could slither inside.

There was enough ambient light from the street to let us see the room in dim form. We put our bags down and took a look around. The basement had been divided from the rest of the house – the whole building had probably been sliced into flats. There was a rank-smelling galley kitchen still filled with dirty pots. No electricity, something green and reeking in the dead fridge. Further along the corridor we found two bedrooms, one devoid of any furniture, the wallpaper damp and hanging down in swathes. The other had a single bed with a pile of eiderdowns on it, and although I couldn't see much here at the back of the house, it looked like there was something shifting about.

"Rats," said Shape. "Don't go near them."

In the main living room (the one by which we entered) there were a few odd items lying around: a khaki bag full of old toys, some framed photographs of a man in uniform, a box of mildewed newspapers, more photos, some women's clothes.

We set up the equipment. It was cold in here. "Too cold," said Shape. "We're going to have to buy the thermal scope. I need to isolate the low temperature spots."

We arranged the motion detectors (which we had swiped from the college) on either side of the lounge, and set two digital cameras in position. We tied the wind chime to the bulb flex hanging from the ceiling rose. Finally, we spread talcum powder over the floor. Then we popped open a few beers and settled down to wait.

After a while, inevitably, we fell asleep. But it was okay because the motion sensors were alarmed.

The next thing I knew, Shape was shaking me. "What's happening?" I whispered.

"Listen," said Ali.

Faint but clear, a small bell was ringing. I sat up. "Is that the chimes?"

"No, it's coming from further away," Shape whispered back. "A classic sign of spirit arrival."

"I don't know, it's sounds like it's coming from outside. It could even be an office alarm."

"The room's got colder – can't you feel it?"

"Christ, what's that awful smell?"

I looked across to the red digital readout on the clock. Midnight. I tried to see into the thick shadows, but maybe one of the street lights had gone out, because it seemed darker in the room now. I had brown spots swirling in my eyes, removing the distinct edges of the room. Ali was kneeling, straining to see. Shape was slowly rising, moving in a careful way that would not disturb the presence. He reached out and turned on the digital cameras. Then we waited. We waited for what seemed like twenty minutes, straining our ears, but nothing happened.

Ali rose and stretched her back. "Well, that was a waste of –" she began, when something rushed into the room with a banshee shriek, a white-wreathed, hunched apparition with a white screaming face and the wide black 'O' mouth and bony claw arms raised above its head, and all hell broke loose. The thing rushed up to Ali and she screamed and suddenly there was a slash and a shocking red cut had crossed the left side of her face, and Shape was backing up and knocking over one of the digital cameras. And then the apparition screamed something that sounded like words but its voice was so distorted that we couldn't understand, and we were bricking it and just wanted to get out of that awful reeking room. And just as quickly the apparition vanished, and we were on our knees shovelling everything back into bags, and clambering out of the window and gone.

The next day we met in the student bar at St Martin's and ran the camera footage, but the cameras hadn't been pointing in the right direction and all you could see was a few frames showing a blur of white. The soundtrack picked up the creature's voice, though. We played it over and over, filtering it until we could understand. It was saying something that sounded like "Alanafga – terror" again and again, until Shape's shouting drowned it out.

"We need to do some research," said Shape with an air of determination, "and find out what these words mean." Shape had a lunch date arranged at his father's club, so he couldn't do the legwork, which meant that Ali and I had to head up to the London Metropolitan Archive in Clerkenwell to research the history of the house.

The archive's a great place. All the documents of London are kept there. There are medical records and high court rolls and maps showing where German bombs fell, but it's always empty except for a few old dears researching their family history. People don't seem interested in their own surroundings, or maybe they are but they're too busy to ever get around to checking them out. We had to leave all our belongings in the red lockers on the first floor, but then we headed upstairs and started looking up the housing history of the Somerstown area behind Euston, where Phoenix Street was located.

Turned out it was a weird old place. A long history of ghostly sightings in an area that had always been incomplete and on the move. Homes were always being torn down to make way for the railway. Even the newborn and the dead hadn't been allowed to linger in their cots and burial plots as the train tracks advanced over the land. Graveyards and hospitals torn up, the poor routed, Victorian philanthropists always ready to preach to the unemployed, the elderly and infirm, dumping a few moralizing Christian tracts on them before shoving them into workhouses to die.

No wonder the grey streets behind the station now housed a largely immigrant underclass. No gentrification here, no luxury lofts and gated communities for this chaotic backstage area of good old London Town, the part the tourists never saw.

It was Ali who found it in an old newspaper, the story of the jilted bride. Ann Matilda Barbary, due to be married at St Pancras Old Church on July 10th 1856, waited in vain to be collected by her father for the short walk to the wedding service, not knowing that her husband-to-be had been killed in a drunken fight at The Tap Inn, Euston, that very morning. She and her husband were going to live and raise a family in one room. From the picture, it could easily have been the basement room in Phoenix Street.

"And that's why she appears in white," said Shape. "She waits for her groom who'll never come and she screams in pain when she finds out he's been killed. This is dynamite stuff. We need to get better footage, though, if we're going to upload it onto a website."

"I don't want to go back there," said Ali. "There was too much anger in her spirit. It's dangerous." The cut on her face was no more than a scratch, but looked livid and sore.

"Then I'll go with Max," said Shape, "it'll be easier with just the two of us."

The next night was a full moon, and although I had no idea why that would make a difference, Shape suggested it was the best time to witness another manifestation. So we headed for Phoenix Street once more, taking only one digital camera with us this time.

"If we can find out what the creature was trying to communicate," Shape said, "we'll have documentary evidence of a link between this world and the next. We could set up a website and make a fortune." How he intended to do this remained an unexplored subject, but I went along with it.

We climbed down into the basement area and found the window still open, so we climbed inside and set up the camera once more. The moonlight had increased our vision in the musty room, and while we waited for a manifestation I went through the photographs in the one of the boxes. I turned over pictures of a couple married in the nineteen thirties, a man in a WW2 uniform, children, grandchildren – an entire family genesis left to warp and molder. The family name of Morgan kept cropping up in thin handwriting on the backs. Jack, Katie, Sally, Sam, Nick, cousins, sisters, aunts.

"The magnetic lines of the earth are holding her here, trapped at the spot where she died," said Shape. "We have to release this poor woman's spirit and set her soul free. Then we can blog about it."

I could never tell if he was joking when he said things like this. Shape hardly said anything that wasn't intended as irony, so you never quite knew where you stood with him.

I turned over more photographs, some clearly recent. Soldiers messing around with a football in a sharp lunar landscape, except that it was brilliantly floodlit. Mailed from –

"I was raised an atheist, but you know, we could find proof of Heaven, how cool would that be?" said Shape, and suddenly I realized he was just doing this to try and upset his parents again. He was thinking how annoyed they would be if he turned in a project based on proof of spiritualism in his degree show. That was all he really cared about.

I turned over another damp photograph of a young man in a sand-coloured uniform, squinting into harsh sunlight. Flipped it to the back and read, 'Alan Morgan Territorial Army Afghanistan.' *Alanafga – terror.*

"Shape, I think you should see –"

And here she was again, wrapped in white, hurtling into the room, disturbed from her sleep, screaming in panic. "Alan – Alan – my son is in Afga –" but she couldn't pronounce the word.

"Your grandson Alan is in the Territorials," I said. But she couldn't hear, whirling insanely around the room. "Mrs Morgan?" And she was running back to her bed on crippled arthritic legs, half-blind and deaf and crazed with fear.

"Not a ghost," I told Shape, "just an old woman. We're in an old woman's home. I think her grandson was looking after her but he's in Afghanistan now."

"Jesus Christ." Shape slammed the camera shut and grabbed his bag. "Come on, let's get out of here."

"No, can't you see she needs help? Something's happened. For some reason nobody knows she's here. Or if they do, they're not doing anything about it. She's been abandoned. Maybe her son failed to notify the Social Services before he left."

Shape brought his face close to mine. "Who gives a fuck? She's just some old bitch. A waste of time, a fucking waste of time." He grabbed me and pushed me toward the window.

"You're the one who makes a big deal about caring," I shouted at him.

"I don't care about her, she's alive. What good is that?" He climbed from the window and headed back to the street.

I wanted to stay and see that she was all right, but I didn't.

I didn't.

I couldn't call the Social Services either, not without leaving some kind of trace. If they tracked us down we could be arrested. I didn't know what to do. And in hindsight I did the wrong thing, I know that now. Instead of finding a way to leave an anonymous trail to Mrs Morgan's door, I thought I'd help her directly. Every evening on the way home from the college, I stopped at the Indian takeaway in Phoenix Street and bought her a curry in a plastic tray, and left it just inside the basement window, together with a bottle of soda water. I pulled the window down as far as I could to stop the room from getting too cold, and every night when I came down again the tray from the previous visit had been emptied, so I just carried on doing it.

One night, I waited by the window to see if she would appear. After a while she shuffled into the room, still wrapped in the dirty sheets from her bed, and grabbed at the tray. Her bony arms were covered with suppurating sores. She dropped the plastic knife and fork on the floor and ate greedily with her fingers. I could not bear to watch a second longer. I was ashamed and confused by my own inaction.

Then, about a week after I had started bringing the food, the hoodie gang returned to the street and stood in front of me at the gateway to the basement, blocking my path. One of the Indian boys glowered from within his blue shiny track suit. He had huge brown eyes, and looked angry. "You're not going down there with that," he said with soft menace.

"Why not?" I asked, but they remained silent. "Why not?"

Finally one of them spoke up. "It's got nothing to do with you."

"She needs the food, she'll die if she doesn't eat."

"Walk away, man, there's nothing for you. Forget what you saw."

"She's an old woman. What did she do wrong?"

"Not her, the grandson, disrespectin' us, innit."

"What did he do to you?"

"Fuckin' us off, man. Shouldn't be here, should he? Wrong postcode for a white army boy, man. You shouldn't be here neither. Less you wanna get cut." Their fists were in their pockets, but they were obviously carrying knives. I knew she was waiting in the basement room. I knew I was her lifeline. But there was nothing I could do. I could no longer reach her.

I went home and tried to forget, to shut out the sight of her desperate face. I tried not to smell that awful smell. I tried to pretend I had never seen her. I told myself it was nothing to do with me.

Two weeks later I picked up a copy of the local newspaper on the bus, the Camden Journal, and on page

14 I found a small article about her entitled 'Wartime heroine found dead in flat.'

The piece explained that Mrs Kate Morgan had been presented with an award for her outstanding work in a nursing unit of the WRAF in 1945 and had spent a lifetime caring for others. It said that her only living relative, her grandson, had recently been killed by friendly fire in Afghanistan. It went on to say that she had been dead for a week before her body was found. Local boys were being questioned. A woman from Social Services trotted out the usual line, that this was a failure of the system and must never be allowed to happen again.

I left St Martin's. I could no longer sleep. I dreaded the nights. Every time I lay in the dark and closed my eyes, all I saw was her terrified face. I never saw Shape or Ali again. If I'd have run into Shape, I don't know what I would have done. Something bad. Later someone told me he was running his parents' bank.

I was twenty-one when this happened. I am thirty now. The nightmares have lessened, but they never go away.

They say ghosts appear because of an injustice. Mrs Morgan was not a ghost before, but she is now. And all my life, she'll continue to destroy my sleep.

THE ROOM UPSTAIRS

SARAH PINBOROUGH

Sarah Pinborough's horror fiction often grabs you by the throat and doesn't let go until you're battered, bruised and utterly terrified (go and read A Matter of Blood *to see what I mean) but for the story that follows Pinborough instead instils a sense of quiet unease that leads to something that is altogether rather moving. 'The Room Upstairs' is a beautifully haunting tale and one that is bound to follow you into your dreams.*

"THERE'S A BASIN and jug in your room, but you'll find the main facilities at the end of the corridor. Use them as you like, of course, but please adhere to the line marked on the bath in order that we don't run out of hot water. I currently have one other guest, Mr Marshall-Jones, and you'll share the bathroom with him. I'm sure you can work out the logistics of timings between you. I hope that's acceptable."

She walked up the stairs with a precision in her movements, as if the approach to each step had been carefully thought out. Jack had an eye for these things. He was sure that if he studied the carpet closely enough he'd see where it was worn from each of those sensibly-clad feet landing in the same place on each trip she took to the second floor. That would, however, take more light than was currently available from the dim bulbs in the wall sconces, that simply cast shadows around them and would leave Jack with the start of a headache were he to look too hard at any given detail of his new surroundings. She paused ahead of him, a prompt to answer.

"That's perfectly fine, Mrs Argyle. No problem there." He smiled, and she moved on briskly, the lining of her skirt rustling against her tights. "I only take a bath every other day. I'll have a good scrub in the basin on the alternates. We kept clean enough in the army that way. No baths then!"

"Where did you serve?" A slight hitch in her pace and then she rounded the corner and continued her march along the straight of the corridor; a sharpness in the tone. Jack followed her, keeping his small suitcase close so that its hard edges didn't scuff the wallpaper as he turned.

"Egypt. Me and Monty. He got all the credit, though." When she once again didn't return his normally quite winning smile, his eyes dropped to the ring on her finger. Her eyes caught his as they fell.

"My husband was in the RAF. He died."

"I'm sorry."

"Thank you. It's not something I like to talk about."

"I understand that," Jack said. He meant it, too. One thing he was quite happy not to talk about was the war. He was good on detail, but learning something wasn't quite the same as actually having been there, and there had always been plenty of people who were ready to catch him out. He kept his war stories to a minimum. Thankfully, the immediate aftermath was done, and unless you got trapped at last orders in a drunken round, most people were ready to put it all behind them now. Rationing was over, music was picking up the beat in a way he didn't really understand, and the next generation were taking over.

She stopped and pushed open a door. "Here we are. It's quite a pleasant room. You get the sun in the morning." It was certainly brighter than the corridor behind him, and the window in the far wall was high and wide. An iron-framed bed sat centrally against one wall and a chest of drawers and wardrobe stood against the other. A large pewter basin and jug sat, as promised, on a small table under the window. It was basic, but more than adequate. On top of that, the room was cheap and until he had his next touch, he'd need to keep an eye on his wallet.

"If you have the window open in the mornings, the smell of the sea can be quite refreshing," she added softly.

"Thank you. I'll bear that in mind." Jack placed his suitcase on the bed and pulled the netting back. The sea was a glimmer in the evening sky, somewhere beyond several rows of houses, a treasure belonging to the horizon.

"But make sure the windows are shut when you go out." The clipped tone had returned to her voice. "Dinner is at six-thirty and breakfast at seven-thirty. I lock up at ten and would rather you were in before then. If you are going to be later, then please let me know in advance, and I would prefer if it weren't a habit."

Jack nodded his agreement. Her words were slightly sharp, but her manner wasn't. She picked slightly nervously at her hands and he wondered how many other guests she'd recited that speech to. He wondered if by imparting all the information she had to very quickly, she could almost forget he was really here in her home. She wasn't a natural landlady. She lacked the practical briskness that came with the role. He should know, he'd moved around enough.

"You'll barely know I'm here," he said.

She nodded, satisfied. "I'll leave you to settle in, then. You've missed dinner but I'll make you a sandwich and a cup of tea and bring it up." An expression that was the ghost of a smile that might have been half-rested on her face and she turned to leave, closing the door behind her.

Jack sat on the bed and loosened his tie, happy to have a moment to relax. He wasn't getting any younger, and the travelling was starting to take its toll on him. One day he'd have to pick a place and stay, but before that happened he was going to need to get a little nest egg together. He hadn't been lying when he'd told Mrs Argyle that she'd barely notice he was there. It suited his purpose to maintain some kind of distance and that was why he hadn't chosen the room in the house nearer the sea. The woman there asked too many questions. She was curious and friendly. You could come a cropper around someone like that.

As much as he stuck to the same set of lies and had told them so often that he sometimes believed them to be true, the devil, as they say, was in the detail. You couldn't account for someone else's knowledge, and the more you talked, the more likely some small piece of information that they knew would emerge and wouldn't quite fit with the lie. Brows would furrow and even his easy grin – more creased now than it had been in the handsome days of his youth, but still effective – couldn't quite dispel the sudden wariness in the eyes. That was fine, if uncomfortable, if the job was done, but could be awkward if not. Also the last thing a man in his line of work needed was to leave a suspicious landlady behind in the wake of a local robbery.

Still, here he was, in a new town to start a fresh job. He waited for the usual fizz of excitement in the pit of his gut, but there was nothing but a hesitant tremor. That would change when he met up with Arthur later. He hoped it would, at any rate. He was forty-five, not yet old enough to retire, and he needed to shake the sense of malaise that had gripped him since climbing onto the train early that morning. This was what he did, and he was bloody good at it. But there was no point in doing it at all without the thrill. Apart from the money, he reminded himself as he sat on the side of the bed. He needed the money. He lay back and closed his eyes. Everything would work out. It invariably did.

HE WASN'T THE only one who needed the money, Jack concluded, as he emerged from the bathroom later that evening, clean and fresh and ready for a good night's sleep. The house was much too large for one woman to manage alone – he'd peered around the end of his corridor and along with another room, which he concluded must be the other guest's – there was another staircase that led up to a second floor. She wasn't a natural landlady, so he wondered why she'd kept the house on. Surely, it would have suited her better to have sold and moved into something smaller?

He glanced around again at the wallpaper, whose dark mauve colouring did nothing to dispel the gloom that hung heavily between the high ceilings, and the carpets, whose threadbare patches were carefully covered with rugs. Perhaps Mr Argyle, the fearless airman, had left her with too many debts to sell. It would explain the lack of photographs of the man. He'd known widows who'd hidden pictures of their dead husbands in the immediate aftermath of war – his own auntie Jean had done so when Fred had died in the Great War – but nearly ten years had passed since Hitler had been done with; Mrs Argyle's grief must have dulled to a point where any photos would bring about a soft smile rather than a fresh bout of tears.

Back in his room, he pondered on his new landlady. She was different, this one. How old was she? Younger than himself by a year or two, he was sure, although the manner she adopted, distant and cool, combined with her prudish clothes, suggested someone older. He turned the light out and let his mind drift towards sleep. Mildly curious as he was about Mrs Argyle, she could wait for another day, and for now the smell of fresh starch in the sheets and the thick warmth of the blanket was all he wanted to focus on. There was a comfort in a well-made bed and a firm mattress, and he was glad that after a long day, the Argyle bed and breakfast wasn't letting him down in that department. He needed to be sharp for tomorrow. Arthur would be waiting.

HE WOKE WITH a start in the darkness. He sat up, allowing the unfamiliar surroundings to settle into recognisable shadows and then reached for his watch. He squinted as, slowly, the hands formed against the white face – quarter to three. A thud came from above him and he turned his head towards the ceiling. Footsteps paced up and down over his head, floorboards creaking with each stride. He swallowed his irritation. Who the hell was up at this time? Was it the other guest, Mr Marshall-Jones? He'd have a quiet word with him at breakfast. He couldn't afford to be losing sleep. Especially not working with Arthur. He didn't allow for mistakes, and tiredness created mistakes.

The footsteps paused overhead, and the floorboards creaked more slowly this time, the echo of a cautious, surreptitious movement. Jack knew sounds. His ear was trained to listen to the tiniest of clicks over his own racing heart, and this sounded like someone crouching and looking at something on the floor. Eyes looking down as his were looking up. He shivered slightly at the thought, and wondered why it disturbed him so. His heart thumped. The tiniest shift from above mimicked him and then there was silence. Jack remained upright. What was the man doing up there? What was –

The sharp and sudden knocking made him gasp and he reached for the lamp. Knocking on the floor? And so loudly? Surely he couldn't be doing that with his bare knuckles? The noise was too solid for that. How could it pass through the plaster and be anything other than just the hint of a rapping? This was too loud. It was as if it was inside his head.

After a furious few seconds, the knocking stopped. Jack's heart was racing, mainly with anger, but also with a touch of apprehension. Was this Marshall-Jones trying to get him to leave the house? Were they both in the same game? They couldn't be, surely. What were the odds of that? But still, it was the only explanation he could muster. Whoever was upstairs wanted his attention. And he wanted him out.

Jack continued to stare up at the ceiling, but after a few minutes it became clear that the game was over. No more noises assaulted him. He turned the light out and lay back down.

"GOOD TO MEET you. You've done well here," Mr Marshall-Jones said, dabbing away a blob of egg yolk from his thick grey moustache. "Nice place. Always clean." He smiled up at Mrs Argyle as she cleared away their plates. She half-smiled back, as if her body was functioning while her mind was elsewhere. She had pretty eyes, Jack thought. Blue with flecks of violet. He wondered how they looked when she laughed. When she *used* to laugh.

"And she's a good woman," Marshall-Jones added, noting Jack's gaze. "Not a talker, and that's rare enough, but she'll look after you. I've been here a month and I've got no complaints."

Jack looked at the portly middle-aged man in the suit sitting opposite and wondered at his game. He looked perfectly respectable in this three-piece and pocket watch, his stomach starting to stretch the fabric, but you never could judge a book by its cover.

"Did you sleep well?" Jack asked.

"Like a log. But then I always do," Marshall-Jones smiled to himself. "My Marjorie doesn't, though. Says I snore like a train." He leaned in slightly. "She likes when I'm away during the week, I think, just so's she can get a good night's rest herself." Jack watched him for any hint of implied meaning, but there was nothing that was obvious. He pressed a little harder.

"It's just that I heard you during the night. Moving around. It woke me up."

"Me?" Marshall-Jones frowned. "I was out like a light by ten and didn't wake up until six-thirty this morning. Couldn't have been me, old chap," he smiled. "And I'm at the other end of the corridor. Hopefully, even my snoring can't reach you from there." He checked his watch. "Good Lord, I must be going. I'll see you at dinner, no doubt. Nice to have another guest here. I'll be off tomorrow, of course – home for the weekend – but good to see you, all the same."

Jack smiled and nodded and shook his hand. If this was a game, then he couldn't quite figure out what Marshall-Jones's angle was. He watched the other man waddle out of the breakfast room and thought again of the footsteps. He was heavy enough to have made that noise, at any rate.

"Would you like more tea?"

He looked up to see Mrs Argyle standing beside him with the tea pot. Under forty, he decided in that instant, the sunlight coming through the front windows and cutting across her face. Too young for this kind of life.

"No, thank you," he said. "I've got to be off myself in a few minutes." She was turning away when he called her back. "Mr Marshall-Jones. Is he on the second floor?"

There were a slight reddening in her knuckles as her hand tightened around the teapot handle. "No. He's at the other end of the corridor from you. Did his snoring wake you?"

"Yes," Jack said. "It must have done."

They looked at each other for a fraction longer than the situation required, and then Mrs Argyle retreated to the kitchen. He watched her go, his curiosity heightened. She was a queer fish, that was for sure. If Marshall-Jones hadn't been moving around in the night, then it must have been her. He remembered the weight in the creaks of the floorboards and the angry power behind the knocking. Could he imagine her slim body creating those sounds? The image didn't quite fit, but it was always possible. Unless, of course, she had a third guest who was keeping himself hidden. Still, hopefully there wouldn't be any more strange noises waking him up. He'd need his wits about him for work, not mulling over the goings-on in his lodgings. He left her to clear the breakfast room, collected his hat from the hallway and stepped out into the crisp autumn air. He had people to meet.

"ARTHUR SENDS HIS apologies, but he's been held up in London for a few days," Scrubbers said. Scrubbers was a weasly man whose suit didn't quite fit and who was too old for the baggy line of his trouser. His hat was tilted back on his head and he smoked constantly. "But it's all right, Jacko," he added with a wink. "The job's still on."

Jack felt his stomach sink. He'd heard good things about Arthur. He could put together a clean job with good planning. He didn't rush things. He was a thinker. He'd never been caught. All these things might be true, but he wasn't convinced by Scrubber's presence. Why would a man like Arthur send a nobody like that to meet him? Jack wasn't without reputation himself.

"I haven't decided if I'm part of the job yet," Jack said, before taking another large swallow of his half of stout. He wasn't thirsty, but the quicker he finished, the quicker he could get away from the man sitting opposite. He lit a cigarette of his own. "And my name's not Jacko."

"No offence meant," Scrubbers grinned. He had a tooth missing at the side. "It's just the way I am. And as for the job? You'll be part of it. No one says no to Arthur."

Jack smiled. "We'll wait and see then, won't we?"

"Arthur says I'm to ask where you're staying. So he can get in touch when he's back."

"Tell you what," Jack leaned in, "why don't we just say we'll meet here at midday every day? When Arthur's back then he'll know to find me here at that time, won't he?"

Scrubbers let out a short laugh, but there was a hint of nervousness in it. He was out of his depth and he knew it. He wasn't one of Arthur's boys. Jack didn't know who he was, but the real faces wouldn't show themselves without their boss. Scrubbers was just a lackey.

"You're cautious, aren't you?" Scrubbers said. "But if that's how you want it to be…"

"It is." Jack drained his glass and stood up from the table. "So unless you've got anything more for me, I'll be on my way. Oh, and one other thing. As Arthur told me to be here today, I shall let him know my lodging costs for the days until he gets back from London. It can come off the expenses. I'm sure he'll understand."

Scrubbers nodded. "I'll see you tomorrow, then."

"No," Jack shook his head. "I'll come here and have a half alone. The only person I want to see here is Arthur. You and me making small talk isn't on my agenda." Jack knew men like Scrubbers. They attracted trouble and attention. He didn't want either.

Still in his chair, Scrubbers shrank into himself slightly. "If that's how you want it."

"That's how I want it." Jack was pleased with Scrubbers' change in manner. Their exchange would no doubt be reported back to Arthur later, and if he was half the brain Jack had been led to believe, then he'd read between the lines and know that Jack wasn't to be messed with.

HE SPENT THE rest of the day wandering around the town and taking in its various attractions, namely three jewellers and two banks. The job that had brought him here would be one of those five businesses. Studying the fronts, he felt the first frisson of excitement, and was relieved. After the meeting with Scrubbers, he'd started to have a bad feeling about the trip, but now he could see that it might be very much worth his while. The jewellers all catered for the wealthy – no cheap trinkets on show in the display cases – and for many of the pieces there simply had small cards alongside them instructing interested parties to 'enquire for the price.' Jack didn't. Instead, he treated himself to a fish and chip lunch in one of the few fish bars open along the front in October, read the paper, and then went for a long, refreshing walk along the beach.

It was a prettier town than he'd imagined, but then maybe that was just because he'd been in the cities too long; Liverpool last and Birmingham before that – grainy, grey places where both the buildings and the people looked miserable and worn. Here, the air was clear and sharp and his eyes stung with the wind blasting across the salty water. The houses, even those closed up for the winter, glinted pleasantly in the afternoon sun. It was a place where people stayed, he decided. An unusual place for a job, however. Perhaps it was Arthur's home town, but he doubted it. No one stole in their own backyard. Certainly not if you lived in a place like this. People would *know* you. In and out and invisible, that's what they needed, to be doing a job like that here. Catch them quietly unawares. In the summer, when the money was rolling in from those making the most of a Saturday or Sunday on the front, then the banks and the jewellers would be on their guard, but not now in the sleepy run up to Christmas.

As the afternoon slipped into early evening, Jack wound his way through the side streets and headed back towards the house. He walked slowly to allow the wind burn on his cheeks to fade and pulled his overcoat tight. He thought about the town, and Scrubbers, and then Arthur. His money was on one of the jewellers being their target and he was long enough in the tooth to know that he'd probably be right.

HE LET MARSHALL-JONES do most of the talking over their dinner of shepherd's pie and peas followed by a very good apple pie, prompting him with questions when the conversation looked as if it might turn his way. Marshall-Jones didn't notice, and was quite happy to talk about his shoe manufacturing business in Northampton and how he was setting up a factory here to serve the south of England. The meal was good, too, and he found he was mildly surprised. Mrs Argyle didn't look like the kind of woman who savoured her food. That was unusual in itself – now that rationing was finally completely over, most people were indulging a little, if they could afford it. Mrs Argyle had the look of a woman who ate to live, not lived to eat. As he finished the last of the pie, he felt a little sorry for her.

Life offered so very few indulgences, and a good meal was one that was available to all.

He said his good-night to Marshall-Jones and retired to his room, to read for an hour before taking a bath. He kept to the instructed fill line but found it provided adequate water depth to soak for a while and relax. He looked up to the ceiling. There were no footsteps above him now. Hopefully the rest of the night would remain as quiet.

HIS HOPES WERE ignored. He was woken suddenly once again by noises from upstairs, and this time he put his light on straight away, flinching at the sudden brightness, even though in reality the lamp gave out a soft, yellow glow. He checked his watch. Quarter to three. He looked upwards and followed the path of the creaking footsteps. Pacing. Someone was pacing in the room overhead, first up and down, and then round in circles. Just listening to those steps made his heart race. There was an anxiety in their uneven movement. For a moment the feet stopped, and in their place came a low moan. A sob. What was that?

He pushed the covers back and stood up on the mattress, hoping to hear more. Music played so suddenly and loudly that he almost lost his balance. It poured through the ceiling as if the plaster and floorboards were nothing but air. It couldn't be the wireless, not at this time of night, and it was too tinny, too metallic. A music box? A jewellery box? He searched his memory to find a name for the music. 'The Dance of the Sugar Plum Fairy'? That was it. The notes washed over him, eerie as they slowed and stretched, as if someone hadn't wound the key tight enough and, so soon after starting, it was slowing to a stop. The moan came again, and more footsteps creaked this way and that above his head. The music stopped. Something smashed. Jack stared. This was ridiculous. What was going on up there? He climbed down from the bed and reached for his dressing-gown. There was only one way to find out.

The air in the corridor was cool and without his slippers on he could feel the cold floor working its way through the thin carpet and into the soles of his feet. He shivered slightly. He looked to his left, but the end of the corridor and the stairs leading down to the hallway and breakfast room had been swallowed up by the gloomy night. As his eyes adjusted to the darkness, he crept carefully in the other direction, laying his feet heel to toe, spreading the weight evenly and listening out for the hint of a groan from the ceiling and ready to shift his position if necessary. He did this out of habit rather than a fear of getting caught. Or rather, he did it out of the habit of the fear of getting caught.

A clock ticked somewhere against the wall. He passed a small side table that barely pierced the night and then, as he rounded the corner, he heard the music again. Softer this time, as if each note were creeping down the far stairs to meet him. They carried heartache and pain on them, and it hit him in such an unexpected wave that he paused for a second. A sob and a moan followed them down, and as he stood, still and suddenly nervous, in the sleeping house, he was sure a sigh brushed against his cheek. He gritted his teeth. He was behaving like a child. He wasn't scared of the dark – in his line of work, the darkness was often his ally – but there was something about the sounds coming from upstairs that set him on edge. They were sounds that didn't exist in daylight. Hidden noises. The music grew louder and he wasn't sure if it was just his imagination, but the notes seemed to have lost some of their softness, now slightly off-key and jagged and angry.

He moved forward, passing a door, from behind which came the far more ordinary sounds of grunts and loud, rattling snores. Marshall-Jones's room. How could the man sleep through the music and sobbing that were so loud in this corridor? Was he just so used to his own nocturnal disturbances that he didn't notice any others? A burglar's dream client. Not that Jack had been a burglar for a lot of years now. He'd started that way, but creeping around through other people's homes had left him feeling like a ghost, and as soon as he could, he'd developed his skills and climbed the ladder.

A *ghost*.

He shook away the sudden superstition that gripped him as another aching sob made the house shiver. Was that a man? Or a woman? Surely it had to be Mrs Argyle, but there was something in the tone that was wrong. It was too deep, too resonant to have come from her. It was followed by a whisper. Words that couldn't quite be heard, spoken in a rush. How could a whisper be loud enough to hear from a floor below? Jack frowned and began the climb up to the second floor. There must be a flaw in the house. A hole in the floorboards that the sound was carrying through. He gripped the banister.

These stairs were narrower than the others, only space for one person at a time, and the temperature dropped further as he crossed the half-way point. It was a clear October night outside and the crisp coldness was finding its way through the brickwork and into the highest floor of the house.

Had this once been an attic, Jack wondered, as he felt his way to the top and then along the banister as the ground levelled out. The ceiling was lower, but he couldn't tell in the dark whether it pointed into the eaves. A shaded bulb hung over head and there was still carpet beneath his bare feet. It felt slightly thicker than that below – less worn, less used. Was this a forgotten place, high in the house?

Closer to the source of the strange noises as he was, he was surprised to find them quieter than they had been only moments before outside Marshall-Jones's door. Footsteps creaked and he froze again. This place wasn't forgotten by everyone. Someone was up here other than him. The music box once again ground to a halt, and he searched in the blackness for the outline of a door. If there was someone inside then surely they would have put a light on? A candle or lamp at least. Who would sit up here alone in the dark?

He knocked against the wood. "Mrs Argyle?" he said softly. "Are you all right in there?" He heard his own breath in his ears, and his heart pounding against his ribs, but the room had fallen silent. He knocked again and pressed his ear to the cold wood. Silence. He wondered if she was on the other side, mirroring his actions – two strangers in the dark with only the wood separating them. He twisted the handle. The door was locked. He knocked again, slightly harder this time, and took a step back. Silence. He shivered in the cold. He was too tired for these games. Whoever was inside wouldn't come out while he was there. He waited a few moments, though, before turning and finding his way back to the warmth of his bedroom, where he quickly fell asleep. The room upstairs remained quiet.

*   *   *

HE STAYED FOR a second cup of tea in the breakfast room the next morning. Marshall-Jones had blustered through breakfast and had looked quite bemused when Jack had asked him if he ever heard anything in the night, strange noises coming from upstairs for example. "Not at all," he'd said. "That's what I like about this place. So much more peaceful than some other boarding houses. No one coming and going late at night. A chap can get a decent night's rest." He'd winked then. "Sure you weren't dreaming, old fella?" Jack had laughed and said he must have been, but his eyes had watched Mrs Argyle as she carried and fetched their plates and cups.

She was a pretty woman, he concluded. There were pale shadows under her eyes, but not the dark circles he would expect to see if she were awake and pacing and doing whatever she did in the room upstairs all night. Perhaps it was pancake make-up covering them up. Women could do all sorts, couldn't they? And women had never been his field. He liked them, and he had his dalliances here and there, but nothing lasting and always with the kind of women who knew that he wouldn't stay. The kind that drank their pain and who carried the knocks that life had thrown at them in the edge of their over-loud laughter. The kind that didn't make him want to stay any longer than the duration of the job. His sadness he could almost cope with – it was their bitterness that was too much.

Mrs Agyle was different. What pain was she hiding, he wondered? How much had she loved her dead husband to drift in this vague nothingness she occupied? It was there in every step and gesture. Mrs Argyle wasn't living, she was simply existing and waiting for her clock to run down and finally cease ticking out this exhausting life. When she looked at him, it was as if he wasn't there at all. Perhaps he wasn't. Perhaps he, too, was merely travelling around until the movement stopped, leaving no significant trace of himself on another human being. But he thought he would still like for her to look at him one day and really *see* him.

She refilled his cup from the pot. "It should be fine. If you'd like fresh, just say."

"It's fine, thank you." He hesitated for a moment before continuing. "Are you all right, Mrs Argyle?"

"Yes, thank you." Her empty blue eyes looked through him. "Why do you ask?"

"It's just that I think I heard you. Last night?" A tight line of confusion ran across her brow. "Moving around in the room upstairs?" *Sobbing. Playing music. Whispering.*

She paused, and he was sure he saw something, some hint of real life, flicker in her eyes. "You must be mistaken," she said eventually, her words falling soft as autumn leaves. "That room is empty. I never go up there."

HE WATCHED HER leave the house from his position on the corner. It was half past nine. He had plenty of time before he had to be at The Red Lion and would only be back in the house for a short while. It had come as no surprise that Mrs Argyle had headed out with her shopping basket first thing. He imagined she was a creature of routine, and why would any practical woman leave fetching the groceries until later in the day, by which time the best might have gone? He wondered what she did with the rest of her days until Mr Marshall-Jones or himself or any of the other guests that had filled her too-large house got home. Did she endlessly scrub floors and polish and change sheets, or did she just sit and stare into nothingness until the inevitable round of cooking and washing could no longer be ignored? Did she go and lock herself in the upstairs room and cry? He envied a husband who could inspire such emptiness in a woman so long after he'd died.

As with the tiredness he'd felt on the train journey to this new job, he felt his own clock ticking loudly more and more these days. Was this all there was for him now? The thrill of the crime? The prospect of gaol? Perhaps he should have lodged with one of the chattier landladies and taken his chances. He didn't have Marshall-Jones's natural bluster. He was a chameleon – he adapted to fit in with those around him, his rogueish charm hiding a calculating mind and an unused heart.

He let himself into the house, pleased to get out of the cold air, and closed the door behind in. Around him, there was the kind of stillness that very few people understood. An invaded quiet that came from being an uninvited stranger in someone else's empty home. He moved quickly, ignoring the large clock that ticked angrily at him. He wanted to know more about Mrs Argyle. He needed to understand her night-time activities.

He moved quickly through the downstairs rooms, carefully pulling open drawers and cupboards and examining the contents. The usual paperwork, bills and bank statements. He didn't look at the figures. He had no interest in that. When he found it, he supposed that at one time her bedroom had been a drawing room of some sort, lying beyond the main sitting room and near to the kitchen and the downstairs bathroom. There was a small dressing-table and a wardrobe and precisely made bed. He looked under it. Nothing. He searched her drawers with precision and the calm professionalism he had employed when he'd started out in this business so many years ago. He felt no titillation at the feel of her underwear in his hands as he moved it this way and that on his hunt. It was just clothing and it was in his way.

He found nothing. Not a single photograph or letter from her dead husband. No snaps of their wedding day. No man's wedding band to match hers. He stared out of the window and into the garden beyond. It was overgrown, even for this time of year. The grass was too long, still left uncut from the summer, and somewhere in the distance he caught sight of a gnome with a fishing rod peering through the blades at him. The unkempt nature of the garden was at odds with the neatness of the house. He was sure that come spring time she would get a man in to spruce it up in case any guest wished to sit outside on a warm evening in summer, but it still struck him as odd that she had let it get into a state of mild disarray. September had been a pleasant month. Hadn't she wanted to sit outside with a book in the warm? Did she even read? There was a full bookshelf in the sitting room, but he had no way of knowing whether they were for her pleasure or the guests'. There was very little of *her* in the house at all. He checked his watch. Any further investigations would have to wait until later.

* * *

ARTHUR DIDN'T SHOW up in the Red Lion at midday, not that Jack was expecting him. If he'd been likely to have been back, then Scrubbers would have said so. Jack sipped two halves of stout and browsed through both the local and national papers, fully aware that Scrubbers had been standing on the other side of the road from the pub for at least ten minutes trying to check if Jack had showed up himself. In the end, he felt sorry for the little weasel and stood up and stretched right in front of the window. Scrubbers had the good sense to duck behind the telephone box he'd been using for cover, and then a few moments later he scurried off.

When he was done in the pub, he found he felt no urge to watch the comings and goings of the jewellery shops, but once again walked along the beach instead. Work could wait until Arthur had arrived and he was on the official payroll. For now, he would treat these few days as a holiday and fill his time with whatever people did when they went to the seaside at the cusp of winter. Given that most of the entertainments were closed, a long walk along the beach was going to have to suffice. As he walked, he found himself thinking of Mrs Argyle's underwear. This time, there was no professionalism in his thoughts, and to fight them he forced himself to walk an extra mile up along the cliff tops before turning back. He hoped the house would remain silent that night. He hoped that would stop the image of Mrs Argyle rising up in his head so often. He hoped that Arthur would be there the next day and he could distract himself with work.

THE HOUSE WAS not quiet that night, but Jack refused to get out of bed and look. He buried himself under the covers as if he was a child and squeezed his eyes shut. The footsteps turned to a loud angry stamping that shook the mattress so hard he was sure he would fall out. Still, he refused to open his eyes. He would not be drawn any further into Mrs Argyle's mysteries. He would not. He would not.

The stamping finally stopped, the tantrum over, and he was just about to let out a sigh of quiet relief when a warm, wet breath filled his ear with an aching sob that whispered at him, too fast for him to catch the words. He sat bolt upright, gasping with fear and swiped at his face, as if he could brush away the spectral mouth. His room was empty apart from him. The house was once again still and silent as if nothing untoward had occurred. Jack's heart thumped loudly in his chest and his face burned in the cool air. He sat upright for ten long minutes, listening out for something strange. Nothing.

He lay back down and stared at the ceiling. Maybe Marshall-Jones was right. Maybe he was just suffering from some kind of night terror. That voice, that awful sobbing, had been in the room with him. It had been under his covers and touching him. He listened to the sounds of the house, which groaned occasionally like a ship at sea, but produced nothing more untoward. Marshall-Jones had gone home to his wife for the weekend, and Jack realised with a creeping dread that there was no one but himself on the this floor. His heart finally slowed to a regular pace, but when he eventually fell asleep again, it was a fitful rest punctuated with dreams of terrible things just out of sight.

* * *

ARTHUR DIDN'T SHOW up the next day either, and the pub was filled with men enjoying a weekend lunchtime drink, checking the racing papers and discussing tips under a thick cloud of cigarette smoke. They looked happy, although Jack couldn't quite figure out how they could be. Most of them would have fought in the war, he decided, taking in the lines and wrinkles on the laughing faces around him. How could they go from that back to this mundane existence of a weekly routine that was invariably the same?

Work, wife, pub. Work, wife, pub.

His own life might be unanchored, but at least there was always the hope that something exciting might come his way. The next job might turn out to be the 'big one.' The retirement job. The one that would provide the fast car, the endless women and the nice pad. What he'd do then, he wasn't sure. Another job probably, but at least it would be his choice.

He looked again at the crowd of strangers around him and wondered when he'd become so maudlin. Was it since he'd arrived at Mrs Argyle's, or had it been creeping up on him through the last few months? It was hard to say, but he was sure lack of sleep and the strange events in the night were taking their toll. Outside, grey rain streaked heavy against the window and he decided to give his walk along the beach a miss. Instead, he headed back to the house and settled into the armchair beside the fire with one of the books from the shelf. Mrs Argyle went out for an hour or so, and then, when she returned, headed straight for the kitchen and started preparing dinner.

At some point, warmed by the crackling flames, Jack dozed off, woken only when the landlady brought him a cup of tea and a slice of cake. He thanked her blearily, and took the tray while she busied herself adding more coal to the blaze.

"Winter's nearly here, I think," she said, in a tone that said she cared neither one way nor the other about the weather. ·

"I think you might be right," he said, "but it's nice and toasty in here." He added his trademark grin. She didn't look up. "If you don't mind me asking," he said, before sipping his tea, "why haven't you sold this house and moved somewhere smaller? It's very large for one person, isn't it? Surely you'd rather not be taking strangers into your home. Pleasant as we are, of course." He smiled again. This time she did look up.

"I can't leave the house," she said. There was a tremor of *something* under her words. Was it fear? "I'd have to take everything with me. I'd have to start again." She got to her feet. "I can't leave the house," she repeated softly, before turning and walking with her precisely even steps back out towards the kitchen. Jack watched her go. What a strange response. He barely saw her for the rest of the day, and when she brought his dinner to the table, she wouldn't meet his eye. He offered his apology for perhaps being too personal, and she'd accepted it with a slight nod, but no further conversation.

It was, however, he concluded when he had bathed and settled into his room for the night, perhaps the closest he'd seen her to having an emotional response to anything, other than the slight twitch of her mouth when she'd first mentioned her husband. He thought again about the feel of her underwear, soft in his fingers. Would her skin feel like that, he wondered, so different to the rough women he'd become used to over the years? It was a different, restless sleep he fell into, plagued with different, hotter dreams, but he woke with a start, just as he had all the other nights. He found it was no longer unexpected.

He didn't allow time for fear to grip him, or for the unnatural sounds (because even he could no longer deny that there was something very *wrong* about them) to play out their angry repertoire, but instead pushed back the covers and stormed out into the corridor and up to the top of the house. He banged on the door, no gentle knocking this time.

"Mrs Argyle? Mrs Argyle? Whatever it is you're doing in there, can you bloody well stop it!" His voice was loud, and it felt good to be combating the noise from within with some of his own. "Stop your bloody crying or come out and talk to me!" Inside, something smashed against a wall and the door shook violently. Jack jumped backwards. "Jesus Christ! Jesus bloody Christ!"

"Mr Hasting?" the soft voice called up the stairs. "Are you all right?"

He spun around as the light on the first floor came on, stretching up towards him. His heart thumped.

"What are you shouting for? Is it a bad dream?"

Jack crept down the stairs and found her standing outside his room in her dressing gown, the cord tied tight around her slim middle. She didn't eat enough, he decided, and with her hair down around her shoulders he could see that she really was a beauty. A rare, hidden beauty. He decided all this in an unconscious instant, storming towards her.

Her eyes widened. "What were you doing up there?"

"Trying to get whoever is in there to shut up!"

She flinched slightly. "I don't know what you're talking –"

"– whoever you've rented that room to is making an infernal racket. Every night. Footsteps. Crying. Breaking things. And that bloody music box going round and round..."

"Stop it," she said suddenly. "Stop it. That room is empty. There's no one up there." She spat the words out at him. "Don't go up there again, or I will ask you to leave."

The sudden fire in her startled him. "I don't care who you've got up there. I would simply like to have a decent night's sleep without being woken at quarter to three every night. I don't think that's too much to ask."

"There's no one up there," she repeated, before turning her stiff back on him and returning downstairs. When she reached the bottom she turned the lights off and left him in the gloom of the corridor.

No one up there? He looked back at the stairs. Something was up there, of that he was not mistaken. Could an animal have got in through the roof somehow and got stuck? No, he decided, as he crawled back under the covers. That wouldn't make sense. They were human footsteps he was hearing, heavy but human. As was the whispering and the sobbing.

He didn't like to think about the whisper that had damply teased his ear under the covers the previous night. Thinking about that would lead to thoughts he didn't wish to have. *Ghosts*. Spirits. Something *other*. He hadn't believed in those when he'd been a child, and he wasn't going to start now. But still, he shivered slightly and hesitated before turning out his light, the chill this time in his bones and soul rather than the air around him. He was going to have to get to the bottom of this. For the sake of his own sanity if nothing else. The night crept round to dawn. He drifted into a half-sleep and dreamed of someone whispering "help me," damp and wet, into his ear.

JACK SLEPT THROUGH breakfast, but found a note in the hallway telling him to help himself to tea and toast from the kitchen if she was still out when he got up. He made tea, but didn't bother with food. All the nocturnal activity had killed his appetite and he had to admit he'd been slightly nervous at the prospect of facing Mrs Argyle after their meeting outside his room. Would she have just acted as if the whole thing hadn't happened?

She was still out when he finally left to walk down to The Red Lion. The heavy rain of the previous day had faded to a fine mist and the temperature had risen slightly, creating a grey fog from which people emerged liked shades and were past each other before eyes could meet. The town was quieter too, and when the church bells sounded out the end of the morning service, Jack shivered at their eerie tones.

The door had only just been unlocked when he arrived at the pub, but he wasn't the first inside, and that cheered his mood. The lights were bright and the landlord grinned from behind the cigarette clamped between his teeth as he poured him out a pint. Jack took it to a table with the paper and sat and watched as the bar slowly filled with men, a couple with women on their arms, dressed in their Sunday best. The women's laughter carried over the men's and as he watched their red lips and tilted necks, he remembered all the women in all the towns from all the jobs. Mrs Argyle was a world apart from them. Once again, the soft feel of her underwear returned to his mind. Mrs Argyle and the room upstairs. They seemed to fill his thoughts. He wondered if perhaps he was going slightly mad. He ordered another pint. It was Sunday, after all.

"I TOLD YOU not to come here," Jack said when he returned to his table to find Scrubbers standing beside it. "Is your memory that short?"

"I've got a message, that's all," Scrubbers said. There was no aggression in his voice, just an edge of disgruntlement. He was a dog who was used to being whipped. He put his umbrella against the wall. "It's Arthur. He's called. He'll be back tonight. He'll meet you here tomorrow."

"Good," Jack said, although he was surprised to find he didn't care much either way. "This isn't really holiday weather."

Scrubbers snickered slightly at that. Jack smiled back. His charming, easy, roguish grin. He imagined Arthur had one similar. "So leave your umbrella. I fancy a walk on the beach." Scrubbers wilted slightly. For a moment Jack thought he might actually fight back, but instead his thin shoulders slumped forward in his jacket. He'd clearly been told to keep the locksmith happy.

"All right. But bring it back tomorrow. My Jean will wonder where it's gone."

As he watched Scrubbers run down the road with his collar up and head down against the increasing rain, Jack wondered why he'd done it. He had a good overcoat. He hadn't even thought about going for a walk in this weather. Still, he had the umbrella now, and he couldn't sit on his own in the same pub all day. Not without drawing attention to himself, and he didn't need that, the day before the job started. A long walk in the fresh air might do him good. If he got tired enough, he might sleep all night even if the house fell down around his ears.

THE BEACH WAS empty and the sea rolled angrily in the distance as it slowly made its way back to shore. Overhead seagulls cried to each other as they wheeled this way and that in the mist. The sound ached with loneliness and even in the brisk wind, he was sure he could hear the echo of "help me" that had plagued his dreams.

MRS ARGYLE DIDN'T speak when she served his supper, and when he glanced up, Jack saw red rims around her eyes. Was that his fault? Had his actions in the night upset her so much? After hours of walking, he had been famished, but now his stomach rolled slightly as he forced himself to eat his pie and vegetables, not wanting to upset her further by leaving a full plate. Although he normally avoided interaction with other guests, he found he wished for Marshall-Jones's irrepressible chatter. At least the other man would be back the next day. Each with their secrets, he and Mrs Argyle were like drifting ghosts in the house together. Talking but never really speaking, and now not talking at all.

Why was she so closed? What was she hiding? What was going on in the room upstairs? He was a good judge of people, he had to be in his game, and she wasn't a natural liar. The air of empty sadness that hung around her lacked the energy for deception. It was almost as if she had separated the lie from herself. And she was lying to him. If not, then why hadn't she just unlocked the room and shown him there was nothing inside? That was all it would take.

He thanked her quietly as she took his plate away and then retreated to his room to read. His mind kept wandering from the thin story, and he wished he'd bought a wireless to break the monotony, but he found that once he'd laid down, the long walk and sleepless nights took hold and he fell asleep, fully dressed, on top of the covers, by eight-thirty.

THE MUSIC WAS louder than it had ever been, and as he woke his hands went straight to cover his ears. The notes turned to wet sobs as the now familiar footsteps creaked over his head. He turned the light on and looked at his watch, even though he knew what the time would be. Quarter to three. He pushed the covers back. His heart thumped. Enough was enough. Something smashed against a wall. For a moment there was silence and then the ceiling shook as the knocking started, and over and under it all was the terrible sobbing.

Jack had his suitcase open and his tools out within minutes. This had to end. Sod showing his hand. Sod everything. He could get into the room, see what the hell was going on in there and be gone before Mrs Argyle had even woken up. Even with the racket upstairs, he felt a moment of regret at the thought. But this could not go on. Something had to be done.

Out in the dark corridor, he made his way up the stairs. The sobbing and whispering seemed more distant, as if it were luring him onwards, and he fought his fear of it and took the steps two at a time. In the grip of the night and alone in the dark, he could no longer deny the possibility of the supernatural at work, and his insides trembled. But his curiosity was stronger than his fear. At the door, closing his mind from the terrible sounds that poured through the fibres of the wood, he crouched and set to work, letting his fingers feel for the click of the lock. It was a ten second job that he could do in his sleep, but with his hands trembling, it took several attempts before he finally felt it give. The noise on the other side fell silent.

Jack stared at the door. His mouth dried. Now that he could, he wasn't sure that he really wanted to see inside the room at all. His hand, sweating in the palm, reached forward and twisted the handle.

"Mr Hasting?" The light in the corridor below came on. He wasn't the only one awake in the house. He stared at the door. This was his last point of return. He could go downstairs and pretend that the door up here was locked and then vanish in the morning. Or he could go in. Go in and *see*. He didn't answer her call. Instead, he turned the handle and pushed the door open.

HE ONLY SAW her for an instant. She was vague, and almost transparent, standing in the middle of the room, sobbing. Her hair was longer and fuller, hanging down around her shoulders and dripping wet. Her soaking nightdress clung to her body, outlining each curve and line of her. On the floor, the music box was smashed.

For the briefest moment, their eyes met and then she was gone, rushing past him and out through the door. He smelled dampness and moss, stagnant water in her wake, and then the pain hit him. Like white lightning in his heart. A terrible, terrible loss.

On the floor below, Mrs Argyle cried out suddenly and then the house fell silent again.

Jack flicked on the light and he *saw*.

On the dresser were several framed photographs. A much younger Mrs Argyle smiling with a handsome man in uniform beside her. Wedding photos. His hand paused as he moved to the next. Mrs Argyle holding a baby, smiling with obviously bursting joy at the camera. In the wardrobe he found clothes, a man's and a child's. A little girl. Small shoes, small skirt. He was no judge of these things, but he guessed the owner at no more than six or seven.

He looked around him. A doll lay on the bed, but boxes lined the walls, stacked high. Two lifetimes were neatly packed away and stored up here. His heart pounded. What had she done? What had he seen rushing out of here? He sat on the bed and listened to the crying coming from below. She cried for a very long time.

IT WAS NEARLY dawn when he heard her coming up the stairs. She said nothing until she'd sat on the bed beside him, her cheeks raw from tears and her hands trembling. There was life back in her eyes, though. It was a terrible, aching life, but it was there.

"He didn't die in the war," she said, eventually. "He came home to us. Me and Millie." Her voice was thick with snot and she wiped her nose with the back of her hand. "He'd changed, though. He didn't speak much. He kept saying he'd seen things. Terrible things. I just wanted to make things better. Like they were."

"What happened?" Jack asked.

"I don't know." Fresh tears filled her eyes. "I woke up early one morning and he wasn't in bed. I knew..." – her eyes narrowed in the memory – "...just *knew*, then, that something was wrong. I could hear Millie's music box playing. It was slowing down. I went to her room and she wasn't there." She paused for a long time, and Jack could hear his heart beating loud. Maybe it was hers. Maybe it was both of theirs. "I found them in the pond. He'd carried my sleeping baby to the water and drowned her. There was an empty bottle of Lysol on the grass and the doctors say he drank it. They said it would have been a very painful way to go. I tried to pull my baby out. But she was gone."

Jack said nothing. There was nothing he could say.

"He must have hated me very much, I suppose. To have done such a thing. To have left me and taken Millie with him. I locked it all up here. Out of the way." She looked at him, and he thought that her nearly-purple eyes had never looked so beautiful. "And now you've let it out. And I'm not sure I can bear it."

Jack put his arm around her shoulders. They sat like that until the morning poured in through the window and she had cried all she could for now.

"I'm a thief," he said, finally. "I break into places and help people steal things. Money and jewels, mainly." Speaking the words aloud was like a boulder rolling from his back. No more locked away secrets. He felt her head move slightly against his chest.

"Really?" she asked, her voice still thick with tears.

"Yes."

"What was the last thing you stole?"

He thought about that for a moment. He thought about Arthur, who would be waiting for him in the Red Lion at midday. He thought about Scrubbers. He thought about all those trains and journeys and inquisitive landladies. He thought about the warm feel of Mrs Argyle leaning into him.

"An umbrella," he said eventually. There was the slightest hitch of a laugh from the broken woman beside him. Only the ghost of a laugh, but he hoped that soon, he'd be able to let that out of its locked room too.

VILLANOVA

PAUL MELOY

The story that follows is genuinely one of the most frightening I have read in a long time. Paul draws you in with characters that are utterly convincing and beautifully realised, before hitting you with a conclusion that will leave you winded. Read this and find out why I think Paul is one of the best writers currently working in genre fiction.

i

BY THE TIME they arrived at the campsite it was dusk. They had been driving all day on foreign roads, and they were cramped and irritable. Ken had misjudged the distance from Calais to La Tranche-sur-Mer; what he'd estimated to be a four or five hour drive through picturesque French countryside incorporating a couple of comfort breaks along the way had turned into a ten hour slog along undistinguished motorways in heavy traffic.

To compound the experience, an inexplicable satellite navigation error had led them off the toll road and on a detour through a town at rush hour with only about a hundred and fifty miles remaining on their journey.

The name of the town mocked Ken: *Angers*. He knew the pronunciation would soften the word but nothing could be done to soften his mood as he cursed and sweltered through jammed and unfamiliar boulevards. He had to make a U-turn but had no idea of the legality of such a manoeuvre. The satnav remained mute on the subject. Finally he summoned his resolve and swung the car around at some traffic lights; no indignant horns blared, so he assumed he'd got away with it.

Finally back on the motorway, Ken had put his foot down and, despite protestations from Katie and Holly, had finished the journey in one go. He refused to stop again and lose any more time. They would have to hold it in.

Holly was almost in tears as Ken swung the car into the campsite. He stopped at a barrier and waited. To the right was a single storey building designated *Reception*. Next to that was a clubhouse. Ken could see the rapid fluttering of lights on a fruit machine. And behind that was a low concrete wall which appeared to encompass the pool. Just visible above the wall Ken could see the bright amber display of an L.E.D indicating the temperature of the water, the date and the time.

"Look at the bloody time," said Ken. "Where is everyone?"

There appeared to be no one about. The barrier remained down. Ken opened his door and stepped out. The ground was dusty and Ken could feel the heat rising up from it through the thin fabric soles of his holiday espadrilles.

More doors opened, and then slammed. He turned to see Katie and Holly hobbling away across the road towards a toilet block. Ken opened his mouth to say something, and then closed it again. He watched them, his face expressionless, and then resumed looking about the campsite.

Further to the right, a short flight of wide wooden steps led up to a glass-fronted chalet. There were notice boards outside and a desk visible inside piled up with glossy flyers. Ken wandered over. One of the notice boards was pinned with timetables for various local amenities: fresh bread was delivered at 08:00 every morning. There was a market in town every Tuesday and Saturday (well, they'd missed *that* for today, Ken thought with a fair bit of ill will), and the Super-U was open every day from 08:00.

Ken went up the steps and slid open the glass door which gave entrance to the chalet. Inside were more leaflets on wire racks and sliding cupboards full of communal toys, board games and packs of cards.

Ken was about to have a look in the desk drawers when a voice said, "Hi! Just arrived, have you?"

Ken started and looked up. A young man was standing on the top step, grinning at him. He was wearing a light blue tee-shirt adorned with the *CampEuro* logo, a pair of knee-length brown linen shorts and flip-flops. He had short, slicked-back hair, large prominent ears and bad skin. Ken stepped around the desk, and as he did so noticed two quite recent-looking burns on the boy's forearms.

The boy must have seen Ken's expression. He held his arms out in front of him, slender wrists turned outwards to better display the wounds. "Accident with one of the barbecues," he said, still grinning. "Got a bit carried away with the liquid fire-lighter. Sorry if it alarms you, but I thought they might heal up better if I got a bit of sun to them. My boss would have me wear long sleeves but they rub, you know."

Ken pursed his lips. "Looks nasty," he said. Should he tell the boy he was a doctor? No, probably not. Ken got a strange sense from just looking at the boy that there was something a bit *needy* about him. He'd had dealings with people who liked to display their injuries. Borderline personality disorders, most of them.

"You're English," Ken observed. Then he added, "Obviously."

The boy nodded. "Yep. We're all English here. Me and the girls. I'm in charge this week, so if there's anything you want, that's cool. I'm Steven, by the way."

Ken looked out across to where his car still sat behind the barrier. "Well, Steven, you could start by letting us in."

"Oh, right. Cool." Steven said. He turned and skipped down the steps. Ken followed, and noticed another burn, about the size of a coffee-cup ring, livid on Steven's right calf. Ken made a mental note to increase his vigilance around the complimentary barbecue set.

Steven produced a thin electronic key from the pocket of his shorts and passed it across the face of a small black box attached to the housing of the barrier. The barrier lifted, shuddering through its elevation with an odd, slow crackling sound, loud in the warm twilight air, and for some reason it made Ken think of hot fat popping on a griddle.

"These must be yours," Steven said.

Ken looked up to see Katie and Holly returning to the car. "Yes," he said. "They're mine. Come on, girls, jump in."

Katie scowled, but Holly, brightened by her evacuations, said, "Hi, have you got *Boggle*?"

Both Ken and Steven appeared to be at a loss for a moment, and then Holly said, "The game? You know? The game *Boggle*? You've got lots of games in that hut. We saw them on the way over to the loos."

Steven laughed and glanced at Ken. "Hah, yes. Of course. I don't know. Maybe. We've definitely got Monopoly!"

Both girls screwed up their faces.

"And Scrabble. Probably."

I hope you're not running the Kids Club, thought Ken. "Let's sort things like that out in the morning," he said. "I want to get unpacked."

"Yes," said Steven. "Let's get you up to your holiday home and show you what's what. Follow me."

Ken watched Steven go around the side of the Information chalet. He emerged shortly, wobbling on an ancient-looking bicycle, waved and indicated a dirt road that forked right and curved away behind the pool. Ken climbed back into the Audi and started the ignition. Holly was leaning forward, her head between the front seats. "Who's that?" she asked.

"He's one of the couriers," replied Ken.

"A what?"

"A member of staff, Holly. His name's Steven."

"Oh. He's a bit of a creeeepo." She said, and Katie spluttered a laugh from the seat behind Ken.

"Don't talk about people like that, Holly," Ken said, trying to sound stern. He then ended up just sounding lame when he added, "We're on holiday." He pulled away and followed the boy on the unsteady bike beneath a thick canopy of trees overhanging the track.

Hidden behind high partitioning bushes and positioned well back on their individual lots, looming like shanties in dim and dusky arbours, were rows of static mobile homes, each with their own wooden veranda and barbecue pit. A few lights burned in the windows, but nobody seemed to be about.

Ken squinted through the windscreen. In the gathering darkness it was getting difficult to see the boy on the bicycle; somehow he kept ahead of the light thrown from the Audi's headlamps and appeared as an intermittent flicker in the road, weaving from one verge to another. Ken wound his window down. It was getting humid. He could see midges fuming around the muted bulbs in the intermittent streetlamps set back on some of the lots.

After another hundred yards, Steven stopped on a corner and indicated a plot to his left. He climbed off the bike and leaned it against the veranda.

Ken swung the Audi off the track and killed the engine. He got out and went over to the courier. Holly and Katie clambered out of the back of the car and joined them.

"Home for the next week," Steven said. If he was smiling as he said it, the expression was lost in the shadow that fell across his face as he tipped his head to peer down at what his hand was doing in his shorts. "Ah, here you go," he said, and produced a yale key on a large red plastic key ring with the *CampEuro* logo embossed on both sides and: Villanova 48 – *Adrienne*.

Ken took the proffered key and went up the plank steps leading to the area of decking which abutted half the length of the mobile home. The door was of a cheap-looking UPVC variety, windowless and scuffed. He tried the key in the lock beneath the white plastic handle.

"We're in," he said. He pushed the door open and

ushered the girls through. There was a light switch on the wall opposite and he reached across the narrow hallway and flicked it on. A low light came on above his head, which did little but illuminate a door to his right and part of a tiny galley kitchen to his left.

"Get some lights on, Holly. Katie – kettle, please. Let's have drinks and settle in." Ken was about to go back to the car and start unpacking, but as he turned, Steven was standing in the doorway blocking him. He was blackened by shadow and for a second, Ken could smell burning. He jumped and the back of his head knocked against the bulb in the low ceiling. He ducked in reflex and where he had been blocking the light, it was now cast back across the young man standing in the doorway, revealing a concerned expression.

"I think you've burned your hair," Steven said. "Against that bulb." Ken reached up and patted the top of his head. Difficult to tell, but maybe there *were* a few crinkled hairs up there, wizened by proximity to the bare bulb.

Ken shrugged and felt himself grin. The poor lad looked utterly bemused. "I'll live," he said. "Excuse me, Steven, I need to go out to the car."

Steven didn't step aside; instead, he went past Ken and moved further into the heart of the mobile home, where the girls were clumping about.

A lamp came on as Ken crossed the veranda and made his way back down the steps. He opened the boot and lifted out a large plastic picnic box. As he turned to go back up the steps another light came on, illuminating the window at the far end of the mobile home, probably one of the bedrooms. That kettle better be on, he thought, and trudged back up to the open door.

He put the picnic box on the tiny narrow work surface next to the cooker. There was a metal coffee pot on the stove and a kettle with a whistle. He lifted the kettle; it was cold and empty.

"Katie!" Ken snapped. "I asked you to boil the kettle."

There was no reply. Then he heard a giggle. It was coming from his right, past the shower room. Ken replaced the kettle on the hob and ducked through the corridor linking the lounge and kitchen to the bedrooms. He was just reaching out for the handle when the door sprang inwards and Holly and Katie came piling out.

"What are you playing at?" Ken said as they tried to squeeze past him and continue their flight into the lounge. He grabbed Holly by the shoulders and looked into her face. Holly's eyes were large and a bit wild. Her cheeks were flushed, hectic blooms on her pale face, and her long dark brown hair was plastered to her forehead and throat with perspiration. "Holly!" Ken said more sharply.

As he spoke, he looked up. Steven was standing in the bedroom. There was a lamp on somewhere in there, probably by the bedside, but its light was meagre and what struck Ken with immediate force was the heat that baked out at him from the bedroom. It was stifling. Ken could feel the hot air rushing out of the room past his face, sucked out into the night through the open front door.

"Steven was showing us a trick," Holly said.

"A trick?"

Holly wriggled free and scampered away into the lounge. Ken heard the kettle clank and the tap run in a hollow sputter as one of the girls began to fill it. He turned to Steven.

Steven was no longer in the bedroom.

Frowning, Ken went through into the small back room. There was a double bed that filled the entire width of the room, and a bank of cupboards built into the wall above the headboard. There was a flimsy wardrobe and a chest of drawers against the wall near the door, and a hairdryer fixed to the side panel of the wardrobe. Ken could see himself reflected in a mirror bolted to the wall above the chest of drawers. The room smelt a bit damp, but then the walls were little more than sheets of plasterboard; you could make them warp just by pressing your palm against them. Ken sidled his body along the foot-wide aisle allowed between the foot of the bed and the chest of drawers and slid open the wardrobe door. It was empty but for a rack of coat hangers fixed to a bar and a couple of shelves. Ken closed the door and stood looking around. The walls were covered with old, faded wallpaper with a tired and oppressive vertical yellow stripe pattern. Ken felt suddenly claustrophobic; he felt like he was in a giftbox that had been wrapped without much love and then turned inside out and thrown over his head. The room was warm, and musty, but no longer contained that fierce heat of moments earlier. It must have dissipated through the rest of the building and out of the door.

Ken went back out into the kitchen. Katie and Holly were sitting on the padded seat that ran in a large L-shape along two walls of the lounge. There was no sign of the courier. Ken took a step back and knocked on the shower room door. No reply, so he pushed the door open. The shower room was dark. Ken groped for a switch, found a light-pull, and yanked the light on. Another dim uncovered bulb lit up the cubicle. There was a shower, a tiny dolls-house sink and a toilet. Ken pulled the cord and turned out the light, and went out onto the veranda. There was a misty half-moon masked by the high leafy branches of the trees that grew in close around the back of the mobile home and along the side of the lot. It had become very dark, very quickly.

Ken noticed movement on the rectangle of grass beside the veranda. He crossed to the waist-high balustrade and saw that it was Steven, standing staring at the barbecue pit. He had his back to Ken, but Ken could see that he was shaking.

"Steven?" Ken said. It came out more sharply than he'd intended, but he was tired and starting to feel a little unanchored by the young courier's erratic behaviour.

Steven started but didn't turn around.

"*Steven?*" Ken enquired again and began to descend the steps leading down to the grass.

Steven whirled around. He held out his hands, which were black with soot. "I was just trying to get this grill off the barbecue for you. It seems to have got a bit stuck."

Ken looked down at the barbecue, which was a small three-sided brick construction with a shelf for charcoal and a metal grill that rested over it, supported by an inch-wide steel lip. The grill was buckled, and appeared to be soldered in places to the steel.

"Don't worry about that now." Ken said. His irritation was returning. Their first holiday in three years and they'd managed to pick a real winner. The plan had been to keep it simple, low-key. No airport stress, no lost luggage, no anxiety. Just a drive and a week of beaches and markets and games in the evening. But now they had arrived late, everything was shut and this *wally* was starting to get on his nerves.

Steven had returned his attention to the barbecue. "I would have done this for you earlier," he muttered.

So now it was Ken's fault? He considered some kind of retort, but then Holly appeared on the decking behind them and called down, "There's no milk, dad."

Ken bit his tongue and stamped back up the steps, leaving Steven still pondering the barbecue.

"WHERE'S MY WELCOME Pack?" Ken's voice was muffled, but his indignation was clear. He withdrew his head from the empty fridge and slammed the door. He stood looking around the kitchen with his hands on his hips. He rechecked all the cupboards but found only the same collection of old pots and pans, mismatched cutlery and crockery and cloudy drinking glasses he had located on his first search. "I've bloody paid for that!" he said.

Three mugs sat on the draining board ready for hot drinks. Behind him, the kettle was whistling with a panicky shrillness, which made Ken think of a lookout at a crime scene trying to get the attention of its gang as the security guards approached.

"No bread, no milk. I ordered tea bags and coffee, butter pats and croissants for the morning. Now we've got nothing until the supermarket opens tomorrow." Ken was fuming.

Steven was standing in the kitchen. He had to hop and scuttle out of Ken's way as Ken rifled through the cupboards.

"I can only apologise again," he said. Ken was starting to sicken of Steven's menial responses.

Ken went to the cool-box and rummaged through the wrappers and tangerine peel and empty cartons.

"Right, girls, we've got a sachet of hot chocolate and a Capri-Sun. *And...*" – Ken paused for effect, slowly withdrawing his hand – "a box of *Tuc*!"

"Great," said Katie.

"Yeah. *Suck*-u-*lent*," said Holly.

Ken could identify with their lack of enthusiasm. He lobbed the box of biscuits onto the sofa between the girls. Then he turned to Steven. "Is the bar still –" he started to ask, but Steven was gone again.

Ken let out an exasperated breath. *If he's fannying about with that barbecue...*

Ken went out onto the veranda but there was no sign of the courier. He went down to the car and opened the boot, looking around as he did so, an unpleasant temper tightening his chest. Then he paused and let out a small, dry, humourless laugh.

Steven's bike was gone.

Ken stepped around the side of the car and peered along the lane. There was nothing to be seen but a few screened off pools of light from the subdued streetlamps amongst the trees. He shrugged and began unloading the last bits from the car, and elected to leave Steven, and his decrepit old bike, to withdraw into the deep charring shadows of the hot French night. He'd deal with him in the morning.

ii

SOMETHING WOKE KEN. He lay in the darkness, eyes wide, heart beating hard. He'd been dreaming about walking through a music shop after a fire. Everything he picked up crumbled to a wet sorbet of coal dust in his hands.

He trod through black puddles and the air was like the end of October. There was a grand piano in the middle of the room. It was burnt through; even the white keys were chunks of charcoal. Ken stood and flexed his fingers. He raised his arms like a virtuoso and plunged his hands down onto the keyboard. The piano exploded around him in a storm of colliery dust.

Gasping, Ken struggled into a sitting position. The bed was lumpy and sunken in the middle. There had only been a pile of thin grey blankets in the cupboard above the bed, and they enwrapped Ken like an enchilada. He found the button on the wall above his head that switched on the reading lamp. The striped walls seemed to pinch in towards the light, and enhanced Ken's claustrophobia; he blinked, trying to dismiss the lingering residue of his dream and the teetering sense that the washed-out golden stripes were piano wires still resonating in the scorched and blistered music shop to a single sustained and pitiable note.

eeeeeeeeeeeeeeeeeeeeeeeeeeeeeeeeeee

Ken shuffled his blankets off and slid himself to the foot of the bed. He pulled on his dressing gown and went out into the kitchen.

EEEEEEEEEEEEEEEEEEEEEEEEE

Ken switched on the light and blinked and drew a breath. The kettle on the hob was shrieking. Still half asleep, Ken reached out and lifted it from the gas ring.

"*Shit!*" he roared and threw the kettle across the lounge. It was red hot. It hit the floor and bounced, emitting a hollow *clang*. Ken nursed his hand. A red line was scorched across his palm. He ran the cold tap and held his hand beneath the tepid water. As he did so he looked around. The gas was off; there had been no flames beneath the kettle. It lay on its side beneath the little folding dining table. Ken wrapped his hand in a wet dish towel and went over to the kettle. He picked it up using the towel.

"Daddy?"

It was Katie. She stood in the kitchen and rubbed her eyes. Ken turned to look at her. For a second he felt suspended in the dream again. She looked so like Elaine it was agonising. Where Holly was all darkness and obscurity, Katie was light. They were like something out of a Bradbury short story. Blonde and blue-eyed, his younger daughter stood and peered into the gloom of the living area, her hair flossed up into a web of spun sugar on one side of her head from where she had been sleeping.

"Hey, sweetheart," said Ken. How odd must he look, standing in his dressing gown with a dishtowel wrapped in his hand, holding a kettle in the middle of the night?

"Heard something," Katie said. She took a few bare-footed steps into the lounge. "Had a dream."

Ken went over to his daughter. He put the kettle back on the hob and scooped her up. She was already drifting back to sleep.

"Come on, love." He said.

"Mmmm."

Ken carried her back to her room, a narrow space no wider than a walk-in wardrobe situated between the toilet and his own room. It contained nothing more than a bunk bed and a side table with a lamp on it. Snuggled up in a ball beneath her ratty grey blankets, Holly snored on the top bunk.

Ken put Katie back on her bunk and covered her up.

"'Night, baby." He said.

"Daddy," Katie said.

Ken paused at the door. "Yes?"

"Had a dream."

"You said."

"Nice."

"That's good."

"Mummy was playing her piano."

"Sweet dreams, Katie," Ken said, his mouth suddenly very dry.

Ken went back to bed and slept without any more dreams. By the time they were all up the next morning, dressed and washed and ready to go shopping as early as he could possibly coordinate, Ken had forgotten about the unsettling synchronicity of his and Katie's dreams. He had also put from his mind the fact that the kettle, picked up from the floor in his dishtowelled fist, had been empty and in no way boiled dry. It had been stone cold.

THE SUPER-U was 500 yards from the campsite, so they decided to walk it, Holly and Katie both carrying canvas Bags-for-Life bought from Tesco back home. Again, there was no one about when they walked past the reception and bar.

When they arrived, the large looping car park surrounding the supermarket was empty. They walked up to the doors and Ken was relieved when they slid open. The first thing that struck him was the smell. It was the brash and unfettered tang of strong cheeses fused with locally-caught fresh fish. The girls wrinkled their noses. Ken thought it was marvellous. You wouldn't get a smell like that anywhere in Britain outside of a nursing home.

Ken had anticipated the layout to be unusual but he wasn't expecting the first aisle to be crammed with such an eclectic array of goods: Beach toys, men's shorts, games, deodorants, gardening equipment, flip-flops, magazines and fruit juice. They wandered past the shelves towards the back of the store, following the stink from the fish counter.

Holly and Katie crowded up against a display in the middle of the tiled floor at the end of the aisle. Upon it, made docile by a bed of crushed ice, was a pile of spider crabs jumbled like a cache of rusty medieval coshes. Holly poked a finger at the spiny haul and gasped when they shifted and flexed their legs in a stuporous response.

"They're *alive*!" Katie said, her eyes wide in surprise.

Ken laughed and came over. He plucked one of the crabs from the pile and held it up so that its artfully articulated underbelly was visible. Its legs curled in on itself, and its claws parried in cantankerous slow motion.

"That's cruel," Holly said, but her eyes were bright and she said it with a rapt expression on her face.

Ken placed the crab onto its bed of ice. "Not really," he said. "They're all dopy this way when you boil them alive."

"*Noooo*!"

"Oh, yes." Ken pressed the heels of his hands together and clawed his fingers and thumbs and wriggled them in the girls' faces. "Aghh, I'm cooking!" Ken cried laughing. "I'm *cooking*!" and then stood wondering whether his pantomime had been a little misjudged. Holly paled; Katie shrieked; both girls turned and fled away up the next aisle, looking a bit sick.

*   *   *

THEY LUGGED THEIR bags to the doors and stopped so that the girls could look at the souvenirs and trinkets on a revolving rack by the magazine counter. It was hung with a variety of nameplates displaying French forenames and their meanings, presumably for children's bedroom doors.

Holly and Katie pored through them looking for versions of their own names. Holly found *Holland,* it's meaning unambiguous: named after the Netherlands. And Katie failed to locate anything close to her own name although she did pour scorn on a number of *Janelles* and *Cherelles,* which she thought sounded chavvy. Ken pointed out that these names were originally French and had been appropriated by the British working classes, thus cheapening them. "Whatever," said Katie.

"Oh, look," said Holly. She held up a nameplate.

Ken looked. *Adrienne,* it said.

"That's our caravan's name," Katie said.

"I *know*," said Holly. "What does it mean?"

Ken translated the simple definition beneath the name.

"Oh," he said.

"What?"

Ken replaced the nameplate on its stand. "It's not as glamorous as it sounds," he said. "It means 'black earth.'"

KEN CARRIED THE bags back to camp. The girls trotted along ahead of him. The road was dusty and the edges of the pavements were bordered by narrow strips of dun-coloured stones. Already it was warm, but there was nobody about. The beachfront was deserted; the sails of the windsurfing boards and small boats ranked along the front fluttered and thrummed in the breeze, and somewhere a line had come untethered and rattled its clips against a mast.

Ken watched the girls as they ran shadowless in the early morning light. The bags weren't heavy but he ached from yesterday's drive and a poor night's sleep. He hoped he hadn't made a mistake bringing the girls away on his own. They were at a strange, baffling age and although his love for them was immeasurable, often he felt as detached from them as he was from images on a screen.

He imagined Elaine's response. *Just persist*, she would have said. *Just keep going. Do normal things. Have fun.*

Ken stopped and looked out across the bay. He could see a bridge, so distant on the horizon it was no more than a misty thread, linking the mainland to an island. He sighed; the emptiness of the beach and the whitewashed promenade was suddenly unbearable.

Ken turned and hurried after his girls.

THEY HADN'T BEEN back long and there was a knock at the door.

It was Steven. He was holding a small cardboard box.

"I found this," he said, offering Ken the box.

Ken reached out and took the box and then he noticed what appeared to be fresh burns on the backs of Steven's hands. He looked down and saw more, nasty-looking pink scabs on the boy's ankles. They couldn't be new, but how had he failed to notice them last night?

"Steven," he said, and against his better instinct: "Let me look at those burns."

Steven reacted with an immediate and unexpected refusal. He stumbled backwards and collided with the balustrade surrounding the veranda, his hands held high above his head.

Ken was stunned by the reaction.

"I'm fine, I'm fine." Steven said. Somehow he kept a sickly salesman's grin on his face. "Really, I'm cool."

"I'm a doctor, Steven. I'm not going to hurt you."

Steven backed away. "I don't need a doctor, thanks. All's well. Just enjoy your holiday." He stood on the grass beneath the veranda. He stared up at Ken, his arms hanging by his side. There were dark smudges on the collar of his *CampEuro* shirt. His bike was leaning up against the side of the mobile home.

Ken looked down at the box he was holding. It was about the size of a shoebox. Ken lifted the flaps that loosely covered the contents.

"Oh," he said. The girls would be pleased.

Boggle.

Ken looked back to where Steven was standing. He was gone.

"Bloody hell," said Ken.

LATER, HE MADE them all *carbonara* for lunch, using the fresh ingredients they had bought from the Super-U. It was very good, very rich and filling. The girls were in their dressing gowns and lay next to him on the sofa playing *Boggle*. Ken thought about going for a beer at the bar. They'd be safe enough for half an hour. He felt the need for some adult company, even if it was just a stranger serving cold beer. He looked at his watch. It was nearly eight o'clock. The girls laughed, the dice clattered. *Where had the day gone?* Ken wondered. They'd done nothing but laze about on the site today. Normally Ken would have considered this a waste, but right now he was glad to do nothing, glad to just relax and enjoy the time with his girls. Tomorrow they could hit the beach.

iii

ELAINE HAD BEEN a concert pianist. She had been due to play a Chopin recital at the *Rudolfinum* in Prague, but on the night she arrived there had been a fire at her hotel and she had died.

The girls were in the shower. Ken sat on the edge of his bed and listened to the sound of them shrieking beneath the jet of water, and the thumps and creaks of the moulded plastic walls giving beneath their weight as they bumped against them.

He looked at his suitcase. He hadn't unpacked; rather he would select items from it as he needed them. He sighed, lay back on the bed and closed his eyes.

He must have dozed, because when he became aware of his surroundings again it was quiet. He sat up. He couldn't hear the girls.

Beneath the mobile home, amongst the leaves and litter and darkness, something moved.

Ken lifted his feet off the floor and sat cross-legged on the edge of the bed. He peered down at the strip of floor between the end of the bed and the chest of drawers.

Again, furtive movement. And then a bump, as if someone had tried to stand up and hit his head on the underside of the mobile home.

Ken stood, slipped on his shoes and went out into the hallway.

"Hi, Dad," Katie said, looking up from the sofa. Her hair was damp and tied back in a ponytail.

"Where's Holly?" he asked.

Katie shrugged and went back to her magazine. "Dunno," she said.

Ken pushed the girls' bedroom door open and looked in. The beds were empty. He knocked on the bathroom door and went in. Holly wasn't in there, either.

Ken strode into the lounge. "Has she gone out?" he demanded.

"She might have," Katie said, still vague. "She didn't say."

"Katie! It's ten o'clock at night. Where is she?"

"Look," said Katie. She was staring past Ken, towards the hall. Ken turned around and saw that the door leading out onto the veranda was open.

Ken frowned and went to the door. There was no moon tonight, just low racing clouds like smoke from a factory chimney. He could smell meat burning on a barbecue. It was still very warm.

"Holly!" Ken shouted.

Something moved to his left. Ken crossed the veranda and peered over the balustrade. In the darkness beneath the mobile home he could just make out the curved shoulder of the gas cylinder that fed the cooker and water heater.

Ken went to the car and got a torch from the glove compartment. He crossed the grass, stepped around the barbecue and knelt down and played the torch beam beneath the mobile home.

Something was under there. Ken leaned further into

the darkness, his shoulder brushing against the pipes that fed the gas up into the mobile home. Suddenly something rolled away from behind the gas cylinder. Ken flicked the torch beam to the right and it slid across the back of something glistening and black. It looked flaky, crinkled, like a bin liner rolled up and melted by a blast of heat. Ken jumped and banged his head on the underside of the building.

He withdrew and stood brushing the dirt from his knees. It had looked like a bin bag; that was probably all it was. There were a few bags, filled with rubbish and loosely tied, still lying in a pile at the side of the barbecue.

Then Ken heard Katie cry out.

He ran around the veranda and up the steps. In the lounge, Katie was sitting with her legs drawn up on the sofa and one hand pressed to her mouth. She was in tears.

"What is it? What's the matter, Katie?"

Trembling, Katie extended her other hand and pointed at the table.

"I don't like it, daddy. Make it stop."

Confused, Ken walked over. Katie was pointing at the dish of lettered dice sitting amongst pencils and bits of scrap paper. He frowned. "Is this a joke?"

Katie shook her head, tears running down her pale cheeks. "It keeps doing it. Every time I shake them they say the same thing."

Ken was about to ask her to demonstrate, to prove what she was saying, but then he heard Holly call from outside.

"Daddy, look. She's coming!"

Ken looked up. From where he stood, he could see through the wide window at the back of the mobile home, along the lane leading back beneath the canopy of trees. A figure was approaching.

With a slow tread, and a tightening in his chest he recognised, Ken walked out onto the veranda. Holly was standing there by the picnic table. She smiled up at her dad, came over and took his hand.

Together they watched as the figure resolved itself out of the dark tunnel of trees. A streetlamp delineated her features, her black dress, and the spray of white lilies she carried in her arms.

"She's still so sad, daddy." Holly said. Ken squeezed her hand.

"So am I," he said.

"Me, too." Holly squeezed back.

Ken and Holly watched for a little longer as the woman approached their mobile home. The ache in Ken's chest became unendurable, and he wept as she placed the bouquet on the ground at the foot of the steps.

"Mummy didn't die in a fire, did she, Daddy?" said Holly, and Ken felt some small comfort for a moment; just a moment.

"I don't think she did, baby," he said.

Inside, Katie called: "Steven's here."

They went inside.

THEY WERE SITTING together in the lounge. The curtains were drawn. Steven, their courier, was standing before them. His arms were spread wide and Ken could see the burns on his forearms. They had grown, consuming the flesh of his biceps and underarms.

On the table their game of *Boggle* was still underway. The lettered dice were in their grid and a pen and paper lay beside them. Ken drew his eyes away from Steven and looked at the sixteen dice and at what they spelled:

B U R N
U R N B
R N B U
N B U R

Ken closed his eyes.

"You come here all the time," Steven said. "*All* your holidays are here."

"No," Ken said.

"You have your own *key*!"

Ken's hand went to his trouser pocket. He felt the shape against his leg.

Steven was nodding. Now his face was gone; his baked-fish eyes looked down at Ken from the black smouldering flesh of his skull.

"I wish I could have saved you," he said, grotesque now, those blind, boiled eyes unable to intimate any of the emotion carried in his voice. "But I'll always be here; I'll always keep trying to warn you."

Warn us? Ken thought, but of course there was no memory of the explosion, of the fire that followed the gas leak from the rotten valves around the pipes beneath them. Pipes that had been knocked loose by Holly, playing under the mobile home while Ken fixed the barbecue. No memory of the lighter fluid, the embers; because they hadn't happened here yet. Not yet.

Ken felt despair crawl through him. He turned to his right and his face crumpled, twisted into a grimace by what he saw sitting propped up next to him. Their heads were together and their fingers were interlocked.

His girls, like scorched china dolls, their skin curling off their muscles like newspaper lifting from a bonfire.

Ken raised his hand and looked at what it held, what was melted to his fist.

Villanova 48. *Adrienne.*

Black earth.

Now he remembered.

He opened his mouth to howl, but the flames had seared his throat to ash.

WIDOW'S WEEDS

CHRISTOPHER PRIEST

The character of the stage magician is clearly one that holds much fascination for Christopher Priest; witness the success of his brilliant novel, The Prestige, *and the later critically acclaimed film adaptation for example. And just as the magician toys with our perceptions of reality and illusion, Priest plays with the concept of just what constitutes a house and a haunting, to fascinating effect. Priest is a real alchemist of prose and the subterfuge and sleight-of-hand within 'Widow's Weeds' will have you coming back to this complex and rewarding story time and again.*

THE ELDERLY VOLVO lurched along the frozen ruts of the unmade lane. The driver hunched tensely over the wheel, struggling to keep the car away from the deep ditches on either side. There was no standing snow, but a thick hoar frost clung to every surface. Dark clouds moved overhead. The heater whined at full strength.

The passenger in the front seat was sitting in a more relaxed way, leaning back with a laptop on his knees. He was scanning his emails, which he had picked up earlier in the day before leaving the hotel in Brighton.

The car was towing a trailer, painted with bright colours and depicting playing cards, an opera hat and cane, a magic wand, some dice and many stars. Painted in flamboyant letters on both sides, as well as the rear, were the words OLIVIERA – THE MASTER OF MAGIC.

The driver halted the car outside two high wrought-iron gates. The trailer skidded as he braked, swinging around at an angle behind the car. The passenger, the master of magic Oliviera, whose real name was Dennis O'Leary, closed the lid of the laptop and put it carefully into his overnight bag.

"You sure this is the place, Rick?" he said, looking doubtfully through the windscreen, which was smeared with frozen droplets of mud.

"I entered the postcode in the satnav. Can't fail."

"Oh, yeah." O'Leary wound down the window on his side and craned out to see beyond the gates. The cold air gripped him about the face. There was a glimpse of a steep slate roof, part of an upstairs window reflecting the sky.

"Last chance," Rick, the driver, said. "Are you really going to go through with this?"

"Ten thousand pounds will last us until summer. That's the guaranteed minimum."

"Rather you than me."

"Yes, but you haven't seen her photograph," O'Leary said, who had.

He climbed out, opened the rear door. He put his overnight valise on his shoulder, then pulled out a larger case. He set the case on the ground next to the car, slammed the door, and walked across to the gates. Peering through, he could see a display board just beyond, mounted beside the driveway. It was supported on two stout timber legs, had a border of astronomical signs, and was fronted with a sheet of clean glass.

At the top, in clear cursive lettering, were the words: THE ATCHIEVEMENTS OF MME LOUISA DE MORGANET. Beneath were several more lines, but a gust of cold wind sent down a shower of frost particles from the tree above, and he backed off. O'Leary returned to the car to collect the case.

"What do you suppose an 'atchievement' is?" he said. "With an extra 't'?"

Rick was leaning across towards him, from the driver's seat.

"A spelling mistake? Look, close the bloody door. You're making the car cold."

O'Leary slammed it, but the window was still open. He leaned down beside it.

"The pub is about a mile further on," he said. "The Shepherd and Dog. Keep the expenses down, okay? You might yet be right about this being a scam."

"You're seeing sense at last."

"Come on, Rick. You stand to gain too."

The two men gripped hands through the window, but they were too familiar with each other to make it seem forced. O'Leary backed off and stood away as the car and its trailer resumed the erratic course down the icily furrowed lane.

O'Leary carried his luggage to the gate and went through. The drive curved between the trees. On each side were lawns, under the frost for now, but they and the flowerbeds around them were neatly maintained. He paused by the display board to read it properly. Beneath the large heading was the following:

Mme de Morganet is well qualified in, and a skilled

tutor of, the following atchievements. Please enquire for more information, and the rates that apply.

Musicianship (including Composition), Foreign Languages (including Translation and Interpretation), Literary Endeavour, Oil Painting, Saddlery and Equestrianism, Astronomy, Aquatic Sports, All Domestic Accomplishments (including Kitchen Skills, Crochet, Needlepoint, Embroidery, Knitting, Sewing), Oratory, Marksmanship, Actuarial Calculations, Tax Returns, Law of Probate, Law of Property, Law of Torts...

FINALLY CERTAIN THAT he had come to the right place, O'Leary continued along the drive, chilled by the wind. The house was a large one, probably Victorian, but in good condition and with up-to-date features. The windows had been tastefully double-glazed, and on the far corner there was an outlet for a central heating boiler. White condensation was whisked away by the wind. He pressed the bell button beside the door.

There was a long wait, longer than he expected, while the chill wind blustered around him, sweeping down from the overhanging hills. The house was situated at the foot of the South Downs, but in this weather the hills gave no shelter at all. Flurries of fine snow were seeding the wind, stinging his cheeks. Uncertainties ran briefly through him: the right address but maybe the wrong day; perhaps he should have phoned ahead...? Finally the door eased open, giving a glimpse of a hallway, a flight of stairs. Warm air flowed out at him.

A woman was there, wearing a thick pullover and jeans and a tweed cap.

"Mr O'Leary, I believe? Otherwise known as Oliviera, the magician?"

"I am," said O'Leary.

"You are most welcome, Mr O'Leary. Madame is expecting you, and has asked me to show you into the drawing room. She will join you as soon as possible."

While she said this she held the door open wide, and O'Leary stepped in. She closed the door swiftly behind him, sealing the house against the wind. A feeling of comfort and welcome swirled invisibly around him. The woman took his coat and his overnight bag, but O'Leary kept hold of his case of magic materials. He never let it out of his sight.

He said yes, he would enjoy a cup of tea, and went through into the drawing room.

As the double doors closed behind him he realized he was in a mausoleum of the past. The enormous room was filled to cramming point with *objets d'art*: busts, sculptures, stuffed birds of prey in domed glass cases, huge screens and lanterns, four immense bookcases, piles of unsorted books on every level surface, a hand-wound trumpet phonograph, a tall birdcage holding several brightly coloured parakeets, two pianos, one of them a concert grand, a harpsichord and several wind and string instruments, two or three music stands, a variety of thick-piled carpets with oriental designs. Swords, lances, shields and ancient firearms were mounted on every wall. In the spaces between were the trophy heads of wild animals: a cheetah, an antelope, an antlered deer. Bric-a-brac had been placed on every remaining surface. The air was suffused with a rich, clean smell: furniture polish, good wood, leather, paper, varnish.

He saw two large armchairs and a settee placed around a hearth. The fireplace was dominated by an enlarged black-and-white photograph of a man in old-fashioned clothes. O'Leary wound his way through the elegant clutter of the room, sat down in one of the chairs, and awaited the arrival of Madame de Morganet.

THE HOUSE, THE circumstances, were not entirely what Dennis O'Leary was expecting, although there had been a clue in the address. This was a select area of Sussex, the strip of land between the South Downs and the Weald, wooded and fertile, with several large houses. An undefined sense of financial well-being had always been detectable in his exchanges with Madame de Morganet, but the opulence of her home was still a surprise.

A middle-aged unmarried man, O'Leary was often lonely when not touring, but loneliness was not a habit he wanted to keep. His career had become a sequence of mild successes – he was a good-enough illusionist and his skill brought pleasure to his audiences and a more or less steady income. He still depended on bookings at clubs and business functions, because he had not done well on television. Two or three of his tricks were unique to him, so he guarded their secrets with care. They were his most valuable properties, but he could not live on secrets.

When not touring, he lived in a small room at the top of a terraced house in Leicester, his car and trailer parked at the rear by arrangement with his landlady. Rick, contentedly married but always hard up and complaining about the meagre wage O'Leary paid him, lived close by. The previous winter, during one such break in work, he had happened upon Mme de Morganet on one of the more restrained internet contact sites (*Responsible Adults seeking Mature Friendship*). At first he had deliberately not selected her link – her self-description made her sound eccentric, or desperate, or weird, and probably all three, while her photograph was ambiguously shadowed.

Rick, when he found out, egged him on. "At least she sounds exotic," he said. "Might cheer you up a bit."

After paying the fee, O'Leary exchanged several tentative emails with her. They elicited enough information from each other to feel a meeting should follow. It took several weeks to arrange, because soon after they made contact, O'Leary began a tour in the north of England. She was a harmless distraction while the work went on. He grew fond of her sometimes bizarre messages, which came as a welcome change in his workaday life.

O'Leary told her all the facts about himself that he knew to be true: that he was unmarried, not rich but not hard up, healthy, sane, not saddled with onerous debts or obligations, and that he was at an age she might consider suitable.

He learned that she was a childless widow, that she had been grief-stricken by the loss of her husband, but that he had left her well-provided-for with a house and an investment income from family securities. She described herself as interested in O'Leary's skill as an illusionist, and said she would love to learn from him. More touchingly, she said that she was lonely and anxious to find a long-term partner. O'Leary told her, shyly, much the same.

Sitting alone in her drawing room, surrounded by the huge collection of antiques, he felt more ill at ease than he could ever remember. But then, unannounced and without any fuss or sense of ceremony, Mme de Morganet entered through the double doors. A gust of warm air followed her in and circled around him, bearing with it the merest hint of patchouli. He stood up to meet her.

THEY SHOOK HANDS conventionally, exchanging names, then Mme de Morganet drew back from him. They stood apart, regarding each other frankly and intently, but not discourteously. Both smiled. Neither of them appeared to feel uncomfortable with this exploratory staring, nor that they were embarrassing the other.

That she was a handsome woman was instantly in no doubt. She appeared to be in her late thirties, although at first sight O'Leary could not be sure. Her raven hair, with a touch of silver, was set off by a bold streak of purple. Her stance was upright but informal, her long gown of dark-grey satin made sombre but also more feminine by black and purple ribbons. She wore a veil, pushed back above her face so that it rested on her hair. She wore black satin cocktail gloves, fingers exposed, with long lacy armlets. Her fingers were heavy with rings, all of them white gold or silver. Their claw settings held dark gems. She had put something on her face, too pale, while her eyes were lined too darkly. Her lips were glossed and deep red.

"Well, Mr O'Leary," she said soon enough. "This is my house and I am pleased to welcome you to it."

"Thank you," he replied. "I am delighted to meet you

at last. I'm sorry it has taken so long to arrange, but I enjoyed your emails."

"And I yours. Please, let's dispense with formalities. You must call me Louisa, and I shall call you Dennis."

He nodded his acceptance of this and they smiled broadly. In spite of the attempt to break the ice, she spoke in measured, almost formal tones, as if reciting aloud, or addressing someone who might not understand. However, far from being intimidated by her, now that he was standing close to her O'Leary felt a sudden mad urge to sweep her into his arms.

She sat down on the settee with a deep rustling of satin, indicating he should sit beside her. He did so, but stayed at the far end. They began to converse, at first remarking conventionally on his journey and the unusually cold weather. The woman who had opened the door to him came in with a tray of tea things. Her tweed cap had disappeared. As they started on the buttered scones and delicate little cakes, O'Leary felt the atmosphere growing more cordial by the minute.

A quiet joy was rising in him. Louisa de Morganet was a mature, beautiful and intelligent woman, a romantic individualist in the way she liked to dress, but obviously modern and open-minded in outlook. Years of experience, and his own deceptive profession, had taught him never to accept at face value anything seen or quickly learned. He resolved to keep this in mind for the time being.

They asked questions about each other. O'Leary had rarely spoken about himself to anyone before. His harmless revelations about his past felt awkward and unnatural at first, but Louisa's manner was so welcoming and candid that his inhibitions began to fade away.

She was in return forthcoming about herself. She told

him how she had met her late husband, François, a Frenchman who worked in the London City branch of a Parisian bank. She indicated the framed photograph above the fireplace. François had a moustache, goatee beard and long sideburns, and was posed stiffly wearing a dark frock coat and with a cane in hand. He looked irritated by being photographed, and glared at the camera, ill at ease.

François, she said, had swept her off her feet, married her, taken her to his family home in Provence, where she discovered he came from a long line of aristocrats. They went on an extended tour of European countries, far to the east – Roumania and Bessarabia – thence to countries bordering the Mediterranean: Lebanon, Turkey and Greece. It was, she said, from meeting members of his family that she developed her taste for knowledge, the learning from others of practical and artistic skills. The de Morganets were academics and professionals, all polymaths. The family was extensive and widely dispersed.

When she and François returned to England they bought this house. She spoke warmly but distantly of him, and O'Leary realized that she must still be feeling her loss.

François de Morganet had contracted tuberculosis while they were on their travels. It afflicted him severely and he died within a year of their return.

Louisa looked mortified by her memories. "He was in so much pain, day and night, terrible discomfort. And the blood – so much blood! I shall never forget, never! *Mon pauvre mari, mon chéri!*"

She was staring into her lap, but then she raised her head, looked at the photograph above the fire.

O'Leary saw tears welling in her eyes, unnerving him, so he left the settee and wandered around the crowded room, easing his way between the many pieces. Soon, Louisa composed herself. She was standing when he turned back to her. She lightly touched his hand as they resumed their seats, and encouraged him to sit a little closer.

Outside, the dark of the evening had closed in, the wind blustering around the gables and roof pinnacles. The open fire, a mound of logs, blazed cheerfully. The serving woman quietly entered the drawing room and went around lighting the lamps, a number of gas mantles, but there were candles too. Once these were alight more scented essences drifted through the room.

"Mrs Acland – did you show our guest to his room?" Louisa said.

The woman was about to leave the drawing room. "No, madame, I brought him straight in here, as you asked." She nodded, then closed the doors.

"Why don't you let her show you where you will be sleeping?" Louisa said to O'Leary. "You must need a rest after your journey and then we will meet for dinner. You will hear the gong."

O'Leary wanted to say that he was not feeling at all tired – indeed, he was energized and alert -- but he decided against it.

"Do you like to dress for dinner?" He shook his head, but vaguely, feeling his way. "I prefer to," Louisa went on. "But it's up to you." She glanced at his case of magical effects and apparatus. "I assume this is not your overnight case?"

"No. These are the tools of my trade. What you asked me to bring."

"Excellent. This evening we shall relax after we have dined, and come to know each other more. But tomorrow I shall be intent on learning about your conjuring. You need have no worries about secrets. I honour all confidences in my quest for knowledge."

"You wish to become a magician?" O'Leary said.

"I intend to add the art of illusionism to my atchievements."

She pronounced the word deliberately, her tongue briefly touching her teeth, making the small but distinct dental sound of the 't.' She was looking closely at him, as if to judge his reaction.

O'Leary headed for the stairs, clutching his case of magic. Mrs Acland, who had been standing in the hall, courteously swung the doors open to allow him to pass through. She led O'Leary to the room on the top floor where he would sleep.

A LOG FIRE had been set in the grate and was burning cheerfully. A gas mantle gave a steady but weak white light into the room. As he entered, O'Leary groped instinctively for an electric switch. One was there on the wall beside the door, and a shaded fitting hung on a flex in the centre of the ceiling, but no light issued from it.

A change of his own clothes was laid out for him, in fact the sharply cut suit that he wore when he was performing. Never normally to be worn in daily life, the royal-blue suit had an inner lining that was a secret network of hidden pockets and slits, loops of thread, elastic bands.

The bedroom was under the steep roof of the house, well-proportioned, clean and furnished in traditional style. The bed stood high off the floor. The dormer window, built out of the sloping roof, was heavily curtained with dark green damask, satin stripes worked into the thick fabric, reaching to the floor, tasseled. A small shower room and toilet lay beyond a white-painted door.

He could not gain a signal on his mobile; no text messages had arrived since he left Brighton earlier. He pressed the handset to the window, hoping to enhance whatever network signal there might be, but there was nothing. He had wanted to contact Rick, tell him how things were working out, but it was not to be.

He booted up his laptop, but there was no wi-fi within range. He looked around the room for a cable connector, without success. He knew that Louisa had repeatedly emailed him, so there must be a landline connection somewhere in the house.

He sat on the edge of the bed, his legs dangling. A stuffed owl, inside a glass case on a low shelf, stared at him with wide orange eyes. O'Leary could still smell patchouli, where a trace of it had transferred to his hand. He ran his fingers beneath his nostrils, smiling to himself. He rolled back across the bed and pedalled his feet in the air with pleasure.

An hour later, when he heard the gong sound from the stairwell below, O'Leary walked downstairs for dinner, dressed in his stage suit.

THERE WAS NOTHING to be seen of Louisa the next morning when O'Leary went early to breakfast. He ate alone, sitting at a long, highly polished oak table. It was in a windowed conservatory, heated by circulating pipes and filled with exotic trees and shrubs. They stood in calm array around him, while outside the trees in the garden and in the woods beyond were bent and battered by a chill, sleet-bearing easterly wind.

When Louisa appeared later in the drawing room, she made no comment or apology. He went in to join her, as she went to the grand piano. She raised the lid, momentarily adjusted the height of the stool, then began playing. She played from memory, without sheet music. Within moments she was entranced by the music, rocking her head to and fro, her eyes tightly shut. O'Leary sat down a short distance behind her, unable to recognize the piece but astonished by her virtuoso skill. At the end she identified it as Liszt's first *Liebestraum* nocturne.

She moved to a music stand, put some music in place, clearly hand-drafted, then picked up a violin. After briefly checking that the instrument was in tune she opened with a dazzling solo, a series of darting clusters and arpeggios, each counterpointing the one it had followed. The piece ended with a shift to a slow, melodic lament, exquisitely beautiful and melancholic.

O'Leary clapped his hands, but Louisa smiled him to silence.

"I am not a show-off, Dennis," she said. "But I want to tell you that I composed and arranged that piece myself. I am not trying merely to impress you, even though the composing and performing of music is one of my many attainments, my atchievements." Again, the deliberate dental sound of the extra letter. "It is important to me that you understand the nature and extent of my atchievements."

He said, "Well, I am extremely impress –"

"No – allow me to demonstrate more. I do have a purpose, to help you understand what might become possible between us." She carefully laid aside her violin, closing it inside its case. "I am a woman of many attainments. I am an avid and successful learner. I executed most of the paintings you can see on these walls. I am an adventurous cook. I am a mathematician, a geologist, a strong swimmer. Would you care to witness my skill as a sharpshooter?"

"I think not." But she was intent upon this purpose. Nothing that passed between them, during the long evening they had spent together the night before, had given him any idea she would act or perform in such a way. Yesterday she seemed gentle, sensitive, enquiring about him, quietly interested in everything he said. Now she was assertive, dominant. "I should love to hear you play again," he said. "Do you know any more instruments?"

She reached behind her, then held out a flute in one hand, an oboe in the other.

"Enough of music," she said, laying the instruments aside again. "I am adept in six European languages and can make sense of half a dozen more. I fashioned many of the collectible pieces you see in this room: I am a skilled potter and porcelainist. I am also a cabinet-maker, and for example I built the side-table on which you are now resting your hand."

She moved towards him and raised her face towards his.

"My dear Dennis, if I may speak to you candidly. I am not seeking to impress you. I am trying to clarify the position in which I have found myself, and now in which you find yourself." Once again he heard the weird incantation of her formal way of speaking, at odds with the more relaxed words they had exchanged yesterday, not to speak of her body language, which he found provocative.

"I am, as you know, a widow," she went on. "In the common parlance of the world I knew with my husband, I would be called a *house to let*. I seek a partner to join me, because the house I have to let is haunted. Yes, haunted by the past, Dennis! I must find someone to be with me, to protect me from the past. Until then I remain in mourning. I am required to wear the *widow's weeds*, this purple, this black, these shrouds of grey and silver.

"Outside this building I display, as you noticed when you arrived, my achievements. Inside, as a house to let, I work constantly to perfect the skills and acquire fresh ones. Until I find the right one to join me, I collect accomplishments." Her face grew ever closer to his and her voice became softer, a bare whisper. "I am a wealthy woman and I seek attainments. I do not mind what I have to spend to make these atchievements. I also seek a partner in life, a shield against the past. Could that man be you?"

Her parted lips were almost upon his. He could feel her breath on his cheek, the light touch of her fingers against his, the closeness of her delicious flesh wrapped in the satin gown. Her dark eyes were narrowed, her lips were moist.

"Yes, I believe so," he said quietly.

"Then what you wish for will be yours! Anything at all, no matter how expensive, or how profound, reckless or shocking!" She swept back from him, staring intently at him. "Teach me how to atchieve the secrets of magic."

*   *   *

THE FIRST LESSON did not go well. Nor the second, after lunch, even though Louisa was, as she promised, a keen pupil. He felt her magnetic presence so keenly that at first O'Leary had to force himself to concentrate.

He always began with a performance of the illusion, then followed it by revealing the secret. She laughed with delight at each effect, but as soon as he began to show her how the trick was done – the sleight of hand, the concealment, the pass, the false shuffle, the fake, the force, the substitution – she was unable to follow. He reassured her that most magicians take years to perfect their skill, and that many went on practising and rehearsing until the end of their careers, but she was frustrated by her failure to learn.

They took a light salad for lunch, seated again at the long table in the conservatory. She sat close beside him, contriving several times to touch him or brush her hand against him. O'Leary was alive with awareness of her. They sat drinking wine together after the meal, all the initial awkwardness between them now gone. A thin mantle of snow lay on the glass panels in the roof, filtering the weak daylight. The wind was still gusting strongly, but it was warm in the house.

"I realize how difficult it is for you to reveal secrets," Louisa said. "You are too used to secrecy. You don't mean to, but you are holding back. Only when you truly *want* to yield your knowledge will it pass across to me."

"I have been telling you everything," O'Leary said. "It's what I'm here to do."

"I believe you, but you are not yielding. We both seek atchievements." She squeezed his hand, then lifted it towards her, resting it briefly on the square of firm bare flesh above her breasts. "Tomorrow it will be easier, I promise you that. When you are willing to yield to me everything I want, then I shall reward you. And I am not talking about money."

She lowered her gaze, and allowed his hand to lift away from her.

They persevered with the magic techniques, but by mid-afternoon they were both tired and agreed to halt for the day. O'Leary locked the various pieces of apparatus into his case. Louisa left the room without saying anything. Some time later, when she still had not returned, O'Leary took a book from one of the piles, then spread himself comfortably on the settee in front of the fire.

THEY MET AGAIN for dinner, but Louisa seemed listless. At the end of the meal, when they had moved to the settee and were hand-warming their balloons of brandy, Mrs Acland came in.

"I am about to retire for the night, madame," she said. "I have placed the package in Mr O'Leary's room, as you asked. I trust that will be all?"

"Yes, thank you. Goodnight, Grace."

"Good night, madame; good night, sir."

The doors closed. O'Leary, pleasantly relaxed after a meal and a day of concentration on his techniques, and by Louisa's heady presence, held up his brandy towards the nearest gas mantle and peered through it, swirling the liquor slowly.

"What package did she mean?" he said.

"Let's call it your atchievement. Tomorrow I shall have mine."

They sat in silence for a while, hearing the sound of

Mrs Acland moving around on the floor above. O'Leary was remembering the £10,000 that had been mentioned long ago during their email period, the fee that had been promised once but never mentioned since. He still wanted it, but just at that moment, money no longer seemed a priority.

At last the house was still. Louisa suddenly revived.

She placed her glass on the table before them, then took O'Leary's and placed it next to hers. She leaned towards him, her lips parted. They kissed. She quickly guided his hand to her breasts, pressing her body against him, encouraging his fingers to explore the curve of her bodice, then to slip gently inside. O'Leary closed his eyes, his senses loaded with her fragrances, the quiet sibilant rustling of her gown, the warm softness of her flesh. She leaned further and further towards him, pressing him back, easing him down to the horizontal. With her weight upon him, she raised her face away from his.

"Tomorrow?"

"What? Yes! But why not now?"

"Because I have not atchieved. Tomorrow, we will both be satisfied. I have promised." Outside, the wind suddenly intensified, rattling the windows and sending a surge of air down the chimney flue. The smouldering logs flared briefly into flame, and a billow of smoke pushed into the room. "Let's hasten tomorrow on!" she said.

She straightened and stood up with a smooth movement. Smiling, she tidied the front of her gown, quickly closing the two buttons that his hand had forced apart.

Still aflame, O'Leary said, "I don't understand, Louisa."

"Soon you will." She was already progressing around the room, turning down gas mantles, snuffing candles. A soft darkness began to spread through the room, from the far wall, to the corners, circling around the fireplace.

The photograph, with François's glaring face, was briefly picked out by the remaining light.

With the fire once more glowing with embers behind the wire guard, she returned to him. He raised his arms to take hold of her, but she warded him off.

"Good night, Dennis," she said. "I asked Mrs Acland to stoke up the fire in your room." She brushed his cheek with her fingertips. "At least that freezing wind has stopped. To hasten our meeting tomorrow, I ask you to sleep naked. Sleep on your back. Sleep deeply."

She twitched an eyebrow suggestively, then slipped away from him, across the shadowed drawing room, stepping around the crowded *objets* and antiques, then through the doors and into the hall. O'Leary collected his case of apparatus and hurried after her. There was no sign of her out there.

THE BEDROOM FELT warm when O'Leary entered. It was as yet much earlier in the evening than the time he normally went to bed. He stood in agitation and frustration for a while, wondering what the hell she was playing at, but eventually he calmed down. He sat in front of the fire in an easy chair, poked the logs a few times to get them flaring again, then read more of the book he had picked out downstairs. He warmed his toes in front of the fire.

Later he went for a shower and came back shivering

into the main part of the bedroom. He stirred up the fire again and added another big log. Flames burst from the bark in a satisfactory way. Wearing only his dressing gown, O'Leary stood before the fireplace, feeling the heat on his back.

When he looked in his valise he discovered a large padded envelope had been squeezed inside. He opened it eagerly and immediately saw several bundles of banknotes. Each wad was wrapped in a paper sleeve imprinted with a bank's logo. With his dressing gown hanging open, O'Leary counted the first of the wads: it was a mixture of £20 and £50 notes, and totalled £1,000 in all. He found another nine, identically wrapped.

There was more. Deeper inside the padded envelope was a small cardboard box, sealed with tape and a note wrapped around it with an elastic band. He put it to one side, because below it, even deeper inside, were many more wads of notes, in their paper sleeves.

He unwrapped the slip of paper and opened the cardboard box. There was a small glass bottle inside, stopped with a cork. The paper had a handwritten message. He sat down beside the fire so that the light from the nearest gas mantle fell on the words. He read:

My darling Dennis – We agreed a transaction, and here is what I promised you. As money does not interest me, and because you have suddenly become special to me, I have in fact trebled the amount we agreed.

This bottle you have found contains a tincture I formulated myself. I should like you to drink about half of the mixture, and spread the remainder of it across the parts of your body you and I no doubt consider most sensual. There is nothing for you to worry about; the mixture is a light alcohol distillation, much diluted with some special herbs and a few secrets I learned from my dear husband. You will adore what this tincture will do to you, and what it will do for me.

As soon as you have read this, apply the mixture as I have described, then take to your bed in the way I asked. There you will wait for tomorrow to come, because tomorrow is when we shall both atchieve what we most desire.

Louisa

THE TINCTURE HAD a sharp taste, but there was so little of it in the bottle that a mouthful was easily consumed. It left hardly any aftertaste. Discovering the package and the note had made him feel somehow observed in that room, and therefore self-conscious. He drank only half the contents and did not follow the second part of Louisa's instructions. He pushed back the cork and placed the bottle on the bedside table. He put his wristwatch beside it, with the face visible. It was now a few minutes before midnight.

He was still not sleepy and wished there was a TV in the room. It was warm now and he lay on top of the bedclothes, his dressing gown open, his back propped against pillows. He turned off the gas light above his bed, and lay waiting for sleep. He heard the calendar wheel of his wristwatch click to the next date, as midnight passed.

Suddenly, Louisa was there. He thought he must have drifted off, because he had not heard her open the door. But there was no mistaking her presence in the room.

"It is midnight," she said. "Tomorrow is today! Let us atchieve!"

She was standing between him and the open fire, which had become the only source of light in the room. He could see the radiance of the fire through the material of what she was wearing – it was some kind of nightgown or shift, made of diaphanous white fabric. He could see the silhouetted shape of her legs, then as she hurried towards him, heading for the side of his bed, he glimpsed the rest of her. The gown barely covered her.

She seized the bottle, shook it.

"You have not used it all," she said, and waved it at him in mock scolding.

"I drank most of it," O'Leary said, amazed and thrilled by her arrival. He was acutely aware of lying exposed before her, even in the half-light. He sensed her perfume, could make out her loosened hair falling about her face, watched her quick hands as she pulled the cork from the bottle. The gown was falling carelessly from her shoulder, revealing one of her breasts. He yearned to have her.

"It must be on you too," she said, and immediately turned over the bottle and sprinkled it across his naked legs, chest and groin.

O'Leary took a sharp intake of breath, because the liquid stung as it landed on him. It was not unpleasant. He was already aroused.

"Louisa ..."

"No. Say nothing."

She clambered up on to the bed, straddled him, raised her gown to her waist and squatted across his body. He reached up to take her breasts in his hands, groping and caressing her beneath the gown, while she found him and eased him into her.

What followed was unhurried.

For most of the time O'Leary had his eyes closed, his senses sated by the physicality of the woman and the fragrances of their lovemaking. But towards the end, while his heart was racing and his breath was rasping in his throat, Louisa suddenly yelled.

"Is he there?" she gasped. "Can you see him?"

O'Leary opened his eyes. The logs had shifted in the grate, bright flames were darting. Across the room, back from the bed and close to the glowing fire, stood the figure of a man. He was young, tall, erect. He held an ebony cane. He was wearing grey trousers and a dark frock coat. His hair was short, tousled, black. He had long sideburns and a goatee beard. He was glaring angrily at O'Leary, and raised his cane.

"Is François there?" she cried again. Her back was turned away from the apparition. O'Leary could say nothing, terrified by the sudden manifestation, but knowing he was at the very moment of climax. "Can you see him?" she said again. "That is what haunts me!"

Their lovemaking came rushing to an end. O'Leary felt the familiar increase of tension, the exciting suspense, the release, but it was more intense than ever he had known it, a voiding, an emptying, a draining, a flow from a deeper source. Where their bodies pressed together, where the tincture had fallen, he felt an almost electrical discharge of energy. Louisa was twisting herself against him, pressing and moving herself deliberately against those parts. O'Leary continued to ejaculate, beyond passion, beyond sexual union, a decanting of himself into her.

From the other side of the room came a man's voice, hollow, dismissive, loudly filling the small room: *"Adieu, monsieur le prestidigitateur!"*

And Louise whispered, *"Au revoir, mon brave."*

O'Leary's consciousness began to fade and the apparition of the dead husband drifted away. Louisa's bodily weight slumped down hotly across him, moist with perspiration, soft and shaking with her climax. Her long hair tangled wetly about him, covering his face and chest. He could not breathe, he was in fearful dark, his senses dying.

He heard her shout, "This house to let, *on s'occupe encore une fois, François, mon chéri.* I am occupied again."

Then there was silence, a muting blackness.

THE ELDERLY VOLVO lurched across the ruts of the unmade lane, throwing up mud whenever its wheels spun as it momentarily sought traction. The thaw had set in during the night. Pools of water lay everywhere and on each side of the lane the ditches were full. The driver, Rick, struggled with the steering wheel, nervous of accidentally sliding to one side or the other. White clouds moved slowly overhead in a sky of wan sunlight.

He came to the gates of the house, but almost passed them by. Since his last visit, a mass of ivy and other creeping plants had grown across the twisted railings. Rick briefly thought that this was not the right place, that it was another entrance, perhaps one that led to an abandoned or derelict house, but he squinted across at the satnav, where confirmation of his destination was shown. He slammed on the brakes immediately, causing the painted trailer behind the Volvo to skid on the muddy surface, swinging around to the side.

He left the car where it had halted and pushed open

the gate. He walked up the waterlogged drive, stepping over several fallen small branches. On each side of the drive the bushes and plants were overgrown and drooping, with weeds springing up all over the surface of the driveway. To one side, what looked as if it had once been a lawn with surrounding flowerbeds was a riot of tumultuous weeds, mostly bare and brown in the winter air.

The house, which he could see ahead, did not look ruinous, but it was clearly in need of urgent repair work. Some of the bricks were loose, with many gaps in the mortar, the painted doors and window frames were peeling, and several slates were missing from the roof. The windows were dull, as if they had not been washed in years. One was broken and had been roughly repaired with cardboard.

There was no sign of a doorbell, so he hammered on the door with his fist. After a long pause the door eased open. Someone peered at him through the crack, then scraped the door wide open.

It was a woman, wearing a woollen pullover, blue jeans and a tweed cap.

"I have come to see Madame de Morganet," Rick said. "I was told she has a package for me."

"And you are – ?"

"Rick. Just say it is Rick."

"May I have your surname?"

"Rick will do. She knows who I am."

"Oh, yes. Of course."

The woman turned away and bent down, and almost immediately came back holding a valise, which Rick recognized as being Dennis's.

"Madame de Morganet is resting and is not receiving

visitors today," she said. "But she has instructed me to tell you that the bag contains everything Mr O'Leary brought with him, as well as what was agreed. You will have to sign for it."

"That's all right."

She handed over a pen and a blank scrap of paper, on which Rick dutifully tried to scribble, resting the paper against the peeling wall of the wooden porch.

"Madame has asked me to convey her sincere thanks to you, Rick," the woman said while he was still trying to get the pen to write. "She was pleased and satisfied with your arrangements."

"Is Dennis here?" he said, as he handed the pen and paper back to her.

"Mr O'Leary left the house during the night." She stared at him noncommittally.

"Left? Where did he go?"

"I'm afraid I can't tell you that. It's a matter for Monsieur and Madame."

He hefted the valise on to his shoulder. "Look, should Dennis turn up, would you ask him to phone me as soon as possible?"

But the door was already closing, the warped old wood scraping against the stone flags. He heard her say, just as the door closed with a double push from inside, "Mr O'Leary's phone is inside the bag."

Rick set off down the drive. As he walked, he eased open the top cover of the valise, and reached inside. He felt the hard weight of the laptop, the plastic case of the mobile phone, clothes and a bathroom bag. He groped deeper and found what he was seeking: many neatly packed wads of banknotes, satisfyingly crisp, down at the bottom of the bag.

He walked past Madame de Morganet's display board, but did not glance at it. He opened the passenger door of the Volvo, put the valise on the front seat, then went back to look.

Unlike the untidy, weed-filled state of the garden, the sign looked clean and cared for, the glass shining in the wintry sunlight. He read her claimed list of 'atchievements,' then noticed the final line:

...Actuarial Calculations, Tax Returns, Law of Probate, Law of Property, Law of Torts, Illusionism and Prestidigitation...

There was a blank area near the bottom, as if to leave room for more skills to be added, then a telephone number.

Rick climbed back inside the car, started the engine and waited for the heater to warm him up. He reached deep into the valise, tossing Dennis's possessions on the car floor, then removed all the wads of notes and counted them. Each one contained £1,000 in mixed notes, and there were thirty of them in all.

He put the money away, out of sight, and sat in the car, thinking. He inspected the laptop, which booted normally when he tried. The mobile phone's battery was low, but nevertheless the handset switched on. There were no text messages for Dennis, he had no missed calls.

Finally, he climbed out of the car and took all Dennis's clothes and personal possessions and placed them inside the trailer. He folded the royal-blue suit neatly. He then locked the trailer, unhooked it from the car and left it where it was, askew across the muddy lane. He put the old Volvo in gear and drove away slowly along the lane, past the weed-filled grounds of the house, beneath the winter-bare trees, against the rising green shoulders of the South Downs, under a brightening sky.

THE DOLL'S HOUSE

JONATHAN GREEN

Some of you may know Jonathan Green better as the mild-mannered author of Abaddon's long-running steampunk series, Pax Britannia, *but within this gentlemen of words beats a dark heart. 'The Doll's House' is in the tradition of the more gruesome stories found in the old* Pan Book of Horror *series, but while there is most certainly a shock here of the most gruesome kind, this is also a meticulously crafted piece of horror fiction; one that will draw you quickly into its dark influence.*

THE HOUSE IS an unremarkable, mid-terrace, Edwardian build that the estate agents described as "a spacious and skilfully extended, four bed period property in a central location." In truth the kitchen is smaller than Jen would have liked, there's no off-street parking, the Tube is a good fifteen minutes' walk away, and the fourth bedroom is little more than a box room.

But it's nice enough, in need of a little repainting – and most of that's upstairs, the previous owners having given the downstairs a sprucing up to get people through the door -- but nothing major, and it's a step up from the two-bed maisonette they moved into before Toby was born. The box room will be big enough for the new baby, when it arrives, and hopefully they won't have to think about moving again for a good few years.

And so they sign on the dotted line and after a fretful few weeks they're finally standing in the hallway of their new home, keys in hand, idiot smiles on their faces, their arms around each other. Toby's already out doing laps of the postage stamp of grass that passes for a garden, squealing with delight.

Chris turns to her, looking like the excited twenty-something she first met at Uni all those years ago. "We've done it!" he says, a boyish twinkle in his eyes again. "We've really done it! I can't believe it's ours!"

He pulls her close, taking care not to squeeze her too tight now that her bump's showing, and they kiss.

They only stop kissing when there is the sharp rap at the front door and a burly shadow appears through the glass panels. The removal men are here.

IT'S THE ISOLATION she finds hardest to cope with.

Toby goes to Nursery three mornings a week and is keen to help her with the re-decorating whenever she'll let him. And although his efforts can only be described as patchy at best, his indefatigable enthusiasm encourages her to keep at it herself.

The two of them paint his room first, choosing the colour scheme together. She even braves IKEA one afternoon, while Chris is at work – he hates IKEA at the best of times – but with Toby in tow, picking out his first big boy's bed and putting it together that same day. When Chris gets in that evening, Jen's just putting on the new dinosaur duvet cover and matching pillow case, while Toby's having his bath.

"Dada! Dada!" Toby shouts, hearing the door go downstairs.

"Alright, buddy?" Chris's voice comes from the hallway below.

Jen smiles, straightening the corners of the duvet cover as she lays it on the new bed.

She hears the thud of Chris's bag on the polished floorboards and the clatter of him kicking off his shoes before he bounds up the stairs to see his son.

"Dada! Dada! I've got a big boy's bed!"

"Have you, Toby?" she hears Chris say over the excited splash of bathwater. "So did you and Mummy go shopping today?"

"Yeah. We went to the big yellow shop."

"IKEA?"

"Yeah. High-KEA. An' I got a big boy's bed and went on the slide."

"You went on a slide?"

And then he's there, slipping his arms around her bulging belly, making her jump. She hadn't heard him come into Toby's bedroom behind her.

"And did Mummy have fun at IKEA?" he asks, kissing the back of her neck.

"Hello," she says, struggling to turn around within his embrace, kissing him on the lips. The aroma of his aftershave still lingers upon him but she can also taste the chocolate muffin he's obviously enjoyed on the way home. "Good day?"

"Oh, you know. Same old, same old. Could've been worse. But enough about me. I want to hear all about your adventures at IKEA."

"It wasn't that exciting." She smiles.

"You don't say. Looks good," he says, releasing her at last and running a discerning hand over the white laminated chipboard.

And then he turns back to face her, concern written large on his face. "You didn't overdo it, did you? Lugging this up here?" he says, eyeing the pile of flat-packed cardboard and broken polystyrene in the middle of floor.

"No, of course not. I'm fine. Anyway, Toby helped me."

"But just the same."

"Don't worry. I'm fine. Besides, you know me. I can't stand sitting around here doing nothing."

He grins again. "You can't stand sitting…?"

"You know what I mean," she says, slapping him playfully on the arm.

"So, what have you got planned for tomorrow? Painting the Forth Bridge?"

"The baby's room."

"Okay, but there is such a thing as doing too much. You don't want to go getting overtired."

"And I won't. In fact I was going to cook us some supper while you put your son to bed, and then I thought I might have an early night."

"Oh, yeah?" her husband says, an excited teenager smile on his face, encircling her in his arms once again.

"Yes, while you go through all those reports, or whatever it is you've brought home with you."

"Oh. Really?" He looks at her with what he clearly thinks are appealing, puppy dog eyes.

"*Really*. You know you'll be annoyed if you have to take them back again tomorrow unlooked at."

"I suppose so."

"And besides, you don't want me getting overtired, do you?"

"Dada! Dada!" Toby shouts from the bathroom. "Watch this!"

"Come on, let me go. Your son wants you."

So MUCH MORE aware is she, now, of the impact the new baby with have on their lives, that she makes the most of that glorious phase between being virtually crippled by morning sickness – with Toby miming vomiting every time he walks past the loo – and being so big she can't even see her own feet to tie her shoelaces.

She and Toby paint the baby's room between them and the three-year-old seems very pleased to have played his part, even if more paint ended up on him than the walls. But by the time the two of them have finished, the box room has been transformed into a vision of soft lavender, finished with cuddly animal-themed detailing.

The last room to see a fresh lick of paint is the master bedroom. The guest room that was put in the attic by the previous owners will have to wait, just as will the clean white canvas that they've inherited on the ground floor.

And then that time is gone in the blink of an eye, or so it seems, and she's feeling like a bloated whale again, the water retention making her curse the celebs that adorn her glossy weeklies with their personal-trainer-and-nanny-bought perfect post-baby bodies.

She can't see her feet anymore and resigns herself to several weeks of back ache, haemorrhoids and half a dozen trips to the bathroom during the night:

*   *   *

THE BABY, WHEN it comes, is almost two weeks late. The labour itself isn't half as gruelling as it was with Toby, and the birth leaves her with a feeling of optimistic euphoria and utter joy. She now has a daughter as well as a son. A matching set.

Chris brings Toby in to see the baby the next day, having had a chance to go home, get some sleep and freshen up the night before while Jen and Emilia – Emmie for short – spent their first night together in hospital.

Toby looks so angelic, with his curly blond locks, and as he kisses his baby sister gently on the forehead, Jen is overwhelmed by emotion.

After only a couple of trauma-free days in hospital – made more comfortable by Chris stumping up for a private room – they're pulling up outside the house to be greeted by a gaggle of curious neighbours, Chris's mum and dad beaming at them from the doorstep.

Toby helped make the banner that's been pinned to the cornicing in the sitting room. It reads 'Welcome Home Emmie' in big bold day-glow letters. Seeing it makes Jen start to cry all over again.

"SO, HOW ARE things?" her mother asks several weeks later.

She's looking well. Jen wishes she could say the same about herself. Her mum's lost weight and has a glorious tan that her white sleeveless top shows off to good effect. But then a six week cruise of the Caribbean will do that.

Jen carefully puts down her coffee on the kitchen counter and takes a deep breath before answering.

"I told you, Mum, everything's fine."

"Are you sure, dear? Only you sounded a little – how shall I put this? – a little stressed when we spoke on the phone."

"Oh you know how it is. Toby had jam all over his face and I didn't want him getting any of it on the new sofa."

"Why you chose a white sofa with a little one around and a new baby in the house, I'll never know."

"It's champagne."

"What is?"

"The colour of the sofa. It's champagne, not white."

Her mother huffs in irritation. "I don't know. Why do they have to make up all these ridiculous names for things these days? What's wrong with 'white'?"

"Because it isn't white."

"Cream, then."

"I told you," Jen says with forced calm, "in the brochure it's classed as champagne."

"Still a silly colour to choose when you've got little ones, no matter what you call it," her mother mutters into her coffee.

Jen takes a deep breath before counting to ten. "Anyway," she says with a sigh, "moving on..."

"Are you sure you're alright?"

"Look, I told you, I'm fine."

"Only you look tired."

"Of course I'm tired!" Jen suddenly snaps. "What did you expect? I spend all day running around after an active three year-old and a six week-old baby. There's shopping, laundry and cleaning to be done, and don't even mention the ironing. I'm more fully employed than Chris is at work! And now Toby's started playing up..." Jen lets out her pent-up frustrations in a loud sigh, her shoulders sagging. "The honeymoon period's definitely over."

"What do you mean by that?"

"I think he's jealous. And he's getting rather naughty."

"Not my little boy, surely? Anyway, I thought he was going to Nursery five mornings a week."

At that moment, heralded by the rattle of keys, the front door bangs open and Toby charges down the hall and into the kitchen.

"Nana!" he exclaims in delight, throwing his arms around his grandmother's legs.

In response, Jen's mother bundles him up in her arms, giving him a huge bear-hug.

"And how's my little sausage?" she asks, kissing him noisily on the cheek and provoking a flurry of giggles.

"Nana, we've been to the park!" the toddler manages to tell her at last, once he's got his breath back. "And I went on the swings and the slide and the see-saw two times. And me and Dada played football!"

"Goodness me, you have been busy boys."

"Hi, Julia, how are you?" Chris asks, entering the kitchen laden down with Toby's scooter and the football. Putting an arm around his mother-in-law's shoulders he plants a kiss on her cheek. "You're looking well!"

"Yeah, well six weeks in the Caribbean will do that to you," Jen mutters under her breath.

"It's great to see you. How was the holiday? Have you been here long? Have you met Emmie yet?"

"No, not yet," Jen's mother says, looking pointedly at her daughter. "Apparently her ladyship is having a nap and Jennifer didn't want to wake her."

"Well you know how grisly she was in the night," Jen jumps in, looking from the baby monitor on the counter to her husband and giving him an imploring look, "and if she doesn't catch up on her sleep now, she'll be grisly all afternoon too, and I couldn't bear that. Besides, it was just for an hour while I caught up with the ironing."

"It's alright," Chris says, squeezing her arm and giving her a peck on the cheek too. "No one's judging you," he adds quietly in her ear.

"You sure about that?" she mutters back.

They hear the baby's cries through the crackle of static on the baby monitor – the green and red LEDs arcing in response – and echoing down the stairs at the same time.

"Well, sounds like someone's awake now," her mother says.

"I'll go," Jen says hurriedly, glad to have an excuse to get away, if only for a moment.

"Right, Chris," she hears her mother say as she climbs the stairs, "could you give me a hand with something?" And then the two of them – mother-in-law and son-in-law – are making their way to the front door, with Toby following, his toddler curiosity as indefatigable as ever.

Jen enters the closed-curtain gloom of the baby's room to be greeted by her darling daughter, her face already near-purple from screaming, tiny fists bunched in impotent rage, legs kicking furiously as if she's trying to bust out of her babygrow, and the unmistakable ammonia aroma of a full nappy.

By the time Jen's cleaned her up and put her in yet another fresh babygrow – the soiled one joining the unending pile of washing in the laundry basket, the allegedly leak-proof nappy having leaked liquid shit all up Emmie's back – and carried her downstairs, everyone's back in the kitchen.

"Here she is," Jen says, passing Emmie into her mother's outstretched arms. "Mum, meet your granddaughter."

"Oh, isn't she gorgeous?" her mother says, nuzzling the baby's silk-soft hair, and then continues in a coochie-coo voice as she stares into Emmie's wide eyes, "Aren't you my darling? Yes, you are. Yes, you are. You're Nana's booful baby girl, aren't you? Yes, you are. Yes, you are."

Emmie gurgles and giggles in response, a cherubic smile on her face, and no sign of the howling banshee that had greeted her sleep-deprived mother upstairs.

"Who's a good girl, eh? Who's a good girl?"

Jen picks up her now-cold cup of coffee and watches her mother with Emmie for a moment, feeling the tension ease from her shoulders a little.

"Where's Toby?" she asks idly, taking a sip of the cold caffeine.

"Over there," Chris says with a nod.

Jen turns and is so surprised she spills half the contents of her mug over herself.

Toby is kneeling at his toy table – which was the coffee table from Chris's old flat, in a former life. He is busy placing the pieces of furniture inside the large doll's house that's open in front of him. His favourite toys have been shoved under the table to make room for the mock Georgian edifice.

Jen recognises the peeling paint façade, the dark lifeless windows and the drab grey tiles immediately.

"Careful," Chris says, eyeing the stain on her top.

"What's that doing here?" she hisses, her voice barely more than an angry whisper.

"It's been sat at the back of the attic at my place for long enough," her mother says, smiling at her grandson as he carefully places a miniature piano in what should really be the bathroom of the house, if Jen remembers correctly – and she does. "Besides, now my little boy's a big brother I think he's old enough to take care of it, don't you?"

"No, I don't," Jen snaps back.

"Whoa, Jen, what's the problem?" Chris steps in, giving her a look. "Toby's loving it. It's very kind of you, Julia."

"My pleasure."

"Well I can't stand the thing." Jen picks up a dishcloth and starts to work at the coffee stain. She soon gives up in disgust. "Something else for the never-ending laundry pile," she growls.

"Don't be ridiculous, Jennifer, you used to love playing with it as a child."

"No, I didn't."

"Of course you did."

"No, Mum, I didn't. I hated the thing. Why do you think Dad put it in the attic in the first place?"

"But it's an antique," her mother goes on. "It's been in our family for generations."

"Well, you can put in on eBay, for all I care."

"Jen! What's got into you?" Chris chides her. "I know you're tired, but –"

"That's right, I'm tired!" She slams her coffee cup down on the counter. The handle comes off in her hand, what's left of the mug tipping over and spilling the rest of its contents across the counter.

She turns to Chris, red-rimmed eyes blazing. "There's pizza for supper or you can order takeout if you want. But I don't care. I'm going to bed!"

"Jennifer!" her mother calls after her. "I didn't mean –"

"Thanks for coming over," Jen calls back, already halfway up the stairs. "We must do this again some time."

WHEN SHE WAKES, sweating, in the middle of the night to a silent house, she knows that she's had the dream again. She hasn't had it since she was a child.

So sudden is her awakening that it even causes Chris to stir.

"What is it?" he mumbles, turning his tousled head and peering at her in the half-light of the room.

"It's got to go," she says.

"What's got to go?"

"That doll's house."

"What? Really? Right now?"

"No. It can wait until the morning, but I'm not spending another night under this roof knowing that it's down there."

"Okay, if you insist," he murmurs, turning over and pulling the duvet tight about him again. "'Night, 'night." Thirty seconds later, he's snoring again.

She looks at the alarm clock on Chris's side of the bed. 03:33.

She gets out of bed. She pads out of the room and onto the landing, and eases Emmie's door open. The elephants, monkeys and other animals that spell out her daughter's name welcome her with broad, painted smiles. The glow of the street-lamp around the edge of the blackout blind reveals her daughter's china doll face. Emmie's snoring, just like her father. Toby stirs when she pushes open the door to his room and she mentally chastises herself for still not having got around to oiling the hinges. Her son murmurs something in his sleep and then is quiet again.

Turning from Toby's door, Jen hesitates, one hand on the newel post at the top of the stairs. She was about to go downstairs, but what would be the point of that?

She stands there, listening to the creaks and groans of the house and the humming of the fridge-freezer down in the kitchen.

At long last, she returns to bed. Chris has stopped snoring, thankfully.

She lays there, her mind full of practical concerns. She needs to buy more nappies and Toby has Nursery in the morning. And then she has to book Emmie in for her two-month jabs at the surgery and there's still a mountain of washing and ironing to be done.

She's just dozing off again when Emmie starts grizzling.

With bleary eyes Jen peers at the clock, the glowing green digits slowly coming into focus.

04:26.

Wearily Jen drags herself out of bed to deal with her hungry daughter.

She doesn't go back to sleep again after that.

THE FIRST THING Toby does, when he comes downstairs the next morning, is go to the doll's house. Usually he'll curl up on the sofa with a bottle of milk in front of whatever's on CBeebies, but today he goes straight to the Georgian-fronted doll's house and starts enthusiastically rearranging the furniture.

And Jen has to admit that it keeps him occupied and out of her way while she gets Emmie up and dressed, without the usual continuous demands for milk or attention. But she still promises herself the thing's going away, at least until her mother drops by again, which hopefully won't be any time soon.

Before she knows it, it's time to take Toby to Nursery. She's halfway there before she realises she's still wearing her pyjamas under her baggy cardigan.

AFTER DROPPING TOBY at Nursery, she pops home to get dressed properly before heading down to the local supermarket. She decides to walk, transferring a gurgling Emmie into her pram, hoping that some fresh air and exercise might help her sleep better tonight.

The two of them don't get home again until almost eleven, by which time Emmie's screaming to be fed. Jen slumps in front of the telly, flicking through the Freeview channels while her daughter gorges herself on her mother's milk, moaning contentedly to herself between hungry gulps, eyes screwed tight shut, making Jen feel like a prize Friesian.

Once Emmie's had her fill and drifted off to sleep, Jen puts her in her cot so that she can finally get around to unpacking the shopping. And then, before she knows it, it's time to get Emmie up again so that they can collect Toby from Nursery.

As she puts her foot on the bottom stair she catches sight of the doll's house, sitting regally on the toy table against the back wall of the kitchen-cum-diner-cum-family-room.

It's now or never. She can't get rid of the thing while Toby's in the house.

The loud rap at the door makes her start and she gives a small cry of surprise.

A dark shape awaits her on the other side of the frosted glass. The sheer size of the figure causes her to hesitate for a moment before she dismisses her doubts as nonsense and turns the latch.

"Post," the hulking figure says, thrusting a parcel into her hands. And then he's gone again.

As she places the cardboard package from Amazon on the key shelf beside the door – it's addressed to Chris – she catches the time on her watch.

12:17.

If she doesn't get Emmie up now, and into the car, she's going to be late picking up Toby.

The doll's house forgotten about again, she heads upstairs.

SHE WAKES WITH a start, her sweat-soaked hair plastered to her brow. It was the same dream; the same nightmare. She looks at Chris's clock.

03:33.

Shaking out her pillow she lies down again, preferring to study the cracks in the plasterwork surrounding the ceiling than close her eyes and see that lifeless wooden face again.

She feels wrung out, but she can't sleep. She listens to Chris's heavy breathing, listening out for Emmie, fully expecting her to start crying for milk at any moment.

But Emmie doesn't start to cry until gone five, on this morning of all mornings, just as Jen is finally starting to drop off again.

She hauls herself out of bed – the duvet feeling like it's filled with clay, and not feathers, as she pushes it aside – going for a pee before seeing to her daughter.

She spends the rest of the night in Emmie's room, lounging in the IKEA-bought rocking chair, her sleeping daughter on her lap, thoughts of the hundred and one things she has to do that day filling her head.

"I'M TIDYING THE playroom," Toby shouts from the far end of the family room, later that same morning, raising his voice in an effort to be heard over Emmie's crying.

"That's nice," Jen says, as she rocks the howling baby in her arms. "Emmie, sweetheart, Mummy would really like you to stop crying now." But the red-faced screams continue.

"Mrs Mulligan doesn't like it when Emmie cries," Toby says, but Jen only half hears him over the baby's bawling.

"I don't like it either, darling. What's wrong, sweetie?" she asks the wailing infant, but the only answer she gets is another purple-faced scream that cuts right through her.

"I've changed you, I've tried putting you to bed but you didn't want to know. You can't be hungry again already. You're not too hot. So what is it, darling, why won't you stop crying?" Jen's rocking of the baby in her arms becomes more vigorous without her really realising what she's doing. Emmie's howls intensify until she almost has no voice left and her face is the colour of beetroot.

"*Stop that screaming at once!*"

The vehemence of the shout makes Jen start and for a moment Emmie is silent, so startled is the baby by the sudden noise. And then the howling recommences with renewed force.

Jen turns to see Toby standing on the rug in front of the doll's house, a look of slack-jawed horror on her face.

That voice, so strict and with such authority, so much deeper than a child's should be, and that accent... It couldn't have been Toby, could it?

"Toby," she says, unable to keep the quaver out of her voice, "was that you?"

The toddler stares at her, an expression of guileless innocence on his cherubic face.

"*Was that you?*"

He doesn't dare blink as he meets his mother's furious gaze, even as the tears start to fall freely down his cheeks.

"Mrs Mulligan doesn't like it when Emmie cries all the time," he sobs.

She looks at the doll held tightly in his small hand; the rough cloth dress, the rattling wooden limbs, the same severe painted face from her dreams.

That voice. That name...

"That name! Who told you that name?" she demands. Laying the screaming Emmie on the rug beside her, she crouches down so that her face is level with her son's, and grabs hold of him by the arms. "Did Nana tell you? Did she?"

But Toby says nothing. He just stares at his mother in fear, those eyes, so big, so blue and so guileless.

"Tell me, Toby! Who told you that name? *You must tell Mummy!*"

"Mummy, you're hurting me," Toby whimpers.

She blinks, suddenly snapping out of the furious trance she's put herself into. It's like waking from a dream; a nightmare.

As she comes to, she looks down at his arms and sees the pinched purple half-moons her nails have made in his otherwise unblemished skin.

And then, the tears pouring down her face, she grabs hold of him again, bundling him up in her arms, squeezing him tightly to her.

"I'm so sorry, my darling," she sobs as she clasps his head to her breast. "I'm so sorry."

"HOW DID TOBY get those marks on his arms?" Chris asks later, when the children are both in bed and he and Jen are sitting at the breakfast bar, an open bottle of wine and half a dozen tin foil trays spread out between them.

"What marks?" Jen asks, feeling the skin on her neck and face flush.

"I saw them when I was giving him his bath. Looked like he'd been pinched."

"That reminds me," Jen says, changing the subject. "Do you know what he did today?"

Chris helps himself to the last piece of chicken shashlick. "What? Was it something bad?"

"He shouted at Emmie to stop crying. He said that Mrs Mulligan doesn't like it when Emmie cries."

"What's so strange about that?" her husband asks, through a mouthful of naan. "I mean I know it's wrong of him to shout at you –"

"But Mrs Mulligan?"

"Sorry, you've lost me. Who's Mrs Mulligan?"

"The doll from that bloody doll's house. The housekeeper."

"Okay," Chris replies slowly, swallowing his mouthful. "You're still going to have to explain to me why that's significant."

"That's what I used to call her. Only I didn't name her. That's what she was called."

"I thought you said you hated the doll's house."

"I did, but this isn't about me. How did Toby know the doll was called Mrs Mulligan?"

"Did you tell him?"

"No."

"Well your Mum must have said something."

"When?"

"Well you must have mentioned it in passing then."

"No, I didn't."

Chris favoured her with a condescending smile. "You remember everything you say throughout the day, do you?" He laughed. "'Cause I don't."

"This isn't funny. It freaked me out, alright?"

"Okay. I'm sorry."

"And there was something else. When he shouted at Emmie to shut up, it…"

She breaks off, suddenly realising how ridiculous what she's about to say is going to sound.

"Go on."

"It didn't sound like Toby."

Chris coughs, putting a hand to his mouth to avoid spraying the counter with half-chewed food. Jen glares at him.

"I'm sorry; it's just that our son's doing impressions now, is he?"

"Piss off!"

"Hey, hey. Calm down."

"Well!"

"Okay, I'm sorry. I just sounded like –"

"I know what it sounded like," Jen snaps. "It sounded like I'm going mad again."

"No, that's not what I meant." Chris puts down his knife, placing a gentle hand on her clenched fist. "That's not what I meant at all. I mean you're doing okay this time, aren't you? I know you've not been sleeping well, but other than that everything's alright, isn't it?"

"Well it wouldn't hurt if you could do a bit more around the house."

"And you know I would, if I could," Chris gets in quickly, "but I'm at work all day."

"I know, and I'm left here all by myself, to deal with everything else. What I wouldn't give for a day back in the office. I should be so lucky."

"Jenny, I know you do a brilliant job. Nobody could be a better mum." He squeezes her hand in his. "I do worry about you, you know? Here all by yourself, day after day."

"Is this meant to be making me feel better?"

He gives her hand another squeeze. "Look, you haven't been sleeping well, so why don't we make it an early night? I'm sure we could both do with one, if you know what I mean." He grins at her, arching an eyebrow in lewd intimation. "I certainly could. And it always helps me get to sleep."

"You don't need any help getting to sleep. You nod off at the drop of a hat."

"So come on," he presses, smiling like a fifteen year-old about to lose his virginity after downing the best part of a bottle of cider. "What do you say?"

"I don't know," she says, resting her head on her hand.

"Look, I'm sure there's nothing to worry about with Toby. Kids give voices and names and characters to their toys all the time. I mean look at Teddy – that's a perfect example. And the name thing's probably a coincidence. He must have heard the name on one of those kids' shows he's always watching."

"You make it sound like he does nothing but watch television all day," Jen counters.

"That wasn't what I meant and you know it. Don't go getting all over-sensitive on me now, okay? Come on, you go on up and run yourself a nice hot bath. I'll clear up down here and then I'll give you one of Chris's special back-rubs. What do you say?"

Jen pushes her half-eaten curry away. She's barely touched her wine.

"I'm sorry, Chris, but not tonight, eh? I'm not in the mood."

"You're never in the mood," her husband mutters under his breath before he has the good sense to stop himself.

"And what's that supposed to mean?"

"Well, what do you think? How long's it been now?"

"Chris, I've just had a baby."

"Yeah, almost two months ago. And how long's it been since we last had sex?"

Jen looks at him, flabbergasted. "I don't know."

"Have a guess."

"Um..."

"Twelve months, almost to the day."

"What is this? Are you keeping score now?"

"Used to be you could hardly keep your hands off me; even after Toby was born we were back at it within a couple of months at most. And that was at your instigation."

Jen stares at him, feeling her neck and face flush in embarrassment.

"But ever since Emmie came along it's like you don't want anything to do with me."

"How can you say that?" she rails, finding her voice

again. "You know that's not true!"

"Well that's how it looks from where I'm standing!"

"What do want me to say? I'm sorry? Is that it? Well, in that case, I'm sorry." Setting her elbows on the counter, she rests her head in her hands. "This wasn't how I wanted this evening to go."

"Me neither."

It's then that Emmie starts to cry, the lights of the baby monitor arcing in sympathy.

Neither of them moves for a minute, and then Chris meets her sulky stare. "Look, are you going, or shall I?"

03:33. ON THE dot.

She goes to the loo, then checks on both the children before getting back into bed, but, try as she might, she can't get back to sleep.

She eventually gives up on the charade and gets up. She checks on Emmie again, but the little one shows no sign of waking up any time soon, so she creeps downstairs.

She easily finds her way in the muted gloom of the hallway, the suffused light from the streetlamp outside shining in through the frosted panes of the front door. She heads into the kitchen.

It sits there, in the darkness, like a malignant shadow. Its windows gleam like obsidian mirrors. The flesh on her arms goose-pimples under her baggy T-shirt, and an icy shiver of unease crackles up her spine. She can imagine the housekeeper at one of the windows, staring out at her from behind the darkened glass, and she can imagine the sort of thing she'd be saying: the cutting, hurtful comments; the chastising tone.

Emmie's hungry mewling stirs her from her reverie and she looks at the glowing red digits of the clock on the cooker.

04:47.

BARELY TWO WORDS pass between her and Chris the following morning when he leaves for work. He doesn't even stop to make himself a coffee and the memory of the argument leaves her in a foul mood for the rest of the day.

She's still stewing over their argument, chopping onions for that night's spaghetti bolognaise, when Emmie's cries stir her from her melancholic reverie, the lights spiking red on the baby monitor. She only went down for her nap an hour ago. She should be good for another half hour at least.

Putting down the vegetable knife and wiping her hands on the tea towel she casts a glance towards the doll's house. Toby's not there.

The doll's house is open, and the sight of it makes her stop and stare. Her three year-old son has arranged the furniture with such precision that everything is in its proper place and not a single piece is missing. Except for one. The housekeeper doll – Mrs Mulligan.

"Toby?" she calls, but there's no reply.

She pokes her head around the sitting room door as she heads for the stairs, but the TV's off and Toby's not there.

Emmie's angry howls continue unabated. She always sounds so angry, as if she's thinking: *How dare Mummy leave me alone up here like this?*

"Toby? Are you alright?"

Still no reply.

Emmie's angry protest is coming at her front two directions now – from the baby monitor in the kitchen as well as down the stairs.

As she makes her way up, she catches a glimpse of the yawning doors of the doll's house again.

She finds Toby in Emmie's room. He's peering through the bars of the cot at the screaming baby, chatting away quite happily.

At first she thinks he's talking to the baby, or even talking to himself. Then she sees the housekeeper doll clenched tightly in his right hand and feels her throat constrict and her stomach knot in fear. The doll is watching Emmie with its black painted eyes, the never-changing expression of disapproval on its face.

"Toby, what are you doing in here?" Jen demands, as she lifts the kicking, screaming infant out of her cot. The air is redolent with an unhappy marriage of diarrhoea and talcum powder. "Didn't you hear Mummy calling?"

She lays Emmie down on her changing mat. Judging by the spreading yellow stain at the thigh of her babygrow, it's another squitty one.

"Mrs Mulligan doesn't like Emmie screaming," he says with candid honesty.

"But she's a baby," Jen says, wearily, "and that's just what babies do. And this one more than most," she adds under her breath.

"Mrs Mulligan says that children should be seen and not heard," the toddler says. "Mrs Mulligan says we'd all be better off if the little blighter had never been born."

She turns on him at that. "Toby! That's a horrible thing to say! I never want to hear you say such a horrible thing again!" With Emmie kicking her way out of the open nappy mid-change, Jen grabs Toby by the arms. "I never want to hear you talk about your little sister like that again!"

Toby cries out in pain and drops the doll. It lands on the carpet, its head turned towards Jen, its painted features set forever in the same disapproving black scowl.

Without thinking, she lashes out, kicking the doll out of the door and halfway across the landing.

Toby starts to cry.

"Go to your room!" she screams at him.

Toby does as he's told, his little body shaking as it's wracked by his sobs.

She turns back to the baby, fists clenched as she struggles to hold in her simmering rage.

There's shit everywhere. Emmie's legs are covered in it, as is the changing mat. Some has even made it onto the wall.

Jen gives in to her own scream of frustration, the baby's yells rising in response in animal panic.

"Shut up! Shut up! Shut up!" she shrieks. And then she stops, exhaustion threatening to overcome her. Her heart's racing. She looks at her hands. She's shaking too.

She just stands there for a moment, letting out her breath in a weary sigh. She doesn't know how long she stays like that, eyes closed, doing nothing, wishing the world away. But the world doesn't go away.

Taking another deep breath, she opens her eyes and sets about clearing up the mess.

"I MEAN, WHERE did he even hear language like that?" she says to Chris over dinner, as she twirls a piece of spaghetti onto her fork over and over and over.

"Not on CBeebies, I take it."

"I wish you would take this seriously, Chris."

"Why? You seem to be taking it seriously enough for both of us."

Her silence is reaction enough.

"Look, you don't know what he might overhear at Nursery. They're caring people, sure, and I've got nothing against them, but they're common as."

"It didn't sound like something they'd say."

"Look, what is it you're really worried about here?"

She hesitates before answering, still twisting the same piece of spaghetti around the tines of her fork.

"I guess I'm worried he might try to hurt her."

"Emmie?"

"Of course, Emmie! Who else would I mean?"

"Alright," he counters defensively. "But come on, be serious. Do you really think that's likely to happen?"

She says nothing.

Chris looks at her, an expresson of burgeoning anxiety on his face. "Clearly you do."

She meets his gaze at last, her tired eyes wide with fearful doubts of her own.

"Look, here's what I think you should do. Call Doctor Pomeroy in the morning."

"Great! So you think I'm going mad."

"No! No, I don't. Not at all. But what harm could it do just to have a chat about things?"

Jen turns her attention back to the congealing meal on her plate. "Everything was alright until she brought that bloody doll's house round."

"Now, come on, Jen. You got ill before and it didn't have anything to do with a doll's house."

"I was right. You *do* think I'm going mad."

She pushes her plate away from her with a clatter of cutlery.

"Look, let's not do this again. Not tonight. I've had the day from Hell and –"

"And you think I haven't?"

"I was just going to say we're both tired, so let's open a bottle of wine and relax. Watch some TV, nothing more heavy than that, and let's see where the evening takes us. No pressure."

"That's your answer to everything, isn't it?"

"What?"

"Alcohol!"

Chris slams his hands down on the breakfast bar and gets up from his seat. "I can't talk to you when you're like this."

"Where are you going?" she asks, suddenly consumed by overwhelming dread.

He's already in the hall putting on his shoes. "Out."

"But we haven't finished supper."

"Oh, I rather think we have, don't you?"

He picks up his keys from the shelf by the door and is gone, slamming the door behind him.

"I'm worried about you, Jennifer dear," comes her mother's voice down the phone line later that evening.

Jen takes a moment to wipe her nose on the balled-up tissue she's been using to wipe away her tears, as she struggles to compose herself.

"Don't be," she manages between sniffs. "I'm alright. Really I am. It's just that I've been so tired and then Chris storming out earlier... I just wanted somebody to talk to."

"Are you sure, Jen? I don't want you to take this the wrong way, but this isn't your old condition coming back, is it?"

"If we're going to rake over the past, Mum, can we at least call it by its proper name? It's not 'my old condition' or 'the baby blues.' It's called postnatal depression. But I'm not depressed!"

"Couldn't you just give that nice doctor of yours a call in the morning? You know, the one you saw last time. What was his name?"

"Doctor Pomeroy. And no, I'm not going to call him in the morning, because I am not suffering from postnatal depression."

"Do you want me to come over, Jennifer? I'm supposed to be going over to Tommy and Sheila's but it's nothing I can't cancel. I mean we've had it planned for weeks now, but if you want me to come over, I'll give them a buzz and tell them I can't make it."

"No, Mum, it's alright. I'm fine. Honestly, I'll be okay."

"Alright, then, if you're sure. But just give Doctor Pomeroy a call for me, will you dear?"

"'Bye Mum."

"'Bye, dear."

She puts down the phone quickly before the tears start again.

IT'S GONE MIDNIGHT before Chris comes home again. The time it takes him to open the door and the way he stumbles about downstairs, in a vain effort to be quiet, tells her he's drunk. He'll regret it in the morning.

She listens as he makes himself some toast and then hears the muffled tones of the television as he moves into the sitting room. He doesn't come upstairs until gone one. She pretends to be asleep as he plants a beery kiss on her cheek, whispering, "I'm sorry," before climbing into bed beside her.

He's asleep within seconds, and she prays his drunken snores won't wake the baby.

But sleep doesn't come for her, even after the day she's had. She lies there tossing and turning for what feels like an interminable age, and the longer it goes on, the more she worries that she'll be up again at 03:33 anyway. It's becoming a habit.

In the end she gives up and sits up. She looks at the alarm clock, already knowing what it'll say.

03:33.

She gets up. There are baby grows and bibs and shirts and God knows what else to iron before the next round of washing begins.

DESPITE HERSELF, SHE tries the surgery in the morning. After getting the same answerphone message what feels like twenty times, she eventually gets through to the receptionist. Doctor Pomeroy is busy, but the girl on the end of the line says she'll get him to give Jen a call after morning surgery.

She feels a little better after that, more clear-headed and more motivated. She puts that motivation to good use, having got Toby off to Nursery. She finishes the ironing, gives the kitchen and the bathroom and the downstairs loo a thorough clean as Emmie gurgles and chuckles contentedly in her baby-bouncer.

She tidies Toby's toys, hoovers the house from top to bottom and even gives Chris's football boots a clean, ready for the pub league game at the weekend. She even has time to make herself another cup of coffee before she has to pick Toby up. And it's then, as she's tidying away the last few toys while she waits for the kettle to boil, that her thoughts turn to the doll's house again.

It's got to go. She doesn't care that Toby will miss it. It has to go and it has to go now.

There and then she decides to forego her cup of coffee, put the doll's house in the boot of the car and make a diversion to drop it off at the nearest charity shop before collecting Toby from Nursery.

She'll deal with Toby, Chris and her mother later, but at least she'll be shot of the bloody thing.

It's then that the phone rings. Its Doctor Pomeroy calling back.

By the time she gets off the phone again, she's feeling better in herself but she's late for Toby. The doll's house will just have to wait until later. But she's decided; it's going, no matter what.

"IT'S NO GOOD, Toby, it's going. It doesn't matter how much you scream and shout; I'm not having that thing in the house a moment longer. Why don't you go and shoot some goals in the garden or play with some of your other toys?" she says, steeling herself as she makes for the toy table. "We could get your paints out if you like."

Screaming like a banshee, Toby throws himself at her, grabbing her arm with his small hands. He digs in with his fingernails, making her gasp in surprise and pain.

"Toby!"

It's then that he bites her.

It is the action of a moment, a consequence of instinct

rather than rational thought. The punch sends him flying across the room to land in a heap on the floor.

He looks at her with hatred in his eyes, his bloody teeth bared in an animalistic snarl.

"You spiteful bitch!"

Jen stares at her son in horror, the moment of appalled guilt and self-recrimination swallowed up by the implications of that one simple statement.

It's the same voice that she heard Toby use before, only now she recognises the shrewish, accented tones for what they are. It's too deep, too old, too malevolent, to be her baby boy.

Her eyes alight on the doll he's still gripping tightly in his little hand.

"Give me the doll, Toby," she says, her voice shaking. "Give me Mrs Mulligan. I'm sorry I hit you, it was an accident, but I want you to give Mrs Mulligan to me *now*!"

"No!" Toby screams at her in his own voice.

"Do as Mummy says!" Jen demands, her heart racing.

"*No!*"

This isn't like him. He's never this badly behaved. And he's never bitten her before.

"Be a good boy and do as Mummy says *now*!"

"*No! No! No!*" Toby yells, running away from her, heading for the hall.

Jen grabs his arms and holds on tight. "Do as you're told, young man. You don't want to make Mummy cross, do you?"

Toby struggles and kicks as he tries to wriggle free.

"Give me the doll – *now*!"

She lets go of one arm so as to take the doll from him, but he continues to resist, putting the hideous thing behind his back in his vain attempt to stop her taking it from him.

"Right, that's it!"

Not holding back now, using her full strength against him, she spins the boy round. Seizing the offending hand, she bends the little boy's fingers back, finally succeeding in prizing the doll from his grasp.

The child's screams of protest have become incoherent howls of hysterical rage and frustration. Emmie adds her own wails of uncomprehending infant fear from where she sits restrained in her baby-bouncer.

Toby grabs hold of his mother's leg as she strides across the kitchen towards the bin.

Jen slams her foot on the bin pedal and the lid snaps open. She holds the scowling doll over the mess of potato peelings, used tea bags and sticky baby wipes filling the black bag, but then stops herself.

Going out with the rest of the rubbish is too good for the old witch. Mrs Mulligan's fate needs to be something more final.

Kicking her son away from her, Jen opens the cupboard under the sink – the one with the toddler safety catch – and takes out the can of lighter fluid and the box of matches she keeps there next to the floor polish and the sink unblocker.

Deaf to the screams of her howling children, she flings open the back door and storms out into the garden. The barbeque is standing there on the patio.

Throwing back the barrel lid, she chucks the doll onto the grill and pops open the can, dousing the thing with accelerant. Dropping the half-empty container at her feet, she takes a match from the box and lights it, watching as the white flare of initial combustion subsides to become a flickering orange flame, the thin stick of wood twisting and blackening in the heat.

Holding the match over the doll, she hesitates, Mrs Mulligan staring back at her with those soulless black eyes of hers, the same bitter scowl of disapproval on her painted wooden face.

The warm afternoon sun is as hot on her face as the match is between her finger and thumb.

And she hears the housekeeper's scolding voice once more inside her head.

CHRIS LEAVES WORK early that night, eager to be home, eager to spend some quality time with his kids, and eager to make amends, desperate to let Jenny understand how much he loves her, how sorry he is, and how much she means to him.

He stops at the front gate, catching the sweet scent of cooking on the air. Some lucky bugger's going to eat well tonight.

He lets himself in, throwing his jacket over the end of the stairs, half-expecting his son to come charging down the hall and throw himself into his father's arms. But he receives no such welcome. They must be having supper already.

"Hell-oo! I'm home!" he calls. But his announcement is met by silence.

They must be in; the car's parked right outside the house. They must be in the garden.

But they're not in the garden. They're in the dining room.

Jen's sitting at the breakfast bar, rocking Emmie gently in her arms, humming what sounds like a lullaby.

The succulent cooking smells wafting in through the open back door are making his mouth water. Having suffered a stinking hangover for the best part of the day, he now feels like he could eat a horse.

"Something smells good," he says. "Are we having a barbeque?"

But his wife says nothing. She doesn't even acknowledge his presence.

"Jenny?" he says, suddenly feeling sick, as if his hangover's returning. "Is everything alright? Where's Toby?"

There's the doll's house, sitting on top of his old coffee table – despite Jen's threats to get rid of it – but there's still no sign of his son.

"Where's Toby?" he asks, his heart pounding.

He makes for the back door, barely registering the fact that Jenny's entertaining the baby with the tatty old thing from the doll's house, or the burns on his wife's hands.

Then he goes outside.

INSIDE/OUT

NICHOLAS ROYLE

There are many rooms in Nicholas Royle's story, both on the inside and the out; all are haunted and it is up to reader to decide on the nature of the ghost therein. If this sounds like something of a puzzle, then that's exactly what it is, for Royle is adept at constructing beautifully realised, deeply unsettling and deceptively complex stories. 'Inside/Out' is a tale that draws the reader into a labyrinth of imagery and symbolism, leading them through the rooms of a house that holds many secrets.

'In its effective development of a surreal atmosphere of Otherness, combined with its imaginative use of the notion of the dream itself, [Natsume Soseki's *Ten Nights of Dreams* (1908)] creates a liminal literary world which is clearly that of the twentieth century. It is a world which Freud or Jung would certainly have recognized in terms of its suffocating representation of such peculiarly modern anxieties as crises of identity and free-floating guilt, expressed through archetypal imagery.'

– Susan J Napier,
The Fantastic in Modern Japanese Literature

HIS FIRST DAY. They gave him the tour. Three floors at the top of a building on the edge of Covent Garden. Hitchcock had shot scenes from *Frenzy* in a similar building close by, a little over ten years earlier.

He saw two women at neighbouring desks, both in white tops, both with blonde hair. They both leaned back in their chairs and looked at him at the same moment, with the same gentle arching of the back, the same hair falling away from the same slender neck. He heard two names, but he had no idea which was which, and then he was whisked away to the next office in this warren of tiny spaces and interconnecting staircases with worn lino and rubber tread.

He would invent excuses to go to her office. He could tell them apart now; Judy was the one who sat nearest the door. She was the one he liked. He didn't *not* like Madeleine, her colleague, but the liking he felt for Judy he felt somewhere inside, in his chest, in his stomach. In his chest *and* his stomach. Her skin was clear, white marble; when she rolled a cigarette, the pink tip of her tongue appeared between her lips. He was both impressed and faintly terrified by her. Rarely was he able to find her on her own, though; Madeleine was generally sat alongside. They didn't always wear the same clothes, but in his mind they did and they looked alike. Identical.

He found it hard to picture Judy without Madeleine's shadowy presence. They were both shy, but Madeleine was shyer. Judy, at least, would laugh at his jokes. She would lean forward over her desk and cover her mouth with her hand because she felt self-conscious about her teeth. He wanted to tell her her teeth were fabulous, which they were, but he didn't. It would take him twenty years to get to the point where he would feel able to tell her that. Twenty years. Most of that time he would spend in another country on the far side of the world in a culture so alien it might as well have been on a different planet.

He never really stopped thinking about her, but he thought about her in the way you might think about Grace Kelly or Kim Novak or Tippi Hedren.

Before he left, before he went to Japan, he contrived to see as much of her as possible, but always in the workplace, always on a pretext, and most of the time with Madeleine as silent chaperone. On one occasion – it must have been Christmas, the office party, oldest cliché in the book – they came into brief bodily contact. She'd had a few drinks, was wearing a dress or a skirt that flared around her wide, strong hips. He wanted to put his arms around her waist. Wanted to, but didn't. He stood facing her and everything else receded, nothing else mattered. For once, Madeleine was nowhere in sight; the woman he was going out with at the time, who was only seeing him while her boyfriend was away, faded from his mind the moment Judy appeared. They came together briefly and he felt the physicality of her. His legs bumped against hers. Momentarily she allowed him to press his mouth against hers and hers yielded and he felt his lips touch her teeth and then she was gone, smiling, eyes shining, an after-image that stayed with him, imprinted on his retina.

THE HOUSE IS narrow and long – tall – with an unusually squarish footprint for a house of that age, often deeper than they are wide. Three storeys – tall and thin. The window on the first floor has a modest bay. What's strange about the house – and it *is* strange – doesn't strike you the first time you see it. Perhaps not even the second or third time.

There's a large block of flats behind it; social housing, as it's now called. One of those unknown streets you walk down in Hackney because there's no Tube and you need to get somewhere else. Hackney is a walker's borough.

He doesn't know what to do, what to say, after so long saying nothing, doing nothing. Or almost nothing. The kiss is long forgotten, he suspects, although not by him. He kept it in a room in his mind, a room at the top of a house with cream anaglypta wallpaper and stripped floorboards and a sash window. It felt like a safe space, even though he didn't know where it came from. He would visualise it regularly and it would help him to perceive the sensation of the kiss, the physical pressure of it, the considered yield and sudden departure. It's like it happened yesterday, not twenty years ago. But he imagines that for her it never happened at all. He was the one who went away; she stayed behind. He was the one who went to a country where he didn't speak a word of the language, where foreigners – *gaijin*, he soon learned – were openly stared at in the street, where the culture continually fucked with your head. Where, for instance, the distinction between inside and out revealed itself gradually, over the years, to be less a quirky social custom, more a pathological obsession. He was unlikely to forget walking into the changing room in the clothing store in Shibuya and being pursued by an angry shop assistant shouting at him for not removing his shoes. "I didn't have to take them off to enter the shop," he argued, but the man just shook his head impassively. How was he supposed to know that shops were an exception to the rule, or that they counted as outside, while the changing room was inside? Even his host had been unsympathetic, his host whose house he never entered without taking his shoes off first.

The red front door opens and she emerges on to the street. He watches her walk, this morning like every other morning, head down, in the direction of Newington Green. He watches her now, he reasons, because he's been watching her for years – from afar even when close up, and then in the intimacy of his memories on the other side of the world. In a sense it's all he's ever done. Watched. From a distance. From the outside. He doesn't feel he has the right to get any closer now, especially now that he is even further away despite being so much closer. He follows fifty yards behind her on the other side of the street. She walks around the north side of Newington Green, crossing only at zebras and traffic lights, where she waits for the green man. She turns right off the west side of the green, as he knew she would, and then, because it's a Monday, cuts through to reach a quiet street of Victorian terraced houses – four- or five-bed houses, decent-sized houses – with profusions of wisteria and rambling rose and honeysuckle, only the former no longer in flower. He waits at the end of the street and watches as she turns up a garden path. He watches her black-and-white-checked coat disappear into an open porch.

Every Monday the same. An hour later she will come out, coat on, and turn right out of the front path and walk to the Tube at Highbury & Islington.

While she remains in the house, he walks down to St Paul's Road, following the course of the New River, which is not a river but still somehow runs underground beneath his feet, and he crosses over to reach the gardens where it emerges into daylight. He walks along it until he reaches his bench, where he sits and waits. He looks at the narrow, shallow navigation and wonders how it could ever have fulfilled its intended function of providing Londoners with drinking water. He watches a mallard that appears stranded, unmoving in the middle of a stretch of vivid green weed, and two crows as they hesitate on the very edge of the bank, as if uncertain whether they will be able to walk on that verdant carpet. At ten to the hour, he leaves the bench and walks back across St Paul's Road. He loiters in the vicinity of Canonbury station until he sees her walking down towards the mini-roundabout and turning right into Grosvenor Avenue, which will take her towards Highbury & Islington. She walks with a slight bias to the right, neither quickly nor slowly, watching the pavement. As always on a Monday, she appears preoccupied. One time, her make-up ran, as if she had been crying. He waits until she is out of sight and then walks up the way she came, turning right into the street of Victorian terraces. When he reaches the house she had gone into, he stops, looking up at its blank windows. There is an empty window box on the first-floor window ledge. The second-floor windows are dirty, as if that floor of the house isn't used. The ground floor allows a view right through the house to the back garden, which seems crowded with mature trees. The front garden resembles a parody of a Japanese garden with dwarf azaleas, wooden furniture, bonsai trees, beds of slate and an isolated stand of bamboo.

He walks up the path and rings the doorbell. After a few moments a large shape appears through the frosted glass and the door is opened to reveal a fat man of average height in late middle-age with fleshy features, bulldog eyes and thinning hair combed back from his forehead. The buttons of his shirt strain over a large belly. Nondescript trousers, lace-up shoes.

"Yes?" he says. "Do you have an appointment? I don't remember…"

"I'm conducting a survey."

"What? A survey. Oh, no, I'm busy, I'm working." He steps back, waving a dismissive hand. The door starts to close.

"It will only take five minutes of your time."

"No, no, no, no," he says. "I don't have time." And the door closes.

What kind of man closes the door on you before you have gone? Before you have even started to turn away? What kind of man does that?

The kind of man, perhaps, who affects a Japanese garden but wears outdoor shoes inside.

He turns and walks away.

THE HOUSE SHE leaves every morning, the house she spends the night in, the house she lives in (safe to assume). That house. That house is tall and thin and has doors on adjacent sides of the building. At the front of the house there is a red door, which opens directly on to the street, and on the adjacent side of the house there is a green door, which opens on to the pavement. It's a wide pavement. The next building, an abandoned pub, is set back from the road. Hence the wide pavement. There's no path to either door, no front garden. She always comes out of the red door. Every morning she comes out of the red door.

So this is the strange thing about the house. The two doors in adjacent walls. One at the front, one at the side. But there's no room in that house for two entrances to two different dwellings. The house is three storeys high, but it's not a big house. It's a narrow house, a shallow house. She always comes out of the red door and walks the same way towards Newington Green. He follows her so far and then lets her go. She's going to work. Except on Mondays, when she goes first to the street of Victorian terraced houses.

ONE NIGHT AFTER dark he goes to the house – he doesn't normally go to the house at night, but he's had enough of outside, wants to get inside – and knocks on the door. The red door. It moves under his hand. It's not closed. He pushes it open a bit further.

"Hello?"

No answer.

"Hello?"

It's very quiet and his voice lands without echo. It's as if it lands on the floor and clings to the walls and the various other surfaces he imagines, the chairs and tables and desks and the tops of dressing tables and wardrobes, as if it sinks into gaps and cracks and tiny holes and into the dust and the grease and it just sinks and dies there.

He steps into the hall, looks down at his feet. He bends down and unties his shoes and removes them. He stands them next to each other in the narrow hall. He advances. The carpet is thin, no underlay. He can feel hard boards or concrete beneath. The walls of the hall are papered with woodchip, painted white. There's a picture on the wall, a cheaply framed black and white photograph of a street scene. Block of flats, wide pavement. Just after the picture, the door into the room beyond, standing open. He stands in the doorway and looks around the room, which is lit by street lighting filtering through a net curtain. An old, squashy sofa on his right, pushed up against the wall. Adjacent to that, a wall with a large window divided into four long separate panes. This is the window that faces the street, the one with the net curtain. An armchair in the corner. The next wall has a door in it. The door that's painted green on the outside. And at the back of the room, a small kitchen, a kitchenette, various reflective surfaces glimmering in the shadows. Old appliances, charity shop toaster, second-hand fridge.

"Hello?" he says.

Still no answer.

He enters the room, allowing his fingers to trail over the old sofa, which feels gritty, as if the windows had been left open, admitting dirt from passing traffic. He walks across the room to the door on the far side. There are deadbolts top and bottom, but each is pulled back. There's a key in the lock and a simple catch. He turns the key and opens the door. Out of habit, having locked himself out of buildings once too often, he operates the snib. The night is still, the road temporarily empty, no one walking by. The street light casts an ivory glow. He is about to step outside when he remembers his shoes in the hall.

A noise behind him.

He turns, alert.

"Hello?"

Nothing.

He pushes the door to behind him. It fits neatly in the frame.

"Hello?"

Still nothing.

He feels his heart rate increase and walks back across the room and into the hall. He turns to face the stairs. They creak beneath his feet. He reaches the half-landing and turns through a hundred and eighty degrees. As soon as he does that, it gets darker. He feels his way up the next flight, the walls cold and damp to the touch. When he reaches the landing, he waits for his eyes to become accustomed to the gloom. While waiting, he becomes aware of a noise ahead of him. A scratching. Four short scratches and a break, then another four, or five, and another break. It sounds loud in the darkness, which, as he stands still and peers ahead of him, gradually starts to lessen in intensity. He can make out two door surrounds, a short distance apart. The landing is only small and narrow, the stairs, behind him to his right, leading up again to the second floor. The door on the left is open, he can now see, and within he can make out a light patch that is vaguely distinct from the darkness.

"Hello?" he says again.

No answer. The scratching continues.

From his pocket he takes out his mobile phone. He presses the button that activates the back light and he points it at the interior of the room. A woman who looks like Judy from behind is standing at the far side of the room facing the wall. Blonde hair, white top, green skirt. She is standing right up close to the wall. He can only see her back, but there's no question in his mind that it's her. The scratching noise is coming from her. He starts to walk slowly towards her. The light goes out, but her white top remains dimly visible.

He says: "Judy?"

She doesn't stop scratching. There's no sign that she has heard him. He's close to her now. He doesn't need the phone. Her blonde hair falls to her shoulders, curtains the sides of her face. He moves round to one side. *Scratch scratch scratch scratch.* As he moves closer to that side, she turns away from him.

He whispers: "Judy?"

All he can hear is her scratching and his breathing. He wants to touch her, to hold her. He wants her to turn around and hold him.

"Judy?"

He reaches out an arm, his hand floating in the darkness, approaching her shoulder. She seems to shrink from him.

FADE

WHEN HE WAS young, he listened to a lot of Joy Division, and the album he played most often was *Unknown Pleasures.* The music – and the lyrics – appealed to a sense of grandiose melancholy within him. Joy Division were different from other bands. They even eschewed normal conventions of the recording industry: *Unknown Pleasures* wasn't split between side one and side two. Its sides were called Outside and Inside. Outside had a back label, Inside was white.

Somewhere along the line, he had lost the inner sleeve, with its track listing information that appeared nowhere else on the packaging, so that he didn't know which of the two sides of the album was meant to be side one and which side two. He decided it was up to the listener and it seemed to him that 'She's Lost Control' was the perfect opener, while 'New Dawn Fades,' with its loaded guns and valedictory mood, was obviously intended to be the closing track.

When he taped it, he recorded it in that order, and it was the cassette he listened to most of the time.

It came as a shock when the album was released on CD, to discover that he had mixed up the sides. That the album opened with the relatively jaunty 'Disorder' and then as early as track two the listener was plunged into the existential horror of 'Day of the Lords,' which in turn meant that the album would conclude with the spare, echoey soundtrack of whip cracks and smashed glass that was 'I Remember Nothing.'

HE FINDS HIMSELF on the landing again, facing the stairs up to the second floor. It's very dark. He can still hear the scratching, but it appears to be coming from in front of him rather than from back in the room where he reached out to Judy and she turned away. If indeed it was Judy. He never saw her from the front, but he knows the shape and size of her, he knows the fall of her hair, the way it sticks out from her head a little on the left-hand side and curls under her chin on the right. Even from behind and in the dim glow of his mobile phone he had been sure it was her. Who else could it be? This was her home.

But the scratching is coming from above. He starts to climb, placing his palms flat against the walls in the absence of banisters. The walls feel drier, but dirty. Covered in a film of dust. He wipes his hands on his jeans. Continues ascending without the use of his hands. At the top of the stairs, the scratching is louder. He can't see a thing. He takes his phone out of his pocket and presses the button to switch on the light. Then he jumps because she is right in front of him and in his fright he drops the phone. If he had taken another step he would have bumped into her. She has her back to him again – this he saw in the split second of dim illumination before dropping the phone – face to the wall right there on the landing.

"Judy?" he says, as he bends at the knees and feels around for his phone. "*Judy?*"

Scratch, scratch, scratch.

"Judy, will you turn round, please?"

Scratch, scratch, scratch, scratch.

He can see the curve of her back now, the fall of her hair.

"Judy, *please*!"

He locates the phone, puts it in his pocket, takes a step towards her, starts to come around to her left. She turns a fraction away from him, to the right.

Scratch, scratch.

He moves to the right, she to the left.

He lifts his hand, takes a final step forward.

FADE

IN JAPAN HE taught English as a foreign language, but took no formal tuition in Japanese. He felt excluded from society. Outside. What he did learn, he picked up from people he met, women he went out with, and from videos and, later, DVDs. He recorded Hitchcock movies off the television dubbed into Japanese, films he knew more or less off by heart, *Rear Window*, *Vertigo*, *The Birds*, and picked up words and phrases, even some constructions, that way.

When the J-horror trend emerged, he watched certain films – those that seemed closer to the suspense films of Hitchcock and others than some of the more supernatural fare on offer, so: *Ringu, Audition, Dark Water* – over and over again in the original language without subtitles.

It got to the stage where he was confident enough to speak to clients and colleagues in Japanese, but he started to get the feeling he was living in a movie – like being in a dream – and then he couldn't shake it.

Finally, he decided, he was inside.

HE STANDS IN the middle of a room at the top of the house. He knows it's at the top of the house in the way that you know things in a dream. But he also knows he is not dreaming.

It is dark.

Scratch, scratch, scratch, scratch, scratch.

He feels bare boards beneath his stockinged feet. He is shaking.

He can see a pale shape in the corner, facing the wall. The faintest glimmer coming off the hair.

"Judy?"

Scratch, scratch.

"*JUDY!*"

His voice is shockingly loud in the confined space, but flat. No echo. He listens to the thump of his heart. He takes a step forward and stops, unable to approach any nearer, incapable of turning away. He becomes aware of a faint square outline on the wall to his left. Curtains or a blind. Against the opposite wall, barely visible only when he doesn't look directly at it, is what appears to be a large quadruped – big head, long body, short legs – or possibly a man on his elbows and knees.

He smells something sharp and sour. Meaty.

From behind him comes a small noise.

Then a hand on *his* shoulder.

FADE

HE COMES TO, curled up on his bench by the New River, teeth chattering. He slides round and sits up, staring blankly at the bright green weed that covers the surface of the water. He pulls his thin jacket around him in an effort to get warm. His shoes, he notices, are undone.

The streets are quiet, mid-morning lull. He walks slowly, more of a shuffle, his shoes still unlaced. He remembers how one of the first impressions he formed of the Japanese was that they shuffled rather than walked. They didn't pick up their feet. It annoyed him at first, and then he got used to it, and soon he didn't mind it. After a few years he no longer noticed it.

Approaching the house from Newington Green, he sees the green door before the red door. He stops in front of it and knocks twice. He remembers putting the door on the snib. He waits a few moments, then pushes on the door. It opens easily. He removes his shoes as he enters and places them just inside, then pushes the door to.

He looks around the room. It takes a moment to register. The place looks different – and not just because he is seeing it in daylight. The sofa is different. Less squashy, it has clean lines and looks firmer, smarter. He walks across the room and places his hand on the sofa. It does not feel gritty. He frowns, backs away, turns to the kitchen. Dualit toaster, Bosch fridge.

He steps into the hall, checks out the framed photo on the wall, which is the same. He recognises the street now as the one he is on – block of flats, wide pavement – only the house he is standing in is not present in the shot. It should be, but it's not.

He faces the stairs and climbs to the half-landing. He feels the walls with his hands – they are clean and smooth. He places his stockinged feet with care, becoming aware of a faint smell of chocolate and ammonia – or something – something acrid and smoky. He turns the corner and continues to ascend. He touches his hand to the wall, which is neither cold nor damp. Stepping on to the landing, he peers into the first of the two rooms directly opposite. Sparsely furnished, it looks like the bedroom of a single woman. He walks softly across to the far wall, which is papered and painted. There are no marks on the wall.

Back on the landing, where the smell is stronger, he can hear a noise, not a scratching but a low murmur. He climbs the stairs. The murmur is a woman's voice. It stops when he reaches the top landing. There are two rooms, just as on the lower floor. He can see into the room on the left. The boards have been stripped and polished, as on the landing itself. In the room, which is flooded with light from the uncurtained, open window, there is a long, low couch like a chaise longue. It is positioned alongside the right-hand wall, exactly where he had thought he had seen some kind of animal. Lying on it, on her back, her blonde hair streaming out over the couch's single arm, is Judy. Standing beyond her with his back to the couch is a man of average height, but, as he starts to turn, well-above-average body mass. He holds a lit cigar in the stubby fingers of his right hand.

"Judy?"

She looks towards the door.

The man with the cigar gives a loud laugh and then says, "Are you conducting a survey?"

"Judy?" he says, ignoring the man with the cigar.

She raises her head and upper body off the couch and rests on her elbows, looking amused.

"Judy," he says, "what's *he* doing here?" He points to the man with the cigar. "You go to *him*. I've seen you. Every Monday. What's he doing *here*?"

The man with the cigar laughs again.

"I think someone came in the wrong door, Madeleine," says the man with the cigar. "Don't you?"

"*Madeleine*?" he says. "Where's Judy?"

"Next door, of course," says the man with the cigar.

"*Judy*," he says, hearing the pleading tone in his own voice.

"Next door," says the man with the cigar.

"What do you mean next door? There is no next door. Just an abandoned pub."

"The *room* next door, dummy."

Madeleine laughs and doesn't raise her hand to cover her mouth.

He starts to back out of the room as Madeleine reclines once more and the man with the cigar turns his back to her again, as if they are about to resume an interrupted session.

On the landing he takes a breath. The stairs down are in front of him. He turns to his left and stands in front of the door to the other room. He sees his hand reach out and grasp the knob and twist it. The door opens on to more stripped pine floorboards. He enters the room and closes the door behind him.

The room is about ten foot square with cream anaglypta wallpaper. There's a sash window, which is open. Standing in the middle of the room, facing him, is Judy. Her hair curls up under her chin on one side, sticks out endearingly on the other. Her lips part. He sees her teeth glinting. A filament of saliva, pulled taut. He leans forward, closes his eyes.

They kiss.

Finally, he is inside.

When he opens his eyes, she's gone and he's alone in the room. He tries the door, but it's locked. He goes to the window and looks out. The wide pavement, two storeys down; cars driving by, a taxi and a bus; the other side of the street, which he has walked down but never seen from this angle before. It's not so interesting. He backs away from the window and approaches the wall to have a closer look at the anaglypta. Right where he's standing, the textured wallpaper shows signs of having been scored with something sharp – a knife, a pen or, at a push, finger nails. He moves along to the left and finds more deep scratches. And more beyond those. He follows them on to the adjacent wall and so on round the room until he is back at the window, breathing fast and shallow. He leans out. The upper floors of the building immediately across the street have silvered windows. They must be at just the wrong angle, because he cannot see a reflection of the tall, narrow house. He cannot see himself leaning out of the window on the top floor. Just the block of flats behind, and the abandoned pub alongside.

He thinks of the photograph in the hall downstairs. He had thought maybe the picture had been taken before the house was built, but the house was older than the block of flats behind it. You only had to look at it to see that. You only had to look at it.

He looked down at the pavement. If the house didn't exist, jumping from its second floor was hardly likely to kill him.

THE HOUSE

Eric Brown

Eric is best known as a science-fiction writer, but I knew, from the depth and strength of his prose, that he would be able to turn his hand to almost anything. Hence, I asked Eric to write outside of his field and 'The House' is the result of that request. If you know Eric's work, then you know he is brilliant at portraying convincing relationships (check out his superb novel Kings of Eternity *for example) and the couple in 'The House' show the strength of Eric's fiction when it comes to matters of the heart. Here we have two people, fighting to stay together in the face of a very unusual haunting.*

CHARLES TUDOR LOOKED up from his typewriter and blinked. It was a second before he came to his senses and realised the source of the interruption: the phone was ringing in the hall. He pushed his chair back and stood slowly. The summons could only be from two or three people – his agent, his editor, or some pre-pubescent girl in the marketing department at his publishers, Greenwood and Worley.

He moved into the hall and picked up the receiver. "Hello?"

"Charles, Edward here. How are you this fine spring morning?"

He blinked. "Spring?"

"It's the first of April, Charles."

"And you've called to play an April Fool's trick, hmm?"

"That's the Tudor I know!" his agent roared. "Droll as ever. No, no April Fool's trick this year. I was wondering –"

Tudor forestalled him. "The answer's 'no,' Edward."

"You don't even know what I'm about to ask."

"I can guess. You'd like me to take part in some wretched publicity event." The third book in the *Tides of Time* series was due to launch in a couple of weeks, and he would be expected to publicise the title.

"For Nigel," Edward wheedled. "You don't know how he's bent over backwards to push the series. It's the least you could do."

"Fuck off."

Edward laughed.

"What?" Tudor snapped.

"You invest that vulgar phrase with such Shakespearian gravitas, Charles." His agent paused. "You do realise you're getting a reputation as something of a recluse?"

Tudor sighed. Is it any wonder, he thought.

Edward went on, "To be honest, it would be a great favour to me as well as to Nigel. And to your readers."

He hadn't been up to London for years, and it would keep the drones at G&W smiling...

"You have a massive fan base out there," Edward said, "all eager to meet the creator of the *Tides of Time* books."

He relented. "One event, Charles. *One*. No more."

His agent chuckled with relief. "That's all we ask, Charles. A signing at Waterstone's, Piccadilly, in a couple of weeks."

"I'll need a drink to get me through the bloody thing."

"I'll have the best French red on hand during the signing, and afterwards I'll take you to lunch."

"The Ivy?"

"Done," Edward said. "Everyone at Greenwood and Worley will be so excited."

"Fuck off."

HE RETURNED TO his study and finished the paragraph, which brought the scene to a close.

He sat back and looked across the room, to where he knew he would see himself, long and grey, in the mirror propped between the bookshelves. He was sixty-five, he realised with a reaction little short of amazement. Where had all the years gone?

He remembered a long, hard walk he had done in his twenties, back from the pub to this very house, long before he'd married Emmeline. Three miles through horizontal sleet, frozen to the marrow. He'd looked ahead and told himself that it would soon be over; soon he would be sitting before the blazing fire, looking back at the labour of the walk... An hour later he had done just that, and had known that his life would follow this pattern, too. One day he would be contemplating his existence from the vantage point of old age, and the long cold walk would seem to have passed in an instant.

The idea had terrified him then, and it was easy to recapture that youthful terror now; though, paradoxically, the terror was temporized by the passage of the treacherous years themselves. The terror had transmuted to bemused acceptance.

The view through the French windows was little changed in forty years. The lawn stretched to the fulsome willow, and squirrels frolicked, twitching, back and forth. He saw Emmeline run naked from her studio, taken by some impulse of her manic phase to disport herself amid nature... He smiled to himself and blinked and she was gone, a vision of utter beauty alive, now, only in his memories. The image of her was replaced by other, later ones, which he tried to banish.

He pulled his gaze from the lawn and regarded the bookshelf beside the mirror. Seventy books bearing the by-line of Charles Tudor filled the four shelves, all of them for children. His first three books, reading editions of his early plays, he had long ago taken out into the garden and burnt along with a trunk of Emmeline's clothes. He told himself that the ranked titles did not make him bitter, did not denote a lifetime of wasted effort that would have been better spent writing serious plays.

But that would have been impossible, he told himself.

He sighed and brought his flattened palms down, once, on the arms of the chair, then stood.

Lunchtime.

TUDOR HAD HATED the stultifying routine of book-signings in his early years as a children's writer, the embarrassment of events attended only by his editor, agent, three sheepish shop staff and a couple of kids disappointed that their favourite writer should turn out to be so... *boring*. Now he abhorred signings because they were so bloody popular.

The children's section of the store teemed with what seemed like a hundred noisy ten-year olds, shepherded by harassed staff who themselves seemed not much older.

He sat behind a low desk and scrawled his distinctive looping signature, personalising the title page to the shy, hesitant Ellas and Bens and Joes who filed past, so many unlined faces with all their lives to live. He could see, in their eyes, something like shock that their favourite author should prove to be so old.

He was half a bottle of pinot noir to the good, his glass topped up from time to time by Charles in grinning attendance. Earlier, Nigel, his editor, had pumped his hand, "You don't know how much I *appreciate* this, Charles..." before rushing off to a 'prior engagement.'

One hour later, the last of the children had left and he was busy signing the remaining stock. A young thing in a Waterstone's tee-shirt danced up, thanked him, and announced they'd shifted over two hundred units.

Tudor exchanged a glance with Edward.

He was about to suggest they bugger off to the Ivy – he wanted to discuss his next project with Edward – when a woman in her fifties approached the desk, clutching a slim volume to her chest. She had evidently been waiting for the children to depart, and then for him to finish signing the stock, before she bothered him.

She wore her five decades with elegance and grace: she was small and trim, with whitening hair and the pale oval face of an emeritus ballerina. He smiled at her, and thought that something about her face was familiar; he wondered if he'd met her once, years ago.

Even her hesitation, as she proffered the book to sign on the title page, was becoming.

He saw with a shock that it was his third play, *The House*.

His hand shaking, he took the book.

"I hope you don't mind..." the woman said.

He gathered himself. "No... Not at all. To...?"

"To Caroline," she smiled.

He passed back the slim play-script. "First time I've seen the thing in years..." And hopefully the last. Even the sight of it, in its uniform binding, brought back the terror.

"I hope you don't mind, Mr Tudor... I'm a journalist, and I was wondering if you might consent to an interview."

He was tempted to tell her that he didn't do interviews, that he had nothing he wanted to say about anything. But something about the woman's smile, her grace, her becoming trepidation, made him relent.

He said, "I don't see why not. But right now I have a meeting with my agent. I don't know... I rarely come up to London. Perhaps, if you wouldn't mind the journey to Suffolk?"

She beamed, and the gesture irradiated her face with something very much like youth. Ridiculously, Tudor felt his pulse quicken.

"That would be wonderful."

He passed his card. "If you give me a ring, we could arrange a date."

"I'll do that. Thank you again, Mr Tudor." And clutching the play-script, she hurried away.

On their way to the Ivy, Edward gave Tudor a lecherous nudge. "You old dog, Charles."

"You know what I'm about to say."

Edward laughed.

He spent the next hour over lunch wondering why the woman had asked him to sign, of all his many titles, *The House*.

HE FINISHED WRITING for the day, poured himself a glass of wine, and stepped through the french windows.

He walked across the lawn towards the willow, the late afternoon sun warm on his back. A squirrel fled at his approach. At the hem of the willow, he turned and looked back at the house.

It had been in the family for almost a hundred and fifty years, an early Victorian mansion with ten bedrooms, a small ballroom, library, billiard room and a dozen others to which he had never ascribed a function. He had grown up here, and the house had easily accommodated his family and that of his uncle. Their respective families had grown and fled the nest over the years, until the late 'sixties when, on his father's death, the house had been left to him. His first thought had been to sell it, despite the many happy memories he associated with the commodious building. Then he had met Emmeline and she had fallen in love with the place, and after that there had been no way he could sell the house.

They had moved in, closed down all the rooms not needed, and lived in the west wing.

The room adjacent to his study, which had been the billiard room, Emmeline turned into her studio; it was south facing and airy, the perfect place, she said, in which to paint.

He stared across the lawn to the studio's long windows, still draped with the sheets he had placed there the day after his wife's death.

He heard a sound behind him – he was sure it was a burst of laughter – and turned.

He thought he saw a sliver of naked flesh between the swaying fronds of the willow, but knew that he was mistaken. He felt tears spring to his eyes.

One morning shortly after their wedding day, Emmeline had come to him with her camera and demanded he photograph her in the garden. She had dragged him from his study and across the lawn, and beside the willow she had pulled off her dress and stretched out on the grass.

Don't just stand there, Charles! Photograph me.

Are you sure? he had asked.

Don't be so bloody wet! I'll develop them myself.

She had rolled onto her back and opened her legs, fingering herself shockingly.

He wondered if it was then, in those brief minutes beside the willow, that he first discerned the seeds of his wife's later illness. Perhaps, as he had told himself many times over the years in an attempt to absolve himself from any responsibility, she had been ill even then.

He closed his eyes and saw her again, lying on her back, her long dark hair smeared across the grass like spilled ink.

He hurried back to the house.

THE BELL CHIMED, loud in the silence of the old house.

Tudor hurried across the hallway. He had made an effort, spruced himself up, even bought a new shirt and jacket. He was old enough not to be nervous at the imminent meeting, nor even apprehensive; but he chastised himself for looking ahead, to a time beyond the meeting when he might come to know Caroline a little more. He was old enough to know better, he told himself.

She was smaller than he recalled, or perhaps it was because she was dwarfed by the dimensions of the gaping porch. She wore a belted fawn mackintosh and a pale blue velvet beret, and her smile was as beautiful as he remembered.

"I hope the journey here was uneventful?"

"Entirely. You live in a beautiful part of the world."

"I couldn't live anywhere else."

"The perfect environment in which to create."

He smiled. That was just what Emmeline had said.

"Something like that," he said.

He took her through to the library, where he had built a fire against the cooling afternoon. He offered her a drink; she said she'd love a coffee. He made two mugs and gave her a short tour of the west wing.

The conversation flowed: he wondered if the interview had in fact begun, or if the easy exchange of information was just that, communication between two like-minded souls.

Stop it, he told himself; you must be fifteen years her senior.

He gave her the history of the house, and she was attentive; then she turned the conversation towards him, asking questions about his life and work.

They were in what had been the conservatory which, in his parents' day, had resembled some transplanted section of the Amazon rainforest. Now it was empty, a vast tiled area invaded by shafts of late April sunlight. They stood gazing out across the lawn to the willow.

He managed to skate over the early years of his writing life, the five years from the age of twenty when he had written his three plays. He told himself that, as a journalist, she would be principally interested in his children's books, which were, after all, what had made him popular, if not famous.

Then he wondered if her interest in the children's books was spurious: was she really here to find out why, so abruptly, he had stopped writing plays?

If so, she ignored the plays and asked about his children's output, and he told himself that he was being paranoid.

They left the conservatory and he found himself pausing before the door to the studio.

He reached out, amazing himself, and turned the door knob. He was to spend sleepless hours, that night, attempting to analyse his motives for doing what he did then.

He wondered if he was trying to lay the ghost... though he knew that it could not be that easy.

"And this is where my wife worked," he said. "She was the artist Emmeline –"

"Emmeline Courtenay," Caroline finished. "Yes, I know of her work."

He hesitated on the threshold of the room, almost felled by a slew of unbidden recollections. "I haven't been in here for years..."

He stopped. She stepped into the room before him, tactfully pretending she hadn't heard the catch in his voice.

He moved to the window and pulled down the sheets. "Emmeline never bothered with curtains," he said. "All that mattered was light."

Now, light flooded the room, dazzling after the imposed twilight of nearly forty years.

Caroline turned a full circle on the heels of her calf-skin boots. Her mouth was open in what he took to be amazement.

As he looked around the room, he shared some of that emotion.

Dozens of brilliant canvases stared at them like windows to other worlds, other times. Most of them portrayed Emmeline, her youthful beauty, her innocence, her joy at the fact of being alive.

He moved to a canvas of Emmeline disporting herself on the lawn, gloriously naked, beaming up at him... Bull-clipped to the top right corner of the canvas was the faded black and white photograph of the original pose.

Caroline said, "She was well respected in her field."

He nodded, made to reply, but the affirmative caught in his throat. He coughed, then said, "Yes. Yes, she was."

"I did a little investigation. She had exhibitions in many of the top galleries." She fell silent. The air was heavy with the weight of her unasked question: *What happened?*

He reached out, touched the accreted oils representing Emmeline's naked flank. Beneath his fingertips the paint felt like old scar tissue.

A week after Emmeline's death, he had entered the studio and arranged her work. He had placed all the early paintings of her naked at the front of the stacks, leaving her more recent work – the portraits he considered a record of her descent into madness – concealed.

He said, "This is the first time I've looked at these in years."

She smiled at him. "It must be hard."

"Silly. It was nearly forty years ago."

They left the studio and he pulled the door shut behind him.

As they made their way to the library, she said, "And you never felt like selling the place, starting anew, after..."

He looked at her. What had she been about to say? "To lose this place, that would have been..." He shook his head. "No. No, I could never have done that."

"Do you think her ghost haunts the house?" she asked.

Not *this* house, he thought. He smiled, sadly. "I sometimes wonder," he said.

He persuaded her to have dinner with him that evening at the Three Horseshoes in the village, and, as there was a last train back to London at eleven, she readily agreed.

He could not recall the last time he had enjoyed a meal, or such company. The conversation was easy; they discovered preferences in common, shared interests. Caroline laughed at his feeble attempts at humour, and he genuinely found her wit infectious.

She let slip at one point the fact that she was ten years divorced, and his heart flew like a love-sick teenager's.

At one point he said, "I hope you don't mind my saying... but from the very first time I saw you, I thought your face very familiar."

She laughed. "I wonder if you've caught me on television, Charles."

"Television?"

"I combine journalism with acting. I did a lot of stage work in my early days, but lately I've had a few minor TV parts."

He smiled. "That must be it. I do admit I watch rather too much television."

He accompanied her to the station in a taxi, then saw her aboard the London train. By the time he returned home, staggering in the silvering moonlight, it was midnight and he was drunk.

He stumbled through the house, laughter alternating with curses, and found himself on the threshold of the studio. He propelled himself through the door, grabbed the closest canvas and tossed it behind him, then moved onto the next one. *You bitch*, he said to himself; *you evil, selfish bitch!*

He stopped, panting, the paintings scattered across the room.

The canvases behind the nudes stood revealed, and he wondered if this was what he had meant to do all along, to punish himself, to exacerbate his guilt and self-loathing.

Emmeline's last work showed a woman who was a tragic ghost of her former youthful self, a wraith tormented by psychological demons. He turned full circle, staring at the revealed portraits; they showed close-ups of her face, horror-stricken, her eyes terrified...

Staring out at him in accusation.

THE FOLLOWING DAY, his heart in his mouth, he rang Caroline and suggested, tentatively, that as he was due to come up to London on business in a few days, well... perhaps she would care to meet him?

"That would be delightful, Charles!"

After that he saw her two or three times a week for the next month.

He travelled down to London and she visited him in Suffolk, staying the night in his small, cramped bedroom. After the first night together he opened up his parents' old room, got a woman in from the village to give it a once over, and he and Caroline slept in the very double bed in which he had been born.

He told himself that he was happy for the first time in forty years.

HE LED HER from his study and across the lawn.

They gravitated towards the willow, as if pulled. It was a blistering summer's day, and they sought refuge in the pool of shade beneath the tree's canopy. He pulled Caroline towards him and held her.

He looked up, to where the trunk separated to form a thick, right-angled bough, old and strong.

She pulled away from him and stared, shocked. "You're crying..."

She wiped the tears from his cheeks and said softly, "Here...?"

He nodded.

She led him back across the lawn, into the study, and she held him and said, "I love you, Charles."

He looked over her shoulder, back towards the willow, and caught a fleeting glimpse of Emmeline's ghost, haunting him still.

A WEEK LATER, while they were dining at the Three Horseshoes, Caroline said, "Charles, I want to ask you about *The House*."

His mouth suddenly dry, he nodded. "Ask away," he

said, with feigned unconcern.

She was forking her meal absently, avoiding his eyes.

After a silence he thought would last for ever, she looked up and said, "Charles, I think it should be performed again."

His heart thudded and he felt suddenly dizzy. "You don't know what you're saying."

"I think I do." She smiled and reached across the table, taking his hand and squeezing. "Charles, I'm not superstitious."

"And nor am I. What happened... what happened had nothing to do with superstition."

She held his gaze, said, "Do you really mean to say that the play was *cursed*?"

"I don't know what else might explain what happened."

"I do! Coincidence! You're a rationalist, aren't you? I've read all your books. They aren't the works of someone who believes in superstition."

"Those books," he said deliberately, "everything I wrote in the years after... after Emmeline died and after what happened subsequently... everything was a frantic attempt to make myself believe in a rational, materialistic universe."

She squeezed his hand. "So what *do* you believe?"

"*I just don't know*," he said.

"It was coincidence," she insisted.

"That's what I wanted to believe, *want* to believe, but..." He took a breath, looked across the table at the woman he realised, then, that he loved very much. "Let me tell you what happened, Caroline."

* * *

THE HOUSE WAS his third play, and his best.

His first two had been popular and critical successes, and the West End was eager for his next one. It took a year, and was the hardest damned thing he'd ever written. He told himself that that was because it was the truest, the most heart-felt of all his work to date. He'd looked deep into himself, into his relationship with Emmeline – but more, he'd extrapolated from the current state of their relationship and written about how it might be in twenty, thirty years. He'd examined his wife's personality, her irrationality, and the portrait he'd painted of her had been far from flattering.

"You see, Caroline, Emmeline wasn't well, even then. What in the early days I took to be delightful quirks of personality, oddities that marked her out from the crowd, that made her 'artistic' or 'anarchic'... well, I came to realise that they were just the early symptoms of her condition."

He stared at his wine, lifted it to his lips and drank.

"It would be called 'bi-polar' now, I suppose. Manic depression. She swung between suicidal lows in which her view of the world was relentlessly bleak, to ecstatic highs when she would think nothing of working twenty hours straight and producing some of her most amazing, life-affirming work."

He shrugged, smiled across at Caroline. "As a writer, how could I *not* write about what was affecting me most?"

She asked gently, "Why '*The House*'?"

"I think the house served as a metaphor. Her middle-aged character in the play was obsessed with the house, and it was failing little by little, bit by bit becoming ever more derelict... just as was Emmeline." He paused, then went on, "She hated the play, of course. Didn't want it put on."

He stopped. He didn't want to tell anyone, not even Caroline, about his arguments with Emmeline over the play.

"It opened at the Lyric just a fortnight after Emmeline died," he said. "And then..."

She squeezed his hand. "I know what happened. You don't have to..."

Just after the curtain fell on the opening night, the actress playing the part of Emmeline had collapsed on the stage and died before the ambulance arrived. Cerebral haemorrhage...

"There was no understudy, as it was a small theatre company with limited funds. I wanted the play to be taken off, and it was my insistence, along with the delay there would be in a new actress learning the part, that persuaded the backers to cut their losses and drop the play."

He looked into her eyes. "So soon after Emmeline's death, and then the tragedy of... I couldn't take the grief. I wanted nothing to do with the damned play. It was easier all round if we just pulled it."

She said quietly, "But Birmingham rep persuaded you to allow it to be staged a year later."

He stared across the bar to the horse-brasses hanging beside the inglenook fireplace. "They did. I should never have listened to them. But I was greedy. I needed the money for the upkeep of the house."

He relented, and the play was staged, and an hour after the opening night's performance, the leading actress was knocked down by a bus outside the theatre and killed instantly.

Caroline said in a soft voice, "Coincidence, Charles. *Coincidence.*"

He stared down at their hands entwined between them. "After that I wanted nothing more to do with the play. My agent sold the rights for a song, but on my insistence he made a stipulation that the play shouldn't be staged before the end of the century." He smiled. "I never thought I'd be around long enough for that date to come about."

"It's now 2011," Caroline said. "Don't you think that sufficient time has passed to allow it to be staged again?"

"No, I don't."

"It's successful production would... I think it would help you, Charles. Free you, unleash you from the demons."

He smiled, bitterly. "I think you're being a little melodramatic, Caroline."

She held his gaze. "Well," she said at last, "I do act, after all."

A combination of facts tumbled in his mind, and something clicked. He said, "*You* want to stage the play?"

"My ex-husband was the producer who bought the rights of *The House* from your agent. He thinks the time has come to stage it again. He's assembled a company and it's now in rehearsal at the Metro."

He stared at her. "And?" he asked.

"And the agreement he and I had, back then, was that if ever he did restage the play, then I should play the part of Emmeline. He contacted me a while ago, honouring that agreement."

He felt suddenly frozen as he stared across the table at her. "You... you had this planned all along, didn't you?"

"Charles..." she began. "I admit, when I first approached you, I wanted to get your permission to

have the play performed. And then I got to know you."
She stopped, reached across the table and gripped his
hand. "What we have together now, Charles, I value
so much."

"I don't know whether to believe you, or feel
betrayed."

She smiled. "I hope you will believe me, Charles, but
I'll also understand if you feel a sense of betrayal. But I
assure you, none is meant."

His heartbeat seemed to fill the room. He said, "I
can't let you do it."

"Charles, I want to prove to you that the deaths were
nothing more than coincidence. I want to *help* you. I
don't believe in mediaeval superstition. The only way to
banish this belief is to stage the play."

He felt desperation surge within him. "Caroline, I beg
you. You don't know what you're saying. Two deaths...
I don't want a third on my conscience. You didn't
know Emmeline, her strength of character. She..." He
shook his head, knowing full well that he was sounding
irrational. "She was insane, and she..."

She stared at him. "What? She cursed the play?
Charles, that's nonsense!"

"I beg you, Caroline. At least think about it."

"Do you think I haven't given it a lot of thought
already?" She was gathering her things together. "I
must go. There's a train at ten."

"Stay the night!" he pleaded.

She touched his hand. "I must go. I have rehearsals in
the morning."

"Caroline, I love you..."

That stopped her. Standing, she reached out and
touched his cheek. "And believe me, I love you, too,

Charles, which is why I'm doing this." She paused, then said, "The play opens a fortnight tonight. I'll be in touch immediately after the curtain. Trust me."

He watched her stride from the bar, a combination of depression and desperation opening up within him like a pit.

HE HIT THE bottle over the course of the next week.

In the days before the play was due to open, he tried to phone her every hour. Each time he was diverted to her answerphone and he left ranting, incoherent messages pleading with her to think again, to abandon the project. He said that if she cared nothing for her own life, then at least consider his own peace of mind. And he begged her to contact him.

He heard nothing from Caroline, and he renewed his barrage of calls. He rang the theatre, demanding to be put through to her, and when his request was refused he asked to speak to the director or producer. Evidently reception had been primed and, ever so politely, he was informed that the people he wished to speak to were either absent or busy with rehearsals.

Then, the day before the opening night, he did get through to Caroline on her mobile.

"Caroline! Thank Christ!"

"Charles, this is most incon –"

"Don't hang up, I beg you! Listen, we must meet."

"That's impossible."

"Then we must talk. Please, listen to me! The last time we met... I didn't tell you everything. I didn't tell you what happened between me and Emmeline, what she said before, before she..."

411

"Charles, none of that matters, now. Don't you see, all that is in the past."

"No, you don't understand. You see, before she went out and –"

"Charles, I really must go now."

He cried, "At least think of me, Caroline! Think of my sanity!"

She paused, then said, "That's exactly what I am doing, Charles. I am thinking of you, your sanity. Can't you see that?"

And before he could think of a reply, she cut the connection.

He hurled the receiver across the hallway, then hurried to his study and poured himself a whisky.

ON THE NIGHT of the opening he sat at his desk and stared out across the moonlit lawn to the dark shape of the willow. He had spent the day drinking in preparation for the call that would tell him that Caroline was dead. He was reconciled to the fact, knew that there could be no other outcome. And then, when Caroline was dead and he had no reason to go on living? He smiled to himself. There was a rope in the garage... His end would be entirely fitting.

He saw movement on the lawn, a fleet figure in the moonlight. He stood, swaying, and knocked over the chair. Staggering, he propelled himself to the French windows, managed to fumble them open and stepped into the warm night.

He saw movement beyond the fringe of the willow tree and crossed the lawn towards it.

He stood and stared, and saw his wife at the age of

twenty, before the years and mental illness had ravaged her body and soul. She peeked out at him from behind the fronds, playfully.

"You!" he said.

He closed his eyes and relived the very last occasion on which he had seen her alive. She was drunk, tormented by the demons of her depression. She was also naked, and perilously thin, as she gestured at him with a gin bottle clutched in her fist.

You'll regret it, Charles! Oh, you'll regret it if you stage the damned play!

He had told her that it was his art, as her paintings were her art; she had no compunction about portraying him in less than complimentary fashion, had she?

That's different! My paintings won't be seen by thousands! They won't know it's you... Your portrayal of me is cruel.

He'd told her that it was an honest portrait of the person she might become... But had he been lying even to himself?

You'll regret it, Charles. Stage the play and you'll live to regret it! I'll haunt it, do you hear! My soul will not rest...

He'd told her she was ranting. Come inside, he'd coaxed; come inside and get warm before the fire. We'll have coffee. I'll hold you...

But she had ran off, laughing, and he had turned and made his slow way back to the house.

Now he opened his eyes, and it was a second or two before he realised what he had heard.

The phone was ringing in the house.

He turned, stumbling, and ran towards the open French windows. The summons became shrill as he barged into the hall and approached the phone.

He stopped, and a cold fear gripped him. He knew what he was about to hear, as he reached out and picked up the receiver.

He heard a crackle, then silence. A voice, so faint, sounded as if from a million miles away.

"What?" he said. "Who is this!"

The line went dead.

He paced the hall, weeping, back and forth, back and forth; he saw Caroline in his mind's eye, her beauty superimposed upon Emmeline's emaciated, mocking face.

He looked at his watch. It was after eleven now. When would the play have ended? More than an hour ago, surely?

The phone sounded behind him like a detonation, shocking him. He grabbed it. "Yes, who is it?"

"Charles! Edward here."

He almost cried out in despair. "What the hell do you want?"

"Charles, are you okay? You been hitting the old – ?"

"I'm fine," he snapped. "What do you want?"

"Just had a call from the US. That film company I told you about – they've made a meaty offer for the rights of the *Tide* series –"

He laughed out loud at the sheer banality of the communication, and slammed down the receiver.

He resumed his pacing. He wanted nothing more than to be put out of his misery. He knew with a terrible inevitability what the next hour or so would bring, and he wanted it to be over and done with.

He willed the phone to ring with the news, then wondered why he was waiting. Why not pre-empt the inevitable? He knew where the rope was stored, and the main bough of the willow would take his weight... Do it now, he urged himself, get it over with.

He hurried down the hall and through the front door. He crossed to the garage beside the house, his way lit by the full moon. He scraped open the garage door, laughing now with relief that the end was so near.

He found the old cardboard box in the corner of the garage and pulled out the looped rope, thick and rough in his grip. It was even tied into an accommodating noose, so he need not spend time trying to form the knot.

He turned and moved to the entrance of the garage, the rope heavy in his arms.

When he heard the sound of the car in the drive, popping gravel, he knew that rather than phone him, someone at the theatre – the producer or director, perhaps – had come to see him personally with the dire tidings.

He stopped by the door and stared out.

A black car, appropriately enough, faced him across the gravel. Moonlight glinted on the windscreen, concealing whoever was in the driving seat.

He steeled himself for the news, and he knew how he would react. He would tell whoever it was that he had begged her not to go ahead with the play, that he had told her she would die. Shunning responsibility, yet again...

He took a step towards the car, then stopped.

The door cracked open and the driver stepped out.

He dropped the coiled rope.

She faced him, smiling. "I told you," she murmured. She looked at the small gold watch on her slim wrist and said, "Almost three hours, Charles, and I'm still alive. And," she went on, "that was the first time and the very last that I'll play the part. An understudy can take over, now."

"Caroline," he said.

He wanted to take her to the willow tree and show her where, almost forty years ago, Emmeline had hanged herself, and he would try to explain the guilt he had carried with him down all the years.

He would sell his wife's early, exuberant self-portraits, he decided, and the later, haunted paintings he would ceremonially burn... and in so doing exorcise Emmeline's ghost from the house, for ever.

Caroline came towards him. "You're free, Charles," she said. "You're free, at last."

He crossed the driveway to meet her in the moonlight.

TRICK OF THE LIGHT

Tim Lebbon

When you think about it, it does seem strange that there aren't more haunted house stories and tales of the supernatural that feature ageing as a theme. After all, ghosts symbolise lives lived and the certainty of death; a revenant is a reminder of what happens to us all. Tim Lebbon's story, then, is unusual in its sensitive handling of this subject, and the denouement of 'Trick of the Light' is as moving as it is frightening.

It was the longest drive she had ever made on her own, and she so wanted the house to feel like home. But when she turned up the short driveway from the narrow country road, and the place revealed itself behind a riot of trees and bushes, Penny stopped the car and looked down into her lap.

"Oh, Peter," she said.

That's okay, Peter says. *I'm here with you. You're a brave little rose, and you'll always be safe with me.*

Penny's hands were clasping together. She forced them apart and reached for the ignition, silencing the car's grumble. It, like her, had never come so far.

She looked up slowly at the house, trembling with

a subdued fear of elsewhere that had been with her forever, but also a little excited too. This was her taking control. Her heart hurried, her stomach felt low and heavy, and she thought perhaps she might never be able to move her legs again. The mass of the house drew her with a strange gravity. For Peter's memory, and the short time she had left, she so wanted to understand.

She had bought it because of its uniqueness. While it had a traditional-enough lower two levels – tall bay windows, stone walls, an inset oak front door, sandstone quoins – a tower rose a further two stories, ending in a small circular room with a conical roof and dark windows. The estate agent had told her that an old boss of the coal mines had used the tower to oversee work in the valleys. The mines were long gone and the valleys changed beyond recognition, but Penny quite liked the grounding of this story. It gave the building a solid history, and that was good. Mystery had always troubled her.

Beyond photographs, this was her first time seeing the house. Her first time being here, in her new home. She knew that Peter would have been impressed.

"I think you'll like it here," she said, and as she reached for the door handle, a movement caught her eye. She leaned forward and looked up at the tower's upper windows. Squinting against sunlight glaring from the windscreen, holding up one hand, she saw the smudge of a face pressed against the glass.

"Oh!" Penny gasped. She leaned left and right, trying to change her angle of sight through the windscreen, but the face remained. It was pale and blurred by dust. Too far away to discern expression or features, she had the impression that the mouth was open.

Shouting, perhaps.

Penny shoved the car door open and stood, shoes crunching on the gravel driveway, fully expecting the face to have vanished as she emerged from the vehicle's warm protection. But it was still there.

"Ah, Mrs Summers," a voice said. A tall, thin man emerged from the front porch, and though she had not met him, she recognised her solicitor's smooth manner and gentle voice. "Is there...?" He rushed to her, his concern almost comical.

Dust, she thought. The shape was much less solid now.

"Hello, Mr Gough." She only glanced at him as she held out her hand, and he shook her hand whilst looking up at the tower.

"A problem?" he asked. "Broken windows? A bird's nest in the aerial?"

"No," Penny said. *I did not see a face at the window.* "No problem. Just a trick of the light."

Mr Gough's affected concern vanished instantly, and his smile and smoothness returned. "It is a beautiful sunny day, isn't it?"

Penny did not reply. She approached her new home, and already she could hear the phone inside ringing.

PETER MOVES HIS food around the plate. Pork chops, boiled potatoes, carrots, cauliflower. He's eaten some of the meat, and picks at where shreds are trapped between his teeth.

"Fuck's sake," he mutters.

"Peter, *please* don't talk like that," Penny says. Sometimes she thinks outright anger would be better, but Peter rarely loses his temper.

"It's just..." He trails off, and she knows what he has to say.

"It doesn't appeal to me," she says. "The heat, for one. Flies, midgies, the diseases they carry. The toilets out there, and you know me and my stomach. And the sun is so strong. I burn just *thinking* about going out in the sun." It makes her sad, this gulf of ambition between them. It has always been present, but where there were once bridges of love and mutual respect, they have petrified as they both aged.

"Fuck's sake," he says again.

Peter gets up and leaves the room. She hears him storming upstairs, opening and closing cupboards, and when he comes down again he is wearing his hiking boots, trousers, and a fleece.

"Where are you going?"

"Somewhere else," he says. The gentle way he closes the front door is worse than a slam.

"I WORRY ABOUT you," Belinda said.

"I'm fine."

"Mum, you don't sound fine."

"It was a long drive, that's all, dear. And you know me, I haven't driven that long in..." *Ever*, Penny thought. *I'm further from home than I've ever been.* She felt suddenly sick, and sat gently on the second stair.

Take a rest, Peter says, tough voice soothing. *Take the weight off.*

A shadow filled the doorway and Mr Gough paused, as if waiting for her permission. She waved without looking, and the shadow entered her house.

"So. The house?" Belinda asked.

"Beautiful. He'll love it." There was an awkward silence.

"Russ and I will bring Flynn down for a visit next weekend. See if you're settled all right, look around. Russ says to make a list of any jobs that need doing."

"I still won't have it that he's dead," Penny said. "You know that."

"Mum, it's been over seven years. He's been declared –"

"I don't care what some strangers declare about my husband. I'd know if he was dead, and I say he isn't. He's... gone somewhere else, that's all."

"What, for a long walk?"

"Bindy."

"Sorry, Mum. But don't talk as if you and Dad had some kind of special bond. We both know that isn't really true."

"It'll be lovely to see Flynn," Penny said. "The garden's big enough to kick his football around. And can you ask Russ to bring some stuff for cleaning windows?"

"I will, Mum." Belinda's voice was heavy with concern and frustration, but Penny was here now. She had made the break. Left her own home, bought somewhere unusual, twelve miles from the nearest town and without bringing her TV with her. The furniture was coming the following day, but she had been careful to bring particular things herself – walking boots, a coat, a map. She loved the symbolism in that.

"It's not much, dear," Penny said. "I know that. It's not Cancun, or China, or an Antarctic cruise, or the Northern Lights, or any of those things he always wanted to do with me. But it's something. It's a small step on a longer journey. He'd be very surprised at me and... proud, I think." She glanced up at Mr Gough, listening and trying to appear distracted. And then she looked around the large hallway, three doors leading off into new rooms, timber floor scuffed, ceiling lined with old beams. "He'll love it here."

"Okay, Mum. Just... call me if you need anything. Will you do that?"

"Of course. Give my love to Russ and little Flynn."

"Love you, Mum. Really."

Belinda hung up first, and Penny could tell that her daughter was starting to cry. She hated hearing that. Which was why she had yet to tell Bindy that she was dying.

"Would you like a tour?" Mr Gough said.

Penny shook her head. "Just the keys, please."

"But you really should look at the tower, it's a remarkable feature, makes the house –"

"Really, I'm fine. Very tired." Penny stood, wincing at the pain in her hips from the long drive. Her bones ached from the other thing.

"Okay, then," the solicitor said. Smile painted on, now. He handed her a bunch of keys, then a smaller set. "Spares." He glanced around. "Lovely old place. You're very lucky, Mrs Summers."

As he turned to leave, a sense of such profound terror and isolation struck Penny that she slumped back against the stair bannister, grabbing hold as the house swam around her. She tried to call out, but her mouth was too dry. *Help me!* she thought, feeling a great weight of foreboding bearing down upon her. *Up there, there's something above, a terrible thing that is pressing down on me now I'm inside. Dusty windows, a trick of the light, but I can hear it up there, I can almost smell it, and I wish I was back in my garden with the roses and rhododendrons.*

Then the feeling started to filter away, and she knew that this was an important moment. She could give in to the terror and run. Or she could remain in her new, temporary home.

There, there, Peter says, his rough working-man's fingers stroking her cheek with infinite care and softness. *Come on, my little rose. Don't be afraid. You never have to be afraid when you're with me.* He has not spoken to her like this since they were in their twenties, madly in love and obsessed only with each other. *I'll never let you be hurt.*

"Thank you, Mr Gough," she whispered. The departing solicitor waved a hand without turning around, indicating that he must have heard. As he climbed into his Jeep, he glanced back at the house just once.

Not at Penny. At the tower. His constant smile had vanished.

SHE GAVE HERSELF a tour of the house and wondered what she had done.

Belinda and Russ had been stunned when she reached a decision to sell the family home. But they had become increasingly supportive as Penny stuck to her guns and insisted that this was just what she wanted. "Maybe your father is right and I *am* just stuck in my ways," she said, and the worry niggled at her that this was hardly a big step. Moving from the home she had shared with Peter for forty years, out into the country, to a hamlet where fewer than a hundred people lived, the house Grade II listed and an architectural oddity that occasionally attracted visitors... it was nothing, really.

The sort of change some people welcomed every couple of years of their lives.

But to Penny, it was the world.

The house was incredibly quiet. So much so that as she strolled through its corridors and rooms, she heard a high, lonely aircraft passing over the landscape outside. *You'll never get me on one of those*, she'd said to Peter when he suggested a simple flight to the Channel Islands to get her used to flying.

Penny opened the back door and paused, head tilted. She smiled. "One step at a time." The garden was wild and overgrown, awaiting her attention. She probably wouldn't have time to do much with it, and that made her sad. But she would make her mark.

The rooms inside were not decorated to her taste, but neither were they worn enough to require immediate redecoration. There was oak flooring throughout and she would have to get used to that, being more at home with patterned carpets. The house smelled unusual, and the sounds were strange – creaks, groans, taps – and she had no real sense of its shape and the space it occupied. It was nowhere near home, and she felt something like an intruder.

When the furniture and boxes arrive tomorrow everything will change, she thought. Everything she owned was packed in a lorry somewhere right now, ready to be transported across the country and deposited in this strange place. In her old house, her belongings had been a network of memories and safety, creating an environment she knew. Packed away, they were just luggage. *Home is where you are*, she'd said to Peter once, but he'd scoffed and gone into a quiet sulk. Later, he'd said, *You're rarely where I am.*

"Everything I have will be here, apart from him," Penny said. Her voice was loud. A bird sang somewhere in the garden, as if in response.

A steady *tap, tap, tap* came from somewhere that did not feel like part of the house.

Penny walked from the kitchen to the hallway, unconsciously matching the rhythm with her own footsteps. She paused at the staircase, one hand on the bannister, looking up. The sound was more distant than the bedrooms or bathroom on the first floor. More hollow, and sadder. She knew the sound. Peter, sat in his armchair with a glass of whiskey in one hand and his eyes distant, while she sat on the sofa and watched the next episode of some TV series she was already losing interest in, and his foot would tap against the wooden leg of his chair. Just a gentle impact, as if he were ticking away the seconds of his life. She would hear, but had never, ever said anything. He was always like this after an argument – a screwed up travel brochure beside his chair, and a dead dream floating in his glass.

He would usually go anyway, but never with his wife.

Tap, tap, tap...

"Peter," Penny breathed. The noise ceased. She held her breath.

Keys in hand, Penny walked slowly upstairs. Each tread had its own feel and sound, and probably its own memories.

Spooking yourself, Peter says. *You always worry too much, my rose.*

Penny reached the landing and stood before the doorway that led to the tower. She had not looked inside on her first walk around the house. Had passed it by, truth be told, because it had felt like the last place she wanted to see. *Too dusty up there*, she'd thought, and she decided that was the one place she'd send Russ when he and Belinda came over the following weekend. Up into the tower, to clean those windows and see what else was there.

"Silly," she said. She reached for the door.

"YOU'RE JUST STUCK here," Peter says. "Don't you see that?"

"But I like it here."

"You used to enjoy travelling. All those weekends we spent down in Cornwall when we were courting. The tour of Scotland in the motor home. Don't you want to do all that again? Don't you ever think about how time just..."

It always goes the same way.

So Peter packs a bag and leaves. He says he is going hiking for a weekend in the Lake District, but he never comes back. His body is never found.

Penny persistently insists that Peter is still alive somewhere, and that drives a rift between her and her daughter. Because there was never any tension between Belinda and her father, and if he *is* still alive, she says, he would contact her.

"No," Penny says whenever the subject is brought up. "He's not gone. Not Peter. He's out there somewhere, waiting for me to join him. And one day, I will."

Belinda never believed that she would. In truth, neither did Penny. But discovering that she only had months to live had changed something fundamental about the way she viewed the world. Before, she had felt safe and secure in her own small bubble of existence. Now, she already sensed that everything else was moving on. Leaving her behind. She was a dead woman walking, and she had one more chance.

SHE PAUSED WITH her hand on the door handle. It was metal, round, and vaguely warm, as if someone gripped it on the other side. It was only a tower, and a room. Perhaps there was a chair up there, and she could sit and look out over the landscape, watch the sun set over a hillside instead of her neighbours' rooftops for the first time in –

Tap, tap, tap.

The sound was closer. Beyond the door, up whatever staircase might have been built within the tower. Peter, tapping his foot impatiently against a chair's leg.

Penny gripped the handle tighter, but was suddenly convinced that there was someone directly on the other side of the door, holding the handle, ear pressed to the wood, smiling expectantly as they awaited her decision.

My little rose, Peter says, *sometimes you're so scared of the smallest things, so fragile and sensitive. It's a hard world, hardy and impartial. But I'll look after you.*

She let go of the handle and took two steps back until she nudged the landing balustrade. The tapping had stopped, but the silence was worse.

"Stupid woman!" she berated herself, and she started singing to fill the space. Still singing, she searched through the set of keys until she found one for the tower door. She locked it, then paused, listening for movement on the other side. But there was none.

"Of course not," she said. "Just an empty room, and dust."

Hungry, thirsty, a little angry with herself for being so easily scared, Penny went down to the kitchen and switched on the kettle. She'd brought everything she needed to make tea and cook a simple meal, but as the kettle boiled she opened the back door to the wild garden once more.

She walked outside, fiddled with the keyring until she had removed the key to the tower door. She threw it as far as she could, turning away so that she did not see where it landed.

"There," she said. "That settles it. The house is way big enough for me anyway." She entered the house again, not once looking up.

And not looking up meant that she felt watched.

PENNY ATE HER fried egg sandwich. She'd speckled it with cayenne pepper, because Peter used to like that, and so spent the next half an hour sipping milk from the bottle and trying to lick the burn from her lips. And she tried to make sense of the house around her as the light outside changed.

She missed her little three-bedroomed home. She had always known where she was in that house in relation to every other room. Her awareness had filled the entire place, when Peter was there with her and, later, when he was gone. It had been more than a home, and sometimes she'd forgotten where she ended and the house began.

Now, the new house hung around her like something waiting to pounce. There was no sense of equilibrium. The first floor felt as though it sought to crush the ground floor. The kitchen was too large, crowding out the dining room, storage room, and pushing into the corner of the quirky living room. Penny felt vaguely dizzy, as if every part of the house was constantly moving, just slightly. Even when she closed her eyes and hung onto the table, the feeling persisted.

And above it all, the tower.

Maybe Belinda was right. Maybe he *was* lying out there somewhere, gone to bones and dust. And he'd have died alone, perhaps with a broken leg or a heart attack, under lonely skies without Penny there with him.

Don't be soft, Penny, Peter says, and she looked around, certain that she actually heard those words spoken. The natural direction for her to look was up. *I'm fine. You know I am. Fine now that you've made the break, and taken the risk. And how does it feel, my rose? How does it feel?*

"I'm not sure yet," Penny said. Even the way her words echoed was unfamiliar. "I'm a little bit afraid."

Don't be, my darling, Peter says. Penny had not heard such love in his voice for many years.

DUSK APPROACHED. IN the valley, it was a wild time. The breeze increased, rustling the trees along the edge of Penny's new garden. Dogs barked from somewhere far off. Birds flitted overhead, and sitting on a stone bench outside, Penny watched them circling the tower. None seemed to land. She could not blame them. There was something so intrinsically wrong there, but she was doing her best to steer her attention away from its upright bulk. To give in to the tower would be to admit defeat.

"I might just as well go home," she said. The overgrown garden dampened her voice, and her words quickly faded to memory.

She walked around the garden with a glass of wine. She never usually drank wine except on Friday evenings, and then only a glass or two after eight o'clock. Now it was Tuesday, barely six-thirty, and she loved the feel of the glass in her hand, the fruity taste of wine on her lips.

The garden was larger than she had thought at first. Either that, or the boundaries were poorly marked and she was strolling across open hillside. She always felt the bulk of the house to her left, but most of her attention was directed downwards, at the twisted vegetation, long grass, and exposed tree roots that sought to trip her. She stepped over and around obstructions, and thought perhaps tomorrow she would walk further into the hills. There was a famous trail up on the ridge, so Mr Gough had told her. Popular with walkers. Peter had been a walker.

"I was a sitter," she spoke to the garden. "A not-doer. A nothing. A... waste of space." She hated the term, because Peter had used it referring to her on more than one occasion. "Waste of space." She looked across at the house, the looming tower, and realised that she now stood in its stretching shadow. The sun touched the hillside beyond, and cast a palette of reds and oranges around the tower's stark lines. The glazed room was exposed to the sunset. There was a solid shadow within, as if a shape was standing in the centre of the room. And Penny wondered what would change were she to suddenly disappear, and what would fill the space she had left behind.

She began to cry. It was dislocation and fear, but also a growing sense that time had passed her by. She had never, ever thought like this before, even when Peter had angrily insisted that he only had one life, and he would not fritter it away waiting for her.

Don't be sad, Peter says. His voice was stronger than the breeze, brighter than the sunset, and more meant for her than the hushing trees and calling birds. *You've done well, my sweet rose. You know not to waste any more time, or time will waste you.*

"Are you coming back to me?" she asked.

You think I ever left?

Penny stared up at the tower room, convinced that she would see movement there, or a face, or a sign that this new home was more than just her own. But still it exuded a weight of wrongness, as if the tower and room had been built onto the house long after it had first been constructed.

"I'm not going there," she said. "The house is plenty big enough without me ever having to go there." No one replied, and she saw that her glass was empty. She did not even remember drinking the wine.

Back in the kitchen, the bottle was empty as well. Penny sat on an old stool and rested her arms on the worktops, her head on her arms. Her bones were full of aches, reminders of mortality. She closed her eyes.

Tap, tap, tap...

"YOU NEVER CALL me your little rose anymore," she says.

"Huh."

"What does that mean?"

Peter looks across at her from the driver's seat. They are stuck in traffic on the way home from the supermarket. She bought food, he bought a CD and a book about Eastern European cuisine and a cheap one-man tent light enough to carry on a hike or a bike. "That was a long time ago," he says.

"So much just fades away," Penny says sadly.

"Huh." The car pulls forward some more, and Penny watches her husband driving. He remains silent, stern. She wishes he would just throw her a glance, a smile, a cheeky, *My rose never fades*. But the rot has set in years before, and now they are simply awaiting dead-heading.

She opened her eyes to darkness, and a cruel throbbing against her skull. The house sat around her, quiet, still, and she felt that it was observing her pained waking. The weight of above pressed down against her, almost crushing her into the stool and worktop. How could the tower have not tumbled long before now? How could it stand, so heavy and dense? Even though she could no longer hear the tapping sound, she could feel it through her hands and feet. Transmitted through the body of the house like a secret message from one room to another. *All about me*, she thought, and she slipped from the stool to the kitchen floor. She unrolled the sleeping mat and sleeping bag, climbed in, ignoring the pressure on her bladder, the need for a drink of water, the fear of what else might be sharing the floor with her in the darkness. She had not been this drunk in decades, but today she welcomed it. Her world swayed. She was protected by numbness, and still feeling that *tap, tap, tap* touching delicately against the flagstone floor, she was pulled back into the dark.

Dawn, and she had dreamed of Peter sitting upright on a chair in the room at the top of the tower. There was no other furniture. Just Peter, seven years older than when she had last seen him, walking boots and trousers and waterproof jacket still on, day pack propped by his side with the flask open and cup steaming coffee, sandwich box balanced on one knee. *So you came?* he'd asked, not sounding surprised. He had always known that Penny, his rose, would follow.

"I have to see," Penny said. She glanced around the kitchen until she saw the set of keys, remembered throwing the tower key outside. Then she recalled the spares Mr Gough had given her. She emptied her bag and snatched up the keyring.

Her head pulsed with each stair she climbed. Her heartbeat matched her footfalls, reverberating through the house. She wondered whether her presence here would become an echo for whoever might own the building after her.

At the door to the tower, she touched the handle again. It was cool. It took a few moments to find the key that fitted the lock, and as she tried she looked around the landing at the closed doors. She had been into each room yesterday, but did not own any of them.

The key turned, and the lock tumbled open.

"Are you there?" she asked, expecting the *tap, tap, tap*. But there was nothing. She pushed the door open.

The circular staircase was made of cast iron and probably worth a small fortune. It did not make a sound as she climbed. She passed two windows looking out onto her garden, but it felt as though she was looking onto a world she had never visited. She saw places she had been, recognising none of them.

The stairs ended on a narrow landing with a single door. It was dusty and cobwebbed. She touched the door handle and it was warm, but she did not wait to think about why. She tried it, then unlocked it with another key, wondering only vaguely why the tower room should be locked away behind two doors.

"Open the door, my little rose," she said, imagining the words on her husband's lips, and she turned the handle. Peter was waiting for her inside, and soon she would hear his voice again.

As Penny pushed the door open she saw something flash across the small room beyond, dashing for cover, terrified of being seen. She gasped, hand pressed to her chest. Her heart beat the *tap, tap, tap* she no longer heard, and as it transferred through her other hand to the door, she saw a smear of light quivering in the room's opposite corner. A window-shaped reflection, brought to life by her fear. She shoved the door a little more, and the reflection disappeared.

She entered the room. There was nothing there. The dusty windows caught the sun's early light and filtered it, casting dust-shadows against the floor and one wall.

The door was closing behind her, and Penny turned to see herself in the mirror hung on the back of the door. Through the haze of old dust covering the glass, she looked nebulous, almost not there.

Also not there, Peter. There was no chair, no husband. The room contained old, old dust, and stale air, heavy with the aromas of age and seclusion.

"I'm here," she said. "I'm here!" Louder. Dust floated down from the ceiling and flitted in pale sunbeams, like tiny flies startled at her presence.

A broken wooden blind hung down across one window, and one end tapped gently against the panelled wall. There were no broken panes, no breeze. Penny closed her eyes and felt a slight dizziness not connected to her hangover. The tower moved, or the world. Now that she was here it did not matter which.

Penny began to understand. She had not come here to die. Neither had she come to try and make amends to her absent husband, or to prove to herself that she was not as he had always portrayed her. She had come because this was another place where she belonged. This empty, barren room was her home, not the house down below. And there was no way she could leave here again, because everywhere else felt so terrible, threatening, and a million miles away.

She pressed her face to a glass pane. At least with dust on the windows, she was shielded from some of the distance.

Soon, she would lock the door, prise a window open a crack, and drop the keys outside. Belinda and her family were not visiting for ten days, so there was plenty of time. Because Penny's was the face at the window. And she was a trick of the light.

WHAT HAPPENED TO ME

Joe R. Lansdale

In many of the stories in this anthology the theme has been of places haunted from within, of threats – supernatural or otherwise – found inside the places where we live. Here, however, we have something coming from the outside to make its presence known in a ramshackle Texan house. Lansdale's story is a compelling blend of the quietly supernatural and full-blown Lovecraftian horror. There is a master at work here, and the final tale in our collection will stay with you for a long time.

I wish I had a story to tell, but I don't.

Not like all of you, and being last to go after all those fine stories is a toughie. I can't make things up like you people, and I'm impressed. So, all I can do is do my best, and admit right up front that this isn't a story, and therefore may be a bit pedestrian because it's something that actually happened to me.

I suppose you could say it's a kind of haunted house story, except it's not a story, and took place many years ago and ends with a not altogether satisfying explanation, if it is an explanation at all. But it does end with a death, I'm sad to say, and some of the things I saw disturb me even now, and I suppose they will do so until the end of my days.

It would be an almost classic story in a way, if it were fiction.

But it's not. It happened, and I'm not going to add any frills, just tell it to the best of my memory, as accurately as I can, and you can judge its worth as my offering for the night.

When I was a young college student attending Stephen F. Austin University, I was poor as the proverbial church mouse. A friend of mine, Clifford, who I called Cliff, was poor too, as was another friend, William, who did not go by Bill. Always William. He was adamant about it.

We decided that the only way we could attend college was to find a place with as cheap a rent as possible, with enough room for three, and go into it together. What we all had to live on were student loans, and they were not large, and after we paid for tuition and books, there was very little to survive on for a semester.

I forget how we came about knowing of the place now, but as it happened we found a house – and get this, because it will be hard to believe in this day and time – but we found a house where the rent was thirty-five dollars a month, split three ways.

Admittedly, thirty-five dollars in those days was worth more than thirty five dollars now, but it was still very reasonable for us, split up like that.

East Texas, even in winter, is generally a warm place. But this winter I'm talking about was unusually cold, at least it was for a while, and considering the house we were about to rent was without gas heat, only fire places, it seemed even colder.

After renting the house, Cliff and I had other matters to attend to in our home town of Tyler, and couldn't be there on the day our rent began. But William could be. His plan was to stay there and we would catch up with him the next day.

Cliff and I drove down together from Tyler in that rare and bad weather I mentioned, and by the time we arrived at the house the next afternoon, the wind was blowing sleet. As we pulled in we were surprised to see that William's car wasn't in the drive.

We were even more surprised to find a note tacked to the door. It was on a piece of notebook paper and said simply: I'VE DECIDED TO GO TO KILGORE COLLEGE.

This was out of the blue, and immediately eliminated one third of our income as far as rent went, but as I said, it wasn't a terrible rent we were expected to pay, so we could bear it. The main thing was we were surprised that he had bailed out on our plans, and had explained himself so thinly with that note.

These days, to find out more, you would pop open your cell phone and give him a call, but then there were no cell phones, and for that matter, the house didn't have any kind of phone, and, frankly, the electricity out that far, especially during weather of the sort we were having, was iffy with all that ice hanging from the lines.

After cussing our partner, we entered the house and found that his bedroll – for there were no beds at this point, and only limited furniture – was still there, stretched out in front of the fire place. There was no fire, but we could see where there had been a recent one, built by William, no doubt, and after discovering that not only had William left his bed roll on the floor, we found he had left a number of other items, including a grocery sack of food, most of it canned goods.

But, let me jump ahead in my story a little, saying that we got over his departure quickly, and that for the first two days things were fine. We were there very little, since we began attending classes. On the weekend we went home to load furniture in a rented van to deliver to the house.

In no time at all we were settled in, and also in no time at all we began to feel uncomfortable. It was nothing radical, and I can't say that I remember being scared, early on that is, but that I did feel discomfort. It was akin to the sensation of thinking someone was peeking in a window at you. And as there were no curtains on the windows at the time, I thought this was most likely a natural sensation of being exposed, though where we were located we could have pretty much gone naked and no one would have noticed.

There were also minor things, such as thinking we had heard sounds, but when we discussed it, we were unable to adequately describe what it was we had heard. One of the more uncomfortable places in the house was the dog run. The house was divided by a long hallway that went from the front porch to the back porch. The front porch was long and ran right and left to the door, but the back porch extended out from the back door on the same path as the dog run hall. Both porches were roofed over and were wide and solidly built, though the back porch creaked whenever you stepped on it.

The dog run hallway, however, was what was most uncomfortable. We assumed this was due to it being separate of the rest of the house, and therefore devoid of heat. Anytime we entered it, it was not only cold, it was foul, as if a dead cat were somewhere within the walls. And the first few nights, when we slept on the floor in the living room, I had the most miserable sensation that something was moving about in the hallway, though I can't say as I remember hearing anything at all. Just this feeling that something was out there, pausing at the closed door that led to the living room. The way those old houses worked, was the front and back door were locked, but as an extra precaution, the door to the hallway could be locked as well from either side of the house; what you had was essentially two houses separated, and yet connected, by a hallway that ran between them and connected to the porches. After the first night, I took to locking the one connected to the living room.

I remember Cliff seeing me do it, and expecting him to laugh or chide me for my extra caution. But he didn't. He merely looked away and went about his business, which gave me the impression that he had the same concerns that I had.

Now, keep in mind, because I know more about what happened later, I'm certainly overselling this aspect of the house, at least early on. I'm merely trying to explain that the two of us were a bit prickly, if not frightened, or even concerned. I thought, as I'm confident Cliff did, it was due primarily to the isolated location, the age of the house, which surely provided noises to which we were unfamiliar, and the fact that we were unaccustomed to being there.

It seemed to me that once we got curtains, odds and ends, our own rooms chosen, that things would be considerably more homey, and this proved to be the case.

At least for a time.

Now, there was another matter. I thought little of it at first, but early on, after we had assigned bedrooms, when the furniture was placed, I had begun to have uneasy dreams; a serial dream actually. You know the sort, where you dream it each night, but it changes slightly.

I would feel myself lying in bed, slowly coming awake, and when I would awake, it would still be dark. Each night I saw a shadow at the window, like a tree limb with branches, hand-like, but much larger than a hand. I would see the shadow curl its 'fingers,' then flex out, as if stretching, and touch the window, and with little effort, lift it.

On one occasion the last part of the dream had been of those wooden-like fingers stalking across the floor, attached to a long branch, an arm if you will, and the fingers had taken hold of my blanket at the foot of my bed and began to pull.

And then I came awake.

This time, as before, there was no branch, and the window was shut. But the blanket that had covered my feet was on the floor in a heap.

This, of course, was easy enough to explain, and I came to the conclusion that during the dream, in fear, I had kicked at my blanket and caused it to come free of the bed and fall on the floor. It was a reasonable explanation, and I accepted it as truth without due consideration.

It seemed so logical.

I also determined that to have peace of mind, I would inspect the windows, to make sure they were fastened tight. I had checked them when we first moved in and found them stuck, as if the window frame had been painted and pushed down before drying, causing it to stick. But when I examined the window I had dreamed about, it was unlocked and no longer stuck. It lifted easily.

It is of also of importance to note there wasn't a tree near the window, so the idea that I might have half-awakened and saw the shadow of a tree limb and its branches against the glass was immediately dismissed. I came to the conclusion that it had been less stuck than previously thought, and I had been mistaken about the lock; in other words human error.

On a day when Cliff had class and I had none, I went out to the barn behind the old house and looked for a hammer and nails to seal that window shut. I knew if I were to sleep in the room comfortably, even if I was only taking care of psychological worries, I would have to seal the window more securely.

The barn was a dusty affair and both sides of it were festooned with all manner of horse-drawn accouterments: horse collars and bridals and back bands and the like for pulling plows. The plows themselves were there, rusted over. There was a big cedar trunk as well, and I looked in there first. It was chock-full of junk, including children's toys and a large note book that I opened. Inside it were a child's drawings. They were of the usual thing, a house with a family. The drawing was done in what I supposed was crayon, or something like it, and it had a blue sky and yellow sun, and dark stick-like figures of a woman and a man.

There was a drawing of a child, placed somewhat at an angle between them, as if the child were falling over, and there was a shadow drawn for the child, but none for the parents. The shadow was crude, but very interestingly drawn nonetheless. There were quite a few other paintings as well, including one of the night sky and what looked like a line of crudely drawn trees. There were other paintings of trees and what I concluded was the barn I was in, and I reached the obvious conclusion that they were the drawings of a very young child. There were quite a few of these drawings, varying only in the fact that in each drawing the trees were closer to the house.

I closed up the notebook, put it back, and went rummaging about the barn looking for that hammer and nails, and finally found them. The nails were in a paper bag and they were an assortment of lengths.

Back in my bedroom, I picked through the bag until I found four, long, thin nails, and used those and my hammer to firmly nail the window shut. There was a part of me that felt idiotic about doing it, but I can say truthfully, that after I had fastened those windows down tight, I felt significantly better than before.

Early afternoon, after class, Cliff drove back to the house and announced he was going home for the weekend, hoping to borrow a bit of money from his parents. I wished him luck, but at the bottom of it all I felt abandoned, as if I had been set adrift on a stormy sea. I'll tell you another thing. I think he too was having discomfort with the house, and had decided to get away from it for awhile. This only added to my discomfort. These concerns soon took a back seat as I decided to stay and study for a history exam.

I sat on the couch in the main room – the one we had begun to call the living room – and studied for my test. I had the books spread out beside me on the couch, and there was plenty of light through the windows, and I was deep into the American Revolution, when a shadow passed over me, darkening the room considerably, and giving me a chill that went beyond the winter weather outside.

I got up and stoked the fireplace, built up the fire, but it did little to heat me up. I pulled on my coat, returned to the couch, but the shadow had swollen to fill the room. The shadow seemed to be nothing more than a reflection of the outside weather seeping in. Clouds had moved to cover the sun. I went to the window to look out, pulled aside the curtains, and saw that it was quite dark for mid-day. I could hear thunder rumbling in the background, and saw a flash of lightning snap out over the thick forest across the road from our rental, giving the trees the brief impression of having been drawn with a piece of charcoal instead of by the hand of nature.

I went back and sat on the couch and turned on a lamp beside it, and began to study again. A short time later, I heard a scratching sound, and then I had what I can only refer to as an impression. A feeling something was on the porch. It was a primitive sensation, something I assume our prehistoric ancestors might have experienced regularly, the feeling that something predatory was near, even if it was unseen, and that it was necessary to be alert.

I glanced toward the row of windows that looked out over the porch. Curtains covered them now, and it would have been necessary for me to go over and pull them back to take a look outside. But I just couldn't make myself do it, so sure was I that something was on the porch, and that there was something to fear about it being there. And then I heard the porch floor creak.

The clouds shifted and it grew darker yet behind the curtains. They were white curtains, but thick. I couldn't see clearly through them, but I could see enough to determine light or dark, and now I saw there was a spot, a shape that had moved in front of one of the windows, and I swear, it seemed as if it were leaning forward as if to try and peek through the windows and the curtains.

I sat there, frozen to the spot. The shadow, which was human in shape, also reminded me of a willow tree, the arms like limbs, the long fingers like branches; it was the thing from my dream, and it swayed with the wind... I must stop here, for to be honest, I can't fully describe it. I'm uncertain how much of what I'm describing is how it actually looked, and how much of it was me having an impression of something I couldn't really see accurately. I know no better way to explain or to describe it than how I have.

The shape moved, and I heard the boards on the porch squeak, and then... I swear to all I know to be true, the door off the front porch opened. I was certain I had locked it, as well as the door to the other end of the dog run, but I was equally certain that I heard it open.

Now I knew someone was out there. It was someone who had arrived with the rain, and not by car. And even as I thought this, I heard the screen door move, and then the screen door and the front door slammed shut in rapid succession.

I glanced toward the door that led out into the dog run hall, and without really thinking about it, I stepped quickly there and turned the latch. A moment later, as I stood at the door, I heard what can only be described as... breathing. The door was generating tremendous cold, and I felt a chill run all the way down my spine.

Someone, or something, was standing just outside that door and they were causing the door to turn cold.

The door knob started to twist, very slowly.

In case you're unclear, I will explain once again that the house was like two houses, divided by that dog run, and that meant that the only way into the house was through the doors on either end of the hallway, with the exception of a back door that led out onto the back porch from the kitchen. Forgive me for repeating this, but it's essential that you understand this so as to appreciate my situation at the time.

That thought occurred to me, about the kitchen door, and as it did, I stepped back and turned and walked gently through the living room toward that door, which was at the rear of the house on the same side as the living room.

I heard movement back in the dog run, and I knew that whoever, or whatever, was there had realized my plan and was rushing toward the kitchen door. My intent was to lock it, for I knew it to be unlocked, and if whatever was in the dog run made it through the hall, out the back door, and onto the back porch, he/she/it might beat me there.

I broke in a blind panic and ran for it. I heard the door to the back porch – general door and screen door – open and slam, in spite of it supposedly being locked.

I glanced to my right as I ran. There were a series of windows against the dining room that viewed out onto the long back porch. I had to pass through the dining room to end up in the kitchen. As I hurried, I glimpsed through those windows. The curtains were pulled back and my view was clear, and I saw the same dark, willow tree shape I had seen on the front porch. But now it was twisting and flowing in a manner that is impossible to describe. But I knew one thing for certain, even if all I had was a glimpse, whatever was out there was most certainly not human.

I made it to the back door and twisted the lock, and immediately the knob turned violently, and then the door began to shake, and there was a moaning like something big and wounded dying out there on the porch. That door shook and shook. I thought it would never end. I heard the wood screech and give a little, and I was absolutely positive that it was about to break and fall apart, that I would then be at the mercy of the thing.

And then, it was over.

The door quit shaking, and the air, which I now realized was cold throughout the house, warmed immediately. The rain was starting to come down, and I could hear thunder and lightning, but I knew as certain as I was standing there, that whatever had been out there, was now gone. It was the kind of thing you could sense.

As an added note, when I had the nerve, I unlocked the door from the living room to the dog run, stepped into the hallway and looked about. Nothing was there, and to make things even more disconcerting, both doors to the dog run were still locked.

Before night settled in solid, I was brave enough to go to my bedroom to gather up bed clothes to sleep on the couch. I found that side of the house, where my bedroom was, incredibly cold. Though I didn't have the impression anything was there, I had an overwhelming feeling that something had been there, and that that side of the house was more its domain. In my bedroom, I grabbed a pillow and some blankets, noted that the window I had nailed down had been lifted, and that the tips of the nails I had driven through the wood stuck out at the bottom like weak little teeth.

I closed the window and locked it, as if it mattered, and with my pillow and blankets left the room. That night I slept on the couch, but not comfortably. Nothing else happened.

That I was aware of.

THE FIRST THING I suppose you might think is if there was something actually wrong with that house, what was its history? I thought of that, and I must also pause here to say that I never in my life have believed in ghosts, and oddly, I'm not sure I do now. Not in the way that some people might think of them. But I took it on myself to visit with the lady who had rented the house to us.

It was Saturday morning, and the moment I awoke, I went to town, dropped by to see her. She had an office on North Street where she handled dozens of rentals. She was a big, middle-aged woman who looked as if she could wrestle a steer to the ground and make it recite poetry. Something I was assured by people around town she had actually done, minus the poetry part. I asked her if there had been unusual experiences reported in the house.

She laughed at me. "You mean ghosts?"

"Unusual things," I said.

"No. Until about six months ago the only thing in that old house was hay. I kept it stocked there, like a barn. No one but you and your friend have rented that house ever. I bought that property thirty years ago from the Wright family. You two are the first renters."

"Is there anything curious about the Wrights?" I asked.

"Yes; they are all very successful and there are no drunkards in the family," she said. "But as for ghosts, or murders, or ancient disturbed grave yards... nothing to my knowledge. Matilda is the only one alive. She was the youngest child of the family, and she's young no more. She was a famous artist of sorts. At least, she was famous around here. She's up in the Mud Creek Rest Home now, and no doubt that's where she'll finish things off."

I don't know if it was our land lady's intent to make me feel foolish, but she did. I had not directly asked about ghostly activities, but she certainly understood that this was exactly what I was alluding to, and had found the whole thing amusing.

I drove home, stopping by the mail box across the dirt road from our house. It was rare I received any mail, outside of a few bills, but inside was a note from Cliff. It wasn't a letter. It hadn't been mailed. It was a note he had left there for me.

Its content was simple. He wasn't coming back. He had dropped out of college and was thinking of starting next semester at a Junior college in Tyler. There was a P.S. written at the bottom of the note. It read: 'There's also the house. It makes me uncomfortable. It might be a good idea for you to leave.'

That was it. I concluded he too had had experiences, but had never elaborated. My guess was he had driven home, felt better being away from the house, and determined not to come back, except to the mail box to leave me a note. He had driven all the way, which was a good two-hour drive, to deliver that note, not waiting to send it by mail, and not waiting until I was home, therefore avoiding having to re-enter the house.

As I considered that, I decided that what was even more likely was he intended to return, but once he arrived, just couldn't go inside again, and had written the note in his car and left it for me in the mail box.

Of course, that should have been it for me. I should have grabbed what mattered to me and hauled out of there, but the truth is, even with two of my roommates gone, I could still better afford the rent there than somewhere else, and I really needed to continue with the semester. If I dropped out, I would lose my tuition. With that very earthly consideration to deal with, I decided that most of what had happened had been in my imagination. It was a decision based on necessity, not common sense, but there you have it. I was determined not to believe what my own senses had revealed to me.

At night, though, I felt differently. I felt trapped, fearful of stepping out into that dog run. I was also equally determined not to believe that the thing had opened locked doors and had paused at the one to the living room, and had not opened it. I couldn't explain that, nor could I explain that I could lock it out from the kitchen, yet it had free run of the porches, and the dog run, and, as I was to discover the next morning, the other side of the house.

I HAD LEARNED to fear the night and any dark days due to rain. Because of that, I always hurried home before dark, and I had learned that as night came the house became colder on the bedroom side. Because of that, I had taken to permanently sleeping on the couch in the living room, and due to that choice, I had not really visited the other side of the residence since Cliff left. In fact, it seemed, with him gone, the atmosphere of dread had compounded, and was focused now on one person. Me.

But the mornings always seemed brighter and less fearful, and it continued that way until late afternoon when the ambiance of the house shifted to a darker and more oppressive tone. It also seemed activated by any grim change in the weather. The ice storms had melted out, but the winter was still unseasonably cold and subject to shifts in temperature and sudden outburst of rain. When that occurred, no matter what time of day, the feelings of dread mounted. Because of that, I was glad I was gone most of the time, and on Wednesdays, when I had a late class, I was at my most nervous on returning. I parked as close to the porch as possible and entered the house rapidly and made my way to the living room, and locked myself inside. The back door from the kitchen to the porch I never unlocked.

But, I was telling you of the morning I went to the other side of the dog run to examine that side of the house. In Cliff's bedroom I saw that all of his abandoned belongings – his books, his clothes – were strewn everywhere, the clothes ripped to fragments, pages torn from books. I was shocked to discover the entire room looked as if an angry burglar had been through it. That was my first thought, actually, or vandals, until I saw that the bed clothes in my bedroom had been ripped from the bed and piled at the end of it in a shape. That's the only way I know how to explain it. Somehow, those blankets had been twisted in such a way as to make a kind of teepee, but one that had no opening into which to crawl; a twisted cone the height of my shoulders. The sheets were ripped in strips and thrown around the room and the glass was knocked out of all the windows. My mattress had been ripped apart and the stuffing was tossed about as if a fox had had its way with a chicken.

When I breathed my breath frosted. This made sense as the outside weather had been let inside, but I had the feeling that the air was not cold from natural atmospheric occurrences. Still, I didn't feel that odd impression of something being in the room or nearby; the cold was more like the residue of something having passed through.

THIS SHOULD HAVE been my absolute cue to pack up, but at this point, to tell it as truthful as I can – I was mad. The idea of being forced out of the house, and the idea of having to pay money I didn't really have for a different place to live, or to consider moving home and losing my tuition loan, was more than I could bear.

I locked the door to the ravaged side of the house as I came out, and then I made sure both ends of the dog run were locked. I followed that by entering the living room side of the house and locking that door. I pulled all the curtains across the windows, and even went as far as to take some of the spare blankets I had moved into that room a few days back, and hung them over the curtain rods in such a way to secure myself from the sight of anything on the porch. I concluded if I couldn't see it, I would be less fearful of it.

I took some peanut butter and a loaf of bread, a plate and a knife to spread it with, and carried it into the living room, followed a moment later with a glass and a gallon of milk from the refrigerator. I closed the door from the living room to the dining room and locked it. I determined I was going to make that room my sanctuary this night.

I didn't have a television or a radio, not in that old house. There were actually only a few electrical outlets available. It had never been fully transitioned from farm house to modern home.

There was a little bathroom off the living room, a kind of guest bath that had once been a closet. It was large enough for a toilet, a sink, and a shower. I took a shower and dressed in comfortable clothes I had laid out, as I had already moved all of my major possession into the living room, and then I prepared myself a peanut butter sandwich, had a glass of milk and, sitting on the couch with an end table lamp at my elbow, began taking a crack at my studies.

As the teacher had cancelled her class for that day, there was no need to leave the house, and I decided not to. Instead, I planned to direct myself to my studies. The house had already taken up far too much of my attention, and to be honest, even at this point I thought that what I might be dealing with were vandals, and that tomorrow, when I went into town, I would file a police report. Mostly, I tried not to think about the other side of the house, and instead concentrate my efforts on my studies.

This went well throughout the day, until late afternoon. I had by this time become a bit more confident – fool's confidence – and I chose to unlock the door from the living room to the dining room and to make my way to the kitchen to see if I might find something more appetizing for dinner than a peanut butter sandwich. As I reached the kitchen I noticed a curious thing; the hinges on the door to the porch were losing their screws;

they were twisting slowly from the hinge. One of them fell to the floor with a small clatter. The hair on the back of my neck spiked up.

I observed this for a moment, until another screw began to move, and then I will admit quite freely, I broke and ran for the living room, closed the door – quietly, lest I somehow aggravate whatever was out on the back porch further – and locked it. I picked up a poker from the fireplace and moved to the couch. After awhile I heard a noise, and I knew immediately what it was. The back door had fallen off its hinges and there was nothing the lock could do for it; the door had dropped into the kitchen, and if that wasn't enough, there was something moving in there now, and even two rooms away, I could hear it breathe.

The breathing became louder as it moved through the house, toward the living room. I gripped the poker so hard I tore the skin on my palm. And then it was at the door connecting the living room to the dining room. I could hear it breathing, and there was a shadow at the bottom of the door where there was a thin crack. The shadow remained for a long time, and then it shifted, and I swear to you that the next thing I saw was a long finger, or what looked somewhat like a finger, slide under that gap in the door and run along its length, wiggling, as if feeling the temperature of the room, which had become almost unbearably cold. Then I saw it wasn't a finger at all, but a limb, or a thin, knobby branch. It clutched at the bottom of the door frame, and then more fingers appeared, and more, until there were far more woody fingers than could be part of a human being, and they began to pull at the bottom of the door. The door moved; it heaved, but after a long fearful moment, it held.

There was a sudden yanking and then a screech so strange and so loud I almost thought I would faint. This was followed by a rush of wind, an appearance of light at the bottom of the door – the artificial light of the dining room bulb – and then there was a popping sound and the light was gone. This was followed by banging and what was obviously the clattering of pots and pans.

And then everything was still and silent and the room warmed up.

I didn't leave the living room until the morning was so bright it bled through the blankets. I unlocked the living room door and made my way through the dining room and kitchen. They were a wreck. The dining room table was flattened and chairs had been thrown through the windows that led to the porch. In the kitchen, pots and pans were tossed about, along with flour and sugar, and there were broken plates and glasses. Some of the plastic glasses I had collected from fast food places to supplement my dishes had been ripped apart as easily as you might tear wet newspaper.

I had a class that morning, and a test, but they were the farthest things from my mind. I drove into town. I went straight for the Mud Creek Rest Home.

MUD CREEK REST Home actually turned out to be Mud Creek Retirement Home. It was a community home where the elderly could have their own rooms and shared facilities. It was very nice, actually. I found out which room was Matilda Wright's. When I came to her door, it was open and there was bright sunlight pouring through her windows and the room was stuffed fat with easels and paints and paintings. Matilda, who I had somehow expected to look ancient and be confined to her bed or a wheelchair, was standing at one of the many easels, painting. What she was painting was a large multi-coloured flower, unlike any flower that actually existed was my guess, and the rest of the paintings were of beautiful, but twisted trees and rivers, all nature paintings.

Matilda was so deeply into her work I hesitated to interrupt her. She was a tall lean woman, and quite attractive for someone I had to guess was in her late seventies. She had her hair dyed blonde, and her face, though creased with wrinkles, looked lively, or at least the side of it I could see. She was actually quite beautiful for a woman of her age, and I could imagine that even twenty years earlier she must have turned quite a few heads. She was wearing a paint-splattered, over-sized shirt and blue jeans, white canvas shoes dotted with paint. She didn't look like a woman who would know about weird things that crept up on the porch where she once lived.

Finally, I knocked. She turned, slightly startled, and saw me. Her face lit up and she said, "Yes?"

"Miss Wright?" I said, not entering the room.

"Actually, it's 'Mrs,' but my husband is long dead. I prefer Matilda. Do I know you?"

I shook my head. "No, ma'am. I live in what used to be your family home, or so I'm told. Would it be all right if I came in and spoke with you?"

"By all means," she said.

She hustled to lift a box of paints out of a chair and offered it to me. I took the seat and she sat on her bed and looked at me. "You live in my old house?"

"I do."

"How interesting. I think about it often. It's where I grew up."

I nodded. "I wanted to ask you a few questions about it. They might seem like silly questions."

"By all means, ask."

It turned out I didn't so much as ask her a question, but broke down and told her all that had happened since I had lived there. I felt, as I feel now speaking to you about these events, a little silly. But I couldn't stop telling her all that had occurred, and she didn't once interrupt me. When I finished, I asked the actual question. "Did anything odd ever occur while you and your family lived there?"

"Nothing of that nature, no. And my family and I were very happy there."

This was a disappointing answer, and I'm sure my face showed it. I said, "I don't know what difference it would make if I knew what's responsible for what goes on there, but I keep thinking if I knew something, then maybe it would make a difference. Though, now that I say that aloud, I can't imagine what it would be."

Matilda looked at me for a moment, as if measuring my character. "I didn't say there was nothing odd that ever happened there."

My ears pricked.

"I said there was nothing of the nature you describe, and that we were happy there."

"Then there was something?"

"Quite different than what you describe. I had an invisible friend."

I was immediately disappointed. "So did I, when I was very young," I said. "Lots of children do."

"That's true," she said. "The thing is, well... shall I take some time to explain?"

"Yes, ma'am, that's why I came."

"When I was very young and we lived in that house, we owned a large amount of acreage. I don't know how much of that is left."

"Ten acres and the house and barn," I said.

She nodded. "It was a hundred acres then. Right behind the barn there were woods."

"There still are."

"The woods were thick, and I often went there to play. And one day I came upon a grove of trees. It's impossible to describe how surprising this was, because they weren't just trees. Here I was in the middle of a forest, quite comfortable walking about, and I came upon what can only be described as a kind of grove. It was broken apart from the thickness of the woods, and there were a number of trees that were clutched together, but they were not like any of the other trees. They were thick limbed, and they didn't grow very high, and they were amazing in the way their boughs twisted, and underneath them it was cool and pleasant. None of the other trees were near them. There was instead a field of flowers, blue bonnets, and they were the buffer between the grove and the other trees. I would suspect that the grove was surrounded by two acres of those flowers.

"The trees appeared very ancient, though I can't say that I knew that at the time; I say that in retrospect. For me then, they were merely odd and beautiful. Thinking back, they seemed to me to be among the first trees to ever grow on the earth. They had not aged like other trees, or grown high, but they were thick, and their bark was soft to the touch.

"I sat under those trees and took a rest, and as I did, a little girl stepped out from between them and looked at me."

"A little girl?"

"Yes. She hadn't a stitch on, but she seemed comfortable with that. She told me her name was Elizabeth. That's my middle name, young man, Elizabeth, so there was a kind of small bond immediately. And here's the interesting part. She looked just like me."

"Your imaginary friend?"

She didn't respond to my remark, she just continued talking. "She was very pleasant. She and I began to talk, and it was amazing. We had so much in common, and pretty soon we were playing together. She wouldn't leave the grove of trees, however, and stayed under their shadow. That was all right. I liked it there, and the grove was large enough to give us plenty of shadow to play under. It was hard for me to tear my way free of her and go home, but night was coming. I became aware of it suddenly, and wanted to go home. I was, as I said, comfortable in the woods, but I knew I wouldn't be comfortable there if night came, as it was easy to get lost, so I told her goodbye. She begged me to stay, but I told her I couldn't, but that I would be back as soon as possible. She finally relented, and as I was about to leave, she stepped between a gap in two of the trees, and was gone. I looked, but there was nothing there but the trees.

"Young as I was, nine or ten years old: I don't remember exactly. But young as I was, I accepted all of this freely. I went home and told my mother that I had met a girl in the forest and that we had played together, and that the little girl didn't wear clothes and had disappeared inside some odd trees.

"Mother laughed at this, and thought I was playing, and didn't take alarm at the matter. I went back the next morning, and Elizabeth was there, but this time she wore clothes. The ones I had worn the day before. Or clothes that were like them. We played that day and it was even more fun than the day before. I don't remember what we played, but there were no girl games of tea and pretending to be married. None of that. Chase, I suppose. I don't remember, but by mid-day I grew hungry and went home. Elizabeth was pouty about it, but I assured her I would be back after eating, and that's exactly what I did. But when night came and I started home, she decided to go with me. As I had played past the time I should have, I was growing frightened of the forest, and I was glad to have Elizabeth as a companion.

"As we went through the woods, I heard my mother calling, and I hastened to reach her. Elizabeth held my hand as we went, and finally when we arrived in the yard, there was my mother, in her apron, worried looking. When she saw me she ran to me and scolded me. I still had hold of Elizabeth's hand. I introduced her to my mother, and my mother smiled, and said, 'So this is your imaginary friend.'

"It was obvious she saw no one and was humoring me. But Elizabeth was there. To shorten this up, she stayed with me for several years, or at least she was with me nights. During the day she told me that she went back to the grove. When I came home from school, after supper, when it began to turn dark, or sometimes on rainy days, she would be in my room, waiting. We had wonderful times together. I finally quit trying to convince my mother Elizabeth was real. This had eventually resulted in me being sent to a doctor – not a therapist, I might add, as there were none available then, least not that we knew of – and frankly, I had come to the conclusion she was not real at all. But, I didn't dismiss her from my memory.

I enjoyed having her around, even if I aged and she did not. In fact, she never changed or changed clothes from the day she walked out of the forest with me. Then, all of a sudden, I was twelve and we were moving.

"Elizabeth was very confused. We had a long talk about it, but she didn't understand. I invited her to move with us, but she said she couldn't. That she had to stay near the grove. And then we moved, and that was it. No more Elizabeth. I came to the conclusion that moving had been an excuse for me to cut the bonds to this imaginary friend I had invented, and though we always had good times together, when she was no longer there, I felt a strange sense of relief. Elizabeth is the only thing odd that I know of that ever happened in that house."

I looked around the room, and back at Matilda. "So many of your paintings are of flowers and trees. Especially trees."

"I like nature," Matilda said. "But that grove... I have spent my life trying to duplicate those trees. Here's something odd. After the night Elizabeth came home with me, I began to paint. It was an obsession. I painted for one reason and one reason alone, and that was to somehow put the images of those trees on paper. Oh, I painted other things, of course, but I always came back to them, and in time, I became known for them, and they became a large part of my career as a painter."

"Did you ever paint Elizabeth?" I asked.

Matilda shook her head. "No. There was no need. I knew what she looked like. She looked like me when I was a child. But where she came from, that intrigued me."

"I think I saw some of your early drawings in the barn," I said.

"Really?"

"Perhaps, or one of your siblings."

"I had two brothers," she said. "To the best of my knowledge they didn't paint or draw."

I sat for a moment, thinking about Matilda's invisible friend, but there was nothing in that story that told me much.

"May I have a look at the old homestead?" Matilda asked.

This took me by surprise.

"Of course, but after what I told you about the house... are you sure?"

"You said it only happened at night and on dark days," she said. She nodded her head toward the blinds and the harsh light seeping in. "It's still very much day and there doesn't seem to be a cloud in the sky."

"Certainly," I said. "I can drive you out for a look, and then I'll drive you back."

Though I had gone in to see Matilda with high hopes – even though I was uncertain what I was hoping for – I was leaving with less enthusiasm. I was in fact thinking I would take her to see the homestead, bring her back, and then use a bit of my fading bank account to stay at a cheap motel. And then, the next morning, I was going to concede defeat. I had already missed a major test to hear about Matilda's imaginary friend. It was time to dissolve my old plan and start thinking of another, as had my erstwhile room mates.

IT WAS COLD outside, but there was no wind blowing and there was plenty of sunlight, so it wasn't unpleasant. Matilda was dressed in a lined leather coat and wore a kind of cloth hat that made her look like the cutest grandmother that ever lived.

She walked briskly, as if she was twenty years younger, and climbed into my wreck of a car without comment, or any obvious examination, and we were off. It was as if we had known each other for years.

When we arrived at the house, the first thing Matilda wanted to do was see the old drawings I had told her about. Out at the barn I found them and showed them to her. She smiled. "Yes, these are mine. Interesting. You'll note that my brothers are not in the drawings."

I smiled and she laughed.

"This one," she said touching the one with the shadow, "is Elizabeth. It's feels odd looking at this, now. I drew Elizabeth like a shadow, my shadow. How unusual for me to see her that way. I had totally forgotten about this."

"You should take those with you," I said.

"I will," she said. "I'll leave them here for now, but when you take me back, I'll bring them. Would you like to see the grove?"

I hadn't the slightest interest, actually, but I was trying to be polite, and to tell you true, I was glad to have company after all I had been through.

"Certainly," I said.

Matilda led the way. The woods were thick, but there was an animal path through them, and we followed it. It was narrow and a little muddy from the rains of the day before, but the walk felt good in the cool winter air.

There wasn't a true trail, and it appeared even the animals were no longer using it, as it was overgrown and hard to follow. I felt certain Matilda would give up shortly, but she didn't. She moved like a squirrel. Far better than I did. The woods were thick on either side of us, and there were an amazing number of brightly colored birds flittering about from tree to tree, singing their songs.

Finally, the trail came out in a clearing, and in the center of the clearing were the trees. They were as Matilda had said. Strange. But I saw them with less warmth than she had depicted them. There were a large number of them. They were squatty in construction, and the limbs had a twisted look. I swear to you, a few of the limbs were actually knotted. The leaves that grew on the trees were black and chunky. The bark had fallen off of them in a number of places; the only way I truly know to describe those trees is to say they appeared cancerous. The clearing around them wasn't spotted with blue bonnets, or any kind of flower, but instead yellow weeds grew knee high on all sides. There were no birds singing now. There were no birds in sight.

"My God," Matilda said. "They have aged so. They look so... sad."

I couldn't disagree with this assessment, and actually, when I think about it, it's a far better description than my saying they were cancerous-looking. 'Sad' is exactly the word, and now that I remember that, and tell it to you, I have to emphasize that no other word would be as accurate.

We walked toward the trees, and as we did I heard them shift. It was not the wind that did it, and I didn't actually see movement, but there was a sound akin to ancient lumber being stepped upon by a large man. Had I not felt I was in some way there to protect Matilda, I would have turned around then and gone back. But she was like a juggernaut. She walked into the shadows beneath the grove of trees. The leaves rustled. The limbs creaked.

Matilda bent down and picked up a chunk of bark lying on the ground and examined it. She dropped it, touched one of the trees. There came that creaking sound, but I swear to you no limbs moved and no wind blew.

"They have suffered so," she said. "Elizabeth, are you there?"

The limbs began to move and thrash about, and one of them stretched long, swept low, and knocked me off my feet. I tried to get up, but the limbs came thrashing down on me like whips.

"Come on," Matilda said. "Come on."

Next thing I knew, she had helped me to my feet, and we were both running. Matilda, in spite of her age, ran spryly, at least until we were away from the grove and back on the trail. She had to stop then and catch her breath. Her face was red and she coughed a few times, leaning one hand against a pine to hold herself up.

I felt like an absolute fool having let her talk me into taking her out into the woods to see a grove of trees, and now that we had seen them, I felt not only like an idiot, but like a very frightened idiot. If there was, anywhere in the back of my mind, an urge to stay on and deal with this odd problem, it was now gone. I wanted one thing, and one thing only. To leave that house and that property.

MATILDA MOVED SLOWLY after that, one arm around my neck as we walked. By the time we made the house she had grown weak, and insisted on going inside. I was ready to put her in the car and leave, but as it was still light, and we were away from that infernal grove, I waltzed her inside and let her stretch out on the couch. After a few minutes she felt better, but she didn't move. I fetched her a glass of water and sat it on the end table, but she didn't touch it.

"Elizabeth, she was there," she said.

"I didn't see her," I said.

"Which would be why I called her an invisible friend," Matilda said. "Actually, I couldn't see her either, but I could sense her."

"What I sense is a change in my plans," I said. "I'm going to leave this house like my comrades, and not come back."

Matilda ignored me. "The trees, they reflect Elizabeth's mental state."

I sat down in a chair and put my hands on my knees and listened.

"I don't now exactly how all this has happened," she said. "But I never truly doubted that she was real, and invisible to others, in spite of what I said earlier. I realize now I lied to you. It was an unintentional lie, but it was a lie. I always felt, on some level, that she was real and invisible. Or refused to reveal herself to others. I can't say. But when we left here I had a feeling not only of sadness and loss, but one of euphoria. It was as if I knew somewhere inside of Elizabeth was something dark, just waiting to take control."

"But how could this be?" I said.

Matilda sat up slowly. "I don't know. I think it may be that Elizabeth is like those spirits of old. That the grove is one of a handful left that hasn't been chopped down and plowed under. Groves like that had to exist all over the world at one time. I don't know any other way to explain it. Trees like those, they're the homes for something that is unworldly."

"You're telling me," I said.

"I remember reading about nymphs in Greek mythology. Some of them were sacred to a particular stream, or lake, or grove."

"You think she's a nymph?"

"An elemental," she said. "One of the last ones left. One of the ones that is connected to the earth when it was raw and new. One of the ones that has survived. I have been thinking about this for years. I've wanted to come back here for years, but didn't for one simple reason. I was afraid I might be right. That Elizabeth might be real. And that she might be angry."

"How could you know that?"

Matilda shook her head. "I don't know. But I always thought there was something dark in Elizabeth, and that it was just waiting to get out. And as I said, I was glad to move away. She was my friend, but I was glad to leave her."

"I think we both should leave her," I said. "I admit defeat."

"Would you consider staying?" Matilda said. "Just one more night?"

"Why would I do that?"

"So I can see her," she said.

"Why would you want to do that?"

"I feel as if I owe her," she said. "I feel somehow responsible for how angry she has become."

"Why didn't she show herself in the grove?" I said.

"The trees were her," Matilda said. "But this house, where she and I were happy, this is her focal point now. She wants you out."

"And I'm more than willing to go," I said.

"Will you stay?"

Until moments before I had been ready to grab a few things, stick them in the car, and drive Matilda back to the retirement home, and drive myself back to my parent's house, but she was convincing.

I gave her a tour of the wrecked house, and even managed to put the kitchen door back in place while Matilda twisted the screws through the holes in the hinges. Then I made us a sandwich of peanut butter, and we sat at the dining room table and ate. About us was the carnage of the night before.

I said, "Why didn't she come in the living room?"

"If I understand what you've told me," Matilda said, "the opposite side of the house is where she's strongest, and that's because that's where she and I played. The back bedroom was mine. She feels comfortable there, as if she belongs. This side was where the family congregated, and she preferred the privacy of the other side of the house. My parents had a bedroom there, and there was my bedroom, but my guess is she associates that side with me, and this side with the family. And another guess is that this is the heart of the house. The part that is most powerful."

"That's two guesses," I said.

"You have me there," Matilda said.

"But she did come on this side, and she broke the door down."

"She's getting stronger and less fearful of coming here. Maybe she could do at any time and just chose not to. Perhaps she didn't have any intention of harming you, but just wanted you to go away, and is trying to scare you off."

"It's working," I said.

"But I believe this is the strong part of the house, where the family was most comfortable. Some people claim all dwellings have a center, a heart, a source of power, something that is inherent, and something borrowed from the living things around or in it, and this place must be it.

"American Indians believed all things had power, that they were alive. Rocks. Trees. They had spirits inside of them. Manitous, they called them. Nymph. Elemental. Manitou. Spirit. All the same thing... what I can't decide is if Elizabeth is angry because I left, or because someone else has moved into the house. Most likely a little of both."

We waited in the living room. The only light was a fire in the fireplace and a single lit candle I had placed in a jar lid on the end table by the couch. The night came, and as soon as the sky darkened, I knew it was coming, and I wished then I hadn't listened to Matilda, and that I had gone away as I had originally planned. There was a change in the air. It became heavy and oppressive, and within moments, on the back porch this time, I heard a heavy sound as if something were dragging itself.

"It's her," I said.

"Yes," she said. "It is."

I looked at Matilda. The fire in the hearth tossed shadows over one side of her face, and in those shadows she looked so much younger. I thought I could not only see the woman she was, but I could almost see the child she had once been.

There was a sudden wailing, like what I would think a banshee would sound like. Loud and raw and strange, it affected not only the ears, but the very bones inside of me. It was as if my skeleton moved and rattled and strained at my flesh.

"My God," I said.

"She is of older gods," Matilda said. "Calling to yours will do you no good."

The next sound was like thousands of whips being slapped against the house, as if an angry slave master were trying to tame it. I heard what was left of the glass in the kitchen and dining room windows tinkle out and to the floor.

And then everything went silent. But I knew it wasn't over, even though the silence reigned for quite some time. When it started up again, the sound was different. It was of the back door to the dog run being flung open, slammed back against the hall. Then there was a noise like something too large for the door pushing itself inside. I glanced toward the living room door to the dog run. It was swelling, and the cold from the dog run was seeping under it; the cold from outside, and the cold from Elizabeth.

The door warped in the middle and seemed sure to break, but it held. And then everything went silent.

I couldn't say where Elizabeth was at that moment, but it seemed to me that she was in the dog run, standing there, or lurking there. The door no longer swelled, but the cold had grown so that it now filled the room. Our candle guttered out. The fire in the fireplace lost its warmth, and the flames grew low.

And then there went up such a savage wail that I dropped to my knees with my hands over my ears. Matilda, she stood there, her arms spread. "Elizabeth," she called out. "It's me, Matilda."

The wail ended, but then the entire house shook, and

the living room door to the dog run swelled again and vibrated.

"It's grown strong," Matilda said, and then the door blew apart in thousands of fragments, one of them striking me in the head as I perched on my knees. It didn't knock me out, but it hurt me badly, and it slammed me to the floor. The way pieces of the house were flying about, I stayed down, was so tight to the ground I felt as if I might become part of it.

Then the thrashing and the howling of the wind stopped. I looked up. Much of the house was in wreckage around me. The fireplace still stood, but the flames had been blown out.

I managed to get up. I called out for Matilda. No answer.

Where the walls had once stood, there was just the night, and beyond I could see something dark moving past the barn toward the woods. It looked like a knot of ropy coils and thrashing sticks, and in its midst, trapped in all those sticks and coils, I got a glimpse of Matilda.

I looked around and saw the axe lying by the fireplace, where I had split a few chunks of wood to start the fire. I picked it up and ran out into the night after Elizabeth. I was terrified, no doubt, but I thought of Matilda and felt I had no other alternative than to help her if I could.

The thing moved swiftly and without seeming to touch the ground. Trees leaned wide as it proceeded, not trees from the grove, but all manner of trees, pines and oaks, sweet-gums and hickory. They made plenty of room for it to pass.

What had felt like a long walk before only seemed to take moments this time, and soon I stood in the clearing, looking at the grove. The mass of limbs, the elemental,

Elizabeth, was already closing in on the place, and there I stood with the axe in my hand, and absolutely no idea what to do with it; I felt small and useless.

I'm ashamed to say I was frozen. I watched as the thing laid Matilda's body on the ground, gently, and then the limbs whipped and sawed in all directions, and the coils of roots and boughs unknotted, and all those loose projections waved at the night sky.

And then, it was gone. In its place was a young girl in simple clothes, and even though I had not seen early photos of Matilda, I had seen that very child in her features. It was Elizabeth, looking as Matilda had looked those long years ago when she discovered the grove. I was seeing Elizabeth in the same way Matilda had seen her; she was an invisible child no longer.

Matilda was on the ground, but now she rose up on an elbow, struggled to sit. She looked directly at Elizabeth. As for me, I was frozen to my spot.

"Elizabeth," Matilda said. Her voice was sweet and clear and came to me where I stood at the end of the trail, looking at this fantastic occurrence; I think I was suffering from shock. "You don't want to hurt me anymore than I want to hurt you."

The little girl stood there looking at Matilda, not moving. Matilda slowly stood up. She held out her hand, said, "We are friends. We have always been friends. Don't be angry. I didn't mean to leave. I had to leave."

The little girl reached out and touched Matilda's hand. When she did, I saw a sort of whipping movement at the back of her head and along her spine. It was like what she really was, was trying to escape.

"We are different, you and I, and both our times are

ending," Matilda said. This seemed like a bad time to bring such things up, but then again, I was uncertain there was a perfect way for dealing with what Matilda had called an elemental.

The wind picked up and the trees in the grove waved at the night air. Matilda continued to talk, but I could no longer hear her. The howling wind was too loud. Limbs from trees, not only in the grove, but from the woods surrounding it, began to fly past me. The air filled with them. I crouched down, but one glanced against my head and knocked me out.

THERE REALLY ISN'T much to tell after that, and as I warned it's not all explained. But when I awoke, Matilda was leaning over me, cradling my head in her hands. I had been hit twice in one night, once hard enough to be knocked out, so I'll admit that my memory of the next few minutes is hazy.

I do remember that I looked in the direction of the grove and saw that it was gone, twisted out of the ground as if by a tornado. But I knew that storm had not been of this earth.

When I was able to get to my feet, Matilda and I walked back to the remains of the house. There was really nothing left of it but that chimney. My car was fine, however, and we sat in it to recover. I got some Kleenex out of the glove compartment and held a wad of it to my wounded head.

"What happened out there?" I asked.

"Elizabeth was lonely," Matilda said.

That wasn't exactly the answer I was looking for.

"I saw her," I said.

Matilda nodded. "Besides me, you are the first. I suppose she no longer cared if she was seen. I can't say, really."

"She was you?"

"She was a form of me. She still is."

"Still is?"

"I made her a deal. I would stay with her forever."

"But –"

"She is inside me. She and I are one. It was my trade off. The grove must go. Her anger must go. And she could be with me until the end of my days."

I was stunned by this revelation, but I will tell you quite sincerely, I believed it; after what I had seen, I believed Matilda emphatically.

"What happens then?" I said. "At the end of your days?"

Matilda shook her head. "I don't know. But you know what? I feel really good having her back, and I know now that though I've been happy all my life, I have on some level still been missing something. That something was Elizabeth. The grove didn't make Elizabeth from its elemental powers, it pulled her out of me and gave her to me. She was another side of me, and she was a side I needed. A friend. I was happy because of her, not in spite of her, and now that the other part of me is back, my middle name, I feel refreshed. It's like having a missing arm sewn back on."

We sat there and talked for a long time, and some of what she said resonated with me, but most of it was merely confusing. Suffice to say, the house was gone, the grove was gone, and I never saw Elizabeth again. Matilda and I claimed the house had been taken down by a tornado, and who was to argue. Who was to guess an elemental force from time eternal had torn it down in a rage, and that what remained of it was now inside Matilda. Or so she claimed.

My head healed. You can still see a scar. I told Cliff the story, and he acted like he didn't believe me, but I think he did. I have a feeling he may have seen something strange there before I did, but didn't want to own up to it. Oddly enough, I never crossed William's path again. But I'm sure he had an experience in the house as well and that's why he left.

What else? Oh, the landlady got insurance money. Matilda and I stayed in touch until her death. I suppose she must have been ninety when she passed. They did discover one odd thing after her departure. Matilda had been confined to her bed, no longer able to walk, and in the last few months of her life, not capable of communicating. But during the night they heard a terrible noise, and when they rushed into her room they found her lying dead on her bed, but the room, well, it was torn apart. The window had been blown out and the bed clothes that had covered Matilda were missing, as if there had been some great suction that had take them away, carried them out the window, along with fragments of a busted chair and all the paintings and easels in the room.

They were all gone, and never found. There were a number of theories, but no satisfactory explanations. My explanation is Elizabeth. I like to think maybe Matilda's soul went with her to some place nice and eternal. Again, I can't say for sure, and I can explain it no further than that.

I don't know what else there is to say. That's my story, and it's just what happened to me. I apologize for it not being a made-up tale, considering so many stories told tonight were good, and highly imaginative, but that's all I've got, and it's true, so I hope it'll do.

ABOUT THE AUTHORS

Nina Allan is a regular contributor to magazines such as *Interzone* and *Black Static*, and her stories have featured in the anthologies *Catastrophia*, *Year's Best SF 28*, and *Best Horror of the Year Volume 2*. She won Ireland's Aeon Award in 2007 and has twice been shortlisted for the British Fantasy Award for Best Short Fiction. A first collection of her stories, *A Thread of Truth*, is published by Eibonvale Press. Her new book, *Stardust*, will be available from PS Publishing in autumn 2012.

Chaz Brenchley has been making a living as a writer since the age of eighteen. He is the author of nine thrillers, most recently *Shelter*, and two fantasy series, *The Books of Outremer* and *Selling Water by the River*. As Daniel Fox, he has published a Chinese-based fantasy series, beginning with *Dragon in Chains*; as Ben Macallan, an urban fantasy, *Desdaemona*. A British Fantasy Award winner, he has also published books for children and more than 500 short stories in various genres. His time as crimewriter-in-residence on a sculpture project in Sunderland resulted in the collection *Blood Waters*. His first play, *A Cold Coming*, was performed and then toured in 2007. He is a prize-winning ex-poet, and has been writer-in-residence at the

University of Northumbria. He was Northern Writer of the Year 2000, and lives in Newcastle upon Tyne with two squabbling cats and a famous teddy bear.

Eric Brown has won the British Science Fiction Award twice for his short stories and has published forty books. His latest include the novel *The Kings of Eternity* and the children's book *A Monster Ate My Marmite*. His work has been translated into sixteen languages and he writes a monthly science-fiction review column for the *Guardian*. He lives near Cambridge, England, with his wife and daughter. His website can be found at www.ericbrownsf.co.uk.

Christopher Fowler was born in Greenwich, London. He is the award-winning author of thirty novels and ten short story collections, and author of the popular *Bryant & May* mysteries. He has fulfilled several schoolboy fantasies, releasing a terrible Christmas pop single, becoming a male model, posing as the villain in a Batman graphic novel, running a night club, appearing in the Pan *Books of Horror* and standing in for James Bond. His work divides into black comedy, horror, mystery and tales unclassifiable enough to have publishers tearing their hair out. After living in France and the USA he is now married and lives in King's Cross, London. His latest novel, *Hell Train*, is due out with Solaris in January 2012.

Jonathan Green is a writer of speculative fiction, with more than thirty books to his name. Well known for his contributions to the *Fighting Fantasy* range of adventure gamebooks, and numerous Black Library publications, he has also written fiction for such diverse properties as *Doctor Who*, *Star Wars: The Clone Wars*, *Sonic the Hedgehog* and *Teenage Mutant Ninja Turtles*. He is the creator of the *Pax Britannia* series for Abaddon Books and, to date, has written seven novels set within this steampunk universe. He currently divides his time between West London and rural Wiltshire. To find out more about his latest projects visit www. jonathangreenauthor.com.

Garry Kilworth has just reached the biblical age of 3-score-years-and-10. As a creative writer he feels he is at his happiest with the short story form. He loves travelling, both inside and outside his own head. Garry lives quite close to the Dunwich in the tale in this collection and frequently walks the long and lonely beach below the cliffs, sometimes running into the ghost of MR James, who also set stories in the same location. On such occasions Garry does not forget to tip his hat to the great writer's phantom and acknowledge that James' story 'Oh, Whistle, And I'll Come To You, My Lad' scared the pants off him when he heard it on the wireless programme *The Man In Black* at the age of 8.

Terry Lamsley's early stories were set in his then-home town of Buxton in Derbyshire, but lately he has widened his horizon somewhat. In 1994 his first collection *Under the Crust* was nominated for three World Fantasy Awards and was given the award for Year's Best Novella for the title story. Since then his tales have appeared in a number of magazines, collections and anthologies, the most recent being *The Very Best of Best New Horror* edited by Stephen Jones and published by Earthling in

2010. For the past ten years he has lived an interesting life in Amsterdam in the Netherlands.

Joe R. Lansdale is the author of thirty novels and numerous short stories and short articles, as well as comic and film scripts. He has been awarded the Edgar, eight Bram Stoker awards, the British Fantasy Award, the Herodotus Award, the Grinzani Cavour Prize for Literature, and many other recognitions. He has been recognized four times by the International Martial Arts Hall of fame, and occasionally teaches writing at Stephen F. Austin State University in Nacogdoches, Texas where he is writer-in-residence. His novella, *Bubba Hotep*, was made into a cult film of the same name, and his story 'Incident On and Off a Mountain Road' was filmed for Showtime's *Masters of Horror*, and he recently was Executive Producer of *Christmas with the Dead*, a forthcoming film based on his short story of the same title. It was directed by Terrill Lee Lankford from a script by Keith Lansdale.

Tim Lebbon is a *New York Times*-bestselling writer from South Wales. He's had twenty novels published to date, including *Echo City* from Orbit, *The Secret Journeys of Jack London: The Wild* for HarperCollins (co-authored with Christopher Golden), *The Island, The Map of Moments* (with Christopher Golden), *Bar None, Fallen, Hellboy: The Fire Wolves, Dusk,* and *Berserk*, as well as hundreds of novellas and short stories. He has won four British Fantasy Awards, a Bram Stoker Award, and a Scribe Award, and has been a finalist for International Horror Guild, Shirley Jackson, and World Fantasy Awards. Forthcoming books include another novel for Orbit in the UK, the zombie/SF novel *Coldbrook*, and the massive short story collection *Ghosts and Bleeding Things* from PS Publishing, as well as several other projects. Fox 2000 recently acquired film rights to *The Secret Journeys of Jack London*, and Tim and Christopher Golden have delivered the screenplay. His story *Pay the Ghost* is in development with a Hollywood studio, and several more of his novels and novellas are also currently in development. He is working on several TV and movie proposals, solo and in collaboration.

Rebecca Levene has neither shame nor pride. She likes writing and rarely says no when someone asks her to do some. This might explain how she's come to write a children's adaptation of *The Three Musketeers*, a *Beginner's Guide to Poker*, an extremely sweary video game and an erotic romance. She's currently working on the third volume of her series of supernatural thrillers. The first two – *Cold Warriors* and *Ghost Dance* – are available from all good bookshops.

Graham Joyce has said of **Paul Meloy** that 'he is one of the best writers of short stories in Britain' and, indeed, Paul has won the British Fantasy Award for his short fiction, much of which has been collected in the acclaimed *Islington Crocodiles* (TTA Press). When he's not dreaming up dark and surreal worlds, he works as a psychiatric nurse.

Adam Nevill was born in Birmingham, England, in 1969 and grew up in England and New Zealand. He is the author of the supernatural horror novels, *Banquet* *for the Damned*, *Apartment 16*, and *The Ritual*. He lives in London and can be contacted through www.adamlgnevill.com.

Weston Ochse absolutely believes in haunted houses. He's lived in two of them. He was able to come to terms with the ghost in the most recent haunted house, a lonely old man who died and was forgotten for months. But the entity that lives in the attic of his first haunted house is another story altogether. Although he was only eight years old when he lived between those vile walls, the entity still haunts him. That his mother has dreams of it too is a cause for worry. Perhaps that's what drove him to write dark fantasy. He's won the Bram Stoker Award for First Novel and been nominated for the Pushcart Prize for Fiction. His work has appeared in comic books, magazines, How-To writing guides, anthologies and most recently, his collection entitled *Multiplex Fandango*. He lives in Southern Arizona within sight of the Mexican-US border.

Sarah Pinborough is a horror, thriller and YA author who has had ten novels published thus far across that range. Her latest releases are *The Shadow of the Soul* (Gollancz, April 2011) – the second of the *Dog-Faced Gods* trilogy – and *The Traitor's Gate*, (Gollancz, June 2011 under the name Sarah Silverwood) which is the second volume of *The Nowhere Chronicles*. Her short stories have appeared in several anthologies and she has a horror screenplay currently in development. Sarah was the 2009 winner of the British Fantasy Award for Best Short Story, and has three times been short-listed for Best Novel. She has also been short-listed for a World

Fantasy Award. Her novella, *The Language of Dying* (PS Publishing) was short-listed for the Shirley Jackson Award and won the 2010 British Fantasy Award for Best Novella.

Christopher Priest was born in Cheshire, England. He began writing soon after leaving school and has been a full-time freelance writer since 1968. He has published eleven novels, four short story collections and a number of other books, including critical works, biographies, novelizations and children's non-fiction. His novel *The Separation* won both the Arthur C. Clarke Award and the BSFA Award while the Hugo-nominated *The Prestige* was adapted for the big screen by director Christopher Nolan. His latest novel is *The Islanders*, available from Gollancz.

Nicholas Royle is the author of more than a hundred and fifty short stories. He has published one short story collection, *Mortality*, two novellas – *The Appetite* and *The Enigma of Departure* – and six novels including *Counterparts*, *Antwerp* and *Regicide*. He teaches creative writing at Manchester Metropolitan University and reviews fiction for the *Independent* and the *Warwick Review*. His small press, Nightjar Press, publishes original short stories in a gothic/uncanny vein as signed, limited-edition chapbooks. Forthcoming from Two Ravens Press is *Murmurations: An Anthology of Uncanny Stories About Birds*, which he has edited, and from No Exit Press a new collection of his London stories.

Robert Shearman is probably best known for writing that episode that brought the Daleks back to the revived series of *Doctor Who*, but ever since then he's been trying desperately to channel his silliness into short stories instead. His first collection, *Tiny Deaths*, won the World Fantasy Award, and the second, *Love Songs for the Shy and Cynical*, picked up the Shirley Jackson Award, the British Fantasy Award, and the Edge Hill Short Story Readers Prize. His latest, *Everyone's Just So So Special*, published by Big Finish, is so new and fresh that Rob can't stop stroking the cover. He has written two series of the interactive BBC radio series *Chain Gang*, both of which won Sony Awards; the third series begins in the New Year. He is currently writer-in-residence at Edinburgh Napier University.

Lisa Tuttle made her first professional sale forty years ago, with the short story 'Stranger in the House' – now the opening entry in *Stranger in the House,* Volume One of her collected supernatural fiction, published by Ash-Tree Press. Perhaps best known for her short fiction, which includes the International Horror Guild Award-winning 'Closet Dreams,' she is also the author of several novels, including *The Pillow Friend, The Mysteries* and *The Silver Bough,* as well as books for children, and non-fiction works. Although born and raised in America, she has been a British resident for the past three decades, and currently lives with her family in Scotland.

Stephen Volk was the creator of the award-winning TV drama series *Afterlife* and the notorious BBCTV 'Halloween hoax' *Ghostwatch*. His latest feature film (co-written by director Nick Murphy) is *The Awakening,* a supernatural mystery starring Rebecca Hall, Dominic

West and Imelda Staunton, while his other movie credits include Ken Russell's *Gothic* and *The Guardian*, co-written with its director William Friedkin. He has also written for Channel Four's *Shockers* and won a BAFTA for *The Deadness of Dad* starring Rhys Ifans. His short stories and novellas, a selection of which are collected in *Dark Corners* (Gray Friar Press), have so far earned him nominations for the British Fantasy Award, HWA Bram Stoker Award, and Shirley Jackson Award, plus appearances in several 'Best of' anthologies. He can be found online at www.stephenvolk.net.

19 NEW TALES INSPIRED BY EDGAR ALLAN POE

POE

Edited by Ellen Datlow

GREGORY FROST · PAT CADIGAN · SHARYN McCRUMB
KIM NEWMAN · LUCIUS SHEPARD AND MORE

UK ISBN: 978 1 84416-652-7 • US ISBN: 978 1 84416 595 7 • £7.99/$15.00

To coincide with the 200th anniversary of the birth of Edgar Allan Poe, this anthology celebrates the depth and diversity of one of the most important figures in literature. Compiled by multi-award winning editor, Ellen Datlow, it presents some of the foremost talents of the genre, who have come together to reimagine tales inspired by Poe.

Sharyn McCrumb, Lucius Shepard, Pat Cadigan, M. Rickert, and more, have lent their craft to this anthology, retelling such classics as "The Fall of the House of Usher," "The Tell-Tale Heart" and "The Masque of the Red Death," exploring the very fringes of the genre.

 WWW.SOLARISBOOKS.COM

Follow us on Twitter! www.twitter.com/solarisbooks

'Menacing
and unnerving'
The Guardian
on Mortality

'Immaculately
sinister!'
TLS on Mortality

Regicide
Nicholas Royle

UK ISBN: 978 1 907992 01 8 • US ISBN: 978 1 907992 00 1 • £7.99/$7.99

Carl stumbles across part of a map to an unknown town. He becomes convinced
it represents the city of his dreams, where ice skaters turn quintuple loops and
trumpeters hit impossibly high notes... where Annie Risk will agree to see him again.
But if he ever finds himself in the streets on his map, will they turn out to be the land
of his dreams or the world of his worst nightmares?

 WWW.SOLARISBOOKS.COM

Follow us on Twitter! www.twitter.com/solarisbooks

CONRAD WILLIAMS

LOSS OF SEPARATION

"Williams possesses a fearless heart
and an absolutely gorgeous soul."
- Peter Straub

UK ISBN: 978 1 906735 55 5 • US ISBN: 978 1 906735 56 2 • £7.99/$7.99

After a near miss in a Boeing 777, pilot Paul Roan opts for a new life running a B&B in a coastal village with his girlfriend, Tamara, but is involved in a serious accident and is lost in a coma for six months. Now Tamara is gone, a child killer is haunting the beaches, and the villagers treat Paul as a sin-eater, bringing him secrets to dispose of. With local nurse Ruth, and Amy, a damaged soul with a special gift, he starts to unearth some of terrible truths behind all these events...

 WWW.SOLARISBOOKS.COM

Follow us on Twitter! www.twitter.com/solarisbooks

UK ISBN: 978 1 907519 95 6 • US ISBN: 978 1 907519 94 9 • £7.99/$7.99

Imagine a place where all your nightmares become real. Think of dark urban streets where crime, debt and violence are not the only things you fear. Picture a housing project that is a gateway to somewhere else, a realm where ghosts and monsters stir hungrily in the shadows. Welcome to the Concrete Grove. It knows where you live...

 WWW.SOLARISBOOKS.COM

Follow us on Twitter! www.twitter.com/solarisbooks

UK ISBN: 978 1 907519 62 8 • US ISBN: 978 1 907519 63 5 • £7.99/$7.99

Jordan helps kids on the run find their way back home. He's good at that. He should
be - he's a runaway himself. Sometimes he helps the kids in other, stranger, ways. He
looks like a regular teenager, but he's not. He acts like he's not exactly human, but he
is. He treads the line between mundane reality and the world of the supernatural. Ben
McCallan's urban fantasy debut takes you on a teffifying journey.

 WWW.SOLARISBOOKS.COM

Follow us on Twitter! www.twitter.com/solarisbooks